SACRED
HEART

Books by Marcel Montecino

The Crosskiller
Big Time
Sacred Heart

Published by POCKET BOOKS

SACRED HEART

Marcel Montecino

POCKET BOOKS

New York   London   Toronto   Sydney   Tokyo   Singapore

This book is a work of fiction. Names, characters, places and incidents are products of the author's imagination or are used fictitiously. Any resemblance to actual events or locales or persons, living or dead, is entirely coincidental.

POCKET BOOKS, a division of Simon & Schuster Inc.
1230 Avenue of the Americas, New York, NY 10020

ISBN: 0-671-01539-7

First Pocket Books hardcover printing November 1997

10 9 8 7 6 5 4 3 2 1

POCKET and colophon are registered trademarks of
Simon & Schuster Inc.

Printed in the U.S.A.

For Eric L.
and the FOBW

Special thanks to those great friends who for years encouraged me to write another novel:

Armand Fontaine. Steve Franklin. Gary Gottesfeld. Judith Paige Mitchell. Zane Cofield.

And to those who assisted me:

My assistants and researchers Julian Plunkett Dillon and Delphine Robertson.

My editor Jane Cavolina.

Pablo Perez in San Julian, Jalisco, who aided me on-line, along with Andrea Alvarado, an *alteña* living in San Jose, California, who did the same.

And especially my agent Cynthia Cannell.

And Emily Bestler and Bill Grose.

Book I

New York City

BULLDOG WAS LOOKING FOR HIS KID.

It was bitter cold. The coldest December in New York since Ought 8, eighteen years before, and the Bulldog and his boys were driving all over Manhattan looking for Tommy Gun. It was closing on to eleven P.M. and the wind off the Hudson was whipping the city like a drunk beating his wife. It was an unfit night for man or beast, truly.

"Jaysus, Bull," Duggan said from the front seat, beside Kearney, driving. "I never felt it so dam' cold since I come ovah. Jaysus."

Duggan was trying to load his .38 with his gloves on and he kept dropping slugs into his lap.

"Do that later, Bill," Bulldog Coyne said simply. Then he took a gold-plated flask from his breast pocket, unscrewed the stopper and took a swig. It was snowing, as it had been for three days now, and the storefronts along Madison Avenue were half-hidden behind the stuff. Bulldog smiled to himself as he felt the golden glow of Toronto's best slip down his throat, penetrate the inner lining of his stomach and hit his nervous system. Duggan, turned sideways in his seat, watched his employer's smile widen.

"Give us a pull, Mr. Coyne, would ya?"

Aloysius "Bulldog" Coyne looked at his bodyguard, but the thoughts behind his eyes were faraway. The Canadian blended he had just tasted was some of the best bonded he had ever swallowed, and after tonight he and his boys could have all they could pick up off the St. Lawrence, load from the barges into trucks, and two-

3

night run back down into the city. The Canadian blended he had just tasted was glory, pure and simple.

"Mr. Coyne?"

Bulldog held out the flask and watched Duggan greedily clutch it, bring it to his lips, then fire the whiskey down with a violent backward jerk of his head. Bulldog waited for the response.

"Goddamn!" Duggan's eyes widened. "Is that Henshaw's stuff? Goddamn!"

Kearney, behind the wheel, stuck out his hand, with a quick glance in the rearview at Bulldog.

"Go on, Kev," Bulldog said. "You'll never taste any better."

Kearney took a shot, then he just gave a quick, short laugh. Kearney was not a man given to superfluous words.

"What did I tell you?" Duggan grinned at the driver, then back at Coyne. "What did I tell you?"

Bulldog kept his smile as he looked back out the window of the Studebaker President at the snow whirling out on the street. The wind was driving the stuff against the glass in a million little wet collisions.

Duggan turned to watch the street like his boss. "Ay, it's a miserable night."

The whiskey had filled Bulldog with a benevolent glow. He had been drinking it all day. "It's a grand night for killin' guineas."

Duggan grinned. "It's always a good night for that."

"Let's find my son."

◄○►

THE TWO WHORES WERE ROLLING ON THE BED, LAUGHING SO HARD THEY were holding their sides.

"Stop, Tommy, I'm going to piss myself!" the smaller one said. She was a small, squat sixteen-year-old from a farm in Ohio, and her large, milky breasts were shaking with uncontrollable mirth.

"Have mercy on us, Thomas!" shrieked the other girl, taller, darker, with a thick Edinburgh burr.

Thomas Coyne was naked except for a bowler hat and an umbrella hooked over his arm, and he was waddling back and forth across the carpet, doing a crude imitation of Charlie Chaplin's splay footed gait, twirling the umbrella like a cane and twisting the ends of a nonexistent little mustache. The whores could not stop laughing.

"For pity's sake, Tommy," the Ohioan squealed. "Please stop!"

Then the Scottish girl, whose name was Georgina, lunged across the bed, reached out and snared Thomas's limp penis in her long, slender fingers. Chaplin had no choice but to come to a sudden, dead stop. A wicked smile spread across Georgina's lips and she began to stroke his cock. She lifted her black eyes and said, "Doesn't Charlie have anything to say for himself?"

Thomas looked down at his cock in her hand, then winked at Mary, the other whore. "How many Chaplin flickers you been to, you ever heard him talk? He can't."

Georgina took a strand of her thick dark hair and held the ends across the head of Thomas's penis, like a Chaplinesque mustache. "He's the quiet type. . . . A man of few words and much action." Mary giggled.

Then Georgina dipped her head, slipped her mouth over Thomas's cock and swallowed its entire limpness. Mary watched with glowing eyes as Georgina began to slide the thickening, lengthening flesh in and out of her circled lips.

Mary jumped from the bed and ran to Thomas's side. She stuck her tongue into his mouth for a moment, then said, "Me first this time."

—◄O►—

ON 126TH AND LEXINGTON AVENUE THE STUDEBAKER PULLED TO THE snow-packed curb, the front passenger window rolled down and Duggan shouted to a man standing in the blue-lighted doorway of a brownstone.

"Hey, Rastus! Come here!"

The doorman, whose name was Joseph, came forward cautiously. He didn't fancy stepping out into the wind, yet he didn't want to ignore a white man, either.

"Boss?"

"You seen the Tommy Gun tonight?"

Joseph, who was so swaddled in coat, scarf and top hat that his dark face and white eyes seemed ghoulish behind the driving snow, hesitated a moment. It was not prudent to speak without thinking to a white gangster. It was much smarter to appear stupid.

"Say what, boss?"

Then the back window rolled down and there appeared the wide, handsome face of Bulldog Coyne, boss of Hell's Kitchen.

"Ain't you the nigger they call Old Black Joe?"

"Dat's me, Boss."

"My boy Thomas been to Fat Sassy's tonight?"

Joseph, shivering, forced himself to smile broadly, showing a mouthful of gold-capped teeth. "He sure was, boss, 'bout eight a'clock, but that boy, he got a appetite for pussy like I ain't never seen." He jerked his thumb back at the doorway, which lead to a stairwell, which led up to Fat Sassy's whorehouse. "He done went tru' all Sassy's whores. He lef' here 'bout ten, saying now he needed him some white girls. I swear, Mistah Bulldog, your boy love pussy worsen' than any nigger I ever met!"

Duggan in the front seat laughed.

Bulldog's eyes searched Joseph's face, and for a moment the doorman thought he might have overstepped his boundaries, but then Bulldog asked, "Did he say where he was going?"

Joseph's body relaxed under the layers of clothing. "Miss Pauline's place on Eighty-second Street, on top that speak. At leas' that what he told the hack driver."

Duggan said back to Bulldog, "Miss Pauline's that whorehouse above Coneelly's?"

"Yessah," Joseph said in confirmation. "Dat's de one."

Without a word Bulldog rolled up the window and the Studebaker eased away from the curb and disappeared down Lexington, into the whirling snow.

Joseph stepped quickly back into the shelter of the doorway and hissed softly, "I hope dey kill all you paddy bastids."

—◀◯▶—

THOMAS WAS SNUGGLED BETWEEN THEM UNDER THE QUILT, SMOKING A big Havana Royale, and watching the snow swirl in the glow of the alley streetlight just outside the window. Downstairs the jazz band, fresh up from New Orleans, was playing "Tin Roof Blues." Slow, melancholy, full of sweet pain. Georgina pulled the quilt up closer around her neck, ground her warm, damp pelvis against

Tommy's hip and sighed. Then for no apparent reason she softly said, "My da can go to hell, for all I care."

Mary from Ohio, pressed against Thomas's other side, was smoking a brown-wrapped marijuana cigarette. She inhaled deeply and stared at Thomas's two silver-sheened, nickel-plated .45 automatics, hanging from a bedpost at the foot of the bed.

"Thomas," she began dreamily, "what's it like to be a gangster?"

"Well, sugar," Thomas teased, "it's just like me."

Mary slapped his arm playfully as she exhaled. "I mean, have you kilt anybody?" She looked at him hungrily and whispered, "They say you kilt a hundred or more."

Thomas clenched the Havana between his teeth at a jaunty angle and peered through the smoke at her. "Nah. Not a hundred. Not nearly."

"How many then?"

Thomas moved the cigar up and down with his teeth, playfully. "I don't know, for sure. Sometimes you can't go back and count the bodies."

Georgina raised herself up on an elbow and studied him. "Are you never afraid of bein' killed yourself?"

He looked at the Scottish girl's breast, hanging down, pressed against the bedsheet. Her nipple was thick, dark, and protuberant. He reached over and traced it absently with his fingertip. "That's what keeps you sharp. Those that forget to be afraid, they're the ones who get it themselves. From guys who ain't forgot."

Mary exhaled another pungent lungful.

"Then, ain'tcha afraid you'll go to the 'lectric chair? Someday."

"That's one thing you can be sure of," Thomas said seriously. "That won't happen to Tommy Coyne." He grinned wickedly. "I never leave any witnesses."

—<o>—

THE STUDEBAKER PULLED INTO THE ALLEY AND STOPPED, ITS EXHAUST fumes billowing in the falling snow. Inside the car, Bulldog patted the pistol in his overcoat, as he always did before entering or leaving wherever he was. "You're with me, Bill," he said to Duggan, then opened the door and stepped out into the frigid cold.

Duggan followed him down the alley, their footsteps making crunching sounds in the ankle-deep snow. "Jaysus, Mary, and Joseph," Duggan cursed, as a blast of wind howled down the alley and jabbed at his face like an ice pick. "Fuck."

Bulldog pounded on the heavy sheet-metal-covered door and then stared at where he knew the peephole was. Duggan stamped his feet furiously and stuck his hands under his armpits. Bulldog kicked the door and growled, "Two-Bit! Open this fuckin' door!"

Immediately there was the sound of a large bolt being thrown and the door swung back and they entered quickly. Two-Bit slammed the door closed behind them and they were standing in a high, arched stone tunnel. Two-Bit—short, thick and misshapen—had built a fire in a sawed-off oilcan and the ice on the floor was melting into slicked-over puddles.

"Snowing so damn hard, Mr. Coyne, I couldn't see it was you." Two-Bit had a scarf around the lower half of his face, earmuffs and a hat. "But I recognize your voice."

"My boy here tonight? In the joint or upstairs?"

"He went in for a drink with Mr. Coneelly, but I think he was headed upstairs. He always is." Two-Bit grinned. His mouth twisted in mirth was not a sight to give anyone else pleasure.

"How's the crowd?"

"It's packed."

Duggan was warming his hands over the fire. "Ye don't say?"

"Yeah, they come in, with dis snow, they never want to leave. They'll be here till morning."

Bulldog slipped his hand into his pocket, came out with a fiver. "Any a' Matranga's greaseballs?"

Two-Bit took the fiver and made it disappear, as if it had never existed. "Carmine Carini and his running-mate, the big guy?"

"Joe Zanca?"

"Yeah, dat's the one. They went in with a coupla Broadway sluts."

Just then a gentleman with puke all down the front of his tuxedo shirt stumbled out of the big iron door that led to Coneelly's speakeasy, momentarily filling the tunnel with light and crowd noise and the sound of the New Orleans band. The man was moving so fast and blindly that without any check in speed he slammed into the opposite stone wall and knocked himself out cold. Someone inside the speak quickly closed the door.

They stared for a moment at the unconscious gentleman sprawled on the stone floor. The two gangsters knew that Two-Bit was anxious for them to go now, so he could roll the gentleman's pockets.

"We'll go around through the kitchen."

"Yessir, Mr. Coyne." It took all the effort Two-Bit had to pull his eyes from the man on the stone floor. "You know where it is."

They left Two-Bit and walked down to the end of the tunnel, to where it doglegged into a short, blind alley. There were a dozen dented garbage cans filled with empties. Bulldog paused by one of the cans, picked up a bottle and looked at the label. "Shit."

Duggan nodded. "It's not that juice Henshaw is sellin', that's for sure."

The kitchen was crowded and cacophonous, and reeked with the smell of fried oysters, broiling beef, browning potatoes. The Chinese head cook stared at them with Asian contempt as they entered and passed through the wide cooking area and into the short hall leading to the speak. They pushed through the door and stood inside a curtained-off area by the service bar. The band was playing something hot and jumpy, and a dozen young women with naked legs and bare arms were singing and mugging for the crowd. The place was underventilated, and the smoke hung in the air in thick, motionless swirls. There was a sense of desperate gaiety about the place. Of mindless celebration and doomsday debauchery. It was loud. Bulldog stood by the busy bartender and peered through the shadows and smoke.

"There," he said. "By the fire exit."

Duggan tightened his eyes and squinted over the packed tables. Across the speak, seated with their backs to the far wall, were Carmine Carini and Joe Zanca. Carmine was small and dark, with furtive Sicilian eyes. Zanca was bigger, looser, born in East Harlem. He had his arm around his latest chorus-line cutie and he was smiling up at the dancers on the stage.

Bulldog stared at them with killing coldness. Duggan felt the ice in his employer.

"You know they're packin'. They say Carini takes his bath with his piece." Bulldog didn't respond. Duggan glanced at him. "We could take them now, boss. It'd be bedlam, and that's a fact."

Bulldog stared at the Italians, but shook his head. "Tonight we cut off the snake's head. Later we'll dispose of the body."

He turned and walked back into the kitchen, toward the stairs. "I need to find Tommy."

◄○►

MARY WAS DRESSING, STUFFING HER AMPLE ALABASTER BREASTS INTO the latest flimsy brassiere with slow, dreamy marijuana movements.

Tommy and Georgina watched from the bed, still snuggled close to each other. Tommy leaned over and knocked the ashes from his cigar into a glass of dead soda water.

Mary pulled up her drawers and reached for a short red dress, hung carefully on the back of a chair.

"Ain'tcha afraid of goin' to hell?"

Tommy grinned behind his cigar, looked at Georgina.

"I mean, all them people you kilt. 'Thou shalt not kill,' that's one of the Commandments. Ain'tcha afraid of all them mortal sins on your soul?"

Tommy crossed his legs under the quilt, pulled Georgina closer, cupping one of her buttocks in his hand. The Scottish girl curled on his chest like a cat.

"Listen to her run on," she said as she watched Tommy inspect Mary's body. "A whore smokin' muggles, talkin' about mortal sin."

Mary didn't even seem to hear her. She slipped the red dress over her head and shimmied it down her hips. It was fringed, and the silk swayed with every flounce of her meaty body. "Well, ain'tcha, Tommy?"

Tommy plucked a shred of tobacco from the tip of his tongue, rubbed it on the sheet. "I got my own Commandments. 'Kill before they kill you.' "

The Scottish whore looked up at him. "That's just one. What's the other nine?"

Tommy considered this a moment. " 'Never trust a cop. Never trust a guinea.' And, 'Blood is thicker than water.' "

Georgina knotted her brow. "That's . . . that's only four."

There was a sound from the other side of the door. A single footfall, a ting of metal. Tommy held up his hand for silence. The smile on his face melted into a lethal alertness.

"What?" Mary whispered, frozen in place, her eyes darting about. As if her word was a signal for action, Tommy sprang from the bed, yanked both nickel-plated .45s from the holsters dangling from the bedpost and flattened himself against the wall, beside the door hinges. Mary hiked up her dress and stooped farm-girl-style behind a washbasin table, as if she were preparing for morning milking. Georgina scooted down and pulled the covers over her head.

Tommy's eyes were fixed on the doorknob. When it started to slowly turn he raised the automatics level with where a man's head would appear. His lips tightened into a thin, hard line. Mary, watching from behind the washbasin stand, hid her eyes in her arms.

The heavy door inched open and the sound of the downstairs

band filled the room—a nervous reading of "Ain't She Sweet." With his thumbs Tommy carefully, silently cocked both pistols. He waited.

Then Bulldog's face in profile cautiously appeared around the corner of the door. He stared at the form under the bed quilt.

Tommy leaned forward until the gun muzzles kissed Bulldog's cheek. "You're dead, Da."

Bulldog's eyes rolled around to the guns before his face turned. Then he looked down at Tommy's dick, limp and still slick from the whores. "Quim'll be the death of you yet, Tom."

Tommy grinned at his father. "It seems to me you're the one with the gats in your mug."

—<◇>—

THE CHURCH OF THE SACRED HEART OF THE BLESSED SAVIOR HAD been built in 1876, and its plumbing was creaky and recalcitrant. The thermometer in the rectory read forty-seven degrees, and John O'Rourke shook his head in wonder and pulled his overcoat closer around him. *The wealth of the papacy,* Father O'Rourke thought to himself with grim irony, and watched his breath hang in the frigid air. It was too cold to sleep, too early to pray, and too late to drink. *The hell with it,* O'Rourke thought, and went to the cabinet where he kept a bottle of Irish whiskey behind the sacramental wine. He took the bottle and a glass through the sacristy door and into the dark church. He paused, his back turned to the altar, and watched the snow striking the big circular stained-glass window over the front entrance. Mary's halo was an eerie, swirling saucer. Her hair seemed to be alive. Without looking, O'Rourke knew that the holy water in the baptismal font would be frozen over. He sat in the first pew and stared up at the altar. An alabaster Jesus, nailed to the cross, eternally looked up to his Father with what O'Rourke felt were the weakest, most sexually ambivalent eyes he had ever seen on a Crucifixion rendering. It always seemed to O'Rourke that a Messiah dying to absolve mankind of all its sins, past, present and future, should reflect that enormity. A burden of wickedness that monstrous, an agony so significant should surely produce hideously bugged eyes, twisted and deformed limbs, lips curled back and teeth bared to the gums in an eternal scream. That would have been a sacrificial suffering. That would have been a true rendering of a Savior. Not this pansy imitation of Christ—donated by the Catholic Ladies of Hibernia, paid for by pennies and nickels stolen from drunken longshoremen's pants pockets by long-suffering wives trying to win salvation for the souls of themselves and their families. This Christ seemed to be looking up to his Father like a neurotic offspring deeply wounded by a cruel comment and seeking an approval he would never receive.

O'Rourke hated the Christly sculpture so much that for years he had berated his Sunday celebrants to dig deeply into their pockets for Sacred Heart's Refurbishment Fund. The money—well over a thousand dollars by now—was kept in a metal box in O'Rourke's desk. He had already selected another Christ from an icon maker in Ireland, but he had never sent the deposit. O'Rourke's parish was so poor, so hardscrabble, that he was loath to spend the parishioners' precious money on statuary.

O'Rourke poured three fingers of whiskey and drank. He shivered as it went down and that made him feel even colder. He buttoned the top button of his overcoat and again pulled it closer around him. He looked up at the statue.

This Christ was not the Christ that had drawn O'Rourke to the priesthood. Who the hell could follow this Christ anywhere? No, the Jesus that had caught the attention of John O'Rourke—in a squalid Gaelic ghetto in the shadow of San Francisco's Telegraph Hill—was a fiery revolutionary who had braved the bullies of Jerusalem, both Roman and Pharisaic, to carry a message so dangerous, so subversive, so liberating, that the rulers, the rich and entrenched, had demanded his death. So fearful of that Christ were they that they had needed to eradicate him to feel safe, or in Pilate's case, just to get a good night's sleep.

That was a Christ to follow. To worship. To devote your life to. But this . . . Who could follow this plaster Christ? Who could fear him? What bullies could he stand up to?

O'Rourke hated bullies.

He drank again, crossed his legs and set the glass on the smooth oak of the pew bench.

—◁○▷—

Tommy hiked up his pants and began to button his vest.

"Tonight . . . ? Are you sure?"

Duggan watched the whores as they threw on a few garments

and ducked out of the room, smiling back at him when they couldn't catch Tommy's eye.

"Aye." Bulldog was pouring out three shots from the silver flask. "For damned sure."

He handed a glass to Duggan, then set another before Tommy on the bureau. Tommy, knotting his silk tie, looked at his father in the mirror.

"Who's setting it up?"

Bulldog looked at his kid. "Try this, Tommy. Tell me what you think."

Tommy stared a moment longer at his father's reflection, then carefully centered the diamond stickpin he had bought from the Goldstein Gang on Delancey Street. "Hanrahan, idn't it? Hanrahan's setting it up."

Bulldog picked up the shooter and handed it to Tommy. He raised his own glass and grinned. "Happy endeavors."

Tommy stared a moment, then started to bring the glass up to toast. Bulldog clinked his against Tommy's, then turned to Duggan. "Erin go bragh!"

They both threw back the whiskey. Then Bulldog looked at Tommy expectantly. Tommy still held the full shot glass.

"*Aaa*, c'mon, lad. Taste the brew."

Finally Tommy brought the shooter to his nose, smelled the clear amber liquid, then with his eyes never leaving Bulldog's, he touched the whiskey to his lips, swallowed some. His eyes widened and then he drank the rest. Bulldog could tell that Tommy knew how good the swill was, what it meant to both of them, to the whole Hell's Kitchen Coyne Gang.

"Aye, and didn't I tell you?" Bulldog was not a man known for his smiles. And the one he wore now he saved for his younger son only.

"Henshaw's? In Toronto?"

"The one and only."

"How much can he deliver?"

"Enough, Thomas, to flood the whole damn Hudson River." Bulldog refilled Tommy's shot glass. "Enough to get all five boroughs of New York City drunk as banshees." Bulldog's smile turned cold. "And give that greaseball Matranga the hangover of his life."

◄◯►

O'ROURKE LIT A CIGARETTE. WATCHED THE SMOKE PLUME OUT WITH his breath. He wouldn't get enough sleep tonight, that was clear.

And all day tomorrow, today really, he would be tired. And today was a Saturday, the busiest day of the week for a Roman Catholic priest. Mass at six A.M. Catechism classes at seven and eight. Mass again at nine-thirty. Lunch with the Women's Auxiliary of the Knights of Columbus. Then confession from two in the afternoon until six. Then dinner at eight with the parish stalwarts—the life-blood of any Catholic community. And ever since Father Byrne had taken leave of absence to be with his ancient, ailing mother back in County Cork, O'Rourke had had to do it all himself. If the old woman didn't die soon, O'Rourke would be joining her in hospital.

He poured another glass and stared idly at the whiskey. Jimmy Peters had brought him a case of the stuff, an Easter Week gift. O'Rourke hadn't asked him where he got it. O'Rourke didn't ask a lot of his parishioners where they got things, or how they paid their rent, or what they were doing last night. It was that way with the Hell's Kitchen Irish. They told their priest what they felt was his province to know, and chose not to burden him with information that would trouble his soul, or be of interest to the New York City Police Department. They would speak in the confessional of their longings, their fears, their petty infractions of the Church's multitudinous regulations. Some of the men would whisper of thefts, robberies, even murder. But they wouldn't give names, specifics, locations— nothing that an Irishman from a strange city, even a priest, might pass along to the proper authorities. Render unto Caesar . . .

And in his turn, O'Rourke would piously admonish them to repent from such behavior, to regret and refrain from activities condemned by both the Church of Rome and the City of New York. Though he never really expected them to. Times were hard in Hell's Kitchen. Wall Street financiers might be drinking champagne from showgirls' pumps on Broadway, but here, among the West Side Irish, men had to do what they could to keep coal in the bin and food on the children's plates. No, all O'Rourke could hope to do was let them and their wives rest easy in knowing that if they were felled by a policeman's bullet while heisting a Thirty-eighth Street warehouse, their souls would pass through purgatory with only the stain of that night's transgressions blackening it.

O'Rourke smiled to himself in the cold church as he thought of a name for what he did—rational redemption.

He had grown cynical since he'd passed his thirty-fourth birthday.

SACRED HEART

—◇—

HANRAHAN SHOVED HIS SMALL HANDS UNDER HIS LEGS AND TRIED TO warm them against the Ford's leather seats. He was one of the smallest cops of the department's twenty-one hundred members— the result of a bribe paid to an Alderman—but very few would be bold enough to say that to his face. Once, just after he'd made detective, a newspaper reporter had done a story about a shoot-out he'd been involved with, and the writer had made the mistake of using the word "gnomish." Hanrahan had stood in hiding outside the paper for three nights, followed the reporter to his favorite speak, made a call to a precinct captain who owed him a favor, watched while the captain's paddy wagons pulled up in front. Hanrahan had then waited by the speak's backdoor while the patrons ran out. When the reporter came out, with nothing but escape on his mind, Hanrahan had coldcocked him from behind with a sap, then proceeded to methodically work over the Hebe with slow, agonizing thoroughness. When he'd finished, Hanrahan had simply knelt by the moaning man and whispered in his ear, "Never make fun of a man's stature, you hook-nosed kike."

Malloy came around the corner of the building and stood by the passenger's side window. His mustache was frosted white, and he was exhaling snorts of white like an overworked mule. He just stood there, looking in at his boss, not even tapping the glass. Hanrahan knew Malloy would wait like that for him until he froze to death. He was country-born, from County Kilkenny, and his value lay in his loyalty, not in his brains. And his loyalty was betrothed to Jackie Hanrahan.

Hanrahan rolled his window down.

"His big Packard's parked around back," Malloy reported quickly, with almost canine servility.

"Matranga's?" The little greaseball never went anywhere except in his own car. The windows were bulletproofed, and there was an extra layer of Pittsburgh steel in the doors and the trunk.

Malloy nodded, waiting for his Detective to tell him what to do next.

"How many others?"

"How many other cars? Two. Maybe three."

Hanrahan thought a moment. That was a helluva lot of dagos to contend with.

"Any sign of the Coynes?"

Malloy shook his head.

15

Hanrahan thought for a moment. It looked good. It looked right. It felt right.

"Get in, Sean. You'll go back and look in a while."

Malloy nodded his head slowly, as though he were making sure he understood what Hanrahan wanted of him, then he walked around the Ford's front end and stepped off the snow-mounded curb and into the street.

◄○►

THE SNOW WAS LESSENING. MORE SWIRLS NOW, DRIVEN BY BRIEF, furious blasts of wind, then muffled, deadened quiet. The City was blanketed by a thick layer of fresh, deep snow. It was two in the morning, numbing cold, and the streets were empty.

Except for the cautious convoy that slowed to a stop in the middle of the block between Seventh Avenue and Broadway on Thirty-eighth Street. The three cars idled, their exhaust plumes billowing in the frozen air. The middle one was Bulldog's Studebaker.

"I've known Jackie since I come over," he was saying. "A lot of business, we've done together."

Tommy, seated in the backseat beside his father, leaned over and pulled out his Thompson from a canvas sack. "He's a flatfoot." Tommy ran his fingertips over the barrel, then held up his hand before his face. By the light reflected by the snow, he could see a thin shine of oil on his fingertips.

"He's a good Irishman, as crooked as any copper I ever seen, and he hates the dagos more than we do." Bulldog clipped his words with a flare of anger, and Duggan in the front seat almost winced.

Tommy took a carefully folded oil rag from the sack, began to stroke the weapon gently.

"I led this gang from a ragtag bunch of dockside brawlers to the brink of takin' over the whole damn West Side," Bulldog said to his younger son. "I think I know what's best for this Mob."

Thomas Coyne knew many things about his father. He knew, for example, that his father had a Jewish girl of nineteen ensconced in an apartment on Crosby Street, and that Bulldog spent as much time with her as he could. Tommy knew that once a month his father gave packets of money to his wife—Tommy's mother—so she could continue to drink herself into oblivion. Tommy knew that

Bulldog had chopped his own father to death with a shorthoe in a County Wexford horse stable after the elder Coyne had broken Bulldog's mother's hip in a drunken frenzy of brutal wifebeating.

And Tommy knew that in pursuit of his dream of controlling the West Side's whiskey trade, his father sometimes let ambition cloud his judgment. He became reckless in his determination, impatient in his planning. That reckless impatience had resulted last summer in the shoot-out on the docks at the foot of Bank Street. The Matrangas had killed three of their boys in the gun battle. Billy Noble, Tommy's best friend, had been one of them.

Tommy laid the Thompson on his lap, took a canister of bullets from the duffel, looked at it a moment, felt the weight of it in his hand. Then he looked over to his father. "Da, I'd follow you to hell, you know that. And I personally want to be the one to blow up Matranga's brains . . ." Tommy switched the weight of the canister from one hand to another. "But Hanrahan—" He shook his head in disapproval. "Look how he sold out Big Jew Gollum."

"Big Jew welched on a deal. He owed Jackie money and he didn't pay the man. You don't do that to Jackie Hanrahan." Bulldog's eyes flashed with righteousness.

Tommy took a moment before he spoke. "He died in the electric chair. Hanrahan got on the stand and said it was Big Jew shot down them two Hunkies in Chinatown, and everybody in the whole damn city knows it was Hanrahan himself pulled the trigger." Tommy held up the machine gun, positioned the canister.

"Big Jew was a Jew," Bulldog said. "He won't do that to us lads."

Duggan in the front seat, turned, ventured support. "He hates the kikes and the wops, does Hanrahan. But I ain't never seen him cross an Irishman."

Tommy slapped in the canister. "He's a fucking cop. He'll do anything."

With that Hanrahan and Malloy came around the corner of the building, moving fast, their shoulders hunched against the cold under their long overcoats.

Duggan rolled down the window, surveyed them a moment, then nodded, saying to Bulldog, "Okay."

Bulldog rolled down his window and Hanrahan's small, pinched face filled the space. His nose was running. It glistened above his lip.

"Bulldog."

"Jackie."

Hanrahan looked over to Tommy, who stared back insolently.

17

Then Hanrahan's eyes went to the Thompson in Tommy's hands. When Hanrahan looked back Tommy smiled.

"You got a nip of that swill you been ravin' about?" Hanrahan asked Bulldog, but kept his eyes on Tommy.

"All out, Jackie Boy," Bulldog answered. "But it's gold, pure gold. It'll make us all lords."

Hanrahan smiled ruefully. "Too bad. It's the damnedest cold I ever felt."

"I ain't never felt it so cold since I come ovah," Duggan said. "Jaysus."

Tommy pulled back the toggle bolt on the machine gun and it made a ratcheting noise. They all stopped talking and looked at him. Then Hanrahan said, "Aye, ye do love that weapon, don't-cha, lad?"

Tommy gave him a cold smile. "I like what it does."

Bulldog moved quickly to get to the point. "Are we ready, Jackie? Is it tonight?"

O'ROURKE BROUGHT THE CIGARETTES AND IRISH WHISKEY BACK WITH him to his rectory. He gave the recalcitrant radiator another fiddle, then surrendered to the cold. He straightened the blankets on his bed, then carefully arranged his overcoat on top. When it looked as inviting as it was going to get, he slipped under the bulk and pulled it up around his chin. Then he reached out and switched off the gooseneck lamp he used to read by.

In the dark, he could see his breath in the cold stone room. Not for the first time O'Rourke thought that the life of a parish priest must be very much like that of a convicted criminal. *Only you get to drink*, he thought and reached for the bottle.

"IF I TOUCH MY HAT, IT'S ON. UNDERSTOOD?"

"What do I look like, the village idiot?" Bulldog growled. Tommy knew his father was sensitive about any question about his intelligence. His illiteracy made him belligerent.

18

They were standing against the wall, the ice crunching under their shoes, the wet cold rising up through the soles. Duggan, Tommy and Bulldog. The two coppers. And strung out along the wall Henry Sheehan, Moon Mullins with his big, sawed-off 12-gauge, the Perkins brothers, and Frankie McGonagle, with the wooden leg he got in the War. Kevin Kearney and the other two drivers stayed in their cars.

"I come out. If everything's okay, I touch my hat, like this." Hanrahan demonstrated again, as if this were all too important to leave to a chance misunderstanding. "If it ain't, I'll put up my collar, like this, and just walk away."

Bulldog just stared at him.

"Why wouldn't everything be okay?" Tommy wanted to know. He hated coppers, and he hated Hanrahan more than any copper he had ever known. Once he saw Hanrahan roust a couple of jigs who had strayed south of Eighty-eighth Street. Just a couple of stupid kids drunk on a Saturday night. Hanrahan had had Malloy and another copper hold each one up, in turn, while he went at them with a nightstick. "Why would anything be wrong?"

Hanrahan stepped away from the wall and stared at Tommy—a copper gesture, meant to intimidate and proclaim supreme power. "Ye want to be careful with something like this. The wrong people could die."

"The man's right," Bulldog said to his son, then to Hanrahan, "Your hat, it's on. Your collar, it ain't." Bulldog grinned with expectation, and it made him look open, friendly, just another mick in America. "Touch your hat, Jackie. Let's all live on Park Avenue."

Hanrahan looked at Bulldog and then smiled back. The smile sent a deep sense of foreboding through Tommy like a shudder. *He's lying. He's fucking lying.*

"Good luck to us all," Hanrahan said. Then he turned to big, dumb Malloy. "Let's go do our job, Sean."

They turned and walked quickly away, leaving huge bear prints in the snow as they disappeared around the corner.

Tommy immediately looked at his father, who was oblivious in his determination.

"Tonight's the night, boys," Bulldog said to the others. "The Coyne Mob takes control."

"Sounds like a fuckin' headline." Stevey Perkins giggled nervously.

"I'm gonna piss in Anthony Matranga's skull," Moon Mullins growled, and jacked a shell into the breech of his 12-gauge.

Bulldog grinned with approval. He liked a murderous attitude in his men when they were about to commit murder. "My Tommy says the head guinea's all his." He looked at Tommy with pride. Pride in himself, and pride in his son. "It's befittin' the future head of the Coyne Mob. We'll be a legend."

Tommy stuck the butt of the Thompson into his hip, holding it one-handed, muzzle up, and stepped closer to his father. He leaned his head forward in their traditional signal for private consultation, and Bulldog did the same.

Tommy paused for the briefest of moments, and then went on and said it.

"It's a setup."

—◄○►—

TOMMY HAD TOLD THE WHORE GEORGINA THAT HE DIDN'T REMEMBER how many he had killed, but in truth he remembered every one. There were seven he had killed alone, plus the other four or five he had had a hand in. The first was Davey Jones, a loose-change burglar from Yorkville who kept coming over to Hell's Kitchen and robbing the old ladies when their men were at work on the docks. He would wait until the women left their apartments to do their laundry or to go to the boot for a pint, and then he would kick in the door and take everything he could grab. Pete Reilly's old lady was home when Davey busted in, and he pushed her around and made her hold his dick, then he robbed her of the Reillys' rent money. The boys came to Bulldog and asked him to do something, and Bulldog put out the word that there was a five-dollar bill and a bottle of his best swill to anyone who broke Davey Jones's legs. Suddenly Mr. Jones was nowhere to be seen. Then a few weeks later Tommy—fifteen at the time, already "graduated" from school and rolling kegs with the niggers, unloading illegal beer from his father's trucks—was down around Bowery with Pool Table Timms and there was Davey, sauntering down the street as if he owned it. Tommy pictured in his mind his father's angry face when he heard of Davey's cheek, and Tommy himself became enraged.

"Davey!" Tommy called out from the cab of the truck. "You gonna be walkin' on crutches, you are!"

Jones stopped dead in the street and ripped out a pistol. He pointed it straight at Tommy and said, "I ain't afraid of any of you fuckin' Coynes."

Pool Table had gunned the Ford's motor and got them out of there. Tommy had stared back at Davey glaring, craning his neck to keep him in sight until they turned the corner.

"Stop!" Tommy had barked at the much older man. "Stop the fucking truck!"

"What?! What?!"

Tommy rose in his seat, threw his leg over Pool Table's and stomped his foot down on the brake pedal. The Ford slammed to a stop and the kegs in back crashed and rolled around.

"Gimme your gat!" Tommy shouted in fury into Pool Table's face, and Table had reached into his pocket for his big, long-barreled Colt. He hesitated before he handed it over. "Bulldog ain't gonna like me givin' ye me gun."

Tommy stared hard at Table, then said softly, "Well, it looks like you ain't gonna do nothing with it."

Pool Table looked into Tommy's eyes, and then softly caught his breath. "Aye, it's your da." Tommy understood, and swiftly took the .45 from Table's meaty paw. He inspected it a moment, not familiar with the weapon. "Is it—?"

"Aye. All six."

"Do you have to cock it?"

"Nah, just pull the trigger."

Tommy threw himself from the truck cab and ran back to the corner. He didn't even hesitate, but came around onto Lafayette with the big pistol held out before him. The street was crowded, a streetcar was passing, and a woman in a window seat saw him and screamed.

Davey Jones, walking swiftly downtown, heard the scream and whirled to see Tommy running toward him, the big pistol raised. Davey again reached for his own pistol and Tommy fired. The first bullet tore out Davey's kidney and exited his back, taking with it a hellish soup of tissue, blood and bone. A tailor's window shattered on the far side of the street. Tommy was only twenty feet away when he fired again, on the dead run. Davey's left shoulder erupted in a geyser of blood, and his arm flopped around limp, hanging by a single tendon. Now the people on the street dropped to the cobblestone, mothers shielding their children, men looking around for the source of the shooting.

Davey Jones continued to raise his pistol, vaguely aware that something terrible had happened to him, but working on instinct.

He had it eye-level, aimed at Tommy's heart, now only ten feet away and closing, when Tommy pulled the trigger again.

And then an incredible thing happened.

Tommy watched as Davey Jones's face disappeared. It kind of folded inward on itself, all the features of his face disintegrating, like dirty water being sucked down a sewer. One moment there was Davey Jones's nose, eyes, lips—and then a blink later there was a gaping raw gaw.

Tommy suddenly realized he was standing in the street over Davey's twitching body. He didn't know how long he'd been there. He felt himself shaking, but it was not with fear. With an all-consuming, flaming *rage*. He raised his eyes to stare at the street full of people, kneeling, lying. It was as if the whole world were holding its breath. Then a fat man scurried to his feet and ran into a butcher shop, shattering the stillness.

Then hands were on him and Tommy spun and raised the Colt.

"No! NO!" Pool Table shouted, holding up his hands as he shrank back. After a moment, Tommy recognized him, stared at him, then turned back to Davey Jones's dead body, just as it stopped twitching. Pool Table looked at the body, then back at Tommy, glowering down at it. "Come on, lad! Quick!" He took hold of Tommy again and pulled him toward the corner. Tommy hung back, glaring at the corpse. "Quick!" Pool Table shouted, and suddenly reality came roaring back into Tommy's head like a freight engine. He started to run.

--<o>--

BULLDOG STARED AT HIS SON, AND FOR THE BRIEFEST OF MOMENTS Tommy could see fear rise like a flare, far back in his father's eyes. Then Bulldog had it under control, replaced it with anger. When he spoke his brogue got as thick as Dublin fog, the way it did whenever he was under stress, or unsure.

"What the hell are ye sayin', boyo?" Bulldog hissed.

Tommy took his father's arm and led him a few feet away from the others. He could feel their eyes on his back. "Da," he said softly, "it don't feel right. There's something wrong."

"*Ahhh*—" Bulldog shook his head in denial. Then his face got mean, the way it always did when there was someone between him and something he wanted. "It's just all that quim you chase got you in a weakened condition. That's all."

"Da—"

"Maybe you should've joined the priesthood, like your sweet maiden of a brother. Then you could get to wear them black skirts."

Tommy stared at Bulldog, and knew there was no stopping him. Whatever was going to happen, was going to happen. That was Bulldog Coyne's great strength, and his greatest weakness. Keeping his eyes on his father's, Tommy slowly raised the machine gun until the barrel was level with Bulldog's face. Bulldog stared at the muzzle, his eyes as cold as the night. Then Tommy clicked off the safety. The other Irishmen watched intently. Everyone stood motionless. A furious blast of wind howled down the street and over them. And then Tommy said, "It's your play, Da."

A slow grin spread over Bulldog's face. "That's my boyo."

—◄○►—

HANRAHAN TOOK A BREATH, THEN RAISED HIS FIST AND TAPPED SOFTLY on the corrugated iron door. It made a hollow sound. Hanrahan waited a moment, then glanced up at Malloy, standing beside him. Malloy was picking his nose.

"Christ, Sean," Hanrahan rasped.

Malloy took his finger from his nose and looked down at Hanrahan with confusion. "What?"

Hanrahan shook his head and started to raise his hand again when there was the sound of a latch being thrown, a moment of stillness, and then the big door slid open an inch, revealing an iron accordion grating and behind it an old man with a dark, shriveled face. The old man inspected Hanrahan up and down as if he were looking at a dead rat.

"He wanted to see me," Hanrahan said.

The old man stared another moment without moving.

"Open the door, it's fuckin' cold out here!" Hanrahan snapped.

The old man reached behind the door with pointed slowness and unlocked something. With surprising strength he leaned against both doors and shoved them partially open. They made a screeching metallic sound as they scraped along the concrete floor. Hanrahan stepped inside, and Malloy dutifully followed. The old man jerked the door shut behind them.

Inside was a partially converted, two-story warehouse. The back wall was white-washed brick, the side walls raw boarding hung on naked two-by-four framing. There were nine men sitting around two tables, playing cards, and the tables were arranged within the heat radius of a cast-iron coal-burner stove against the right wall. A man in shirtsleeves and a bowler hat was stirring a pot of soup cooking on the stove top. The odor told Hanrahan it was minestrone. Another man stood beside the man in the bowler hat, holding a cup of coffee. Everyone in the room seemed to ignore the two Irishmen who had just entered.

Hanrahan studied the two card games a moment, looking for Anthony Matranga. *Fuckin' guineas all look alike*, he thought; then a man looked up at him, and he saw that it was Matranga. Hanrahan approached the table. Malloy followed closely, as if he were trying to hide his big bulk behind his detective's diminutive frame.

"It's fuckin' freezin' out there," Hanrahan said across the table to Matranga. Matranga was a small man, shorter even than Hanrahan himself, and that always made the policeman feel a kind of a kinship with the gangster whenever they were in each other's presence. Even though Hanrahan loathed the Italian in all other matters.

Matranga stared at him a moment, then said something in Sicilian to the four other men at his table. They laughed, looking up at Hanrahan, and he felt himself flush with anger and humiliation. It was Hanrahan's belief that Sicilians were the repository of all that was twisted and dark in the human race. They had ruined New York, and left unchecked they would infect the whole damn country.

"If you have a joke, say it in American English, so we can all have a laugh." Hanrahan stared at the table until the smiles had all faded. He wasn't going to let these wops intimidate him. Life wasn't that precious. "I heard one the other day, about a bride at a dago wedding."

Now the men stared darkly at Hanrahan. One, with sandy hair and a pencil-thin mustache, threw his cards down on the table. Hanrahan heard Malloy, behind him, move a step closer.

"I been havin' trouble," Matranga said to him, moving to defuse the situation. "I been havin' trouble with you *Irish* on Forty-seventh Street." Hanrahan knew that by "Irish" Matranga meant the department. "I pay you good money this don't happen. What is this shit?"

Hanrahan felt himself relax. Shaking down dago gangsters was something with which he was quite comfortable. He allowed himself a small smile. "People are spendin' money like there's no tomorrow. It's a big party." Hanrahan started to stroll around the tables, asserting his rights as a New York City detective. "The other day this big Wall Street Jew told me the bottom's gonna fall out the stockmarket. This year, next year for sure. Whattaya think of that?"

Matranga's eyes followed him as he sauntered around the table. "I don't give a fuck about no stock market. What I give a fuck about is I pay you to keep Forty-seventh Street quiet, and you Irish come in my joints, shake down my bartenders, make my customers nervous. What is this shit?"

One of the players at the table began to shuffle the cards.

Hanrahan kept his smile. "I told you. People are spendin' money. Then they're always needin' more money. I can't control that." He had reached Matranga's chair. He stopped. "It's a free country."

Matranga stared up at Hanrahan with anger, then looked around at the men at the table and shook his head with disgust. Fucking Irish. "Get the fuck outta here. You make me sick." Matranga looked at the man with the deck of cards and tapped his hand on the tabletop. The man with the cards started to deal. Hanrahan didn't move. Matranga picked up his cards, inspected them slowly, revealing to himself just the corner of each one. Then he looked back up at Hanrahan. "What?"

"I don't come out on a night like this for nothing."

Matranga stared up at him with disbelief, then he looked at the table and said in the thick Sicilian of his home village, "These people have no shame."

The sandy-haired man with the mustache, knowing the policemen couldn't understand him, said, "They sleep with their own sisters. They are pigs."

"We could kill them now, right here. Two less to worry about," another man said.

Matranga smiled at that man, as if he liked the idea. Then he looked at Hanrahan.

Hanrahan's glare was Shakespearean, perfected on a thousand frightened young men. "I'm still waitin'. And it's still fuckin' cold outside."

Matranga shook his head again, then fingered loose a quartet of twenty-dollar bills from the bottom of the stack of money on the table. He folded the money over and held it in two fingers, his hand resting on the tabletop. Hanrahan had to lean over another gambler, stand on the balls of his feet to pluck the money from Matranga's contemptuous grasp.

"Now," Matranga said. "Get the fuck outta here."

—◄○►—

THE DOOR SCREECHED AS THE OLD MAN PULLED IT ACROSS THE CON-crete, jolted shut with a clang and an iron shudder. Hanrahan raised his hand to his hat, lifted it a few inches from his head, then settled it back down. He turned to his right and quickly walked away from the warehouse, Malloy beside him. Hanrahan turned to Malloy and said, "Fucking guineas gonna be laughin' trough their asses when the Coynes get trough with them."

—◄○►—

SALVATORE HAD NEVER KNOWN SUCH COLD IN HIS LIFE. SALVATORE had never known such cold existed. He took his hands from the mount of the Browning automatic rifle and blew into them. He had seen photographs, of course. Of the Alpine crests in Switzerland, in northern Italy. A picture book about Germany. But he had never experienced it. Three weeks before he had been sipping grappa in his home village in the mountainous region of Sicily called Adrano, and now he was squatting behind a Browning in the empty office of a closed-down garment factory, and he was experiencing cold such as he had never known.

"Is it always this cold in America?" he said to the man next to him, a man named Umberto from a fishing village on Sicily's African coast.

"Maybe only in New York, I think," Umberto said.

Salvatore blew into his hands and thought that tomorrow he would ask if he could have a pair of gloves. For a week he had been sleeping on the floor of an unheated fifth-floor walk-up on Mulberry Street with two other young men. Food, beer and ciga-rettes had been brought up to them by a man named Carmine. A very important man, who everyone said worked for an even more important man. The legendary Matranga, a name to be spoken in a reverential tone, like a saint's.

"Do you have any more Luckies?" Umberto asked.

Salvatore turned and looked at him in the darkness. "Signóre Carmine said we were not to smoke."

A moment passed before Carlos, with the 12-gauge, said, "We have been here for twenty-seven hours. We piss in the corner and it freezes. We shit on the stairs and it freezes. There has been no coffee since this afternoon. And we can't even have a Lucky?" In the week they had been here Umberto and Carlos had fallen in love with American cigarettes.

Salvatore looked past Umberto's form to where Carlos's voice was coming from.

"But we are working for *Il Capo Matranga*," Salvatore said as if that would justify any hardship.

The other two seemed to consider this in the silence that followed. Then behind them there was the sudden, jarring sound of a door yanked open as silently as possible, and for a moment the shuttered office was filled with the dimmest of light. Salvatore turned to look and saw two men enter the office's back door. The taller form Salvatore knew to be *Signóre* Joe, the American who spoke bad Italian. *Signóre* Joe was always with *Signóre* Carmine.

"I could hear you fools talking at the back door," Carmine growled.

The three young men said nothing for a moment, then Carlos, the most outspoken of them all, asked, "Is there coffee, *Signóre* Carmine? It is very cold."

Carmine moved past them to the iron shutters and began to carefully, silently unlock them. Salvatore could see *Signóre* Carmine had a shotgun slung over his back, as if he were going boar hunting.

"It's about to heat up," Carmine Carini said in English, as he opened the shutters.

—◇—

THEY HAD JURY-RIGGED A SNOWPLOW TO THE FRONT BUMPER OF AN OLD Ford truck with New Jersey plates, and the snow was so high it kept piling up between the teeth and spilling over. Duggan was driving. Bulldog walked on the driver's side, Tommy on the passenger.

They turned the corner at a clumsy, slippery run, and it was only a long half block to the big iron door. Tommy's head swiveled as he tried to look down every alley, through every blackened window. Tommy glanced across the truck's hood at his father and saw that Bulldog was grinning at him, slashing clumsily through the snow, his big Colt held high. Tommy tried to smile back, but he couldn't. Then his eyes looked past his father to the other side of the street and Tommy saw a movement, something, in one of the windows, and he was about to shout something when Duggan downshifted and the truck lunged forward and roared into the sliding metal door. The metal buckled and the truck ripped through the accordion grate and into the warehouse, its headlights reflecting off the whitewashed brick walls and back out into the street.

Tommy paused behind the truck, half-enveloped in its exhaust smoke, and peered intently at the ground-level garment factory office across the street. He had seen something. Something had moved. Then Duggan shouted from the truck cab, "They ain't here!"

Tommy didn't hesitate. He raised the Thompson and started firing at the windows of the garment factory. He heard someone scream, and then the narrow snow-covered street echoed with a deafening barrage of small-arms fire. It sounded as if every pane of window glass on the block was shattering. Bullets struck metal with the sound of a hundred ball peen hammers. All over the street snow was being kicked up by automatic fire. Someone in the garment factory was shooting a Browning. Just to Tommy's left Henry Sheehan seemed to rise up out of his shoes and fly backward, his severed legs moving and spouting blood all over the snow. Tommy shouted and raked the garment factory with submachine fire. Then a round whistled by his ear from above and behind. They were shooting down at them from the roof of Matranga's warehouse. Tommy turned, just in time to see Moon Mullins stagger out of the warehouse, his 12-gauge open, pulling out the spent shells.

"Fuckin' setup!" Moon screamed at Tommy, as he slammed in two new cartridges, then he made a noise like the wind being knocked out of him and his insides sloshed down the front of his overcoat. He fell against the truck's fender and toppled over.

"Da!" Tommy shouted as he reached for another canister. "Da!" Then he saw movement from across the street and he turned to see a thick, heavyset Italian rushing at him firing a pistol. Tommy stooped by Moon's body, with his left hand picked up his still-breech-opened 12-gauge, slammed it shut with a violent jerk and pulled both triggers. The Italian seemed to explode before his eyes.

From the roof behind someone was cursing him in Italian. Tommy jammed in the round canister of shells, turned and fired furiously at the roof line.

"Daaaaaaaa!!!!" Tommy bellowed over and over. "Daaaa!! Daaaa!!"

Whoever had the Thompson in the garment factory was shooting continuously, and the withering fire was chewing up everything in the street. Tommy ducked around behind the truck, threw himself over the hood and into Matranga's warehouse. Tommy spun around and he saw Duggan slumped behind the wheel, a gaping hole where his right eye should be, the truck's windshield shattered.

"Da!" He fired a burst at the whitewashed wall, because there was no one there.

"Tom." It was coming from under the truck. Tommy ran to the driver's side, and Bulldog was half-under the running boards, trying to reload his Colt. His hands were dripping with blood.

Tommy began to pull his father out from under the truck. Bulldog looked up at him and for the first time in his life Tommy saw true terror in his father's eyes. "Me legs," Bulldog whispered. "Me legs." Tommy lifted his father's considerable bulk onto his back, then picked up the Thompson and ran back out into the street.

He fired the whole canister at the garment office, then threw the Thompson away. He ran, slipping, through the blood-soaked snow. In front of his face was Bulldog's red hand, clutching the Colt revolver.

"Don't let them get away!" someone shouted from the garment factory, and Tommy heard the Browning start up again. He was almost to the corner, hugging the buildings, when it felt like someone picked him up and threw him against the wall. He scrambled to keep his footing, his father on his back, then he rounded the corner and the street was quiet, the snow white and pristine. And empty. Kevin and the other drivers had left, saving themselves.

"You sorry sons a bitches!" he shouted. "I'll kill all of youse!"

Tommy ran to the next corner, then the next. At the third a cab was idling at a cab stand. When the cabbie saw Tommy running toward him, carrying Bulldog, he immediately threw the car in gear and started to pull away from the curb. Tommy shot him twice with one of his automatics, then pulled him from the cab and dropped him to the street. He plopped Bulldog down on the front seat, sat down and floored it, went into an out-of-control swerve all the way across the street, and crashed into a row of parked cars. Without taking his foot off the gas, he yanked the wheel and the cab ripped away from the parked cars and careened down the street.

—◦—

FRANKIE MCGONAGLE WAS SITTING WITH HIS BACK AGAINST THE WALL, screaming at the street. "Don't one of you fine Italian maidens have the balls to put an Irishman out of his fuckin' misery?!"

Joe Zanca—tall, big, *American*—trotted back down from the corner. He looked at Frankie McGonagle, then said to Carmine, who was watching Frankie scream. "Can you fuckin' believe it? The Coynes got away."

Frankie took a deep breath, threw back his head and bellowed.

"The fuckin' Huns got the best of me, now you greaseballs got the rest!"

Carmine shook his head and looked over at Salvatore, who had the disassembled Browning over his shoulder.

"He ain't gonna like that," Carmine said to Joe Zanca.

"May all of you rot in hell for all eternity!" Frankie McGonagle's good leg was now as useless as the shattered stump he had picked up in a Belgian trench. He also had a gruesome head wound that had produced a lot of blood. He was blinded by the stuff. "I put a curse on all of youse!"

The snowy, blood-sloshed street was littered with bodies—the whole Coyne Mob except for the old man and his kid. And three Italians, two of them Carlos and Umberto, who had come over on the boat with Salvatore a week before. Carmine looked down at Frankie McGonagle again.

"Would one of youse fucking greaseballs have a pint on you, by any chance?" Frankie roared.

Carmine shook his head again. "These people are unbelievable."

Then a car came around the corner and stopped. Out of the Packard stepped a diminutive man in a fur-collared overcoat. Salvatore knew immediately that this was the famous Matranga. He walked toward them, just as Frankie McGonagle hollered, "I can't see you goddamn guineas, but I can smell you, you garlic-eating sons of bitches!"

Matranga stared at McGonagle a moment then nodded, and Carmine swung up the shotgun and blew Frankie's head off.

With Frankie's bellowing silenced the street was quiet—the hum of Matranga's armored Packard, the howl of the wind.

"Everybody but the Bulldog and his boy," Joe said to Matranga.

Matranga looked at Joe, then Carmine, and finally his eyes settled on Salvatore. "Then we ain't finished, are we?"

—◁○▷—

WHEN THE SHOOTING STARTED, MALLOY HAD BEEN JUST UNCORKING A little jug he'd gotten from a Jew boot down on Rivington Street. He grinned at Hanrahan. "Listen to that, would ya?" The two men in the police car listened intently to the battle going on a few blocks away. "Jaysus. The Coynes are tearin' 'em up."

Hanrahan took the little jug from Malloy's hand and threw back a long swallow. The distant gunfire hadn't slackened a bit.

"Jaysus," Malloy said again.

—◀○▶—

"DA!" TOMMY FOUGHT TO KEEP CONTROL OF THE CAB ON THE ICY streets as he tried to unbutton Bulldog's collar. "Da! Hang on!"

There were several doctors on the Coyne payroll who treated members of the mob without question or hesitation. Tommy's benumbed, screaming mind ran through their names and locations. There was one close-by in Hell's Kitchen. A butcher of a drunken Dubliner.

"Don't die, Da!" *Please don't die!* "I'm gonna get you there!"

Tommy knew he'd been shot, that the seat of his pants was wet with blood, but he didn't have time to stop and examine it now. He worked the clutch and the brake, tried to keep the car from overturning on the ice and snow, as he skidded into the sanctuary that was Hell's Kitchen.

—◀○▶—

AT THE CORNER OF NINTH AVENUE AND FORTIETH STREET A THIRTIETH Precinct police car, responding to a phone call to the precinct about a pitched gun battle on 38th Street, screamed south across the intersection, just as Tommy drove in from the east. The police car plowed into the back door of the cab, overturning it, and the smashed police car became entangled in the cab's undercarriage and driveshaft. The two cars, their metal enmeshed, intertwined, spun in a circle across the icy intersection and crashed into the show window of a department store. The police car's gas tank ruptured and gasoline began to spew out from beneath like fearful urine.

Tommy, holding up his father, kicked open the cab door, clambered out onto the cab's upturned side and began to pull out Bulldog. The two cops were screaming. They were trapped in the

31

crushed police car, and they could smell the gas. Tommy hauled his father from the cab, pulled him onto his back and ran back into the empty aisles of the department store. The squad car blew then, and Tommy and Bulldog were lifted up and thrown across a counter into men's haberdasheries.

—◁○▷—

THE FIRE ENGINES ARRIVED FIRST, AND THE FIREMEN IN THEIR SLICKERS started to fight the blaze that was gutting the bottom floor of Gould's Department Store. The police came next, and when they saw the flaming squad car and the charred remains of their brother officers the word went out and Ninth Avenue quickly became jammed with squad cars. It was almost three o'clock and the night had turned numbingly, impossibly cold, even as the snow had slacked off.

The cops searched for the cab driver's body, and it wasn't until Hanrahan came on the scene, Malloy in tow, that anyone linked the crash with the gun battle on Thirty-eighth Street. Hanrahan motioned to Malloy and they snaked their way past the firefighters and up the dead escalator onto the department store's upper floors.

On the fourth floor Hanrahan found a trail of blood, and he knew that the Coynes were somewhere above.

"DON'T DIE, DA!" TOMMY, BATTERED AND BLEEDING, DRAGGED HIS FATHER across the vast wood-slat floor of the seventh-story loft of Gould's. "Please don't die." Bulldog's limp body left a wide, thick smear of blood on the lint-dusted floor as Tommy dragged him through the long rows of Singer sewing machines. The seventh floor was where Gould's tailors did their alterations, and beside each sewing station were piles of clothes and fabric, like artillery ammunition.

"Da!" Bulldog's eyelids twitched at Tommy's shout, and he knew his father was still alive, somehow. "Don't die on me!"

Smoke was beginning to drift out of the stairwell. Tommy left his father and ran to the tall, grime-encrusted windows that lined one wall. Down below, the street was packed with city vehicles. Firemen and cops were running around frantically, and the flames from Gould's first-floor fire danced across the storefronts, giving the wintry night a hellish brightness. Tommy ran to the back-wall windows and through the decades of dirt and pigeon droppings he could see a flat, snowy rooftop only one story below. Tommy tried the window and it was stuck. He was pushing on it when from behind him Hanrahan shouted.

"Bulldog! You up here?"

Tommy whirled, whipped out both of his silvery .45 automatics.

"Bulldog?" Hanrahan shouted again. Then through the smoky haze he emerged from the stairwell across the loft.

Tommy cocked both guns, and Hanrahan's eyes snapped to the sound. "Tommy?"

"You stool-pigeon bastard! You set us up!"

"Tommy, no!" Hanrahan held up his hands. "I didn't do that!"

"How the hell'd Matranga know we were coming?" Tommy's arms shook with rage and fatigue.

"I don't know!" Hanrahan shouted, as Malloy appeared out of the smoke beside him. "Where's Bulldog?"

"You friggin' copper!"

"I didn't do it! One of your boys must be on Matranga's pad!"

"You're fuckin' lying!"

"No, I ain't!" Hanrahan moved into the loft a few feet, looking around. His right hand was under his overcoat. "I ain't! Now, where's Bulldog?"

"Here," came weakly from the gloom of the loft.

Tommy was heartened to hear his father's voice. He realized he'd been afraid he wouldn't ever hear it again. But when he looked to him, his spirits sank. Bulldog Coyne, using every bit of the determination and resolve that had gotten him his name, had pulled himself upright and was tottering against a tacking table. His legs were all twisted in wrong directions, useless and slack, and he was covered in blood.

"Jesus, Da . . . "

And then Hanrahan swept up a tommy gun from under his overcoat and fired a quick vicious burst. Before Tommy's eyes Bulldog's upper torso jerked in a deadly Saint Vitus' dance then crumpled like a doll with its stuffing spilling out. Tommy froze for a shocked shard of a moment, realizing he'd just watched his father die. Then he threw himself behind a fitting dummy just as Hanrahan's tommy gun chewed up the floor where he'd been standing.

"Jackie!" Malloy gasped in disbelief. "What the hell ya doin'?!"

Hanrahan ducked his small form down below the level of the sewing machines and moved quickly down a center aisle. Tommy's two arms appeared over another remnant table, the .45s firing furiously. Malloy took one in the shoulder, spun around and went down. Then Hanrahan fired a long continuous barrage across the loft. When Hanrahan stopped to dig another canister from his overcoat pocket, Tommy stood and ran pell-mell across the splintered floor, snatched up a bolt of thick velvet from a table, and using the cloth to shield his face, jumped straight up at the round-topped back windows. He crashed through the glass and fell the twenty feet to the rooftop below. He landed in three feet of snow and it cushioned him like a pillow as he landed and rolled. Then he was up and slogging toward the fire escape and Hanrahan was in the window firing down. The freshly fallen whiteness sucked at Tommy's shoes, pulled him back, and he could hear the bullets plowing into the snow just behind. He was at the edge and over, just as the rounds started pinging on the fire-escape steel.

"Damn!" Hanrahan cursed. "Damn!" He turned and moved quickly down the rows of sewing machines to Malloy, who was sitting stupidly on the floor, holding his shoulder like an injured adolescent.

"Jaysus, Jackie. What the hell—"

His words were cut off as Hanrahan stuck the muzzle of the tommy gun into Malloy's chest and without hesitation squeezed the trigger.

—◁○▷—

FIFTEEN MINUTES LATER THERE WERE FIFTY COPS IN GOULD'S LOFT. IN THIRTY minutes, there were a hundred and fifty. The fire had risen to the third floor before it had been extinguished, and all the cops, who had arrived to grimly witness the chilling sight of two fellow officers burned to cinder in what had obviously been a pursuit situation, had by then coughed their way up the stairs to see the carnage and outrage in Gould's loft.

"Poor Sean was beggin' for his life," Hanrahan said. "On his knees, for God's sake." He repeated the story every few minutes, for the benefit of the newly arrived.

"I was runnin' back down for reinforcements, lookin' for some of youse guys"—as if somehow they shared in the guilt—"when I heard him. He was beggin' for his bleedin' life, he was." Hanrahan looked around at the grim Celtic faces. "That little Coyne bastard laughed. He fuckin' laughed!" Hanrahan paused for dramatic effect. "He executed him! He shot him like a mad dog."

"Jaysus," a young rookie breathed softly.

"Sean Malloy," an old veteran said. "I walked a beat with him for two years."

"The best cop ever put on the uniform."

"Aye, the best."

There was a commotion at the back of the crowd of cops. A rustle of importance. Then the policemen parted and the Commissioner pushed through. He looked at Malloy's body, chest ripped open, then at Bulldog's, crumpled twenty feet away. Then the Commissioner looked at Hanrahan.

"Tell me what happened."

⟨○⟩

TOMMY HAD CLATTERED DOWN THE FIRE ESCAPE, THEN STUMBLED SEVEN blocks north on Ninth Avenue, then turned east. He could again feel bleeding in his lower back. He gulped in huge drafts of frigid air that tore at his lungs like an ice ax, even though he was soaked with perspiration. In the middle of the block on Forty-seventh he lurched into an alley, tripped over a step and tumbled headlong into a stand of garbage cans, mounded with snow. He lay among the cans a moment, trying to catch his breath, when light suddenly spilled into the alley and a man whose sleepy face looked vaguely familiar appeared in a doorway. He looked down at Tommy with concern.

"Are you all right?"

Tommy didn't answer. After the events of the night the man's solicitousness seemed out of place, otherworldly.

John O'Rourke stepped out into the snow-drifted alley, leaned over, and started to reach out to help Tommy up.

Just then a police car bulldozed through the snow on Forty-seventh Street, its siren echoing off the buildings. There were shouts out on the street, and a pair of cops ran past the alley on the other side of the street.

Tommy acted quickly. He pushed himself to his feet and stuck a .45 into O'Rourke's face.

The man registered surprise. He was going to say something

when Tommy pushed him back through the door. "Keep your mouth shut or I'll blow your fuckin' head off!"

Tommy quickly locked the door behind him, then turned back. He looked up at the vaulted ceilings, the altar. He realized where he was.

O'Rourke peered at him through the church's gloom. "You're Frank Coyne's little brother."

Tommy pushed him quickly down the left aisle, under the Stations of the Cross. "Are all the other doors locked?"

"There's only one other. I like to leave them open"—Tommy had O'Rourke's arm in a tight grip, moving him quickly—"but Mrs. Cohalon always locks them after she cleans the—"

"Shut up," Tommy said, as they neared the front entrance. Suddenly someone tried the door from the outside. Tommy yanked O'Rourke behind a pillar and pointed the gun at the door. Someone rattled it again, but it wouldn't open.

"I guess it's locked," O'Rourke said.

Then there was a shout from outside the alley door. Then another. Someone started pounding on the front door.

"Open up! Open up!"

The pounding stopped for a moment, and the church was calm and silent. Tommy breathed heavily and his breath frosted in the coldness of the stone church. Then the pounding started again.

"Father! Open the door!"

O'Rourke looked at Tommy. "What have you done?"

Tommy kept looking from door to door. "I told you to shut up."

"Because I have friends on the Force. Whatever it is—"

"Father O'Rourke!!" That was followed by a fresh frenzy of hammering. Tommy looked at the priest, then dragged him quickly to the front door.

"Tell them everything's all right. Tell them you're alone."

O'Rourke stared at the door a moment. The pounding had ceased, but there was a sense of activity behind the aged oak. "I can't do that."

Tommy cocked the automatic and shoved the muzzle under O'Rourke's chin. "I'll kill you quick as anyone else!" Tommy hissed.

O'Rourke looked into Tommy's eyes. "I can see that."

The pounding started again. "Police! Open this door!"

"Tell them to go away."

O'Rourke nodded, then said loudly to the door, "I can't let you in!"

There was a long moment of silence, then, "Father O'Rourke?"

Tommy jammed the muzzle tighter against the priest's throat. "Tell them if they try to come in you'll be the first to die."

O'Rourke hesitated.

"Fuckin' tell 'em!"

"You don't want me to say that."

Tommy stared at him with amazement. "Are you bugs?"

"If I tell them that, whatever trouble you're in, it'll only worsen your predicament."

"Worsen my predicament!"

"Father?" the voice shouted from the other side of the heavy door. "Father, are you all right?"

Tommy whirled O'Rourke around and smashed his face against the ancient oak. "Do you want to die, priest?"

"It wasn't in my day's schedule."

He pressed the automatic against the base of the priest's skull. "Cause you don't mean nothing to me. I'd kill you as soon as look at you."

As well as he could, O'Rourke nodded into the door.

"Now you do exactly what I tell you to do."

"Father?" It was a different voice. *"Father, this is the Commissioner of Police!"*

"My God," O'Rourke breathed, "what did you do?" Then he understood and said softly, "Kill a cop . . . "

THE COMMISSIONER WAITED A MOMENT, THEN TURNED TO LOOK AT THE street. The unseen sun had turned the sky a dark slag-heap gray, and the patrol car headlights glinted behind the shifting legs of the scores of uniformed cops who were stamping the street's snow into a muddy sludge.

"You're sure he's in there?"

"He's in there." Hanrahan stood close to the Commissioner's arm, moving with him every time he did.

The Commissioner turned back and stared at the door. "I have never been so cold," he said, almost to himself.

Hanrahan lifted his fist and looked at the Commissioner for confirmation. The Commissioner nodded. Hanrahan pounded with urgency on the door.

"Father O'Rourke?" the Commissioner bellowed. "You'll have to open this door."

There was no answer. The Commissioner looked up at the church steeple, then at the rooftops of the surrounding buildings. A cop with a Winchester carbine waved down at him.

"If he shows even half a face," Hanrahan said, "we got him."

—◄○►—

O'ROURKE SAT IN A BACK PEW, WHERE HE HAD BEEN TOLD TO STAY. Tommy came back from the rectory—O'Rourke's cramped living quarters.

"That's it? Just these two doors?"

"It's an old church. They bricked in the back wall when they built the shoe factory." Then he said, "You're bleeding. It's all over the floor."

"There's no other way in or out?"

O'Rourke studied him. "Your brother Frank was an altar boy here. So were you, weren't you?"

"I told you to shut up."

Tommy slumped into a bench and looked up at the stained-glass rose window over the front door. "What about the bell steeple?"

O'Rourke shook his head. "It's too narrow. I told you, Sacred Heart's fifty years old."

Tommy looked slowly around the church. "If I die in here, priest, you're gonna die with me."

"How do you expect to get out?"

"I don't."

"Then you're just buying time?"

"You in a hurry to die, priest?"

"No, I'm not," O'Rourke said. "Let me make a suggestion."

—◄○►—

BY EIGHT O'CLOCK THE SNOW ON FORTY-SEVENTH STREET BETWEEN Eighth and Ninth, the whole block, had been churned into an icy, muddy slush. Reporters from all eight daily New York newspapers were catching cold behind police barriers set up in a rough square in front of the church. They kept taking photographs of the Church of the Sacred Heart, from every conceivable dramatic angle. The Greek coffee shop across the street was doing breakneck business filling thermoses and wrapping ham-and-egg sandwiches. The news of the massacre had spread through the neighborhood like a legend, and the Irish inhabitants of Hell's Kitchen had bundled up to see where the coppers had run Tommy Gun Coyne to ground. The last survivor of the feared and homegrown Coyne Mob.

The Commissioner took a cup of coffee from his sergeant assistant and immediately scalded his tongue. It felt good. "Do you think it's going to warm up? I have never felt cold like this."

Hanrahan stamped his wet feet in impatience, but kept his voice low and deferential. "Commissioner, we oughtta just bust in the door and rush the place. That Father's as good as dead anyway."

The Commissioner looked at Hanrahan with a sense of wonder. "Do you think he'd actually kill a priest?" He was impressed. "Jesus."

A reporter for the *Daily News* shouted out from behind the barricade. "What are you going to do, Commissioner? What's your next move?"

Then there was a flurry of activity behind the reporters as a pair of newshounds from the *Herald* pushed their way to the barricades. Between them was a blowsy-looking woman in her fifties. One of the *Herald* reporters whispered something to a cop, and the cop let them slip by the barricades. The cop hurried to the Commissioner.

"Commissioner," he said conspiratorially, "they got his mother."

The Commissioner stared at the patrolman. "The priest? They got the priest's mother."

"No, Tommy Gun's."

He looked at the woman then. And she stared back with unfriendliness. The reporters, sensing their scoop would be accompanied by a quote from the New York City Commissioner of Police, moved her forward quickly.

"Mrs. Coyne?"

The term seemed to affront her. She glared at the Commissioner with the judgmental eye of an early-morning drinker.

"Aye."

"And that's your son in there?"

The reek of whiskey seemed as much a part of her body odor as the mothball stink of her cheap overcoat.

"Nah. That one's his father's. Always has been."

The Commissioner looked to the reporters, as if for help, but they were busy remembering every word.

"Do you think he'd listen to you?"

"He never has. Why should he start now?" She bobbed her head in angry agreement with herself. "I knew he would end up bad, just like his goddamn old man. Drinkin', whorin'. Killin' n' bootleggin'. Hell, they did it together." Her face flushed red with resentment and cold. "I'm glad the bastard's dead."

It took the Commissioner a moment to realize she meant the elder. Bulldog.

"Then you don't think—"

"It's my other boy you should have a crowd for. For Frank you should have a goddamn parade."

The Commissioner looked to Hanrahan, but he wasn't saying anything. Then the sergeant behind him said, "The other one's a priest."

The Commissioner turned completely around to look at his sergeant assistant. "There's another one, and he's a priest?" This was getting complicated. "Maybe if we got him down here he could—"

"He's in the jungles, convertin' the heathens," Peggy Coyne said with pride. "That one does God's work. But he writes me regular, he does. That's the one you should—"

"Commissioner!" one of the patrolman at the church door shouted.

—◦—

THE MAKER OF THE BIG OAKEN FRONT DOOR OF SACRED HEART HAD, with Catholic irony, cut into the wood a tiny, latticed peep-door, like the screen of a dollhouse confessional. It had no purpose, since anyone who knocked on Sacred Heart's big door was always allowed in—until now—and as far as O'Rourke knew, the wicket had never been opened. He opened it now. Amazingly, it only required a strong yank.

A cop's shocked face stared at him, inches away.

"I'm Father O'Rourke," he told the cop, who immediately turned and shouted for his Commissioner. A moment later the Commissioner's face appeared behind the latticework screen. The Commissioner's eyes tried to peer around, through the tiny sightlines. "Where is he?" the Commissioner whispered.

"He's in here," O'Rourke replied.

"Has he harmed you, Father?" The Commissioner's naturally pleasant face turned grim. "He's already killed three of our boys."

O'Rourke stared at the Commissioner a moment, stunned.

"Is he in the back?" the Commissioner asked. "Open the door, Father, and we'll take care—"

"He's asked for sanctuary," O'Rourke said quickly, to have it said.

It was the Commissioner's turn to be stunned. "What?"

"Thomas Coyne has asked for sanctuary. He's requested the protection of the Church."

Hanrahan's voice came from the Commissioner's side. "That's a crock of shit!"

"What the hell are you talkin' about?" the Commissioner barked. "Open this door, Father!"

O'Rourke steeled himself. He knew this was only the beginning, and he had no idea what the end might be. "Thomas Coyne has appealed to me as a representative of Rome. He believes that if he gives himself up, his life will be in jeopardy—"

Hanrahan snorted derisively.

"—and that he won't be given justice under the law."

"Aye, and did he give Sean Malloy justice?"

O'Rourke knew Sean Malloy. He was a parishioner. His children had been confirmed here at Sacred Heart. O'Rourke had been in attendance at the confirmation.

"You can't do this," the Commissioner said. "This isn't legal."

"The ancient rite of sanctuary goes back a thousand years—"

"This is New York!" Hanrahan was livid. "This is fuckin' America!"

"The Church's mercy has no borders," O'Rourke said, and felt like a fool.

"Father O'Rourke," the Commissioner said slowly, "the man you're protecting is a cop-killing gangster. He wouldn't think a whit about killing anyone, including yourself."

"He's asked for sanctuary, and I've granted it."

There it was. O'Rourke slowly closed the wicket. His heart was pounding. He turned to Tommy, pressed against the door beside him.

"It worked."

"Yeah, we'll see," Tommy growled, and lowered his .45.

◄○►

THE MORNING PAPERS RAN LATE EDITIONS, AND THE AFTERNOON PAPERS printed early runs. The *Herald* and the *Globe* put out two extras,

because the news coming in was more and more bizarre and sensa-
tionalistic. *"Coyne Mob Wiped Out"; "Coyne Mob Plugged"; "Bulldog
Bites Bullet."* Then, *"Tommy Gun Tommy Guns Cop"* and finally, *"Cop
Killer Coyne Asks Church Sanctuary."* The eight major New York
dailies vied with each other for the most lurid headlines. *"Massacre
on 9th Avenue."* By midday the story had gone out on the wire to
the rest of the country and the whole world, knocking off front
pages political clashes in Berlin, a sunken ferry in Indochina, unrest
in Mexico.

Just after noon the Mayor and his entourage arrived on Forty-
seventh Street. He stepped from his car and surveyed the crowd
with a politician's reassuring gaze. Then he saw the Commissioner,
pulled his tailored overcoat around his narrow-hipped figure, took
a step out of the slush and waited for the man who owed him his
job to hurry over.

"What the hell have we got here?" the Mayor asked. His eyes
were red and swollen. There had been a party at Flo Ziegfeld's last
night, and the Mayor had played and sung until just before dawn.
Irving Berlin had sat next to him on the piano bench and they had
even done a duet together.

"Coyne's definitely inside. The pastor has granted him
sanctuary."

"What the hell is 'sanctuary'?"

One of the Mayor's Ivy League–educated aides, standing close-
by, saw his chance. "An ancient Catholic tradition of protecting
anyone who—"

"I know that, for Chrissakes!" the Mayor barked. "Is it legal?"

"There's no precedent for it in America. And it hasn't been used
in Europe since the mid-eighteenth century."

"Goddamnit! I need a straight answer! Is it legal?"

Everyone was staring at the aide, as if somehow all of this were
his fault. He wished he'd never spoken up. "As . . . as that church
is in the borough of Manhattan, and therefore a part of the City
and State of New York, under jurisdiction of the laws and statutes
therein—"

"Is it legal?!"

The aide looked around at them. "No."

The Mayor turned to the Commissioner. "Then go in there and
get him out."

The Commissioner didn't move. He was wondering if the perfume he smelled had rubbed off the Mayor's latest showgirl con-
quest or whether the little dandy dabbed it on himself.

"Look, I can't have a killer and a do-gooder priest hold my administration for ransom."

Hanrahan elbowed his way closer. "That's exactly what I been saying, Mr. Mayor."

The Mayor looked at Hanrahan as he would a noisy child, then repeated his order to the Commissioner. "Go in there and get him out."

The Commissioner shook his head slowly.

"What?" the Mayor barked.

"I'm not going to be the one to lead an infantry charge on a church. Not in Hell's Kitchen."

The Mayor looked around at the large crowd of voters that had gathered. Laborers in work clothes, their collars turned up against the numbing cold. Women in shapeless overcoats, watching the church with a sense of reverential morbidity. There was a kind of personal Greek tragedy about the whole thing. Every Irishman in New York either knew someone in the Coyne Mob or knew someone who did. And now they were all dead, except for the devilishly handsome and wickedly dangerous young Tommy, and his future seemed short and bleak. This was better than Broadway. This was better than the moving pictures.

"If I send my boys in shooting," the Commissioner was saying, "the priest is going to get it. And he's real popular around here. Hell, so's Coyne."

"The kid killed Sean Malloy," Hanrahan said quickly. "Let's not forget that. Or them other two poor boys."

"That's right," the Mayor said. "I was elected on a promise to crack down on gangsters."

"Then crack down on the Italians, but don't ask me to blow the door off an Irish church."

The Mayor stared at him a long moment. He'd only been in office a year, but he'd already formulated an effective way of handling problems. Let other people deal with them. He turned to his Ivy League aide. "Get the fucking Archbishop down here."

◄○►

TOMMY, LYING FACEDOWN ON THE FRONT PEW, FINGERED THE .45's trigger nervously until O'Rourke appeared again, coming back through the rectory door. The priest was carrying a small leather case and the bottle of whiskey. As he neared he saw the suspicion in Tommy's eyes, and the automatic's muzzle pointed in his direction.

"I told you, the back's all bricked in."

Tommy's expression didn't change. O'Rourke set the case and the whiskey down on the pew in front of Tommy's face. Tommy picked up the bottle and drank a long, deep draft.

"In the trenches, we chaplains sometimes had to administer emergency medical." He opened the leather case. "U.S. Army issue." From the case O'Rourke took out a short surgical knife. Tommy jammed the muzzle of the .45 against the priest's kidneys.

"I'm going to cut off your trousers," O'Rourke said in a small voice.

Tommy cocked the .45.

"Look, you're bleeding badly."

"What difference does it make? I'm never going to live through this day anyway."

O'Rourke didn't know what to say. The kid was probably right.

"But when I go"—Tommy pressed the .45—"I'm going to take some sons of bitches with me."

"Then you won't be wanting to pass out, and if that bleeding isn't stopped, you will."

Tommy considered this. The priest hadn't been anything but a right guy to him since he'd forced his way into the church, but Tommy wouldn't allow himself to feel anything but rage, tamped down repeatedly until it was hammered into cold, hard hatred of everybody. He felt totally alone in the world, and that was a situation he'd never had to experience before. He'd grown up surrounded by his father's mob, and now they were all dead in the snow in front of Matranga's warehouse, and the Bulldog was a corpse in the loft of Gould's Department Store. *Hanrahan*. The vengeful fury that coursed through his body made his skin tingle. Tommy didn't want to die before he killed Hanrahan.

O'Rourke saw the tightness transform Tommy's face. He saw him turn from a handsome young man into a demon, and it frightened the priest. Then he saw resolve, and Tommy relaxed and uncocked the .45.

"Okay. But remember, it don't mean nothing to me that you're—"

"—a priest. Yes, I know."

O'Rourke cut away the blood-soaked trousers and stared down at Tommy's buttocks. There was a raw, gaping gash diagonally across the right cheek. O'Rourke began to wash away the encrusted blood with a cloth soaked in alcohol. Feeling the sting, Tommy didn't wince, but twisted to look back fiercely.

"It didn't hit an artery." O'Rourke touched the riven flesh. "I don't think the bullet's even in there." He cut away the rest of the trousers and ran the cloth through his fingers. "Ah." He dug at the material and then held up a short, squashed piece of metal. "Browning. We saw a lot of these in the Ardennes. You're very lucky."

Tommy gave a short, bitter grunt. "Yeah, I'm a fuckin' four-leaf clover."

⸺◈⸺

THE MAYOR AND THE COMMISSIONER HAD GONE INSIDE THE COFFEE shop to get out of the cold. Hanrahan stood in the alley next to the church and watched as two patrolman hurried toward him. They had wet swatches of snow on their blue shoulders and knees.

"We can get onto the roof from the shoe factory in back," one cop said breathlessly.

"Just run a two-by-ten from one roof to the other," the other one offered.

Hanrahan mulled this a long moment. In his overcoat pockets his smallish hands continually worked at the contents—bullets and loose change in the right, a lead-filled sap in the left.

"Can you get a clear shot down through the bell tower?"

The first cop took a few slushy steps, peered out the alley at Sacred Heart's slender, Protestantistic steeple.

"It's pretty narrow . . . We won't know until we're up there."

This wasn't the answer Hanrahan wanted, and his cold glare made the cop look away. "I want this paddy bastard dead. Get up there and blow the top of his fuckin' head off."

⸺◈⸺

O'ROURKE PULLED THE LAST SUTURE TIGHT, THEN SNIPPED OFF THE END. "This'll stop the bleeding, but you need a doctor."

"You keep talking like I got a future or something."

O'Rourke said nothing as he repacked the small leather case.

Then, "I'll get you some clothes to wear." He rose and walked back to the rectory.

Tommy sat up and grimaced when his buttock touched the cold hardness of the pew. He stared around, suddenly aware he was half-naked in a church. He picked up the whiskey bottle and tilted his head back to take a drink. That's when he saw the plaster-of-Paris Jesus over the altar, staring down at him. Tommy swallowed the whiskey and glared back.

O'Rourke came back from the rectory carrying pants, shirt, underwear. He set them down on the pew.

"If you want to surrender, I'll go out with you. I'll ride to the station house. I won't leave you alone for—"

"Forget it. The only two choices out there for me are a copper's bullet and the electric chair, and I ain't havin' either one."

Tommy started to pull on the black pants.

"I hope you're not thinking about taking your own life, because—"

"Sell that garbage to the bead-rattlers." Tommy tore off his bloody-tailed shirt. "I ain't buyin' it."

He pulled on the collarless shirt. "Besides, suicide ain't my specialty. Homicide is. When I bite the pill, some coppers are biting it with me. Maybe a priest, hey!" He looked down at himself. "Priest clothes."

"It's all I've got. I can't afford regular garb."

Tommy picked up the whiskey bottle and shook it. The liquid gurgled. "But you can afford whiskey."

"It was a donation from a parishioner."

Tommy sat down on the pew. "Probably some boot, huh?"

"It's very possible."

"Well, he shouldn't be *donating* hooch in the Kitchen. That's Coyne Mob terri—"

Tommy stopped as he remembered there was no more Coyne Mob. There was just him. He took a drink, then rested the bottle in his lap. O'Rourke held out his hand, and Tommy realized the priest wanted a drink. Tommy hesitated, making him wait, then handed over the whiskey.

"How long were you an altar boy here?"

Tommy gave a bitter smile. "For about half a minute. That old bastard—"

"Father Skelley."

"—caught me emptying the poor box. He slapped the piss out of me. Then he told my Ma, and she beat me with a broom handle. That's when I went to live with . . . Bulldog." Again, the terrorizing realization on Tommy's face.

"Your brother Frank—"

"Frank was already planning for the seminary by then. Frank was *born* with a fucking Daily Missal in his hands."

O'Rourke pulled from his pocket a creased, yellowed envelope. He held it in his hand and looked down at it.

"What's that?"

"It's a letter from Frank. I got it a couple of years ago, and it was a year old then."

Tommy stared at the letter in O'Rourke's hand. One half of the envelope was covered with bright exotic postage stamps. "From South America?"

"Mexico. That's where Frank is completing his mission." O'Rourke smiled. "He's a Jesuit, now."

O'Rourke dug into his other pocket and pulled out a pack of cigarettes. Tommy reached over and plucked them from his hands. O'Rourke watched him shake out a cigarette. "They were having a lot of trouble down there, you know. There's a revolution been going on for over ten years."

Tommy threw the pack back to O'Rourke. "Gimme a light."

O'Rourke took out a box of matches, struck one, and leaned over to light the cigarette. Tommy froze. "What was that?"

"What?"

"You hear that?" Tommy eyes went up to the church's vaulted ceiling. He stared at it a moment, motionless.

"I didn't hear—" O'Rourke started to say, and Tommy held up his hand, demanding silence.

And then there was a barely audible footfall from above.

"They're on the fuckin' roof!" Tommy snatched up the .45 he had laid on the pew and rushed to the front of the church.

"Let me talk to them!" O'Rourke shouted as he stood.

"Shut up!"

Tommy ran through the small open doorway that led to the narrow curving staircase up to the bell tower. In the bell tower it was cramped and medieval, and only thin shafts of dirty gray light slanted across the icy stone walls. Tommy leaned back against the wall and held his .45 over his head, its muzzle crowding out Sacred Heart's single iron bell. A moment later a rustle of snow struck his face. He pulled back the gun's hammer and waited. From above came a barely heard wisp of whispered conversation, and then a shadow fell across the slat of light. Tommy fired and the bullet struck the bell. Tommy fired again, and again the bell rang.

—◄○►—

OUTSIDE ON THE STREETS THE CROWD GASPED. THE WOMEN QUICKLY crossed themselves. "Dear God! He's shootin' in the church!"

"He's killin' Father!"

"Jesus, Mary, and Joseph!"

Then a wedge of snow tumbled from the roof to the street below, and a blue-uniformed cop slid over the side of the eaves and hung there, frantically grasping at the snow and ice.

The bell continued to toll, slowly, softly, as it swayed from the bullets' impact.

The Mayor and the Commissioner hurried out of the coffee shop and stared up incredulously at the patrolman scrambling to keep from falling. The news photographers jumped over the barriers and crowded against each other, snapping off shots.

"What the hell is he doin' up there!" the Commissioner bellowed. "Who sent that man up there?!"

Hanrahan, a few feet away, said nothing.

Then the head and shoulders of another cop slowly appeared over the lip of the roof. He clutched the other cop's coat and started to carefully pull him back onto the church roof. Another heavy wedge of snow and ice tumbled down and splattered on the sidewalk below.

"He's shot the priest!" someone from the crowd shouted. "He's killin' everybody!"

The dangling cop clambered onto the roof and out of sight. Then he reappeared and gave a sheepish wave to the street. The other cops started to applaud, but when the crowd didn't join in they stopped.

"For Christ's sake, he's shootin' Father O'Rourke!" a woman shrilled. "Can't you do nothin'?!"

The Mayor gave the Commissioner a look that asked the same question, and the Commissioner strode quickly across the street to the church door and banged on it loudly.

"Father O'Rourke! Are you all right? Father?!"

When there was no answer the Commissioner turned to speak to the Mayor, then was startled to realize he had crossed to the Church alone and that everyone else was standing on the other side of the street. He looked at them a moment, wondering what to do next, when, for the first time, Tommy's furious voice came through Sacred Heart's wicket door.

"You try another funny page like that, and the priest dies!"

The Commissioner involuntarily stepped back a few steps and to the side. Then he caught himself and shouted in his best official-domistic manner, "How do I know he's not dead already?"

"Maybe I'll just shoot you!"

The Commissioner moved quickly to flatten himself against the church wall and a few people in the crowd tittered. He looked out at the Mayor, the reporters taking pictures, the crowd, then he said, "This is the Police Commissioner!"

"Then I definitely want to shoot you!"

The crowd laughed again.

"Listen, Coyne. I want to speak to the priest, right now! Right now, or we come in shootin'!"

"Well, come on in, Commissioner. I got a bullet for you, I had the priest bless it!"

There was an audible collective gasp from the people gathered across the street. Cop-killing was one thing to the Kitchen's Irish, blasphemy another. The Commissioner was at an impasse. He really didn't know what to do next. He'd figured from the beginning that a man who had taken lair in a church was eventually going to give himself up. Barring that conclusion, this thing had no way of ending up any way but bad.

Just then O'Rourke's voice came through the door. "Commissioner, this is Father O'Rourke! I'm okay, I'm unharmed. Don't do anything imprudent!"

The Commissioner felt a wave or relief. Maybe there was a way to negotiate a politically satisfactory end.

"Coyne, listen to me! Your situation is hopeless! Why don't you just give yourself up, lad?!"

"Oh, yeah?" Tommy shouted. "You're going to go to bat for me, right? You'll put in a good word with the judge?"

The Commissioner saw the logic in Tommy's irony, but he still had to try.

"If you come out now, you still have a chance, but if you—"

Tommy's bitter laughter shot through the peephole and the Commissioner stopped short. Then Tommy shouted, *"Hanrahan!"*

Hanrahan, standing in the slushy street, shivered when he heard Tommy bark his name. He felt everyone's eyes on him. He was taking a step backward when Tommy shouted again.

"You're dead, Hanrahan! I'm going to fuckin' kill you!"

By early afternoon, just before the Archbishop arrived, newsboys descended on Forty-second Street hawking early extras of the *Evening Graphic*. The front page was black with screaming headlines and *composograph* photos of last night's and this morning's events. They'd found an actor with Thomas Coyne's general features and coloring, and they'd posed him snarling with a machine gun over a dead uniformed cop's body. *"Boy Gangster Slays Beloved Policeman."* Another shot had the same actor kneeling before a gray-haired priest, seeking absolution. Then the next showed him hiding behind the priest, as the priest held up his hands to a heavenly light. *"Takes Refuge, then Takes Hostage."* The crowd snapped up all the copies and passed them from hand to hand, knowing they were all playing a part in this Passion play.

The Archbishop's long black Cadillac was instantly recognizable, and an electricity surged through the crowd. Something was going to happen now.

The Archbishop stepped from the sedan still wearing under his overcoat the long vestments he'd been in when summoned from the formal Mass he'd been celebrating at St. Pat's. The hemline of his robe dragged in the muddy slush of the street and his acolyte rushed to lift it.

The Mayor moved forward quickly, both hands outstretched—public obsequiousness for the voters.

"Your Grace," the Mayor said, gripping the Archbishop's hand in both of his. *Get us out of this one.* "Thank you for coming."

The Archbishop was a good-looking Irishman with longish silver hair. When he was younger the other priests gossiped that when he said Mass the women left the pews warm.

The Archbishop looked at the church. The Archdiocese of New York boasted three seminaries, twenty-four orphanages, twenty-nine Catholic hospitals, and four hundred and forty churches. For the life of him, the Archbishop couldn't remember this narrow little Sacred Heart.

"Have you been apprised of the situation?" the Mayor asked.

The Archbishop slowly turned his eyes from the church, looked fully at the Mayor. He was a man accustomed to having people endure his deliberate pace, and he certainly wasn't going to be hurried here, not by this frivolous dandy.

"I'd like to hear it from you."

—◄○►—

O'ROURKE HAD FRIED SOME EGGS AND SAUSAGES HE'D FOUND IN THE icebox. Mrs. Cohalon's doing. He brought the two plates out to the front pew, and he and Tommy sat beside each other and ate. The .45 was on the pew, on Tommy's other side. The hot food smoked in the chill air.

"I don't remember it being so goddamn cold in here," Tommy said as he wolfed down bread and sausage. "Is it always like this?"

O'Rourke held a forkful of food in front of his face. "Only in wintertime."

Tommy stared at him, then broke into laughter. It echoed off the stone walls.

"You know," he said, breaking up his eggs with his bread, "you got a lot of balls, for a priest. What's your name?"

"John O'Rourke."

"Well, Johnny Boy, you got a lot of Irish. And you make good eggs." He looked down at the egg-drenched bread. "This might be my last meal."

O'Rourke put his plate down beside him. He reached for the cigarettes, shook one out.

"I think I know a way out of this for you."

"Don't start that stuff again."

"Last year," O'Rourke began slowly, "we had a major flooding problem. This big pipe that runs under the church burst." He lit the cigarette, exhaled. "I saw some city workers pull up a concrete slab and get right at that pipe."

Tommy stopped chewing. "Where?"

"Right under my desk."

Tommy stood up. "Show me."

—◄○►—

IN O'ROURKE'S SPARTAN OFFICE THE TWO OF THEM PUSHED AWAY THE small cluttered desk and beneath was a single three-foot-square slab of concrete. They tried to lift it, but it wouldn't budge.

"How many guys did it take to move this thing?"

"Five, six."

Tommy looked around the room, then at O'Rourke. "You got a crowbar?"

O'Rourke thought about this. "No, but . . ." He turned and walked from the room. Tommy hesitated a moment, then slipped the gun from his waistband and followed.

In the sacristy behind the altar O'Rourke was pulling something from a small jumbled closet. It was a long iron pike, with a wick on the end used to light candles. "Midnight Mass on Christmas Eve," O'Rourke said, and he started unscrewing the metal base of the wick. "The altar boys always complain it's too heavy." O'Rourke got the wick off, tossed it into the closet, then dug around for a moment and came up with an ancient square-handled hammer. He laid the pike on the stone floor, held it tightly, slammed the hammer down on the end. The metallic blow echoed off the walls. O'Rourke looked up at the open door to the church. "You think they can hear that?'

Tommy moved quickly to the door and closed it. O'Rourke began to pound. In a few minutes the end of the pike was flattened and sharp.

Back in the office they jabbed the pike into the crevice around the concrete slab. After a few tries it seemed to find a groove and slipped under. O'Rourke pushed in on the pike for all he was worth, then started to push down. Tommy got on the end of the iron rod and joined him. They strained and grunted but the slab didn't budge. Tommy started to slack off and O'Rourke said sharply, "No! It's getting ready to move. I can feel it." Tommy pushed down harder and the slab slowly began to lift.

IT TOOK THEM THE BETTER PART OF AN HOUR, PUSHING, STRAINING, inching, shoving, but eventually they had the slab moved away enough for a man to wriggle through. Their clothes were soaked with perspiration, and their sweat cooled in the frigid church. O'Rourke fished out a damp cigarette and hung it on his lip. "Can you get through there?"

Tommy sat on the edge of the slab and slipped his legs through. His feet struck something solid. "I need a light." O'Rourke was already holding out a flashlight. He snapped it on. Tommy looked at the torch in the priest's hand, then up at O'Rourke. He took the flashlight, then twisted his body and shoulders down through the crevice.

Beneath the church was a six-foot-square chamber. Half-buried under fresh dark dirt was the top of a pipe. By the looks of it, a pipe large enough for a man to stand erect in. Tommy shone the flashlight over the pipe, then around the chamber. There were smaller iron pipes running everywhere. Tiny condensation icicles hung from the rust. Then he shone the light back on the pipe in the floor. It was new, but had already started to stain in the dampness beneath the church. He kicked it. Then he looked up and O'Rourke's face was in the narrow opening.

"Gimme that rod."

O'Rourke disappeared for a moment, then the end of the pike slipped through the crevice. Tommy took it in both hands, positioned the top end to get leverage, then raised the pike and slammed it down on the pipe. The pike went right through it. Tommy grinned and pulled it out. It left a perfect circular hole. "Clay," Tommy said up to O'Rourke, then raised the rod to strike again. Then he heard a faint echo reverberate through the chamber. Tommy froze and listened, then realized he was hearing someone pound on the church's front door. It was audible down here, moving through the ground.

"They're at the door."

O'Rourke turned his head. With the office door shut, he couldn't hear it. He looked back at Tommy. "I'll handle it." Then he was gone.

Tommy hesitated a moment. He felt the weight of his .45's in his shoulder holsters. Then he raised the rod and began to beat down furiously. On the seventeenth blow the brittle clay pipe shattered.

O'ROURKE WAITED AT THE FRONT DOOR, LISTENING TO TOMMY'S assault on the pipe. They were pounding on the door from the other side.

"Father O'Rourke! Are you all right in there?"

Then, suddenly, there was silence from the rectory. O'Rourke took a deep breath, then opened the wicket covering. "I'm here."

There was no one visible through the latticework. Then the Commissioner's voice came from one side, away from the peephole. "What's happening in there?"

"We were talking," O'Rourke said quickly.

"Does he want to give himself up?" the Commissioner offered hopefully.

"Anything is possible at this point."

The Commissioner thought about this. "Father, I have someone here wants to speak to you."

There was a moment, then a familiar voice said, "Father O'Rourke, this is the Archbishop."

O'Rourke knew then that he wasn't going to get through this

thing unscathed. No matter what he did, his life would never be the same again.

"Your Grace."

"I feel ludicrous talking to you through a door, but they won't let me come in," the Archbishop said. "The police."

"I wouldn't be able to open the door anyway, Your Grace."

"Are you all right, son?"

"Yes, Your Grace."

"He hasn't . . . harmed you?"

"No."

There was a short moment of silence, then the Archbishop said, "I'd like to talk to him."

"He's in the rectory," O'Rourke said, then lied. "He's praying."

After another brief moment, the Archbishop said, "Are you sure you can't open the door?"

O'Rourke took a breath. "That's not possible, Your Grace."

There seemed to be something happening on on the other side of the door, then there was silence. Then the Archbishop said, "Father?"

"Yes?"

"We're alone now," the Archbishop said through the door. "The Commissioner has gone to the other side of the street. We can speak in privacy."

O'Rourke put his face close to the latticework peephole and could just make out the Archbishop's light blue eye through the cracks.

"Father, the modern Church doesn't recognize sanctuary. You know that."

"Yes, Your Grace."

"We standard-bearers of the Roman faith have to be very careful in dealing with secular issues. In other parts of the country there is a growing anti-Catholic movement." The Archbishop paused, as if he were making a point in a sermon. "This man you're protecting is a multiple murderer."

"I know that, Your Grace—"

"The Church can't be construed as aiding and abetting criminals, especially those who were born into the faith."

"Your Grace, Thomas Coyne is afraid that if he gives himself up, the police will kill him."

ON THE OTHER SIDE OF THE DOOR THE ARCHBISHOP TURNED AND looked across the street. There were a hundred police on the street— grim-faced and vengeful—all staring at him. The little bantam cock of a cop who hung at the Commissioner's elbow seemed to radiate malevolence. He even took a step forward when the Archbishop's eyes fell on him.

The Archbishop sighed.

It would have been a miserable afternoon anyway. His first scheduled appointment was to have been with a committee of Upper East Side Jews—always a contentious lot—who were petitioning him to speak out against a priest in Staten Island who was delivering anti-Semitic diatribes from the pulpit. Next would have been a group of Catholic women pressuring him to take a more definite stand on the ongoing Prohibition. With the wave of gangsterism and violence resulting from bootlegging, an active repeal movement was aborning. These ladies wanted nothing of the sort, and they wouldn't be timid in their demands for O'Connor's blessing. Certainly the events of last night and today wouldn't help their reactionary cause.

The Archbishop's last appointment of the afternoon was to have been with a contingent of refugee priests from Mexico desperate to enlist the American Church's support in their troubles down there. The Archbishop didn't think any of them even spoke English.

But that had all been canceled now, because of the pastor of this narrow little Hell's Kitchen church.

"YOU'RE NOT FROM HERE, ARE YOU, FATHER?" THE ARCHBISHOP'S voice came through the wicket.

O'Rourke wondered why he was asking the question. "San Francisco."

"Ah," the Archbishop said softly, as if that were an explanation. "Father, our vocation in life is to tend to spiritual matters, not to impose ourselves on society's events."

O'Rourke felt an unexpected wave of anger charge through him. "So, I should wait until they lead the boy to the electric chair," he snapped, "and I can walk with him and comfort him in his final moments."

There was silence from the other side of the door. Then, "You're a young man, O'Rourke. You have your whole vocation before you. I wouldn't want you to do something now that will tarnish you for the rest of your life."

O'Rourke knew the Archbishop was trying to help him. "Your Grace, I don't understand all that happened last night, and I know there's been a lot of death and suffering . . ." He didn't know where to go. "But . . . but what would it profit justice, or society, to have another young death before he can even have a fair hearing?"

"The Commissioner of Police is right across the street. I'm sure he wouldn't allow—"

"He'll be DOA when he gets to the Tombs. Attempted escape. You and I both know that."

O'Rourke could feel the Archbishop weighing his impertinence. Maybe he had gone too far. And what did it matter now?

"If you can get the boy," the Archbishop began, "if you can get the boy to surrender to me, I personally will take him in." O'Rourke turned quickly and looked back toward the rectory. "I'll accompany him all the way to the precinct house. I'll see that he's not beaten or mistreated in any way."

O'Rourke listened for any sound of Tommy in the rear of the church. There wasn't any.

"Why don't you go speak to him, Father?" the Archbishop said, as if reading his thoughts. "Tell him he has my word."

O'Rourke nodded, even though no one could see him. "I'll be right back."

—◁○▷—

WHEN THE SEWER PIPE SHATTERED TOMMY GUN STEPPED BACK AND listened. He could hear O'Rourke's voice talking to whoever was on the other side of the church's front door. Somehow he felt instinctively that the priest was on his side, that he wouldn't betray him. For the first time since last night Tommy didn't feel completely alone.

He got down on his knees and stuck his head and shoulders through the large hole in the sewer pipe. The cold down here was shocking, deadly. Tommy turned on the flashlight and peered in. The pipe was huge, large enough for a man to stand in, with another man on his shoulders, and it was surprisingly clean. Where the oozing dampness on the curving walls had frozen, thin sheets of milky ice reflected the flashlight's gleam. Tommy pointed the light deep into the pipe's blackness. It seemed to go on forever.

Here was a way out.

Tommy slipped out of the hole and pulled himself back up into O'Rourke's office. He could hear the conversation at the door at the front of the church, but he couldn't understand what was being said. Tommy hurried through an entry into a spare, sparse sleeping

56

area. There were two single beds flush against opposite walls. One of the beds was in tangled, slept-in disarray. O'Rourke's bed. The other was made up, with folded clothes stacked neatly at the foot. Priest clothes, with clean clerical collars perched on top like the crowns of humble kings. Tommy snatched up the clothes and stuffed them under his arm. In a scarred wardrobe in an alcove he found a black overcoat, a black suit coat, a black hat. Back in the office he listened again to O'Rourke's voice speaking through the door, then quickly rifled the desk they had pushed into a corner. The top drawer was crammed with record books, writing paper, a mono-grammed Daily Missal. In the second, lying on top, was a weathered leather document folder. Tommy tore it open, ripped through the contents. It was O'Rourke's personal records. A California birth cer-tificate. His graduation certificate from St. Mary's College in Los Angeles. And a new-looking passport. Tommy opened the passport and O'Rourke's photograph looked up at him. He studied it carefully. O'Rourke was nine or ten years older than Tommy, but their hair color and complexion were very similar. It might be resemblance enough to get Tommy out of the country. The only stamps in the pass-port were an entry into and departure from Italy, a year ago. Tommy tied up the document folder and stuffed it in with the clothing.

Then he knelt and yanked open the third drawer. This is where old Father Skelley had kept the collection-basket money. Sure enough, there was the same dull metal lockbox. Tommy laid the lip of the lockbox on the edge of the desk, as he had done fourteen years before, and pushed down hard. The lid bent back readily, forming a kind of chute. Tommy turned the box over and shook it. Some change and loose dollar bills tumbled out. Then a neatly rubber-banded roll of tens and twenties bounced off the desktop. He caught it, flicked through it quickly. There was over a thousand dollars here. He didn't stop to think about why there was so much money in a poor parish's collection box, but rammed the money into his pocket. On the floor beside the desk was a small, worn black leather satchel, a little smaller than a doctor's bag. Tommy popped it open and dumped the contents on the floor, then gathered up the clothes and the document folder, stuffed them into the satchel. He pulled on the overcoat, shoved the flashlight under his belt, touched his two shoulder-holstered automatics, as if to reassure himself, then jumped down into the hole. In the cavern beneath the church he could hear O'Rourke's voice reverberating as he carried on the conversation through the door. He threw the satchel down into the pipe and eased himself in, hung for a moment, then dropped down.

Tommy's feet plunged through the thin sheet of ice over the six inches of water that covered the floor of the pipe. The frigid wetness soaked his socks and a shiver raced up his legs. He grabbed up the satchel and started to run into the yawning blackness.

—◄◦►—

O'ROURKE ENTERED THE RECTORY AND KNEW INSTANTLY THAT TOMMY had robbed him. He paused a moment, surveying the office. The bent lockbox lay on its side on the desk. That meant the parish Refurbishment Fund was a memory. He could see through into the sleeping area, to the open wardrobe. The hanger where his overcoat always hung was empty. O'Rourke stepped around the desk and saw the yanked-open drawers. His document folder has been taken. At his feet lay the spilled contents of his sacramental satchel. He stooped and picked up the crucifix, the blessed oil, the holy water, the pyx containing the host. He carefully placed them on the desktop, then went over to the hole in the floor, peered down into the blackness of the sewage pipe.

Back in the church he waited by the door, thinking about what he was about to do. Then he reached up and opened the peephole.

"Father?" the Archbishop said expectantly. The cold had reddened his face, and he'd turned up his collar.

"He'll give himself up."

The Archbishop started to grin, then he stopped himself. "Now?"

"No," O'Rourke said. "At six o'clock."

"At six?" The Archbishop pulled out his watch.

"He wants time to think. . . . He wants to make his confession. . . . Then we're going to pray together."

The Archbishop looked up from his timepiece. "It's quarter after two. Will it take you that—"

"He'll walk out of here at six. He'll give himself up."

The Archbishop stared through the latticework wicket. Then he nodded. "Good work, Father." He looked toward the Commissioner, the Mayor, waiting across the street. "I'll tell them."

—◄◦►—

HANRAHAN WATCHED THE ARCHBISHOP CROSS THE STREET FROM THE church and approach the Commissioner's group. This whole thing

58

had become a mess, a bloody Irish mess. It should have been finished last night, with the rest of Bulldog's mob. But this young, murderous Coyne son of a bitch didn't do anything you'd expect him to do. And he had more lives than a shithouse cat. And the longer this thing went on, the more likely it was that Hanrahan himself would be splattered by the mud. This thing had to be closed down, and quickly.

Hanrahan roughly elbowed his way past the outer circle of City and Church officials. There were a few audible complaints, and the Commissioner shot him a reproachful glare. In the few hours since the patrolmen had screwed up on the church roof Hanrahan had been relegated to outsider status in this municipal melodrama. The Commissioner would deal with him later, he knew, but that meant very little to Hanrahan now. Coyne was the important thing.

The Archbishop was saying something to the Commissioner and the Mayor and whatever it was, it brought a look of relief to their faces. Hanrahan shoved someone aside and edged his small body into the center of the group.

"All you have to do is wait," the Archbishop was saying. "And no more bloodshed."

The Mayor seemed even more elated than the Commissioner. He turned to his aide and asked openly, "Do I have to be here? There's a new show opening at the Ziegfeld, and now that the storm's over I promised Flo—"

"I think so, Mr. Mayor. I think it's unavoidable."

"Wait for what?" Hanrahan demanded of the group in general, but no one even seemed to notice him.

"Damn," the Mayor said, a look of true disappointment on his face.

"It'll be over at six," the aide offered. "You'll still have time to go home and change for dinner."

"Excellent." The Mayor grinned broadly. "I'll make tomorrow's morning edition and tonight's opening."

"What'll be over at six?" Hanrahan wished he could pistol-whip the information out of these lace-curtain assholes.

"Once again, Your Grace, you've performed a miracle," the Commissioner said with oily unctuousness. "Thank you."

"Now, I've assured Father O'Rourke," the Archbishop said solemnly, "that once in custody, the boy won't be harmed in any way. I've given my word that none of your men will take justice into their own hands when he walks out of that door at six o'clock."

Hanrahan immediately turned and began to elbow people aside. "Get out of the fuckin' way!"

"Your Grace," the Commissioner was saying, "how could you think otherwise?"

Hanrahan pushed out of the back of the crowd and into the coffee shop. He took quick angry steps to the pay phone in the back. A large man in a tweed cap was using it. Hanrahan shoved his badge into the man's face and yanked the receiver from his hand. "Get outta my way or I'll smash your fuckin' kneecaps." The man shrank back against the wall and Hanrahan worked the crank furiously. "Ascot four-two-six," he threatened into the mounted mouthpiece. As he waited for the connection he noticed the big man in the tweed hat was still there against the wall, watching him. Hanrahan slapped him hard, backhand. "I said get the fuck outta here!" The man turned and ran out the coffee shop's back door.

Then a voice came through the receiver and Hanrahan said, "Tell the man I gotta talk to him."

—◄○►—

THE BIG PIPE COURSED FAIRLY STRAIGHT FOR LONG STRETCHES, THEN SEEMED to make small adjustments at coupling intersections where water from melting ice formed lacy sheets of downpour. Soon Tommy was drenched and shivering, but he kept moving forward, his sutured buttock aching, his shoes crunching through the frozen sheet of ice that sheathed the floor of the sewer. Tommy limped for what felt like six blocks under the surface of the city.

Then there was a dim light up ahead, and a low rumbling hum that seemed to vibrate up from beneath. Tommy slowed as he came into a huge underground cavern where seven or eight massive pipes like the one he was in fed into some kind of pumping station. Rushing water coursed below in a turbulent gray sea. High in the upper reaches of the cavern a thin shaft of wintry light bled out of a dripping tube. A rusted steel ladder arced up the curved wall to a narrow catwalk. Tommy waded through the bone-chilling waist-deep water, then clung to the ladder with one hand and both knees as he negotiated the treacherous climb up to the catwalk.

Tommy stood under the tube and looked up. Above him, through a manhole grate, was a gray patch of late-afternoon sky. There seemed to be no traffic of any kind. His teeth chattering, Tommy ripped off his soaked trousers, dug out new ones from the priest bag, pulled them on, then snapped on the clerical collar, his hands shaking violently. He slipped his holstered automatics over his shoulders, pulled on the black suit coat, the black overcoat, then shaped out the homburg and placed it on his head. He picked up the valise, looked up at the grate at the top of the tube and started climbing.

—◄○►—

TWO SMALL BOYS WERE PLAYING ESKIMO IN AN ALLEY OFF FORTY-FIRST Street. They were taking turns pulling each other up and down the snowbound alley on an apple crate. Then one of the boys saw something and stopped.

"Hey, whazzamatta!" the kid in the crate complained. "Mush! Mush!"

But then he saw what his buddy was looking at and stood up in the makeshift sled, spellbound.

A priest was emerging from a steaming manhole twenty feet away, in the mouth of the alley. The priest looked around for a moment, saw them, seemed to reach for something under his overcoat then thought better of it. He took a few steps toward them and the boys shrank back.

"I just come up from hell," the priest said. "And if you tell anybody about me I'll fucking kill your whole fucking family." Then the priest turned and walked out of the alley.

The kid in the crate, who was Jewish, saw his buddy, who was from Alsace, make a desperate sign of the cross, and the kid in the crate suddenly realized he should be afraid.

—◄○►—

SALVATORE TWIRLED THE SPAGHETTI AROUND HIS FORK, LIFTED IT FROM THE plate, gave it a slight, distinctive double dip before he slipped it into his mouth. He was unconscious of the lifelong gesture, but the thick-hipped girl serving slabs of Italian bread spied it from across the room and thought it the most alluring thing she had ever seen in her sixteen years of life. Salvatore saw her watching him, and the look was all the more stirring because of her unsmiling boldness. Salvatore momentarily returned the look, then dropped his eyes. It wouldn't do to be noticed showing interest in someone who might be another man's woman. Not now, just when America was beginning to get so good.

When they entered this building just off Canal Street, Salvatore had been unsure of what awaited him inside. Back in his home village the local mafiosi soldiers told each other stories of young assassins who had been imported to New York to do a particular job, then afterward were themselves executed and their bodies disposed of forthwith. It made perfect sense, the soldiers said. The killers were brought in without documentation, used like mules, then made to disappear without a trace. It was like disposing of a murder weapon. Nothing incriminating, nothing connectable. It was even more logical in his own case because the other two torpedoes brought over with Salvatore had been killed in last night's gun battle. Carlos cut in two in the street by the young American's shotgun, Umberto bleeding to death three hours later from wounds inflicted by the same man's Thompson. He had been lethal, this ferocious young American, and Salvatore thought that if all the gunmen in New York were like him this place must be very, very dangerous.

These were the thoughts that crowded Salvatore's cautious mind as he entered this spacious, high-ceilinged apartment. The first things that struck him were the polished furniture, the whiteness of the doilies on the rich upholstery, the thickness of the carpet. Back in Sicily Salvatore had only glimpsed such wealth while standing hat-in-hand at aristocrats' back doors.

The next sight Salvatore registered was the women cooking in the kitchen. If there were women, then he hadn't been brought here to be murdered. At least, not today. Salvatore had relaxed.

He was twirling another forkful of spaghetti when he felt a hand slap his shoulder. He looked up into the big, friendly face of *Signóre* Joe.

"Hey, kid, how you doing?"

Salvatore, not understanding the American language, and again not wishing to offend in any way, simply nodded slightly to show respect and obedience.

Zanca laughed and tousled the kid's hair with a familiarity unthinkable in a native-born Sicilian. "You're a helluva man with that Browning, kid." Then Zanca turned and called across the room to Carini. "Hey, Carmine! Ain't this kid a son of a bitch with that Browning?"

Carini was eating at the big dining table. This was his apartment, and his wife who had supervised the cooking. He looked at Salvatore, and Salvatore dipped his head in respect.

"You're a good man," Signóre Carmine said in Sicilian. "You have a future."

Zanca moved to tousle his hair again and Salvatore had to stop himself from pulling back. "Helluva man with a Browning." He grinned. *"Mangia, mangia.* The Coynes ain't eating today."

Salvatore recognized the name Coyne. He understood that was the name of the enemies of Matranga they had battled and killed last night. Except for the young one who had battled so ferociously. That one was still alive. Salvatore wondered if he would be given the task of killing that one, that "Coyne." It would be a dangerous assignment, but one that would further strengthen his position with the great Matranga if he was successful. Salvatore liked what was happening to him. He liked New York. He would kill the Pope to continue this.

"More bread?" The girl was standing before him, the basket balanced between her hip and breast. She stared at Salvatore with that same open-eyed frankness and it stirred his genitals.

"Sí, grazie." He took the bread from her hand and their fingertips touched.

"Anna María," Zanca said, "have you met Salvatore?"

She didn't take her eyes from him. "No, I haven't, Mr. Joe."

"Anna María Matranga, this is Salvatore—what's your last name, kid?"

"Benedetti. Salvatore Benedetti." She was a Matranga. Somehow related to the great man.

"Welcome to America, Salvatore Benedetti," the girl said, and Zanca saw the look between them and grinned.

"Tell him, Anna María," Zanca said, "that Italian girls are for marrying. Tell him if he wants to cat around I'll take him down to Broadway."

Anna María didn't smile, but an amused light sparked in her eyes. "No, Mr. Joe, I don't think so."

Then there was a knock on the door and the men immediately stopped eating and stared at it. Salvatore put down his plate and put his hand into his pocket, where the .38 they had given him lay resting. Anna María watched him with interest.

Two men stood on either side of the door, while a third carefully unlocked it and looked out. He quickly swung it open and three men in long overcoats pushed in, brushing the snow from their shoulders. The second one was Anthony Matranga.

Anna María saw Salvatore's eyes follow the small man's every move. "He's my uncle," she said, and somehow the statement was pregnant with the same sexual boldness she carried in her eyes.

Matranga threw a look in their direction and Zanca quickly left Salvatore and Anna María and walked across the room. Carini rose from the table and the three of them conferred quickly. At one point, Carini looked over at Salvatore, and Salvatore stood to make himself ready. Then Carini nodded at him.

"There'll be more food when you come back," Anna María said.

—◄○►—

TOMMY SAT IN A CAR A HALF-BLOCK DOWN FROM CARMINE CARINI'S building. The low midafternoon sky was as gray as a cadaver. The snow had largely ceased, but every five or ten minutes there would be a swirling flurry lasting a minute or so and then dying rapidly to the freezing nothingness. Tommy ran his finger under the tight clerical collar. O'Rourke's neck was a half-size smaller than his, and the starched fabric chafed against his skin.

Tommy had stolen the Model A from in front of a settlement house on West Thirty-ninth.There was a renegade boot who sold cheap mulekick slush from an office on the second-floor rear. Tommy had waited only a few minutes before a red-faced customer had pulled up, leaving the motor running in the subteen temperatures. The whole transaction would have taken less than two minutes, but when the drunk got back to the street he would find only the empty, snow-shoveled street.

Tommy watched as a family came around the corner across from Carini's building. There was a short, squat mother and three children under ten, swaddled against the wind and cold. They waddled hurriedly across the street, the mother somehow holding hands with all three of her brood as she navigated them around the icy puddles, between the mounds of dirtying snow. As they passed the Model A the mother noticed Tommy and said, *"Buona sera, Padre."* Tommy nodded as they passed, then he saw Joe Zanca come out of Carini's apartment building with a handsome young man. Tommy could tell by the cut of the guinea's coat that he was a "Mustache Pete," right off the boat. The young man tried to emulate Joe Zanca, looking up and down the block, but Tommy could tell the torpedo had no idea what he was looking for. Then Joe gave a short wave of his hand and Carmine Carini and Tony Matranga walked out of the apartment house and into Matranga's Packard, parked and running by the curb. Zanca and the torpedo got into another car and the two cars pulled away.

Tommy already had one of his .45s in his hand, but there wasn't time. He started the Model A and followed, a half-block behind. Matranga's two-car convoy took Bowery to Delancey, then slipped into the slow-moving traffic inching across the icy Williamsburg Bridge to Brooklyn.

◄○►

CALVARY CEMETERY WAS SMOTHERED IN A THICK QUILT OF UNSULLIED white snow. It lay peacefully on the crosses and tombstones, softly blanketed the stone Saviors and granite Marys. The snow-choked lanes between the graves were smooth and untouched, like frosting on the sides of cakes. No one had been buried in the cold earth this day. Any bodies would be kept in waiting until the weather was more tolerable for the living. Calvary's gravediggers were all somewhere else today, keeping themselves warm with fire and steam and alcohol.

Hanrahan lit another cigarette as he watched a solitary car passing on Greenpoint turn on its headlights. He was standing beside his Ford, wondering if he should get back in. The man was supposed to be here twenty minutes ago. Hanrahan was nervous. Maybe Matranga was setting him up, as he himself had set up Bulldog. It didn't figure, but working with dagos you never knew. You had to remember their favorite way of dealing with any problem was simply to eliminate it. The fucking greaseballs would just as soon rub out one of their own as any mick or Jew. Still, they usually didn't kill coppers unless there was no other way, and Hanrahan had delivered the Coynes up just as he'd said he would. Cleaned and plucked. Except for that fucking kid. The fucking dagos had let that punk get away.

Hanrahan pulled out his watch and cursed. No matter when Matranga arrived, Hanrahan wouldn't make it back to Hell's Kitchen by six o'clock, when Tommy Coyne was scheduled to give himself up. Hanrahan took another agitated drag on his cigarette. That fucking kid was going to be a major problem. Hanrahan had considered staying put, shooting him as he came out of Sacred Heart with the priest. But the Commissioner was going to be there, the Archbishop, maybe even that pussy-eating Mayor. Even pleading temporary insanity brought on by grief over Sean Malloy's murder, Hanrahan was looking at a manslaughter stretch, and prison time was not something Jackie Hanrahan had ever planned on doing.

Two cars turned onto Greenpoint, their headlights on. They pulled up to the curb a half-block away and waited, exhaust plumes billowing out behind them.

"Finally," Hanrahan mumbled to himself, then dropped his cigarette, pulled up his collar, and crunched into the calf-deep snow of the cemetery.

—◇—

"LEMME GO WITH YOU," CARMINE CARINI SAID. HE WAS WATCHING Hanrahan's small figure disappear between the statuary and memorials.

"He only talks to me," Matranga said. "He don't want nobody else around."

Carmine shook his head and looked back at his boss. "I don't like you going alone, Tony. This guy'd sell his own mother."

Matranga didn't speak for a moment, then he smiled grimly. "Whose he gonna sell her to? They all dead, the Irish bastards."

Carmine took out his .38 and checked the cylinder. "I ain't letting you go alone."

"Stay here. I'll take the kid with me."

Carmine looked at his boss again. "That's good. He's good."

Tony and Carmine got out of the Packard and walked back toward the second car. Joe Zanca got out quickly.

"What's doing?"

Carmine went around to the back of the car and opened the trunk. "The kid. He's going with Tony." Carmine opened a compartment in the trunk and took out a sawed-off 12-gauge.

Joe ducked his head and said to Salvatore, "C'mon, Sal."

Salvatore, in the front seat next to the driver, had been looking at the snow-covered cemetery. He had never seen anything like it in his life. Rows and rows of crosses and angels, blanketed by a foot of soft white. It was miraculous. Then Mr. Joe motioned to him and he opened the door and stepped out.

Carmine handed him the short 12-gauge and said in Sicilian dialect, "This man is your patron." He nodded at Matranga. "Protect him with your very life."

Salvatore nodded. He understood. Carmine handed him a handful of shells and Salvatore put them in his pocket. Then he cracked the shotgun and loaded both barrels. He looked at the great Matranga then, who was chewing on a cigar. Matranga stared at him a moment, then grunted. He turned and walked into the cemetery, leaving footprints a foot and a half deep in the virgin snow. Salvatore walked beside him.

—◁○▷—

IT WAS SIX O'CLOCK. THE ARCHBISHOP LOOKED AT THE COMMISSIONER, who looked at the Commissioner, who looked at the Mayor, who was miffed because he was already late for the Broadway dress rehearsal.

"Let's get this done," the Mayor said.

The Commissioner nodded to his underlings and a phalanx of patrolmen and detectives encircled them and they crossed the street and walked up to the door of Sacred Heart of the Blessed Savior Roman Catholic Church.

"Father O'Rourke?" the Archbishop called out. There was no answer. The Commissioner raised his fist to pound on the door but before he could there was the hard metallic sound of the lock being thrown. Then the door slowly opened and Father O'Rourke stood there. They all craned their necks to look past him.

"Come in," O'Rourke said to the Archbishop.

No one moved. Then the Commissioner asked softly, "Where is he?"

O'Rourke stared at them a moment, then took a deep breath and said, "He's not here."

—◁○▷—

TOMMY DIDN'T KNOW WHAT TO DO WITH THE PRIEST'S VALISE. IF HE left it in the Model A and he lived through what was about to happen, there was absolutely no guarantee he'd make it back to the car, or that he'd even want to. And he couldn't carry it because he was going to need both of his hands free. But he was going to need the priest's identity and passport if he was going to have any chance at all of getting out of the city. Finally, he unlaced his shoes, tied the shoelaces together, then strung it around the handles of the valise. He slipped the laces over his shoulder and the bag hung down at his hip. He could pretend to carry it, then let it hang free when he needed his hand.

Tommy pulled out both of his silvery nickel-plated .45s. Somehow he'd gotten through the events of last night still in possession of his weapons. He checked their magazines. He had six in one and nine in the other. He popped a bullet out from the clip with nine and put it in the other. With a round in each chamber he had fifteen shots to get it done, eight in one, and seven in its mate. He cocked both guns, slipped them into the pockets of the priest's black overcoat. Then he opened the Model A's narrow door, grimaced as he steeled himself against the pain shooting up from his buttock, and stepped out into the street.

—◀○▶—

THE EPITAPH ON THE HEADSTONE WAS BARELY READABLE UNDER ITS quilt of snow. "Gerald Payton Hanrahan—1865–1912 Always Remembered."

"Yeah," Hanrahan said aloud, then thought, *I remember. I remember how you used to come home soused every fucking night and—*

Hanrahan looked up as he saw two overcoated figures come into his row. One he recognized as the man he wanted to see, Matranga. The other he didn't know. Their pants below the knees were damp and dusted with snow. The guy Hanrahan didn't know was carrying a sawed-off, cradled in his arm like a baby. He was making no attempt to hide it. Hanrahan unbuttoned his coat and moved his hand closer to his gun, holstered on his belt. As they neared Hanrahan growled, "Who the fuck—?"

"Shut the fuck up," Matranga said. "He's fresh off the boat. He don't know nothing. Besides, you the one called this meeting, out here in the middle of nowhere. In a fucking graveyard."

Hanrahan eyed the shotgun, then looked at the man. A goodlooking wop kid. Can't be twenty. "You fucked up. You didn't get the son. Now we got problems."

"What problems I got? You, maybe. Maybe you got problems."

"He runs his mouth, we all got problems. He runs his mouth I set up my own people, I ain't safe nowhere in the city."

Matranga smirked. "You could hang yourself like Judas did."

Hanrahan glared at him. "This is how you take care of your own?"

"You ain't my own. You're a fucking Irish pig copper."

Hanrahan wanted to shoot him then, and Matranga knew it. Salvatore could feel the tension between them. He moved his thumb back to the shotgun's twin hammers.

"I done good for you, Tony," Hanrahan said softly. "I handed you New York on a silver fucking platter."

"What do you want me to do? He's in that church. You want I should blow up the fucking church?"

"He's coming out at six. They'll put him in a paddy wagon and take him down to 100 Center Street."

"Yeah?"

"That mariah can't ever get Downtown."

Matranga gave a short, bitter laugh. "I hear the fucking Archbishop is gonna be riding with him."

"So?"

Matranga shook his head. "You are some piece of work, Jackie."

And that's when they heard the shooting start.

—◁◯▷—

CARMINE WAS NERVOUS. HE DIDN'T LIKE HIS BOSS OUT IN THE OPEN where he couldn't see him. Joe Zee was standing on the Chrysler's running board, keeping his shoes out of the sidewalk slush.

"I wonder who Hanrahan is selling out now."

Carini didn't respond. He was staring into the gray mist of the cemetery, where his boss had disappeared.

"Hey, look at this," Zanca said, and when Carini didn't respond, "Carmine, look."

Carini turned. Fifty yards away a priest was walking toward them. He carried a black satchel. He was hunched against the cold and his hat was pulled low over his eyes.

"Fucking priest out on a day like this," Zanca said. "That's fucking devotion."

Carini turned to look back into the cemetery.

"Whattaya think he's doing here, praying for somebody or something?"

Carini was becoming irritated with Zanca's endless blather. He turned to say something, and that's when the priest lifted his head and he saw the priest's eyes and Carini jammed his hand inside

6 9

his overcoat but the priest was already firing, a silvery .45 automatic in each hand. Carini was killed instantly, struck by two in the chest. Joe Zanca didn't have time to get out his gat either, before a bullet tore off the top of his skull and he was thrown sprawling over the Chrysler's roof.

Tommy ran to the two parked cars and fired two into the second car's back window. The driver slumped forward on the wheel. Matranga's driver started to get out of the Chrysler and Tommy ran around the back of the car and shot him as he stood up. The driver spun and Tommy shot him again.

Then he continued running around the front of the Packard and into the cemetery's thick snow.

"Seven," he said to himself. He had eight rounds left.

◄○►

AT THE SOUND OF THE FIRST ROUND, MATRANGA AND HANRAHAN whipped out their guns. Matranga looked at Hanrahan, to see if he was being set up, but when he saw Hanrahan's face he knew that wasn't true.

"Who?" Hanrahan shouted. "What the fuck?"

Salvatore took a step toward Matranga and Matranga said, "Stay close to me!" Salvatore nodded and moved between his boss and the snow-muffled echoes of the last gunshots. Then it was very quiet. Hanrahan looked back at Matranga.

"What the fuck?" he asked again.

Tony Matranga was scared. He couldn't remember the last time he'd been afraid of anything. He moved from behind Salvatore's protective body and shouted toward the mist-shrouded street. "Carmine!" There was only the silence of the snow-choked graveyard. Matranga felt a wave of impending doom wash over him. "Joe!" he shouted, even louder. When there was no answer he touched Salvatore's back and said in Sicilian, "The other way. Let's go!"

The Sicilians were already disappearing into the foggy veil covering the cemetery when Hanrahan turned and saw them. "Hey! You can't go that way! It goes on for miles!"

Hanrahan watched them slip out of sight then he looked back in the direction of the street. His car was parked that way. He'd only taken a few steps when he heard the gun battle erupt behind him.

SACRED HEART

—◄○►—

TOMMY HAD CLAMBERED THROUGH THE SNOW, RUNNING AS FAST AS HE could in the sucking whiteness. He heard voices behind the tombs to his left, two rows over. He heard Matranga shout out for Carini, then Zanca. *They can't hear you*, Tommy thought as he plodded through a drift and came up behind a big square sepulchre. A granite angel stared mutely down at him, her hands in a position of impossible repose. Then he heard quick, heavy footsteps thudding in the snow. Under the tip of the angel's wing he saw a fleeing flash of dark overcoat through the maze of crosses and Christs.

Tommy ran down the line of graves, then crossed behind a small mausoleum a wealthy Catholic clan had erected to honor the founder of the family fortune. The mist here was thicker. It clung to Tommy's face like frigid webbing. He came around the side of the crypt just as a young Sicilian carrying a shotgun emerged from the haze. There was a brief second of recognition in the young Sicilian's eyes, then the shotgun erupted and bits of marble exploded up from the tomb and struck Tommy's face. Tommy fired both .45s simultaneously and the young Sicilian rose up from the snow and flew backward. Behind him Matranga was already scrambling to turn and Tommy shot him just as he submerged back into the mist.

Tommy wiped his face with his gloved hand. There were light flecks of blood. He moved forward cautiously into the spectral cloudiness. A few steps farther, and the snow was stained with a thick swath of dark blood. Then there was Matranga, inching forward on all fours, clutching at the snow like a child learning to crawl. The side of his overcoat was blown open and blood gushed out like a fountain.

Tommy stood over him a moment, then kicked him in the wound. Matranga screamed.

"I guess you didn't win, did you, greaseball?" Tommy sneered.

Matranga started to crawl forward again. He was making whimpering sounds, down in his throat.

"Fucking king of New York," Tommy said. Then he leaned over and put the muzzles of both .45s against the back of Matranga's skull.

"My da'll be waiting for you in hell," Tommy said, and pulled the triggers.

71

MARCEL MONTECINO

◄◦►

HANRAHAN HEARD THE SHOTGUN BLAST. THEN THE .45S, TOGETHER AND the single shot. He stood stock-still, like a dog smelling the wind. Then there was another volley that sounded like the .45s fired together again.

This can't be happening! Hanrahan thought. *This is impossible!*

As Hanrahan stood there, trembling not from the cold, the mist drifted in from deep in the cemetery, settled around and engulfed him. Hanrahan stirred himself and ran for the street. He'd only gone a few steps when he slammed right into a headstone and pitched forward on a snow-mounded grave.

JesusMaryandJoseph! He scrambled to get to his tiny feet. The mist swirled thickly around him, mixing with a few stray snowflakes. Behind him in the snowy haze someone slapped a fresh clip into an automatic and Hanrahan whirled and fired at the sound. He peered with terror into the white nothingness, then there was a footfall to his right and Hanrahan fired again, and then again. Then behind him came a ghostly laugh. Hanrahan whipped around and aimed at the sound. Then the mist parted and a priest stood before him. Hanrahan was so astounded that he started to lower his weapon and the gun in the priest's hand flared and Hanrahan was lifted up and thrown back into the outstretched arms of a larger-than-life Christ, supplicating His Father for mercy on all mankind.

Hanrahan sprawled back in his Savior's stony embrace, looked with amazement at the big, bubbling hole in his gut.

"Fuck me, Molly," he breathed as he pressed his hands around the spurting wound. "Fuck me, Molly."

Then a shadow fell across Jesus and Hanrahan looked up at Tommy's vengeful face over the white collar.

"You're supposed to be at the Church," Hanrahan said to Tommy in the most reasonable of tones.

"Nah," Tommy said, and pressed a .45 against the wound and fired. The blood spurted all over the snow-covered Christ. "I wanted to be with you."

Hanrahan settled back against the statue as he whispered again, "Fuck me, Molly," and died. His warm blood ran in steaming rivulets that dripped from the statue's hands.

Tommy glared at Hanrahan's dwarfish corpse. He wished he could bring him back to life and kill him again. Then his eyes drifted up to the imploring Christ. He stared.

"Fuck you, too," Tommy said, and it was the closest thing to a prayer he'd ever uttered.

72

Book II

—◄◇►—

Mexico

TERRAZAS STEPPED OUT ONTO HIS BALCONY AND LOOKED OUT across the city of Guadalajara. It was still early enough that the pleasant odor of breakfast cook fires hung in the air. Terrazas sipped his thick coffee and breathed in deeply. Below him, in an open area before the presidio, Indian women were making tortillas in a wide clay skillet on a tripod of stones. They patted the cornmeal into a small, flat cake, then laid it on the skillet, patted the next cake, set it next to the first, then turned over the first. Terrazas, who had just eaten a European-style breakfast, longed for one of the women's warm tortillas, dipped in a bowl of *menudo*.

"That's Mexico," Terrazas said. "Not the army, not the government. Certainly not the generals." He turned and looked into the dining room. "That. That is the soul of Mexico."

Several of the men rose from the long white-clothed table and carried their coffees out onto the balcony. The Mexicans looked down at the Indian women and were unimpressed. The foreigners stared with interest, trying to discern the elusive true soul of Mexico.

"I understand," the Spaniard Muñoz said. "When I was studying surgery in Moscow, we would see the peasant women out in the fields, harvesting the beets." Dr. Muñoz nodded down at the Indian women. "That was the soul of Russia."

Hernández, with dark skin and Aztec features, stared at Muñoz. "And if we had *conquistadores* who would go down there and rape those women, would that be the soul of Spain?"

Muñoz, who was a physical coward, quickly averted his eyes.

75

Terrazas watched with hidden pleasure. He used Hernández to say the things he chose not to.

"General Terrazas," the Englishman began, "how do those women down there feel about the new laws?" He set his cup down on the balcony railing. "Do they still pray? Have they renounced Christianity? Have you asked them if they still love the Virgin?"

Terrazas smiled. The *inglés* wanted a quote. Something he could wire back to London for next week's Sunday *Times*.

"For four hundred years the *campesinos* of Mexico have been force-fed a poisonous diet of superstition and fear. That kind of sickness can't be reversed overnight."

"So you're saying the common people of Mexico are not in favor of the new laws?"

Terrazas looked at the English reporter and frowned.

"Mr. Lancaster, if you're going to write about my country perhaps you should be better informed about your facts. The laws you speak of are not new at all, but in fact were Articles included in the Revolutionary Constitution of 1917. It's only now that we have a *presidente* with enough *huevos* to inforce them."

"Calles?"

"Sí, Presidente Calles."

Lancaster casually took a step closer to Terrazas—a hound snuffling for a scent. "General, what do you know about the rumors that Calles's wife secretly has Mass said at the Presidential Palace? And do you approve of this kind of hypocrisy?"

Terrazas imagined a fat, pale Englishman in Coventry reading Lancaster's story over a breakfast of kippers and tea. "Mexico hasn't outlawed religion, Mr. Lancaster."

"Just the Catholic Church?" Lancaster shot back.

Terrazas ignored him. "It's the priests who have decided to become outlaws. If this fictitious worship you speak of was conducted by any priest who registered with the federal government in Mexico City, as dictated by the Special Order of December seventh—"

"But none of them registered. Not a single priest, bishop or archbishop in the whole country." Lancaster waited for a reply.

Terrazas shrugged. "Then those priests must be apprehended and punished, just like any other criminals."

"Criminals?" Lancaster asked. "To conduct Christian worship is a crime?"

Dr. Muñoz flared in his Communist zeal. "Aren't you yourself hypocritical?" he demanded of Lancaster. Muñoz was young and thin, with a full dark beard and the absolute conviction of a rationalist fanatic. "Didn't your beloved England toss out the same corrupt and rapacious Church four hundred years ago? And it wasn't just over Henry's lechery. Didn't the King expropriate vast land holdings the thieves of Rome had accumulated in a thousand years of skullduggery and greed? Didn't the lords of England take baths in tubs of gold in castles seized back from the Church?"

Terrazas threw an amused glance at Hernández. They had come through the Revolution together, survived the decade-long warfare and bloodletting, and they had no respect for a theoretician like Muñoz. But he did have his uses.

"Is that what war is about?" Lancaster countered. "A chance to get at the Church's wealth in Mexico? Is that why all Church property has been confiscated by the State?"

" 'Repossessed' would be a more proper term," Muñoz snapped back. "The Catholics have robbed and raped this land since the first conquistadors stepped off their ships."

Hernández grinned at Muñoz. "*Spanish* conquistadors."

Terrazas raised his hand to quell the argument. "Why shouldn't Mexican land belong to the Mexican people? Why should fat, fornicator priests own their own vast ranchos?" Lancaster started to say something and Terrazas stopped him. "The Roman Catholic Church is a European institution imposed on this land and this people by European invaders. Did you know, Mr. Lancaster, what Cortés's second act was when he stepped ashore at Ulúa?"

"He—he claimed these shores for Spain."

"That was his first act. To steal the land. His second was to baptize a score of Indian women and then give them to his soldiers to amuse themselves with."

Lancaster didn't speak.

"So," Terrazas continued, "first he stole the land, then he filled the people with superstitious fear and made whores of our women. In this way Mexico was enslaved. And so it has been ever since. The Revolution was the Mexican people's heroic victory in throwing off those final vestiges of slavery. And this counterrebellion"—he waved his hands at the mountains in the distance—"is the death throes of the enslavers."

Lancaster wasn't going to let an opportunity like this go unmined. "So you admit Mexico is in a civil war? Especially in these Los Altos regions."

There was a commotion inside. The officers having their coffee around the long table were congratulating two teenage boys who had just entered the room. They were wearing dark blue uniforms, exact replicas of the one Terrazas had on.

"Ah, *mis hijos*," Terrazas said and his face filled with pride. He left the balcony and moved back inside. "Gentlemen," he said, and the others followed him in. "Gentlemen, I would like you to meet the two newest officers in my army. Colonel Antonio Terrazas"— he put his hand on the back of the neck of the older, taller boy, who grinned with embarrassment—"and Captain Francisco Terrazas." The younger boy couldn't have been fourteen. His face was round and thick, like his body. He couldn't even raise his eyes.

Lancaster couldn't hide his astonishment. "They're just . . . boys."

Dr. Muñoz moved forward smiling. "This is good, *mi general*. This is excellent. Make them soldiers of the Revolution as young as possible." He nodded with approval. "That's what they're doing in the Soviet."

Terrazas moved between the boys and tousled their hair, grinning. "Captain Paco and Colonel Tonio." He roared with laughter and pulled them tightly to him as he cast an eye at Lancaster. "You thought maybe that an old anticleric like me would name them something like Diablo and Lucifer, like the Governor of Tabasco calls his sons?" Terrazas shook his head. "No, that's a valid political statement. But it shows the boys no respect, eh?" He looked to each of his shy sons in turn, and *his* respect was obvious. "Captain Paco and Colonel Tonio," he said softly. Then, "Dr. Muñoz, you are an educated man. A man of ideas. You've been to Russia and seen how successful a secular state can be. I ask you, would you teach my sons what you've learned, so they can better be of service to the continuing Revolution?"

Hernández gave a short, bitter laugh. "A Spaniard *giving* something to Mexico."

"General," Muñoz said solemnly, "I would consider it an honor. Thank you for allowing *me* to be of service to the Revolution."

Just then there was a shout from the street. "General Terrazas!"

Terrazas looked to each of his sons, his face growing serious. "Now you will see firsthand the cold responsibilities of leadership."

IN THE DUSTY STREET STOOD A GRIZZLED VETERAN OF THE REVOLUTION. His chest was crossed with bandoleers; his boot heels jangled with silver spurs; his flared leather pants bore the cracks and creases of a thousand hours in the saddle. Over his shoulder he loosely held the American-made Winchester that was never far from his trigger finger.

"*General Terrazas!*" he bellowed again, looking up at the second floor of the *alcalde.*

On the balcony Terrazas appeared, flanked by the others.

"*Mi general!* Good morning to you!"

"Good morning to you, Severo, old friend!" Terrazas shouted down. "What kind of morning do you have lined up for me?"

"A glorious morning! We are going to execute five enemies of the Revolution!" Severo Salazar gestured back at the five men roped together with leather bindings lined up behind him, under heavy guard. Four of them were priests.

And the last priest in line was Tommy Gun.

OUTSIDE GRAND CENTRAL STATION THE NEWSBOYS WERE ALREADY hawking the late extras. "*Tommy Gun Escapes Church!*" "*Citywide Dragnet!*" Tommy pulled his hat down over his eyes, lifted his overcoat collar and pushed through the doors. There were uniformed cops just inside the entrance. Tommy tightened and was moving his hands toward his guns when the cop saw his collar and looked past to the next traveler entering Grand Central.

He stood in line, waiting to buy a ticket, glancing over his shoulder at the teams of detectives moving through the crowds. Then the guy in front of him hurried away and the ticket seller smiled at him.

"Where you going, Father?"

For a moment Tommy could only stare at the guy. Then he realized it was the ticket seller's warm smile that was throwing him. "Mexico," Tommy said finally. Then he remembered the brightly stamped letter in his pocket. He drew it out and read slowly. "Guadalajara," mispronounced with a hard *J.*

The ticket clerk opened a drawer, pulled out a booklet and a roll of tickets. "That's a long way, Father." He ran his finger down a row of printing, fixed on a line. "We'll get you to Laredo, then you have to repurchase over the border." He looked up at Tommy.

"That'll be twenty-three dollars. With the clerical discount." Again the broad smile.

Tommy counted out the money from the bills he'd taken from O'Rourke's metal box, then started to take the ticket from the clerk's hand. The clerk wouldn't let go.

"You didn't forget your passport, did you, Father? You're going to need it at the border."

Tommy made himself form a grateful smile and patted his breast pocket. "It's right here. Thank you, my son."

The ticket clerk leaned over a bit and whispered slyly, "I bumped you up in class. No extra charge." He winked and released the ticket. "Have a good trip, Father." The clerk looked up at the big concourse clock. "Track Twenty-eight, departing in twenty minutes."

Crossing Grand Central, Tommy was hit by the odor of browning onions and frying meat billowing out from the dining room. His stomach rumbled hungrily, but Tommy pressed forward through the crowd. The blizzard had stalled travel for most of three days, and now everyone was hurrying to get where they should have been sooner.

There were a pair of coppers at the entrance to the tracks, and several more on the platform, leaning against the walls, surveying passing faces. Tommy tipped his hat to one fat copper who stared at him a little longer than the others, and the fat policeman nodded and looked away.

A tan-skinned porter saw Tommy heading for the train. He stepped down and offered Tommy a helping hand and that same warm smile. "Bum leg, Father?" Tommy realized he was limping from the bullet tear in his buttock.

"Football injury." Tommy nodded, and then when he raised his foot to step up on the train hot pain shot up his spine. The porter felt him falter and took hold of his arm.

"There we go, there we go," he said softly as Tommy climbed the three metal steps. The smile again. "And you such a young man. Lemme see your ticket, Father." He examined the ticket as he said, "My wife's Catholic. She's Cuban. She makes me wear this." He opened a button to reveal a small oval on a chain, then said, "Mr. Conductor, could we see you a minute?"

Tommy looked quickly up the aisle at a florid-faced Irishman heading his way. "Mr. Conductor, the Father here got a bum leg." The porter held up the ticket. "Anything we can do for him?"

The conductor looked at the ticket in the porter's hand, then at

Tommy. Then the *conductor* smiled. "How's a private compartment sound to you, Father?"

Of course, Tommy thought. *That's the ticket I should have—*

Tommy froze as he saw two detectives he knew out on the platform, walking toward the train.

"If you're worried about the extra expense, Father," the conductor was saying, "don't. It's on the railroad." The conductor took his arm and began to lead him down the aisle. The two detectives had stopped and were talking to a pair of uniformed flatfoots. They were eyeing the train. "There's a coupla extra compartments the company keeps open for VIPs. And to me, 'tis no one more important than the Church's own." They passed into the next car. "Father, I've told no one about this," the conductor said, dropping his voice. "I'm a family man, with eight kids, all in parochial school." The conductor looked at him with a sudden sense of urgency. "I'm a good man, Father. I've never raised my hand to the missus, and I give up the drinkin' ten years ago. Give it up cold." The conductor stopped at a compartment and opened the door, but stood in the doorway. "But there's this waitress in St. Louis, where I layover—" The conductor seemed stricken. "I can't keep my hands off of her, Father." The detectives were walking the length of the train, peering into the windows. "I sin with her every chance I get."

Tommy kept his eyes on the detectives; they were nearing. "Is she a blond or a brunette?"

The conductor's eyes widened with surprise. "Why, she's— she's redheaded."

Tommy smiled. "I'm giving special dispensations for redheads this week. It's not a sin."

The conductor's eyes filled with tears. "Ah, Father. Thank you." He reached out and gripped Tommy's shoulder. "Thank you for understanding."

Tommy used the opportunity to move the conductor aside. "Is this where you want me to be? Because I'm very tired." He turned and looked back out the train windows. The detectives were almost abreast of them, out on the platform.

"Yes, Father." Tommy entered the compartment and started to close the door, but the conductor's foot was in the way. "Father, could you give me your blessing, I would really—"

Tommy raised his hand and quickly etched a cross in the conductor's face. "Bless you, my son." He pushed the door and the conductor moved his foot. "Thank yo—"

Tommy shut the door and locked it. Then he crossed to the window and pulled down the shade. He went back to the door and stood there, listening. There was a garbled shout from somewhere. Tommy yanked out a silvery nickel-plated .45, stepped back and aimed it at where a man's head would appear in the door. A half-minute elapsed, then a minute, then the train lurched and started to move forward. The train was well out of the station and coursing through the city's tenement backyards when Tommy finally relaxed. He sat on the edge of the bed, wincing at the pain in his buttocks, and stared at the door. After another long moment he lay the .45 down on the bed. A wave of unendurable weariness swept over him. He carefully lifted his feet onto the mattress and stretched out. Within seconds he was asleep.

⊲○⊳

THE TRAIN TRIP TO LAREDO TOOK JUST UNDER THREE DAYS. TOMMY slept for much of the first. The porter with the Cuban Catholic wife woke him with sandwiches and a pint of 'leg just outside of St. Louis. Tommy ate and drank and peeked around the shade at the crowded platform. The New York cops might have alerted the Missouri flatfoots to be on the lookout for him, and he wanted to stay out of sight.

The conductor with the waitress girlfriend stopped by to strut manfully and say good-bye, and to introduce Tommy to the conductor for the next leg of the journey. This one was a Polack, big and respectful. Tommy told him he didn't want to be disturbed, he needed to pray. The Polack nodded in awe and backed out, shutting the door in his own face.

Tommy slept for another ten hours, and when he awoke and raised the shade he saw an America he'd never seen before. Wide and flat, stretching to forever; the winter grass brown and dry in the wide patches free of snow. Tommy watched it for hours, slipping past his compartment window. He'd spent his whole life in the brick, concrete, and steel constraints of New York City. He had never grown accustomed to seeing the horizon, to experiencing the vast oneness of the country, even in its most rudimentary sense. Watching the Texas flatlands rush by, Tommy felt as if he had spent the twenty-five years of his life as a rat in a maze. He gawked at the immensity of the world and felt more and more alone.

Then he tired again and slept some more.

SACRED HEART

—◄ ○ ►—

T ommy had killed his second, third, and fourth men all on the same night. It was a sultry, still Friday in July, and Bulldog had sent Tommy and Fightin' McGillicuddy down to Essex Street to collect final payment on a shipment of Scotch delivered to Jakey Silverberg. Jakey was young and tough and took no shit, and though only a year or two older than Tommy he was already running his own little mob in the free-for-all the Jews called their rackets. Tommy liked Jakey, and after business had been transacted Jakey took Tommy and Fightin' McGillicuddy to a cathouse where all the whores were Jewish. Tommy wasn't even seventeen, but he had already become his father's right hand, and Jakey wanted to show the Coyne kid a good time in his neighborhood. They had fucked straight for three or four hours, switching whores, sharing, pairing, until even Jakey said he couldn't get it up anymore.

As they walked out of the cathouse, a Dodge had come around the corner and a wop shouted out, "Is that you, kikey!" and then he'd opened fire with a tommy gun and Fightin' McGillicuddy caught it first and went down big, then Jakey kind of rattled a moment and his right arm detached from his body and dropped into the street. The wop had just started shooting at Tommy when the Dodge ran right into a milk wagon crossing Houston from a side street. It plowed into the team of dray horses, killing one instantly. The horse's belly burst and its guts spewed out onto the hood of the Dodge. The far horse had two broken forelegs and lay in the street screaming, pumping its hindquarters in a futile attempt to get up. The driver of the Dodge slumped over the wheel.

The wop with the tommy gun lay sprawled in the street, thrown from the Dodge, and Tommy ran to where the submachine gun had skidded, picked it up and ran to the Dodge. He stuck the muzzle into the automobile and sprayed the whole inside of the car. When he turned back the wop in the street had gotten up and run away. It wasn't until he read the papers the next day that Tommy learned there'd been three of Matranga's men in the Dodge, counting the driver.

Tommy's reputation was made that night. And the enmity with the Matranga mob cemented.

83

THEY PULLED INTO LAREDO ON A CLEAR, MOONLIT NIGHT. THE NEW conductor, this one a Protestant who'd stared blankly at Tommy's collar, knocked gruffly on the door and declared that all passengers had to disembark for Mexican customs. Tommy stepped out onto the rude platform, the first time he'd left the train since he gotten on in New York. The air was clean and cold. The land stretched out low and undulating in all directions. Across the slow-moving, sorry-looking river dozens of open fires glowed in the bright night.

"Is that Mexico?" Tommy asked the passing conductor.

By way of answer, the conductor nodded to the small group of passengers forming at the end of the platform. "Get your ticket from the Mexican inside, then get in line over there. They'll take care of you."

Inside there was only a fat brown man leaning on a plank counter. He glanced up as Tommy entered, then looked back and stared as he limped across the scarred wood floor.

"Guadalajara," Tommy said, wondering why the fat man was staring at him. The fat man hurriedly tore off a ticket and collected thirteen U.S. dollars and thirty-seven cents. Tommy turned and limped back out, and the fat brown man fished a silver medal from inside his shirt and kissed it.

Tommy carried his satchel bumping against his good leg and moved stiffly to the back of the score of people gathered before a small table set up under an umbrella. A single bare electric light poured down a startling circle of glare. A Mexican Army lieutenant in a dirty dun-colored uniform inspected each traveler's passport or visa, then passed along the papers to a civilian official seated beside him, smoking a cigarette. The civilian in turn scrutinized the papers with self-importance, then slammed down a stamp. Arrayed against the wall behind them, three Mexican soldiers slouched, waiting for a command.

Tommy stole glances at the people around him. They were all foreign-looking. Some resembled the wops back home in New York, but most had darker, sharper faces, with large hawk noses and piercing black eyes, and straight black hair that gleamed in the unshaded light.

Indians, Tommy suddenly realized with a start. *Fucking Geronimo Indians.*

A few of the men wore oddly tailored suits, but most were working people, with laden blankets slung over their shoulders and rope-woven bags. They inched their feet forward as they moved up in line.

Tommy was the only white man.

Then Tommy stepped before the table. The lieutenant saw his collar first, then his eyes moved up to his face. They stayed a moment, coldly searching; then the lieutenant turned and looked at the civilian official.

Tommy felt a premonition of something bad coming, and he pressed his arm against the weight of his .45.

"Why are you coming to our country, priest?" the civilian official asked in Spanish.

Tommy, not knowing what to do, simply offered his passport. The two Mexicans stared at it.

"We don't need any more like you in Mexico."

"Maybe you're fucking crazy," the lieutenant spoke for the first time. Tommy didn't understand any of what they said, but he absorbed the antipathy radiating from both men. He wondered what had caused them to hate him so, and he wondered what would happen after he killed them.

"I don't speak Mexican," he said, finally.

The civilian official glared with hatred, and Tommy knew the official had understood what he'd said. For a moment, Tommy thought they knew who he was, that they'd been alerted by wire or telephone to detain him, but he quickly dismissed that thought. If the U.S. officials had known where he was going, he would never have gotten this far.

"I have a brother in—"

"Father, the old man is waiting for you." An Indian woman, thick with childbearing, pushed her way through the crowd and stood next to Tommy. "We can't hesitate." Tommy looked at her, but knew enough not to show his surprise. Then the Indian woman spoke to the two behind the table in swirling, slurred Spanish. She seemed to go on forever. The two Mexican men at the table were impassive. They alternately stared insolently at the woman, then glared at Tommy. Finally the civilian official spoke, cutting off the woman in midsentence.

Without a breath she turned to Tommy and softly said, "Take off your collar, Father."

"What?" He thought he'd heard her wrong.

"Take off your collar." She said it with such whispered urgency that Tommy did as he was told. As he was unbuttoning, the Indian woman said, even more softly, "Do you have any money?"

"Yes."

"Give them each a large bill. Two five-dollar bills, if you have it."

Tommy quickly put away the clerical collar, then loosened two bills from his roll while his hand was still in his pocket. The bribery of public authority was something he'd learned early in New York. As he fumbled in his pants he could feel the hard weight of his holstered automatic pressed under his arm. The lieutenant watched him carefully, moving his head slightly to alert his soldiers, who stood up straighter and tightened their grip on their rifles.

Tommy brought out the two bills. There was a five and a ten.

"Good, good," the woman said, indicating there was no way to rectify the situation now that the bills had been seen. She quickly palmed the money, then reached for Tommy's passport. The civilian official looked at Tommy one last time, then stamped the passport and handed it to the Indian woman, taking the bills from between her fingers as she drew her hand back.

"Quickly, Father, the train is about to go," the Indian woman said loudly as she took Tommy's arm and walked him past the table and into Mexican jurisdiction. The train was inching forward, and the other passengers were getting on. "The old man is hanging on, waiting for your arrival. It's not far. Just a few miles—"

"What're you talking about? What did you tell them?"

She bustled him along to the train.

"I told them the old rancher McClary was dying, and he wanted an American priest to give him the last rites." She glanced back quickly at the table. The lieutenant was watching them. "That gringo bastard has been dying for ten years, and everyone knows he hates Mexicans." Then she pushed him onto the train landing. The lieutenant turned away. The Indian woman grabbed his hand and kissed it. "Bless you for coming, Father, but be very, very careful." The train was picking up speed. With her back to the Mexican officials she made a tight sign of the cross and whispered, "*Viva Cristo Rey.*" Then she walked away from the train without looking back.

⟨◦⟩

TOMMY HUNG ON THE LANDING AS THEY CROSSED THE BIG STEEL BRIDGE over the river. He watched the lights of Laredo fade behind him as the cold air whipped at his face. He didn't understand what had just happened back at the border crossing, but he realized fully for the first time since he'd begun his flight from New York that he was leaving behind more than his crimes. He would have to learn a new way to speak, a new way to think—and he was going to be an outsider for the rest of his life.

When Tommy got back to his coach, it was occupied by two of the well-dressed Mexicans he had seen on the platform. They stared at his cheap, wrinkled black suit, and said something sharp, and Tommy quickly closed the door and moved down the aisle. In the Pullman the people had dispersed themselves through the car and settled down. Some were already asleep. Tommy picked a place away from the others, stuffed his bag into the overhead netting, and sat down on the hard-backed seat. A dark-skinned woman with a shawl over her head looked at him, then when Tommy stared back she looked away. Before long the lights in the train went out and Tommy slept.

—◆◇◆—

HE AWOKE JUST AS THE SUN WAS BREAKING OVER THE LOW MOUNTAINS TO the east. He sat without moving and watched the land reveal itself. Before, he had never thought much about Mexico, just as he had never given much consideration to anything beyond New York, women and the whiskey trade. He had seen grainy front-page photographs of some kind of revolution down here. Dago-looking men with long, bushy mustaches, in white cloth pants and huge floppy hats, holding their weapons like extensions of their dicks. They always seemed to glare out of the newspaper with the fiery guinea haughtiness that Tommy had grown to hate since he was a young boy fighting in the streets of the Kitchen.

And somewhere Tommy had picked up an image of Mexico as a land of steaming Tarzan movie jungles. But what he saw outside the train's dirty window was a wide expanse of brown and bare. Bare, but not empty. The rising sun illuminated a sparse sprinkling of adobe farm buildings, grouped together as if answering some herding instinct; cattle, large and rangy, stubbornly grazing over the open, fenceless land; narrow dirt roads along which small, dark men moved in pairs and small groups. It was a huge, uncrowded country, but it wasn't unpopulated.

—◄○►—

IT WAS WELL INTO MIDDAY WHEN TOMMY ALLOWED HIMSELF TO REALIZE he'd made it. He'd escaped the fate cast for him when Bulldog had ignored his advice and walked into the trap in Matranga's warehouse. A sense of lightness cautiously crept into Tommy's heart. He had no idea what his new life was going to be like—except it wouldn't include summer nights strutting among the crowds on brightly lit Broadway, surrounded by the rest of the Coyne Mob, steeped in youth and power and money. There wouldn't be notes sent backstage to painted and eager Cotton Club showgirls. Solomon & Fleischer's wouldn't be taking any more orders for a dozen double-breasted suits, no cuffs, with a slight flare. There wouldn't be any more champagne breakfasts at the Plaza, the waiters rushing to light his Havana. That was all gone. But Tommy smiled inwardly with the satisfaction that he'd escaped the New York cops and the other Sicilian gangs. He'd wiped out the Matrangas and Hanrahan—and he was still alive.

—◄○►—

THE TRAIN SEEMED TO STOP IN EVERY TOWN AND VILLAGE. INDIAN women, their children trailing behind them, moved down the platform, selling bright blankets and sweets and some kind of little meat pies, passing them up through the windows. The sides of the stations declared the names of each town in peeling paint—names long and heavy in vowels—Salamanca, Irapuato, Arandas.

There were troops in every town, and crowds of heavily armed horsemen, crisscrossed with belts of bullets, lazing in their saddles as they glared at everyone and everything. Tommy sat warily behind the window glass and watched them. He recognized their manner, their insolence, their contemptuous power. They were gangsters.

During the first day, on three occasions a Mexican official came through the train, staring at faces, asking questions. Each time, Tommy slumped against the seat and pretended to be asleep. On the morning of the second day a slow-moving convoy of army trucks paralleled the train for over an hour. That afternoon a line of cavalry raced beside the tracks, the troopers shouting and waving their hats.

Around sunset of the second day on the train Tommy saw the land outside the windows begin to climb. The pine trees and the mescal cactus grew fuller and greener. The train crossed deep gorges on precarious trestles that trembled beneath the rumbling iron wheels.

Just after dawn on the third day in Mexico, on the crest of a mountain pass, the train began to slow. It huffed to a halt in the middle of nowhere. The wind moaned. Tommy grew uneasy; he flattened his face against the glass and looked forward. Through a distorted view he saw several large men carrying canvas packs leave a trackside shack and approach the train. One of them smoked a curved-stem pipe. Another wore a dented bowler. They moved in a manner that was instantly familiar to Tommy, all the more so since he hadn't seen it since he'd crossed the Rio Grande.

They were Americans.

They walked alongside the train beneath Tommy's window, then disappeared from view, then a few moments later the train starting moving again. The track slipped down from the mountaintop and curved around and down into a valley. Tommy heard their loud, confident voices before they even entered the car.

"The best run I ever saw, back in '21. Kadinsky took the handoff from Stodelmeyer, and he just ran through the Notre Dame line like a hot knife through butter."

"Shut up about that damn game. You sound like a broken record."

They stomped heavily into the car, ignoring the few male passengers and staring openly at the women.

"Over here."

From their gear—which they stacked in the middle of the aisle— they were miners or engineers. Five of them. They arranged themselves around themselves and sat down.

"Gimme that flask, I'm freezing."

"Fucking greasers don't know what a heating system is, they can't put a match to it."

A big miner with a beard and pocked cheeks took a long pull on a flask. He grimaced. "I'm convinced they make this shit from bull piss, is what they do."

The guy with the bowler, who was small and reddish, said, "We'll be in Guadalajara in three hours. Then we'll get at some whiskey."

"And some Cuban rum."

"And some whores. I'm gonna rip me up a whole slew of fat little monkeys."

The eldest of the group, gray-haired and scowling, pulled from his coat a creased and fraying newspaper. He carefully unfolded it and Tommy saw it was a *Police Gazette.*

"Damn, Ted, you gonna read that damn thing again?"

The gray-haired miner carefully adjusted a pair of frameless glasses on his nose. "Yeah, for the last time. I'll get fresh editions in G.D."

Tommy, stealing glances at the miners, saw them start up a poker game played on the seats. Before the first hand was won he noticed one of the miners was staring at him. He was fair and blue-eyed, and he kept handling a baseball, fingering it, tossing it from hand to hand. Tommy's first impulse was to stare him down, but he quickly looked away, out the window.

The miner with the baseball kept staring at him. "That's an American over there," he said to the others. He had a West Side accent.

"Where?" They twisted in their seats to look at him. Tommy kept his eyes on the mountains slipping by beyond the glass.

"Hey!" the big bearded one said. "You a gringo like us?"

When Tommy didn't reply the big beard shrugged and turned back to his game. "He's a monkey, he just don't look like one."

"Half the greasers around here look white," another said. "They say it's because of Maximilian's soldiers."

The blue-eyed New Yorker shook his head slowly as he slammed the baseball into his palm. "No, I seen him before." He rose from his seat and walked toward Tommy. The others watched.

"Hey, pal." He loomed over Tommy. "Hey." He prodded Tommy with two fingers. Tommy forced himself to empty his face of emotion before he turned to the New Yorker.

The guy's blue Kitchen eyes inspected him closely.

"Don't I know you?"

Tommy didn't react to the guy's words. He just stared up blankly.

"I seen you before. You from New York?"

Tommy resisted the impulse to shake his head. He slowly turned back to the window.

"Aw, leave him alone, Gunny. He's just another Mexican," the bearded miner said.

Gunny cocked his head and stared down at Tommy. "No . . . I seen him before. Hey, pal, you speak English?"

Tommy didn't respond.

"Gunny, you in this hand, or what?"

Gunny gently tossed his baseball from one hand to the other. "I'm in." Then he started to turn back to the others but instead quickly underhanded the ball at Tommy. Tommy caught it easily, reflexively. Gunny grinned in triumph. Then Tommy pasted an idiot's smile on his face and offered back the ball, nodding his head in supplication. Gunny's grin faded.

"Just another greaser," he growled and plucked the ball from Tommy's palm. Gunny walked back to his seat and picked up his cards. "He looked like somebody, but he's just another damn greaser."

For the next half hour Tommy tried to keep from looking at the miners, but every time he did steal a glance he was met with Gunny's suspicious blue glare. And the Mexicans on the train, understanding only that Tommy had tried to deny what he was, stared at him with curiosity.

Then the conductor passed through the car, calling out, "Santa Maria. Next stop, Santa Maria." Tommy unhurriedly gathered his suitcase from overhead. He had to get off the train. Gunny wouldn't stop staring at him.

The train slowed to a stop and Tommy wincingly stepped off the train onto the stone platform. The conductor gave him an inquisitive look, then climbed back onto the train. As the train started up behind him, Tommy looked out over a wide street that ended at the platform. The train was pulling out of the station before Tommy realized what was wrong. It was deserted. There were no people. Then the train was gone, its whistle echoing as it slipped around the next mountain pass. A brief, brisk wind howled across the platform and was gone. Tommy had never felt more isolated and cut off from the world than he did at this moment. Then he heard a human sound—a hammering coming from one side of the plaza. He stepped from the platform onto the hard dirt ground. He had taken only a few strides when he saw to his left a burned-out building. It was a yawning hole of blackened timbers and ashes, in stark contrast to the neat Spanish-style structures on either side. It didn't belong there. Then the hammering started up again, just ahead and to the right. As Tommy took a few steps forward he saw another ruined building, this one of brick. The walls had been thrown outward as if from an explosion within, and the bricks were strewn about the street before it. Inside two men were tearing at the standing remains of the walls with sledgehammers. Behind them another two were painting over words scrawled on the soot-blackened bricks. Tommy looked at the workers a moment, trying to fix on something about them, and then he realized—they were prisoners. The heavy way they moved; their silent resignation; their disinterested air. Tommy looked around for their keeper and found him staring down from the bare cubicle on the open second floor. He was sitting on the edge of a desk in what had once been an office, belts of bullets snaked around each shoulder, a rifle across his lap, and he was silently watching Tommy. He must have been watching ever since Tommy got off the train.

Tommy looked away quickly. Then he saw the church bell tower behind the facing row of buildings. If he was going to get to his brother Frank in someplace called Guadalajara, which the miner had said was only a few hours away, then he would somehow have to enlist the local priest to show him the way. He had taken a few steps when he realized what the scrawled words the prisoners were painting over said. *"Viva Cristo Rey."* That's what the Indian woman in Laredo had whispered to him. Tommy stared at the words, wondering what they meant. The guard on the second floor got to his feet and propped his rifle on his hip. Tommy moved on.

The empty street fed into an even emptier plaza. On the far side of the square stood an ancient church, small but resolute. Tommy started across the square. There were no cars, no horses, no carriages—just a wide expanse of gray, iron-hard ground, with a gurgling fountain in the middle. Tommy took the priest's collar from his pocket and snapped it around his neck. Even if he didn't speak Mexican, Tommy figured he could point to the letter and the collar would get him to his brother. He was halfway across the square when he noticed a dark apparition slip out of a door and race across the plaza toward him. Tommy put his hand under his coat and slipped his finger through the trigger guard. The thin wraith turned out to be an old lady, clothed in black, and unbelievably fleet in her distress. She ran to Tommy and began to tug at his arm, hissing in Spanish as she looked in terror around the square.

"I'm sorry, I don't understand," Tommy tried to explain. As the old lady babbled on, another panicked figure materialized from an alley, then another and another. They were all women of advanced age, and they rushed to him and began to pull at him with fierce urgency. Tommy could not have been more shocked.

"Leave me alone. Please. Please. *What the hell are you doing!?*" he shouted finally. The women suddenly froze with an audible intake of breath and stared off across the plaza at something they seemed to have all heard. Then like a flock of crows they skittered away across the square—their blacks skirts rustling like wings—and disappeared into their cubbyholes.

Tommy turned around, but there was nothing there. Just the wide expanse of the empty plaza.

What the hell is goin' on?

Tommy moved the weight of O'Rourke's satchel to his other hand and started up the low steps into the church.

The tall double doors of the church were ajar. Tommy thought of the door to Sacred Heart back in Hell's Kitchen. Then he stopped short when he saw the bullet holes in the wood—a neat, splintered grouping of five, just at the height of a man's heart. Tommy was again awash in the disquieting certainty that something was happening around him that he didn't understand.

Tommy pushed the door open and slowly stepped into the cold darkness of the church. He had only taken a few feet when he saw the church had been desecrated. The narrow wooden pews were overturned, some of them tossed up against the wall as if by the hand of a giant. A holy water font had been overturned, its stone pedestal smashed to pebble. The other font held a vile, yellow liquid, and the stink told Tommy it was urine. Tommy stared in amazement. He'd seen three men blown apart as they tried to construct a bomb. He'd watched as his father strangled a stool pigeon with the sash from his own smoking jacket. But he'd never before seen piss in the holy water.

Then he looked at the walls.

They had once been covered with murals that if Tommy had had an education, he would have known had been centuries old when Manhattan was still a forest. Images painted with all the devotion and exactitude of impregnable faith—all the more moving in their New World simplicity.

But now they had been made demonic.

The Virgin sucked on an enormous bulbous penis that had been scrawled beside her face. Christ stumbled under the Cross while St. John buggered Him from behind. Mary Magdalene clasped her hands in prayer and raised her eyes skyward to a hairy, dripping vagina crudely fashioned just above her halo.

Icy revulsion moved under the surface of Tommy's flesh. He turned slowly to the altar.

Anything of value—the gold chalice, the altar's ciborium, the tabernacle—had been stolen and in their place were mounds of human excrement. The shit had hardened in the church's chill, and a greenish mold grew over its surface.

Tommy felt overwhelmed, as if he were in the company of a great evil. Even more evil than his own.

He took a step forward and his shoe dipped into something thick and slick. There was a congealed pool of blood on the polished stone of the church floor. Tommy slowly raised his eyes to find, hanging from the rafters, what had once been a priest. Above the noose his face had blackened and his eyes had popped out. His cassock was rended in a hundred places. They had hanged him, then used his twisting body for target practice.

Tommy stood in stunned awe, seeing the murder in his mind, feeling the fury of the killers.

Then something snaked before his eyes and before he could react he was yanked backward off his feet by the lariat hoop that tightened around his middle.

Colonel Salazar, the *agrarista* chieftain, laughed and spurred his big blood-bay stallion out of the church.

"*Ay yi yi,*" he shouted as he bounced Tommy down the church stairs and into the square, which was no longer empty. A score of horsemen watched with delight. "Look what the wind blew in!"

Salazar raked the stallion with his silver spurs and galloped across the plaza, dragging Tommy across the dusty stones.

"They are like flies," one of the horsemen laughed. "They always come back to their shit!"

Salazar wheeled the big red bay around the fountain. Tommy tumbled over and over until the rope bolted him forward. Salazar raced back to the church steps and yanked back so hard on his reins that the stallion almost sat on his haunches in obedience to his rider.

Another *agrarista* deftly dismounted and pulled his pistol from his waist holster. "They're more like roaches. You have to step on them to kill them." He put the muzzle of his weapon against Tommy's skull and cocked back the hammer.

"No!" Salazar shouted as he swung from his saddle. "This one is for Terrazas." The big red stallion backed up, keeping the rope taut. "This one is for Terrazas," he said again. "He wants to put on a show."

Stunned and bleeding, Tommy was struggling to reach his .45s, but the rope kept his arms pinned. Salazar kicked him in the face. "What are you reaching for, priest?" He grinned at the others. "Your beads?" They all laughed. He knelt and stuck his hand under Tommy's arm. His face grew very hard. "This is not a rosary." He held up the shiny nickel-plated automatic for the others to see. They stared down at Tommy with killing eyes. Then Salazar pulled out the matching gun from Tommy's other holster. He admired them in front of Tommy's face.

"Did the Archbishop bless these, the better to send us to hell?"

Tommy didn't understand the words, but the hatred was clear. "I'm gonna fucking kill you," he rasped between his bloody lips.

"A foreigner!" Salazar exclaimed with delight as he stuck Tommy's .45s into the wide belt around his middle. "An English!"

"No." Another *agrarista* had torn open O'Rourke's satchel. The clothes were strewn about the plaza. He was looking at O'Rourke's passport. "An American!"

"A gringo!" Salazar grinned. "Terrazas will be very happy."

At the distant far side of the square the four workmen prisoners were being led into the plaza by their keeper. The guard shaded his eyes and tried to see what his compadres were doing with their prisoner. From another direction an ancient flatbed truck roared loudly into the plaza.

Salazar waved his hat at the truck, and it turned sharply and bumped toward them.

The guard spoke to his four prisoners and they moved back to the wall.

"Terrazas has the others," a man on a black gelding said. "Let's kill this one now and hang him from the bell, so everyone can hear." He smiled shyly. "I've always wanted to do that."

One of the workmen turned to the wall and knelt to pray. The guard told him to stop.

Salazar tied Tommy's hands behind him with a short piece of leather, then yanked him to his feet. "Terrazas," he said simply.

When the man wouldn't stop praying, the guard bolted a cartridge into his rifle chamber and shot him at the base of the skull. The man slumped against the wall, still on his knees. The guard said something to the other three workmen and they held out their arms and touched their fingertips, arranging themselves military-style.

Two of Salazar's *agraristas* dismounted, lifted Tommy by his arms and threw him into the bed of the truck. There was a young priest, barely out of his teens, already in there. He was trembling so violently his heels rattled on the bare boards of the truck bed. Tommy looked at the young priest and then tried to get to his feet. An *agrarista* slammed the butt of his rifle into the back of Tommy's head and Tommy folded against the side of the truck. The Mexican laughed.

On the other side of the square the guard methodically executed the three remaining workmen.

—◄ ○ ►—

WHEN TOMMY OPENED HIS EYES, IT WAS NIGHT. HE LOOKED UP AT GAS-lights and telephone lines crisscrossing the moving sky above him. He heard the sounds of a city—automobile traffic, a streetcar bell, and jubilant cheers. He started to raise his head and an angry jolt of red hot agony shot from the back of his brain and seemed to squeeze his skull like a vise. He slumped back against the truck-bed floorboards.

The truck moved slowly through the narrow streets of the city's central zone. The mounted *agraristas* rode proudly on either side; those in front carried flaming torches to light the way. The side-walks were thinly lined with approving citizens. Their faces were joyous and vengeful. They shouted out encouragement to the horsemen. These were ancient grudges they were redressing. A pha-lanx of young *comunistas* ran alongside the truck, red kerchiefs knot-ted around their throats.

A small street urchin with a crooked right leg and clouded eye dashed into the street before the parade and shouted, "Butcher the black pigs! We'll have a feast!" The *comunista* youths roared with victorious laughter. The *agraristas* shot off their guns into the air. The boy ran lurching beside the truck and threw stones at the two priests in the back.

And from doorways and windows, others watched silently, grimly, and turned away in shame.

At a large gray building, gates were opened and the truck drove through. Inside was a prison, clean-swept and stone. The prison guards moved toward the truck but the *agraristas* stepped in their way. The priest prisoners were theirs, and they would deliver them.

The young priest started to mew with terror as soon as the truck's tailgate was let down. The grinning *agraristas* told him they were going to fuck him in his mouth and his *culo.* As soon as one of them touched him he started to scream. They laughed and carried him away down a corridor. Tommy was yanked from the truck by two tall *agraristas* who whispered similar perversions to him as they dragged him into a large, straw-floored cell. They propped him against the barred door and for several minutes took turns punching him. Tommy passed out after the first few blows and one of the tall Mexicans had to hold him up through the bars while the other beat on him. Finally they left him bleeding in the dirty straw and went away.

SACRED HEART

---◄ ◊ ►---

WHEN TOMMY CAME TO HE OPENED HIS EYES AND SAW AN INDIAN watching him. The Indian was seated on a concrete slab in a circle of candlelight, eating rice and tortillas. He was small and thin and hawk-nosed handsome, with intelligent black eyes that surveyed Tommy with curiosity. He carefully folded a tortilla and bit into it, never taking his eyes from Tommy.

Tommy's body glowed with pain, and he knew better than to make any quick movements. He turned on his side and crawled to the barred cell doors. Grimacing with every movement, he gripped the latticework bars and pulled himself to his feet. He took a deep breath and shouted, "I want to speak to an American!" His shout echoed off the damp prison walls. He took another breath. *"What the fuck is going on here!"* The only answer was a derisive burst of laughter somewhere deep within the bowels of the prison. Tommy leaned his brow against the bars to try and quiet his throbbing head. It had exploded with every shouted syllable.

"You from Texas?" the Indian said, and Tommy whirled and stared at him. It wasn't the fact that the Indian had spoken, but that Tommy had understood him that was startling.

"They called you a gringo." The Indian chewed. "I figured maybe you was from Texas." It *had* been English the Indian had spoken.

Tommy threw himself at the bars again. *"I wanna talk to an American! This is all a big mistake!"*

The Indian shook with quiet laughter. He wore black trousers with flared bottoms and shiny nickel-plated ornamentation. His shirt was coarse white cotton.

"That's a good one, *padre.*" He grinned over his plate.

"Hey! Somebody!" Tommy shouted and shook the bars. From somewhere down the corridor a jailer shouted out angrily.

"He says, *padre,* if you don't shut up he's gonna come shoot you right now."

Tommy turned and stared darkly at the Indian, then he lurched across the cell and plopped down on another straw-covered slab. He slowly shook his head and then stopped when it began to hurt.

The Indian wiped up the last few grains of rice with his tortilla. His hair was long and straight and hung down his back to his waist. He eyed another plate of rice and tortillas on the floor.

"*Padre,* you gonna want your food?"

Tommy didn't even look up. The Indian got up from the slab

and squatted down over the plate, *campesino* style. He ate from it hungrily.

"I been to Texas a lot, when I was running guns for General Villa. I been all over Texas. El Paso. Odessa. San Antone." He paused and smiled. "Good lookin' women in San Antone." He made a pumping motion with his fist. "*Chingando* all night long."

Tommy slumped back on the slab, holding his head.

"I remember in San Antone, there was this one little *gringita*, her name was Josephine—"

"Shut up," Tommy said from behind his closed eyes. "You talk too much."

The Indian grinned again. "That's 'cause of this little schoolteacher in Galveston. *Una negrita*. Her skin was just 'bout same color as me." He shook his head with treasured remembrance. "What a woman. *Chingando* all night long." He filled his mouth again. "She gave me my English. She was schoolteacher in the nigger school there in Galveston."

The Indian paused for a moment and belched. He looked at the half-empty plate.

"*Padre*, you sure you don't want nothing to eat?"

Tommy didn't move, so the Indian started to eat again, using the tortilla as a shovel to scoop up the rice.

"I want you to talk to these guineas for me," Tommy said finally, still not opening his eyes, "make them understand that this is all a big mistake."

The Indian cocked his head doglike as he contemplated what Tommy had said.

"I'll tell you what to say, you just tell 'em what I say in Mexican." Tommy opened his eyes and looked at the Indian. "All right?"

The Indian shrugged. "I'll try, *padre*. If that's what you want me to do, I'll try."

Tommy shut his eyes and lowered his head onto to the slab.

The Indian took another few mouthfuls, watching Tommy closely, then seemed to tire of the food and wiped his fingers on his pants. He squatted there, looking at Tommy, for several long moments.

"*Padre*, I want you to do something for me."

Tommy didn't respond.

The Indian rose and slowly approached Tommy. He stood at the foot of the slab, then raised his eyes and crossed himself. He knelt and touched Tommy's arm. "*Padre*."

Tommy raised his head with a start and jerked away his arm. "Whaddaya want?"

"*Padre,*" the Indian said solemnly, "I wish to make my confession."

"Go away. Get the fuck away from me!"

"*Padre. Por favor.*"

"Get away!" Tommy moved away from the Indian.

"But I wish to confess my sins."

"What's that got to do with me?"

The Indian was confused. "You're a priest."

Tommy stared at him a moment, then got off the slab and limped to a concrete trough in the corner of the L-shaped cell. The trough was lined with a bronze tub, and the bronze had turned green. The tub was filled with stale, standing water, and a rusted spigot leaked a steady stream of droplets onto its scummy surface. Tommy pushed away the thick film, filled his cupped hands and splashed the water over his face and throat.

"I ain't no priest." Tommy dunked his whole head into the water, then lifted it, dripping.

The Indian watched him carefully, his head tilted in that way. Then he smiled.

"*Padre, padre . . .*" He shook his head as he smiled.

"What?"

"It's too late. There's no good in—"

"Look," Tommy turned to face him. "I ain't a priest."

The Indian squatted back on his haunches, inspecting him.

"It's because of this goddamn—" Tommy ripped off the torn remains of the collar.

"In these times," the Indian said, "anyone would say he wasn't a priest. But who would pretend he was, who was not?"

Tommy looked at him. "I came looking for my brother. *He's* a priest."

"What's his name?"

"Coyne. Father Frank Coyne."

The Indian thought a minute, then shook his head, indicating he didn't know him. "They probably killed him."

"What do you know?" Tommy flared. "You don't know that."

"If he's still in Jalisco. All the foreign priests pulled up their skirts and ran like women."

Tommy considered this awhile. The Indian wouldn't take his eyes off him. Finally, seeming to reach a decision, he said, "*Padre,* please hear my sins."

"Goddamnit, I told you, I ain't no damn priest."

"*Padre*, this isn't going to change anything. They're not going to believe you. This trick is useless and disgraceful."

Tommy glared at the Indian and said nothing.

"You took an oath. You received the sacrament of the cloth. You have responsibilities."

There was a long moment during which Tommy and the Indian looked at each other. Then the Indian rose. "I know how to do it in English. Bless me, Father, for I have sinned."

"I'm not a priest."

"I'm going to get hanged in the morning, and I wish to meet the Virgin with a clean soul."

Tommy looked at the Indian, considering what he'd said. "What are they going to hang you for?"

"For sleeping with the *alcalde's* daughter."

"They're gonna swing you for jazzing somebody's daughter?"

The Indian shrugged. "And his sister. His wife also."

"Well, I'm sure you have a lot to talk to a priest about, but"— he turned away—"I'm not—"

The Indian reached out and gripped his arm. "Don't turn away from—"

Tommy pivoted on his good leg and hit the Indian flush against the side of his face. It was a solid barroom Irish Sneaky Pete, and the Indian went down as though someone had snapped his backbone. The effort caused hot pain to shoot up Tommy's leg and through his badly beaten midsection and to the back of his head, and he hobbled over to the slab and sat down. After a while the pain subsided and Tommy looked at the Indian. The Indian hadn't moved.

Tommy picked up the empty plate, walked to the tub and filled it with water, then walked back to the Indian and stood over him. The Indian was thin and light, and the punch had caught him unaware, and he was still not moving. Tommy threw the water on him and pushed him with his shoe.

"Hey. *Hey.*" The Indian began to stir. Tommy turned away and walked back to the basin. He leaned over it and began to wash away the dried blood from the back of his head. Suddenly the Indian was on him, cursing in Spanish and shoving his head under the water. Tommy struggled for a moment, then reached back and caught a handful of the Indian's long hair. Tommy yanked as he threw himself backward and slammed the Indian into the stone wall. The Indian grunted and Tommy whirled and caught him with two right crosses.

This time Tommy waited for the Indian to come around on his own. When he opened his eyes Tommy said, "You got a name, Indian?"

The Indian felt his jaw. "If I had my knife I would cut your heart out." He sat up on the jailhouse floor. "If I had a *pistola,* I would—"

"Well, you don't. And if you come at me again I'll smack your brains out of your head." Tommy tapped the cement slab. The Indian spat on the floor, and his spittle was thick with blood. He shook his head like a dog with an itch, then looked at Tommy.

"Quintana. I am called Quintana."

"Well, Quintana, I'm sorry they're hanging you in the morning, but it ain't my fault. And I can't hear your confession 'cause I'm not a priest. I wish I could do something for you, but—"

Tommy stopped because Quintana had started to laugh. He rocked back and forth and giggled, shaking his head.

"What's so fucking funny?"

"You don't understand," he said gleefully. "You don't understand."

Tommy had that uneasy, uninformed feeling again. "I don't understand what?"

Tears streaked down Quintana's face. "They gonna hang you, too."

THEY CAME FOR THEM JUST BEFORE DAWN. ONE OF THE GUARDS HAD A flashlight, but the *agraristas* carried kerosene lanterns and torches. They took Tommy and Quintana out into the prison yard, where there were three other priests waiting in the gray light. Tommy wouldn't stop talking.

"I'm not a priest. Listen to me, I'm *not* a priest!"

The guards prodded him and told him to shut up, but Tommy wouldn't.

"Tell 'em, goddamnit!" he hissed at Quintana. "Tell 'em!"

Quintana looked at him and for a moment Tommy thought he wasn't going to help, then Quintana said to an *agrarista* guard, "The *yanqui* says he's not a priest."

"Tell the *yanqui* to be quiet or we'll cut out his tongue."

Quintana looked at Tommy, then back at the *agrarista*. "I think he's lying, too, but he's adamant."

The *agrarista* was tying them together with a lead line. "Perhaps you should be quiet, too."

Quintana nodded in understanding.

"What did he say?" Tommy asked. "Did you tell him?"

Quintana told him what the *agrarista* had said, and Tommy looked at the *agrarista* and shut up.

Then they led them out through the prison gates and into the early morning streets. Colonel Salazar sat waiting for them, astride his big red bay, the other *agraristas* arrayed down the street. The whole party began to walk slowly along the wall of the prison. Salazar rode up beside Tommy. He grinned down at him.

"Have you said your prayers, Monsignor? Are you ready to die?"

Tommy wished he had his .45s. "You fuck your own mother, you greaseball guinea bastard."

Salazar stared down at him. He had heard the threat in the tone. With one swift motion he slashed Tommy across the face with his rawhide quirt. Tommy lunged for him, then fell over when the lead line pulled him up short, dragging the others down with him. One of the priests was enormously fat and floundered in the dust of the streets. The *federales* and *agraristas* roared with laughter in their saddles. Salazar trotted the stallion to the head of the column, snatched up the lead line and wrapped it around his saddle horn. The other prisoners rushed to lift the fat priest and they trotted around the corner of the prison and into a wide boulevard.

After a few blocks the fat priest slumped to his knees, dragging down the others, and Salazar and the *agraristas* again sat their saddles and laughed.

People were starting to come out to see the hanging of the priests. In other parts of Mexico, in Tabasco or Chiapas, the sidewalks would have been as crowded as a fiesta-day parade route, but here in Jalisco, where the people were the most European and their Catholicism the most undiluted, the ranks of the priest-haters ran to Marxist students, radical unionists and the government.

The fat priest had collapsed in front of a brothel and the women came out on the balconies to watch. When they saw that Quintana was leashed with the others some of them started to wail.

"No, Quintana, *noooo!*"

"*Pobrecito!*"

"What will we do without you?!"

Quintana grinned up at them. "Mourn for me, my loves! Remember me!"

Salazar started to walk his stallion forward and Tommy helped to lift the fat priest to his feet and carry him along.

"We'll always remember you, Quintana."

Quintana lifted his bound hands in salute to the whores, and he saw Tommy looking at him.

"We all have to die. Better to die with women crying over you, eh?"

In a third-floor window a naked American looked down at the passing procession. After a moment he leaned out the window and shouted across the brothel.

"Hey! Gunny! Gunny!"

Gunny appeared in another window, a young whore under each arm. "What?" he shouted back, but was already watching the street.

"Ain't that the Mex from the train? The one you thought was a white man?"

Gunny squinted at Tommy and the others marching past below him.

"Yeah Where they takin' him?"

"My whore says they hangin' em. They're priests and they're hangin' 'em all."

Gunny watched them move on down the street. Then the other American shouted, "Don't seem right, hangin' priests."

Gunny had a whore's breast in each hand. He looked into each of their faces in turn. They smiled. "Well, it ain't like they're white, is it?"

Tommy, in the street, heard the shouted words and the American accent and started to look around, but then something bounced off his chest with a thud.

The boy with the bent leg and the clouded eye—the one who had taunted Tommy on the truck the night before—pushed through the ranks of onlookers and dashed crookedly into the street. He had a pocket full of smooth, round stones and he lurched along beside them, throwing them at the priests.

"Black pigs!" he shouted. "Leeches!" He sent another stone at them and the crowds cheered and egged him on. He ran under the *agraristas*' horses and around the guards, his eyes dancing. "Make a miracle! Call on your phony god to save you!"

"Why do you shout blasphemy?" Quintana said. "What has God ever done to you?"

"What has he ever done for me, except make me a cripple?" The boy launched another stone and Quintana ducked and the rock hit

Tommy in the forehead. He looked at the boy as a trickle of blood seeped down his temple. The boy ran close to taunt him.

"Hey, *Padre Gringo*. How do you like our country now?"

Tommy looked at the boy and said to Quintana, "Tell this little bastard if I wasn't tied up I'd rip off that fucking leg and shove it up his ass."

Quintana grinned and shook his head. "It doesn't matter."

They passed from the wide boulevard into the three massive, connected plazas. Across the way was the bullet-pocked cathedral. Its stained-glass windows had been shot out and the burned and gutted interior was visible from the street. The flames had licked out and blackened the walls above the windows. Across the front of the church, rising above it, was a latticework of scaffolding. They had been renovating the cathedral when the rebellion broke out. Hanging from the scaffold, above the parapet wall, were five hangman's nooses.

Salazar led them to the *alcalde*'s mansion, then pulled them up short. He dismounted, pulling his rifle from the saddle scabbard. He shouted up at the mansion's balcony.

"*General Terrazas!*"

A few moments later a tall, light-skinned man in a tailored uniform with polished leather Sam Browne belt stepped out onto the balcony. He looked down at Salazar, the five prisoners.

"Good morning to you, Severo, old friend! What kind of a morning do you have prepared for me?"

"A glorious morning! We're going to execute five enemies of the Revolution!"

The others—the foreigners, the officers, and Terrazas's sons—came up behind Terrazas to stare down at the prisoners. Terrazas watched the foreigners closely as they took in the square. Thousands of the city's inhabitants had been herded into the plaza to witness the executions. Their expressionless faces were in stark contrast to the grinning, exulting *callistas* in the front ranks. The *agraristas* danced on their spirited horses, looking like the mountain brigands and highwaymen they were.

"And *this* is Mexico," Terrazas said to Lancaster and Muñoz.

—◇—

THEY WERE LINED UP ON THE SCAFFOLD, THE NOOSES DANGLING OVER their heads before them. Behind them, the roof of the cathedral had collapsed and all that remained were blackened timbers crisscrossing over the ashes and rubble.

Salazar jumped nimbly back into the saddle. He was handed up a list of offenses, and he in turn handed it to one of his lieutenants, a youngish *agrarista* on a dun-colored mare. This man could read.

"Juan Sánchez de Álvarez," the young *agrarista* read softly.

"Juan Sánchez de Álvarez!" Salazar bellowed at the square, then pointed up at the boy priest. The young priest was shaking so violently he couldn't keep his feet, and when his name was called he slumped back against the soldiers holding him up. They dragged him forward to the noose.

Quintana turned to Tommy and shook his head in disgust. Tommy's eyes were darting all over the plaza.

"Charged with sedition, counterrevolution, crimes against the Constitution—"

Severo Salazar loudly repeated the charges and the young priest started to sob.

"—conducting religious training as forbidden by Article 33 of the Constitution of 1917—"

The young priest began to wail like a child. He crumpled to his knees in languageless howls of fear.

Quintana said to Tommy, "Is that any way for a man to die?"

Tommy looked at him as if the Indian were an escapee from a madhouse. "You're bugs."

Quintana frowned, then said to himself in Spanish, "It's disgraceful. A man shouldn't have to die with people like that."

The priest at his right, a dark middle-aged *mestizo* with graying temples, had been calmly praying. He looked at the screaming young priest and nodded. "No, a man shouldn't."

Salazar had finished shouting the charges. He swiveled in his saddle to look up at Terrazas.

Terrazas held up his hand for a moment, making sure all were watching; then he dropped his hand and shouted to the plaza.

"This man is a traitor." He paused dramatically after each proclamation. "He's a traitor to his President, his pueblo and his people. . . . He would teach us, and our children"—he waved his hand at his sons—"to give their allegiance to a mystical god, to a foreign religion, to a European pope. . . . These he puts above his own kind. These he puts over his own country."

The young priest shouted for mercy, dissolving again into incoherent sobbing.

"He would turn back the calendar. Back to the time when the

porfiristas and the priests conspired to keep the land for themselves. And to keep us ignorant, superstitious, and bound to the *hacendados* like slaves. He is a traitor to the Revolution!"

The young priest lay on the scaffolding boards, quaking.

"And for that your government has declared this traitor must die."

Salazar spurred his horse to the cathedral and shouted up at the guards.

"Let the sentence be carried out!"

The guards lifted the screaming priest to his feet, slipped the noose over his head and simply stepped him off the scaffold. The priest dropped and was brought up short. He died instantly.

Quintana turned to the mestizo priest. "I wish to make my confession."

The mestizo priest kept his eyes on the hanged man just below them. "Are you sorry for all your sins?"

Quintana thought a moment. "In some cases, a man doesn't have much choice."

"You are absolved. Your soul is clean. You may meet the Virgin."

Quintana turned to Tommy. "If I'd known it was going to be that easy I'd of done more."

"I'm an American!" Tommy shouted as loudly as he could. *"I'm not a priest. I'm American!"*

The Englishman turned to Dr. Muñoz. "What did he say?"

The mestizo priest asked Quintana the same thing.

"This is all wrong! I shouldn't even be here! I'm not a priest!"

"He claims he's not a priest," Quintana said. "What do you think?"

"I'm American!"

The mestizo priest leaned forward to look past Quintana at Tommy. He studied him. "It doesn't matter what I think."

Quintana nodded. "Exactly." He liked the mestizo.

"What is that man saying, that he's American?" Lancaster wanted to know.

Terrazas looked down at Salazar, and the two men had known each other so long that Salazar immediately stood in his stirrups and shouted to the *federal* officer nearest Tommy. "Silence that man."

The *federal* lieutenant stepped from the parapet onto the scaffolding, glanced down at Salazar, who nodded, then the lieutenant unholstered his pistol and slammed his gun butt into Tommy's stomach. Tommy sank to his knees, fighting to keep his balance.

"Forgive me, *padre*," the *federal* officer whispered, and through his pain Tommy heard the soldier's repentant tone.

The lieutenant stepped back onto the parapet and Salazar shouted out, "Alfredo Castillón!"

Two soldiers took hold of the fat priest's arms and stepped him forward. The scaffolding bowed under his immense bulk.

"Alfredo Castillón, you are convicted of sedition, counterrevolution, and crimes against the Revolution and the federal government."

The priest was so obese he seemed to be from another race of men. His face was lost in folds of shiny, sweaty fat, and his tunic was dark from terrified perspiration. He was praying continuously, his lips emitting a humlike chant just audible over the shouted charges.

"—with fornication with young girls sent to you for religious training!"

Quintana eyed the priest's elephantine bulk. "It doesn't seem possible."

"—fornication with young boys given to you for religious training!"

"Regrettably, it is," the mestizo priest said.

"Look at him!" Terrazas shouted to the assemblage. "This is the church they want to you believe in! This is the 'Right Hand of God'!" The front ranks of the crowd laughed. The crook-legged boy wobbled forward and launched a stone. "Look how fat he's grown from your labors! While you feed your hungry children tortillas and beans, he eats veal and candies! Then he repays you by molesting your precious babies in this temple of debauchery! Look at him! Look!"

Salazar nodded up and the soldiers pulled the noose down, slipped it around the fat priest's throat, then one of them pulled back on the rope with all his weight while the other put his boot into the fat priest's back and kicked him off. The upper supports of the scaffolding bowed and creaked but then the immense weight hit the end of the rope. The soldier holding the rope was jolted from his feet but the rope held and then the head of the fat priest ripped from his body and his soft fat torso fell two stories and plopped down into the thick padding of straw that had been spread in the street to absorb the blood from the firing-squad executions against the side of the cathedral.

The headless body flopped into the straw and then immediately bounced up and lurched forward like a decapitated chicken. Separate streams of blood geysered up out of the grisly gaping maw and the fat priest took a few more steps, his hand grasping like a baby's. The crowd—even the priest haters who had cheered the death of the young priest—gasped and flowed backward like a tide. Then the horrific torso stumbled and fell. It lay quivering for several moments, and then it relaxed and was still.

In the stunned seconds that followed people automatically and openly crossed themselves and there was a communal murmured plea to the Virgin Mary. Then there was a silent stillness. A few people in the plaza sank to their knees in fearful worship. Salazar was the first one to break the breathless instant. He spurred his stallion into the crowd, slashing his quirt at the prayerful.

"Get off your knees! You're breaking the law! Get up!"

The people rose slowly, but there was a dark mood among the faithful, as if the events this morning in this plaza were transcending even the sacrilege of priest killing. As if they were witnessing something demonic and they didn't like it.

"Anyone making the sign of the cross will be shot!" Salazar turned the red stallion in a constant circle, glaring at them. "Anyone kneeling will be hung along with the pigs!"

Then Tommy, on his feet again, shouted, "I'm an American! I'm not a priest I'm an American!"

Terrazas was angry. He had intended to show the foreigners the resolve of the Mexican people to throw off the yoke of the Church, but instead they were witnessing a barbarian spectacle. He could imagine the Englishman's story of bloodthirsty savages and Aztec rituals. Terrazas moved to wrest control of the plaza. He pointed at Tommy and Salazar shouted, "The gringo!"

The *federal* lieutenant who had struck Tommy and then asked for forgiveness now stepped forward slowly, taking Tommy's arm. He was ashen under his tan skin. "Father, please understand, I have no choice."

Tommy looked to Quintana, who said, "He wants your blessing."

Tommy looked at the pistol holstered at the lieutenant's waist, the one the lieutenant had struck him with. "Tell him to untie me and I will."

Quintana looked at Tommy, then quickly said, "He can't give a true blessing unless you free his hands."

Salazar motioned to the crippled boy. "*Niño*, come here." The boy hesitated. All his bravado had been drained by the sight of the walking headless priest. "Here!" Salazar ordered, and the boy took a lurching step forward. Salazar reached back into his saddlebag and brought out a soft leather bundle. He held it out to the crippled boy.

"Bring these up to the general."

The boy looked dumbly at Salazar, then at the bundle.

"Quickly, *chico!*"

The boy took the bundle, then ran in a sideways lope into the *alcaldo*. A few moments later he was led onto the balcony by one of Terraza's officers. He handed the bundle to Terrazas, who laid it on the low railing of the balcony and folded back the corners.

"*Mi general!*" Salazar shouted so all the plaza could hear. "These articles were found on the prisoner when he was arrested!"

Terrazas stared down at the bundle's contents. Then he picked up the passport and opened it. He read loudly to the plaza, "John O'Rourke." He pronounced it *oh-roo-kay*. Then he looked up and surveyed the people with righteousness. "Yes, he is a gringo. Sent down here to do what?!" Terrazas held up the stack of dollars and shook it at the crowd. "Sent to our country to buy guns for the rebels! To bribe and corrupt! To make whores of our daughters!" The crowd was silent. Terrazas lifted the two gleaming .45 automatics above his head so all could see. "I wonder which sacrament required these!" Some of the people turned to inspect Tommy more carefully. "I wonder how much Mexican blood the good father intended to spill with these!"

"Father," the *federal* lieutenant was saying to Tommy, "none of this is my doing. I'm only a soldier. I have orders."

"There are older orders," Quintana hissed. "God's orders."

"I don't want to lose my soul," the lieutenant pleaded. "I beg you for your forgiveness."

Tommy motioned with his bound hands. "Cut me loose!"

Salazar galloped his stallion under the scaffold and shouted up at the lieutenant, "Prepare the prisoner!"

The *federal* lieutenant stared down at Salazar a moment, then reached up and drew down the hangman's noose. His hand was shaking. He took Tommy's arm.

"Please, Father."

"He curses you," Quintana rasped, eyeing the lieutenant's holstered pistol. "He curses your whole family. He says the Virgin will personally see to it that all of you will spend eternity in—"

"Lieutenant!" Salazar shouted up. "What's the problem?"

The lieutenant stepped Tommy from the parapet onto the scaffold. He slipped the noose over Tommy's head and tightened it around his neck. The moment he felt the coarse rope against the flesh of his throat, Tommy unconsciously breathed in a lungful of air and held it. Everything seemed to slow. The plaza became as silent as a sepulcher. It was as if the place had become a painting, or a frozen frame of a moving picture. Tiny fragments of the square seemed to stand out from the rest, as though viewed through field glasses: a red-haired woman in the crowd; pigeons on the tile roof across the way; a '22 Hudson parked before an alley, its windshield glinting in the morning sun. Tommy opened his mouth to shout again and the lieutenant said, "Forgive me, Father," and pushed him off the scaffold.

Tommy fell through the air, saw the world start to rush upward before his eyes, and then the rope went taut and the scaffolding beam above him—weakened by the strain of the fat priest's weight—splintered and Tommy fell two stories to the straw. He lay in the blood of the decapitated fat priest, looking up at the sky, confused. Was he dead or alive? He raised his head and Salazar on the red stallion was only a few feet away, watching him. Tommy rolled over and pushed himself up to a kneeling position and the whole plaza gasped.

"*Un milagro!* It's a miracle," they whispered and crossed themselves. A hundred people knelt without thinking.

Salazar leveled his Winchester and fired into the crowd. A man was struck and his head exploded brains and blood all over his neighbors. Then someone in the back of the crowd shouted, "*Viva Cristo Rey!*" and someone else answered with "*Viva la Virgen!*" and Salazar plowed his stallion into the people, emptying his rifle at those he thought had shouted. A teenage girl went down, blood spurting from her breast. There were screams all over the plaza, a Greek chorus of muttered threats. Salazar pulled his pistol, wheeled his stallion, and rode back out of the people. A battalion of *federal* troops ran double-time into the plaza and formed a half-circle perimeter around the cathedral and the *agraristas*, facing out at the crowd.

Quintana turned to the mestizo priest and said, "Have you ever seen a morning such as this?"

The mestizo priest shook his head slowly. "Never." He was looking at Tommy.

Salazar galloped back to Tommy, leaned down and took up the hanging rope. He looked at Tommy and said in Spanish, "Get up, bastard!" Tommy rose dumbly to his feet. Salazar rode him into the ruined cathedral and shouted up to the *federal* lieutenant on the parapet.

When Tommy appeared again on the cathedral parapet shouts rang out from all over the plaza. "No! It isn't right! Let him live!"

Salazar barked an order at the *federales,* and they knelt and took up a firing position.

"Citizens of Guadalajara!" General Terrazas shouted. Then he shouted it again. The plaza quieted slowly, then the only sound was the sobbing of mourning women. The Englishman had started to jot down notes in a half-sized ledger. The Spaniard's eyes were wide with alarm.

"My compadres!" Terrazas shouted. "This is no miracle! There are no such things as miracles!"

"Please!" he beseeched the plaza. "Listen to me! They have filled you with fear and superstition!" He threw his pointed finger at Tommy, like a spear. "This man is not your savior! This man is not your friend! He's a criminal, an enemy of the Revolution!"

On the cathedral parapet, the lieutenant stared at Tommy with awestruck wonder. There were tears coursing down the *federal's* cheeks.

"He would take you back to the old days!" Terrazas reasoned with the people. "He would keep you poor and ignorant! He would deny you the *land!*" Terrazas stressed the last word, as if that were the ultimate condemnation.

"Please, *mi padre,*" the lieutenant whispered. "Give me your blessing."

Tommy was staring out at the plaza. He didn't seem to be aware of what was going on around him.

"Unbind him!" Quintana said with urgency. "Quickly!"

The lieutenant looked at Quintana then.

"Now!" Quintana said.

The lieutenant nodded dumbly and began to tug at Tommy's bonds.

Below them, Salazar took his eyes from General Terrazas and looked up at the scaffold. Quintana saw the moment Salazar saw what the lieutenant was doing.

"This priest is special," Quintana said quickly. "He has been sent by Christ."

The lieutenant nodded and pulled at the leather bindings.

Salazar walked his horse to get a better view. Terrazas was still speechifying. "Lieutenant?" Salazar said up to the scaffold.

Quintana saw the bindings start to loosen. *"Gringo!"* he barked, as if the lieutenant weren't there. *"Gringo!"* Tommy slowly turned his head to Quintana, and at that moment the bindings fell away.

"Give me your blessing, *padre*," the lieutenant said and touched Tommy's arm. Salazar fired up and the bullet entered the lieutenant's lower back, tore through his heart and exited his throat, blowing a fist-sized hole in the soft tissue. Tommy was washed with his blood and flesh, and the man's body slammed against his, almost knocking him from the scaffold. Tommy's hand closed over the lieutenant's pistol grip, and Quintana saw him return from wherever he had gone and Tommy flung away the lieutenant's body and took quick, careful aim down at Salazar and fired. The *agrarista comandante* was thrown back over the blood-bay's rump and bounced like a rag doll, his feet hooked in the stirrups, and the animal galloped into the ruined cathedral.

One of the soldiers down in the plaza, excited by the gunfire, pulled his trigger and two men in the crowd went down. Then the whole line of kneeling soldiers fired and twenty-three people in the square were dead and wounded. People began to flee in all directions and the soldiers fired again.

On the scaffold, the soldier to the right of the mestizo priest lifted his rifle to shoot Tommy and the mestizo priest clubbed him with his bound fists and then Quintana was there and pushed the soldier into the air. He looked surprised as he went down. Then another soldier aimed at Quintana and Tommy shot him between the eyes and the soldier's head exploded and Quintana managed to catch the rifle as the soldier fell. Then Tommy turned and aimed at the balcony of the *alcaldo* and everyone on the balcony ducked.

"Gringo!" Quintana shouted as he jumped from the scaffold onto the cathedral parapet. "This way!" The mestizo priest was already running for the stone stairs. Tommy looked back at the *alcaldo* with regret, then jumped onto the parapet.

The red bay was stamping at the black debris on the cathedral floor. Salazar's body still hung back over the horse's rump, where no man's weight should be, and the horse's eyeballs rolled and his nostrils flared as the animal blew air.

A *federal* was trying to climb over the debris to escape through one of the shattered windows in the rear and Quintana shot him from across the cathedral as he would a startled deer, and the stallion whinnied excitedly and started to run in circles and Quintana caught the reins. Speaking to the horse, Quintana righted Salazar's body, then pushed it out of the saddle as he caught the horn and pulled himself up. He did all this with his hands still bound before him.

"Gringo!" Quintana shouted as there was a fresh volley of gunfire from the plaza. Through the doorless entrance he could see the panic in the plaza. "Gringo!" Tommy came down the stone stairs just as Quintana reined in the stallion before him. Quintana nodded to the bay's rump behind him, "Let's go!" and Tommy clumsily jumped from the stairs and gripped Quintana tightly and the Indian spurred the stallion and made for the window the *federal* had been trying to reach. The stallion clambered over the burnt pews and the *federal's* body and Quintana spoke to him and the stallion jumped up and through the window and they came down in the street crammed with running people. An *agrarista* started toward them, riding over the screaming people, and Tommy shot him and he fell from the saddle and the people trampled him as he had them.

—◄○►—

FRANK COYNE HELD UP THE EUCHARIST AND CLOSED HIS EYES. HE paused for a moment, as he always did, anticipating what was to come. Then he intoned the ancient Latin words *"Summunt boni, sumount mali, Sorte tamen inaequali,"* enunciating each syllable carefully, singly, precisely, and felt the presence of God flow into him. It was the moment Frank lived for. It gave his life purpose and power. In this instant Frank knew why he had been born. He was the bridge between God and the world. He was the conduit. He was God's gatekeeper. He was the door to salvation. They had to come through him.

He slowly turned to face the congregation, opened his eyes, and was once again startled by the wall-less view. The washed blue of the sky, the mountain range to the east, the smooth table of the valley floor below. Sagrado Corazón was an inconsequential village, and its small church had reflected the pueblo's lack of importance, and the *agraristas* riding through two months before had simply pulled down the walls of the church with their horses, smashed the altar and drunk the sacramental wine and then ridden on, leaving behind only a few standing support columns and the clay floor. That's how Frank had found it when he'd walked up to the village two weeks ago.

Because the communion rail had been smashed by gun butts, Frank stepped down from the slapped-together platform that served as an altar stone and moved among the kneeling communicants. At each one he lifted the wafer ceremoniously from the chalice, etched a cross in the air, signifying Christ's gift of His body to achieve everlasting life, and then slipped the Host between the communicant's lips. A light-haired boy moved beside him, holding a simple pottery plate as the paten. The worshipers accepted the Host gratefully, hungrily, and Frank thought again, as he had uncountable times since he'd come up to the Los Altos region, that these light-eyed *alteños* were the best Catholics he'd ever encountered.

Frank paused as he moved among the people and, departing from the Latin liturgy, said aloud in perfect Spanish, "I say unto you, Except you eat the Flesh of the Son of Man and drink His blood, you shall not have life in you." There were murmurs of agreement, some nodded their heads humbly. A little theater—and what was the Church if not theater?—went a long way with the Mexicans, even these pure-blooded *alteños,* and in these Satanic times Frank had determined to use whatever tools he could find to combat the evil afoot. He continued moving among the kneeling people, dispensing eternity, then passed through what had once been the church door and out into the street, where a hundred people knelt, waiting for Communion. They had been coming up into Sagrado Corazón for days now, ever since the federal government had instituted its policy of *reconcentración*. First a trickle, then a steady flow of the faithful—fleeing the godless *federales*.

A dog trotted up to the edge of the gathering, looked in at the humans, then sniffed a column and was lifting his leg when a woman rose quickly and sent the dog yapping with a hard slap. She paused and watched four horsemen come across the plaza toward the church, and then she quickly went back to her place in the street and knelt.

The riders reined in and sat their saddles, watching. Frank, glancing at them, could see they were a father and three sons. And from the way the people in the street regarded them, they were men of importance. Frank went among the congregation, until the last communicant had been given the Sacrament. There were still a few fragments of wafer at the bottom of the chalice and Frank paused again and said, "If anyone eat of this Bread, he shall live forever." There was a vague rustling and shifting of weight. Some among them intuited what was happening and watched closely.

The elder rider touched his horse and the animal moved forward, stepping carefully among the kneeling. The three sons followed. When the rider was near Frank turned to him and said, "We're celebrating Mass."

"I know that." The man had blue eyes, Frank noted. These *alteños* were the least *mestizo* of a nation that defined itself by its mixture of bloods.

"This street is my church," Frank said.

The man with blue eyes looked at Frank, and then slowly took in the kneeling worshipers. Then he said, "I am Victoriano Rojas, and I wish to take Communion."

Frank had lived in this country for six years now, and though he was well accustomed to the machismic arrogance of the Mexican male, these *alteño rancheros* were in a class all their own.

Rojas turned back to Frank and fixed him with those clear light eyes. He sat straight in the saddle with an aristocratic bearing. His face was bronzed from the sun and as creased as a teamster's wallet.

"Myself and my sons."

Frank examined the rider carefully, frankly. He sensed this Rojas was important, that this exchange was important, that it would set in stone the parameters for all further dealings between himself and the ranchers. It was imperative he not show any deference; it was paramount he remember he was speaking for God.

Frank looked into the cup as if he were seeing the remaining scraps of wafer for the first time. "I'm pleased, Señor Rojas, that with the Devil so busy in this land, there are still many good Catholics eager to attain a state of grace."

Rojas nodded almost imperceptibly, then leaned forward a little. He expected to be given the Sacrament in the saddle.

Rojas was not unique, he was simply quintessential. The men of Los Altos prided themselves on their horsemanship and did nothing on foot they could do on horseback. They took fierce pride, also, in their independence, their honor—and the readiness to fight for it. They were proud of their womanizing and their religion, as long as it didn't interfere with their womanizing. They reminded Frank of the men he'd grown up among. They reminded Frank of the Hell's Kitchen Irish.

They reminded Frank of his father.

He looked up at Rojas and frowned. "*Señor,* you expect the people of Jalisco to fight and die for Christ, and you won't even get off your horse?"

Frank saw a flicker of doubt flash across Rojas's handsome face. The man glanced about.

"I am a representative of Jesus Christ and his Eternal Church," Frank said softly, as a man might threaten a bureaucrat. "If you wish to partake of Christ's salvation then you must show devotion. None are higher than the Living God."

Rojas stared down at him. "You are a foreigner. Is there a Mexican priest here?"

Frank shook his head. "They shot him."

Rojas looked about at the destroyed church, at the kneeling faithful murmuring their prayers as they eavesdropped on the conversation between the priest and the *ranchero*. When Rojas had allowed a sufficient amount of time to pass he hung his reins over his saddle horn and dismounted. His sons did the same.

Frank dipped his fingers into the chalice and withdrew a sliver of communion wafer. He held it over the cup and stared at Rojas.

And then the *ranchero* and his sons knelt in the street and received Communion.

—◇—

"MY GREAT-GRANDFATHER WAS A FRENCHMAN," ROJAS WAS SAYING. "A sergeant in the army of the Emperor Maximilian." They were walking below the pueblo, just where the mountain began to descend sharply. Rojas's sons followed at a respectful distance. "When it became obvious the Emperor was a fool and the *juaristas* would prevail, my great-grandfather deserted." The mountain was rocky here, stones scattered over the red clay slope a hundred million years ago, and they picked their way carefully. "He came up here to hide and fell in love with the land. He met my great-grandmother and married her. He never left." Rojas stopped and picked up a stone. It was jagged on one end, smooth on the other. Rojas turned it in his hand, examining it. "She was a Rojas. He took her name to avoid Maximilian's deserter hunters." Rojas spun the stone out into the valley below. It bounced a half-mile down the hill. Frank didn't respond, but he knew Rojas was probably lying to protect his great-grandmother's honor. They began to walk again. "We up here in the high, lean lands, we have never bothered much with Mexico and the federal government. Presidents come and go. Diaz, Madero, Huerta, Carranza . . . They're all the same. And the generals are *campesino* clowns in pretty uniforms. We pay as much attention to them as we do to their taxes. . . . But this time, this president . . ." Rojas shook his head. "He attacks Christ. He would make himself God, his governors apostles, and his generals avenging angels. This Terrazas—"

"Terrazas is the anti-Christ," Frank said firmly, expressing his true belief. "He must be stopped."

"Truly, he must." Rojas looked at Frank and nodded.

Then the *ranchero* turned to look back up at the mountaintop. The *montañas* of Los Altos were gently rising, rolling affairs, but this one was different. It was the highest for fifteen kilometers in any direction, and the steepest, and at its summit was a nipple, six times as high as the cathedral in Mexico City, and the front of the nipple had collapsed hundreds of thousands of years ago and had formed a kind of amphitheatrical bowl. In this bowl the village sat. The people of Los Altos called the mountain La Corona. The Crown.

"This is a good place to take a stand. It can only be approached from this direction, which is very defensible." He turned back to look out over the distant valley below. "You will see any *federal* army hours before they get here." He looked up the slope again. "And you have the springs." La Corona had a series of cold springs that bubbled up from some deep underground source. The Indians who had once lived up here had settled around the unlimited source of fresh water. Then the Spanish founders of Sagrado Cora- zón had dug wells, constructed a town fountain, but still the water seeped out from between the rocks and trickled down the moun- tainside. There was a rivulet coursing twenty meters from where Frank and Rojas stood.

"This is a very good place to make a stand," Rojas said again.

As they watched, above them two nuns came out from the white- washed walls of the pueblo carrying straw baskets and stooped beside the rivulet and began to wash bloody sheets and bandages.

"I don't intend to just defend, *señor*," Frank said. "We have to take the fight to them." Frank fixed Rojas with a hard look. "We have to let them know they can't make war on God and get away with it."

Rojas returned Frank's stare, then something down in the valley caught his attention. "There's a single horseman coming. Coming fast."

Frank shaded his eyes and looked down the mountain slope.

"Padre Francisco," Rojas said, "why are you in our country? Why are you not in your own? Are there not enough Catholics there you can minister to?"

Frank smiled at the question, then his smile faded. "I am here because God has called me to fight for Him. I'm here because God wants me to be."

*   *   *

117

FORTY MINUTES LATER THE HORSEMAN WAS RACING UP THE STEEP MOUN-
tain road. Then there was a shout from one of the nuns and Frank
and Rojas looked up to see she had dropped the wicker basket and
the white sheets were spilling down the mountainside. The other
nun said something to her, then hurried after the laundry.

Rojas turned back quickly to look at the horseman. The *caballero*
veered off from the road and headed for them. The horse was magnificent—big and red, a stallion. The *caballero* was Indian, with his
long, wild hair streaming behind, and he rode like a Yaqui, Rojas
thought. Rojas rested his hand on his pistol and cocked back the
hammer.

Frank heard the cocking mechanism and looked at Rojas's hand
on his weapon then looked back at the rider, who reined in amidst
a flurry of dust and pebbles. The stallion was lathered, winded and
wild-eyed from the gallop up the mountain.

The Indian looked at Frank, then at Rojas, then back again to
Frank, closely examining his face. The stallion danced.

"Padre," Quintana said, "I have your brother!" He pointed out
into the valley. "Down there!" The bay stallion blew wind through
his nostrils and the Indian wheeled him and came back around. "I
think he's dying."

—◇—

THEY HAD GALLOPED OUT OF THE CENTRAL ZONE AND THEN THROUGH
the treelined avenues where the government dignitaries and the
industrialists lived behind high ornate gates, then down the dusty
dirt lanes between squalid squatters' shacks and out into the countryside and away. Word of what had happened in the plaza, what
Tommy had done, spread over the city's rudimentary telephone
system, and by the time they were pounding through the outskirts
the people had come out to watch them ride past and to shout
encouragement.

"*Viva Christo Rey!*" they cupped their hands and yelled, and "God
cannot be killed!" And they galloped by—the big red stallion, the
wild *norteño* Indian, and the *yanqui* priest who had defied death
and killed the hated *agrarista* Salazar.

"*Viva Christo Rey!*" And then a mule skinner had held the reins
to his six-mule team and stood in his wagon and shouted, "*Viva*

Padre Pistolero!" And that was the first time anyone had ever said those words.

—◄○►—

THEY RODE HARD FOR THE REST OF THE MORNING AND THE LAND BEGAN to rise gently and then more steeply, and the blood bay was a wonder. He responded to his new master with flippant head tosses and ever-increasing effort. Whenever Quintana leaned forward in the saddle and said something to him, the horse's ears would prick up, as if trying to catch every nuance.

They stopped at midday at a crossroads lean-to that sold food and drink and animal feed, and Tommy slipped off and leaned against a sheltering eucalyptus tree. A woman in the yard before the lean-to was dropping strips of pork into a massive kettle of boiling grease, then dipping the meat out with a big wooden spoon she held against the side of the kettle to drain off the grease. Across the top of the kettle she had laid a narrow board and on this she cut the meat. Several rail-thin dogs sniffed excitedly around her sandals, looking for scraps. A short, thick man came to the door of the lean-to and watched them, drinking tequila.

Quintana dismounted and the stallion watched him carefully. Quintana grinned and said, "He smells my Yaqui blood. He's never been ridden by an Indian before." Then Quintana turned to Tommy and saw that Tommy's pants were soaked with fresh blood.

"Qué pasó, gringo? Did you get yourself shot?"

Tommy nodded his head, then slipped down the eucalyptus tree and slumped against the base. The woman left the kettle of boiling grease and came over. Quintana was leaning over him. He started to pull off Tommy's pants, and Tommy put the dead lieutenant's pistol against the Indian's temple and cocked it.

"I think you will find that it's empty." Quintana said something to the woman and she went back to the kettle and the chopping board and came back with her knife.

"Are you sure?" Tommy asked.

"Sí. I counted."

Quintana took the knife from the woman and Tommy pulled the trigger and when the hammer came down on the spent cartridge Quintana started and glared at Tommy, his hand tight around the hilt of the knife. Then Tommy smiled and after a moment Quintana grinned and then started to laugh and then Tommy laughed, too, and then he passed out and slumped over.

The woman went inside the lean-to and came back out with a blanket. She laid it in the dust under the eucalyptus tree and helped Quintana carry him over.

"Is he a priest?" She eyed the lieutenant's brain matter dried over his face and shoulders.

Quintana began to cut away Tommy's trousers, being careful to follow the seams. "You should have seen him," Quintana said. "He was incredible."

"And they shot him?"

"They'll shoot you, too, woman," the man said loudly from the doorway. "They'll shoot you just for the blanket."

"He was like an avenging angel." Quintana looked at the woman. "He killed Severo Salazar." He nodded at the stallion as if to offer proof. "That's his horse."

The woman crossed herself quickly at the mention of the snake-hiss of a name. "Virgin protect me," she murmured.

"They'll shoot you, too. Just for making the cross, foolish woman," the man in the doorway shouted, then went inside for another tequila.

Quintana cut away the bloody pants and the woman knelt beside him and wiped away the blood with her apron, and they both looked down at the wound in Tommy's buttock. O'Rourke's crude sutures had burst; the wound had erupted. It smelled badly. It was the odor that made Quintana frown.

"I can make a poultice, draw it out," the woman said, and then Quintana saw three horsemen riding from the direction of the city and he stood and went to the red stallion and pulled the rifle from Salazar's saddle scabbard and jacked a shell into the chamber.

One of the horsemen raised his hand and shouted, "It's all right."

But Quintana laid the rifle over the saddle and took careful aim, speaking softly to the quivering red stallion. The horsemen saw him, but rode on in anyway.

"*Viva Cristo Rey*," they said as they reined in. "We are believers."

"We were in the city. We saw what happened." They looked down at Tommy, unconscious on the blanket. "*Qué pasó?* Is he dead?"

Two of the men were in business suits; the other was a *charro*.

"Where are they? How far back?" Quintana kept the rifle on the lead rider.

The lead rider looked at his *compadres,* then dismounted. The other two stayed in their saddles, watching Quintana.

"They aren't coming. Not yet, at least. The people in the city gave them bad directions. They pointed them everywhere." He stooped to look at the woman carefully cleaning Tommy's wound. "He can't die," he said to the woman, as if passing the responsibility to her. Then he looked up at Quintana. "Actually, I don't think he *can* be killed. He was magnificent."

Quintana finally relaxed and slipped the rifle back into the scabbard. "That's what I was saying. He was incredible."

The man looked at Tommy, then at Quintana a long time, and then he asked, "Hombre, do you think it was a miracle?"

When Quintana didn't answer the man looked around at all of them and said, "I think it was. I think it was *un milagro.*"

—◁◯▷—

A FEW MINUTES LATER TWO MORE RIDERS CAME IN FROM THE CITY, THEN six more, then three. And within a few hours there were fifty horsemen standing around in front of the lean-to, watching the woman make a poultice from leaves and dark earth and passing around bottles of tequila. The man came out from the lean-to and cooked the rest of the pork in the boiling grease, adding wood from time to time to the fire under the oilcan kettle, and the horsemen wrapped the chunks of pork in tortillas and chewed them as they watched the woman apply the poultice to the infected bullet wound. Some of the horsemen dropped their tortillas into the grease and then fished them out with knives and ate them, wiping their greasy hands on a rag hanging from the eucalyptus tree. None of them paid anything to the man from the lean-to, and after a while he went back in and let the horsemen do their own cooking.

A cart pulled by two old oxen and laden with watermelons came in from the south and the horsemen waved it over. The man on the cart hesitated and then the horsemen moved toward him and he had no choice. The men formed a line and unloaded the watermelons, laying them carefully under the eucalyptus tree. When the owner of the cart complained, saying, "What am I going to do? How will I get my watermelons to the city? Who's going to pay for my cart and my oxen?" Then one of the horsemen dropped the watermelon he was holding and it split on the hard ground and burst open.

"We could pay you now, if you like," the horseman said coldly, and the cart driver went to stand by the door of the lean-to with the other man. They watched without speaking.

When the cart was empty the woman turned over the straw bedding with her hands, arranging it until she was satisfied, then four men lifted the blanket into the cart. Quintana made a shelter of sticks of wood and a rain slicker he found in Salazar's saddlebags. He mounted the big red stallion and looked at the woman, who was standing by the cart, looking through the slats at Tommy.

"We're going to the sierra."

The woman nodded, then looked back at her man standing in the doorway.

"This is a war," Quintana said. "Your skills would be valued." He looked at the man in the doorway. "Does he value you?"

The woman looked at Quintana, then dropped her eyes. She went back to the boiling kettle and threw the scraps of pork fat to the dogs, then the board for them to lick, then she went into the lean-to. The man followed her in. After a while Quintana thought she wasn't coming but then she came back out with a cloth bundle and another blanket and climbed into the cart, settled on the seat and took up the reins.

"*Andale*," she said, and the animals began to move forward. The cart rolled out of the lean-to yard and Quintana rode beside the cart and the fifty horsemen rode after.

The owner of the oxcart stood with his watermelons under the eucalyptus tree and the woman's man stood in the doorway of the lean-to and they watched as everyone rode away.

—◀○▶—

THEY CAMPED THAT NIGHT BESIDE A CREEK RUSHING DOWN FROM THE mountains and the woman stayed up all night changing Tommy's poultice and bathing him in water-soaked rags and in the morning his fever had risen and he was starting to shiver. Six riders set out for the nearest town to find a doctor, but they came back two hours later saying the town had been swept by *federales* and the entire population driven on the road to another, larger pueblo where there was a garrison. The town was empty.

In the early afternoon Quintana and the others watched from a pine forest as on the neighboring mountain a village was reconstituted. In the shelter of the trees they could see the line of carts laden with household possessions leaving the pueblo in a continuous thread moving like ants down the sierra road—cattle, pigs, children, women laden like pack animals walking beside the equally burdened burros, men together in groups, closely supervised by the *federal* soldiers. A horseman close to Quintana pointed and said, "Look there," and they watched as outside the village church *agraristas* executed a score of villagers. There were a few young women among the prisoners and they were kept till last, and then raped and sodomized before they were shot.

"*Agraristas*," a man on a spotted horse said, and then he spat.

Quintana watched grimly, and thought that at this distance it was like watching a puppet show.

Tommy came out of his delirium then, for a few surfacing moments, and looked weakly up at Quintana on the big red horse and asked, "Where—where are we going?"

Quintana nodded his chin upward, toward higher elevations, and said, "Los Altos. Catholic country."

—◄○►—

IN THE AFTERNOON TOMMY'S FEVER SEEMED TO HAVE GONE DOWN BUT as the sun set he got even hotter. The woman let the oxen walk along on their own and got into the back of the cart and alternately put water-soaked cloths on his forehead and covered him with the extra blanket. Just before dark a hundred men rode in from the north. They were *alteño* each and every one, and their mouths were hard-set and they bristled with weapons of every description and their chests were crisscrossed with bandoleers of ammunition. Their pueblos had been reconcentrated and their homes burned and their women defiled, and they were looking for an army to join. In some of the villages the *agraristas* had not allowed the people to take even a cooking pot. They had shot the dogs and the goats and the cows and left them in the emptied streets to swell in the sun. They had pillaged the houses while the *pueblerinos* stood outside under the *federal* rifles and watched, and whatever the *agraristas* didn't want they piled in the street and burned. The men from one pueblo said that the hated *agraristas* had shot anyone found wearing a religious medal. The men from that pueblo said this fact in a soft monotone, as if they themselves still could not believe what they had seen.

Among the incoming horsemen were many women, walking beside, riding behind, crowded in carts. They had seen their husbands and sons murdered, their daughters taken for sport, and there was a hard determination in their eyes, harder even than burned in the eyes of the rough men they had taken up with.

Also with the horsemen were a few surreys and carriages, expropriated from the estates of wealthy *hacendados.* In one surrey, pulled by a matched pair of white geldings, rode the mestizo priest and the crook-legged boy. Quintana saw the priest first, and they stared at each other for a long time, as if they had survived a great battle together. Then Quintana saw the boy and his face hardened. He pulled him from the surrey and tightened the fingers of one hand around the boy's throat and with the other reached for the small of his back, where he carried his knife.

"You little bastard! I'm going to slit you from—"

"Let me go!" the boy flailed at Quintana's arms and tore at the fingers on his throat. "Let me go!"

Quintana's hand felt for his knife, but it wasn't there. The *agraristas* had taken it in Guadalajara. He began to beat at the boy's head with his fist.

"*Señor!*" the mestizo priest said. "Don't do this."

"This little *agrarista* monkey threw rocks at us! He spit in our faces as we walked to our death! Don't you remember?!"

"Yes, he did these things. But he's sorry for his actions. He has been transformed."

Quintana glared at the struggling boy, then shook him and threw him to the ground. The boy rubbed his throat and whined.

"Shut up! Or I'll give you something to really cry about."

The boy silenced himself and glared up at Quintana. Then he asked, "Is he here?"

Quintana stared down at the boy, then looked at the mestizo priest. "He wants to see him," the mestizo priest said. "So do I."

"So do we all," said a coarse-bearded horseman with a raspy voice.

Quintana looked at all of them, then nodded at the cart. "He's there." The boy leapt to his feet and scrambled up into the surrey and then jumped down, a leather bundle in his hands. He ran lurching to the cart.

"He's sick," Quintana said to the mestizo priest and the others. They began to move toward the cart. "He's very sick."

They crowded around the cart, looking down at the pale shivering, sweating man in the blanket-covered straw.

"Is this the *pistolero* priest?" the raspy-voiced man asked.

"*Sí*," the mestizo priest said. "This is the one."

The other horsemen dismounted and pushed forward to get a look, until the mestizo priest held up his hands to them and they stopped where they stood. The mestizo priest turned back to look down at Tommy. "He cannot die," the mestizo priest said.

The crippled boy hung on the side of the cart, looking wide-eyed at Tommy. He started to climb in and the woman reached up and struck him and he stopped, surprised. "I have his things!" the boy cried, shoving forth the leather bundle. "I brought them for him!"

The woman went back to wiping Tommy's face. The boy quickly clambered over the side of the cart, keeping a wary eye on the woman, and settled down like a loyal dog beside his master. After a moment he reached out and touched Tommy's arm. The woman raised her hand to strike again and the boy cringed but didn't move, and the woman lowered her hand.

———◄○►———

THEY PASSED BY THE CART, EACH IN TURN, THE HUNDRED NEW *CRISTEROS*, and each in turn paused to see this wondrous American priest they had heard about. The news of what had happened in the plaza in Guadalajara had spread like spilled water over the red dirt highlands, and the events had already taken on mythic proportions. The mestizo priest, whose name was Moreno, taking up with the *vaqueros* in his flight from the city had told of the gringo priest who had been sentenced to death by the dreaded Terrazas, had been hanged and resurrected by divine intervention, and then had killed the hated Salazar with a single shot and had escaped the city ringed by *federales* and *agraristas*, riding like the wind on Salazar's blood-red stallion with a wild Yaqui Indian beside him in the saddle. Those who had been in the plaza three days before and had seen the hanging and the resurrection mingled with the men from the country and embroidered the tale with miracles and superstition. They sat around fires in the dry camp they made there in the open and some of the men from Guadalajara claimed the *Virgen* had appeared on the scaffold and had Herself taken the noose from the American priest's neck. Another man swore he saw an angel swoop down and catch the gringo priest in his arms as he fell from the scaffold, cradling him and settling him down on the strewn straw, just like the infant Jesus. Several other city men said yes, it was true, they saw the angel, too.

It went on like this as they ate jerky and cold tortillas, sprawled around dozens of small campfires. Jesus was there, a scarred veteran of the Revolution declared. He had slipped the *pistola* to the gringo priest and said, "I have chosen you to fight My battle." Another man said he too saw Jesus, but it was the Infant not the Savior, and He had said to the gringo priest, "Go and slay Mine enemies." The men traded miracles and appearances and drank coffee and pulque and they were hard men who should have known better but the times had disconcerted them and they grasped readily at anything that made them believe they were not alone in their rebellion.

The women came to the cart and looked in at Tommy and the woman from the lean-to under the eucalyptus tree. The women offered advice and they argued in whispers and then they reached an agreement and a new poultice was prepared and a strong tea made from bark laced with tequila and mint and Tommy's head was gently raised and as he stared around wild-eyed the woman put the cup to his lips and made him drink. He immediately retched and vomited and the women nodded in approval and the woman from the lean-to under the eucalyptus tree stroked Tommy's fevered brow and cooed softly to him.

During the night Moreno the mestizo priest came to the cart and saw that the crippled boy had fallen asleep in the straw, one arm wrapped around the leather bundle, the other outstretched, his hand touching Tommy's foot. Moreno lifted the boy from the straw, his eyes locking for a moment on the still-awake woman's, and then he carried the boy to the fire he and Quintana had built and laid him on a comforter he had found in the surrey. He slipped the leather bundle from the boy's hand and sat on the ground beside Quintana and unwrapped the bundle and inside were Tommy's nickel-plated, pearl-handled .45 automatics and O'Rourke's passport. Quintana picked up one of the guns and examined it with admiration. He read aloud the name on the barrel. "Colt." Moreno picked up the passport and stared at the grainy photograph inside. He stared at it a long time then he handed the passport to Quintana, saying, "Is that him?"

Quintana moved closer to the fire and looked for a full minute at O'Rourke's photograph, and then he looked at the mestizo priest and shrugged.

"You said he said he wasn't a priest," Moreno said.

Quintana looked again at O'Rourke's likeness in the starched clerical collar. "That's what he said."

"Maybe he isn't."

"Maybe he isn't."

Moreno stared at the flames of the campfire a moment, then looked at the crook-legged boy snoring lightly on the horse blanket. "He's called Miguelito."

Quintana closed the passport and wrapped it with the guns in the square of soft leather.

"He has no other name. Just that." Quintana handed the bundle back to Moreno. "He's lived his whole life in the streets, like an animal . . . In the gutters like a rat."

Quintana shrugged again. He'd seen that and worse in the north. "Tell me, *padre*," Quintana began, "yesterday morning, when we were on our way to the gallows . . . did you ever think any of this would happen?"

Moreno shook his head. "No, *compadre*, I did not. I thought I was going to meet my Lord. I thought I was dead."

Quintana nodded. "We owe our lives to him, truly."

"Truly."

The two men watched the flames in silence for a few minutes. Then Quintana looked around at all the sleeping men and he said softly to the mestizo priest, "Tell me, *padre*. What happened in the square . . . was that a miracle?"

Moreno slowly brushed the knees of his black trousers in a habitual gesture. "I don't know." He idly picked up a stick and pushed it into the fire. "I've been in the priesthood for twenty-four years, and I've never witnessed a miracle before, so I don't know what one looks like." He held up the burning stick and watched it smoke. "I know I've never seen anything like what happened in that plaza."

"Did you see the *Virgen*? Did she appear to you?"

Moreno smiled. "What I saw on that scaffold was a man whom God would not let die."

Quintana considered this, and then slowly nodded in agreement.

—◦—

WHEN LOURDES SAW THE BIG RED HORSE GALLOPING UP THE MOUNTAIN, she felt a clawed fist of terror grab her intestines and rake her womb. Horror crawled over her scalp and flashed up her backbone. Her legs wavered. She gave out an involuntary shout and dropped the straw basket of soiled linen she was carrying. The bloody sheets and pillowcases spilled out into the rivulet of cold, rushing water and began to swirl in stops and starts down the mountainside.

"Sister Lourdes!" the other nun cried as she rushed after the sheets. *"Qué pasó?!"*

The big red horse clattered up the stony incline, then veered off and began to pound for Father Francisco and the rancher Rojas. Lourdes was about to scream out a warning when she saw the Indian mounted on the big red horse. She held her breath and the Indian reined in before Father Francisco and said something to him, and Father Francisco said something to Rojas and they both hurried up the mountainside toward the pueblo. The Indian walked the big red horse beside them, riding silently.

"Sister Lourdes!" Manuela hissed as she hurried after the sheets washing down the rivulet.

Lourdes's legs were trembling but she made herself move. She scrambled over the rocks, stooped and pulled a sodden sheet from the rushing water, then speared another with her foot, then she looked up and Father Francisco was hurrying past. He was deep in conversation with Rojas and then he turned and threw a question up at the mounted Indian. And then, for the briefest of seconds, he fixed his eyes on Lourdes and she looked away quickly. Father Francisco always appeared to be displeased with Lourdes and even in the midst of something as important as the appearance of the big red horse the priest seemed to find time to let her know of his disapproval. Lourdes grabbed at a pillowcase but it slipped from her fingers. She rose and dashed forward, catching the pillowcase just as it was about to sweep down the mountain. Then she saw the red horse's hooves before her splashing through the rivulet and the terror raged over her body again. She froze and slowly raised her eyes. The big red horse walked past her, his eyes on her. Lourdes fixedly returned the animal's stare. Then she looked up at the Indian in the saddle and he was watching her, too, with a quizzical expression. Lourdes turned slowly to watch them—the priest, the rancher, the Indian on the red horse—move up the mountainside. The Indian turned once in the saddle to get another view of her and then he kicked the horse's flanks and the animal trotted past the two hurrying men.

"Sister!" Manuela hissed. "Don't stare after him like that!" She had piled the soaked linen on a rock and was starting to work at a piece in the cold water. "It looks improper." The short, squat nun threw a disapproving glare after Quintana. "Besides, he looks like a Yaqui, and you don't want to encourage those northern beasts."

Lourdes knelt by the side of the rivulet and held a pillowcase under the surging surface. Scabs of dried blood and bits of fecal matter separated from the linen and dissolved in the water and for a moment there was a tint of pinkish brown and then it was washed away.

"Do you know that Yaqui?" Manuela's voice was colored with suspicion.

Her hands still trembling, Lourdes quickly lathered the pillowcase with a bar of coarse soap and furiously scrubbed the material together. Manuela glanced at her but said nothing more. Then the soap slipped from her grasp and Lourdes snatched after it, missing it twice before she had it again. She allowed herself to sit back on her haunches under her habit and bury her face in her knees. Manuela watched her closely. Then Lourdes raised her head and looked at the older nun.

"I know the horse."

Then Father Francisco was calling down to her.

—◌—

"GET YOUR MEDICINES," FRANK SAID TO THE YOUNG NUN WHEN SHE was standing before him, her eyes downcast. "There's a sick priest." Frank was excited. He kept looking out into the valley, as if any moment he would see the sick pastor.

"Sí, padre."

In the infirmary there were six patients the two nuns were tending to, all of them victims of *agrarista* cruelty. One man had been shot in the back of the head, execution-style, and yet he still lived, clinging to a senseless life, feces dribbling from his anus. Another had had his throat cut and had walked up to the Sagrado Corazón with the stomach of a slaughtered goat wrapped around his neck, holding in his blood. Still another was a teenage girl whose breasts had been sliced off. She lay on her side and cried endlessly, day and night, and she was crying still when Lourdes entered the converted residence and hurried to the cabinet where Dr. Villanueva kept his valise. The physician had fled so hastily at the *agraristas'* approach that he'd left behind his medical bag. His name was embossed in gold lettering just below the clasp. Lourdes had never met him, but his office was filled with photographs of the doctor and his family, and they were all of religious events—marriages, christenings, First Communions. The doctor was a good and active Catholic, and that's why he'd fled. Lourdes wondered what had happened to him, and to his three daughters.

Hastening out the front door of the infirmary, Lourdes came up short again with a gasp as she saw the red horse stamping his hooves at the plaza's paving stones. The Yaqui had not dismounted, the people of the pueblo had gathered around him, and the animal was nervous.

Lourdes felt herself start to swoon, her vision clouded, and then she was brought back into focus by Manuela's rebuking hiss. "Sister Lourdes! What is *wrong* with you?!"

Lourdes shook her head and stepped out into the street. "Nothing," she said softly. "It's nothing."

"Sister Lourdes," Father Francisco called. He was seated in a buggy and he motioned for her to hurry. Lourdes moved quickly across the small area that served as Sagrado Corazón's plaza, gathered up the skirt of her voluminous habit and climbed up into the buggy. Frank held her arm to steady her, but it wasn't necessary. Lourdes was strong and young under the folds of black.

"We must hurry," Frank said. "There's a fellow priest out there, on the brink of death, from what this man says." Lourdes looked at the Indian, then looked away quickly when she saw his curious eyes on her.

Frank clucked and slapped at the horse with the reins and the buggy bumped across the irregular stones and started down the mountainside. Quintana rode just ahead and to one side, and following behind were a dozen horsemen from the pueblo, including Rojas and his three sons.

Lourdes couldn't avoid looking at the big red horse. Its fiery haunches rippled and muscled right before her eyes. The Yaqui turned in the saddle and looked back at her and Lourdes looked down at the buggy's floorboards.

"*Qué pasa*, Sister?" Father Francisco asked, a little perturbed. "What's the matter?"

Lourdes started to say something, but she knew if she spoke she would cry, so she simply shook her head and kept her eyes averted.

SACRED HEART

—◁○▷—

LOURDES HAD JOINED THE CONVENT OF SANTA MARIA AT THE AGE OF fourteen. It was a nursing order, not that far from her hometown of León. She had wanted to be a nun since her earliest childhood. Her father was an architect, a builder of markets and warehouses, a creator of the prosaic, and the Hidalgo home was large and dark and cool, like a church itself. And like a church it was festooned with representations of the numinous. Intricately carved wood crosses for every Hidalgo death; Madonnas and Madonnas with Child—some pale and bloodless and chaste in the European manner, others dark and rustic, fashioned by *mestizo* and Indian artisans—her father collected them. It was while looking into a mirror between two Indian Madonnas that Lourdes—at the age of three—first became aware of her deformity.

At the Convent of Santa Maria, the other nuns hardly looked at her distortion and never once mentioned it. There were several sisters there with disfigurements of their own—crossed eyes, a twisted limb; they were the unmarriageable daughters of good families, and those families were grateful to have a place to tithe away their genetic mistakes. But that wasn't the case with Señor Hidalgo. When Lourdes stood on the chair in the upstairs hallway, shrieking at her reflection in the big, ornate oval mirror, her father came running from his study, afraid his beloved daughter had broken a limb. But when he saw her sobbing with horror into the mirror he understood she had become aware that she was different. He held her in his arms, cooing softly until she had quieted enough for him to explain it to her. It was a miracle, Señor Hidalgo said. Lourdes was a miracle. The little girl looked up at him between her teary gulps for breath. Yes, Señor Hidalgo said. You see, when you were born, when God delivered you to the Virgin Mary to bring to this world, the *Virgen* looked down and saw how beautiful you were and she felt such happiness that her eyes filled with tears, and one tear, a single pearllike tear, fell from the Madonna's eye and it landed right there, and slipped down . . . Enriquez traced his finger down the slurring of flesh that coursed down the left side of Lourdes's face, from above her eye to the corner of her lips. He kissed his daughter's mouth. So, you see, this is to show the world how much the Virgin loves you, how much her son Jesus loves you.

"HOW MUCH FARTHER?" FATHER FRANCISCO CALLED OUT TO THE YAQUI. Quintana turned in the saddle and pointed out to the southeast. There was a plume of dust far in the distance. He looked back at Frank and then his eyes fell on Lourdes. She was staring at the horse.

⸺◇⸺

THEY HAD RIDDEN UP TO THE CONVENT GATE AND SAT THEIR SADDLES, laughing and passing around jugs of liquor. After a while they began shouting at the gate, saying that unless someone came out they would set the whole place on fire. Lourdes and the other sisters peered out at them through the peepholes they had poked in the adobe walls when they had heard of troubles at other places.

"That's Salazar!" Sister Cleotilde gasped with horror. The name was like the hissing of the serpent.

"Which one?" Lourdes whispered.

"The one in front. The one on the devil horse." It was a tall, fire-red stallion with black mane and tail, black fetlocks and hocks, and its muscles bunched and quivered under its scarlet hide like throbbing sexual organs. Lourdes looked away quickly in shame, feeling—after what Cleotilde had said—that she had somehow glimpsed a bestial manifestation of Satan.

"They say he eats babies," Cleotilde whispered breathlessly.

"The horse?" Lourdes gasped.

"No, Salazar!" Cleothilde admonished. "They say he rips out their hearts and—"

"Get away from the wall!" *La Madre Superiora* moved quickly down on them, her hand raised as if to strike. She was a tall, angular Irishwoman in her early seventies, and though she had been in Mexico since the early '80s this was the first time she was frightened for her nunnery. "Get to your hiding places!"

Lourdes turned to run and Mother Superior's clawlike fingers caught her sleeve and held her tightly. "And don't come out, no matter what!" She spoke to Lourdes in English, with the same Cork brogue that painted her Spanish. Lourdes tried to pull away but the old Irishwoman yanked her back. "You are the ripest!" she rasped. "They mustn't see you!" Then she shoved Lourdes with surprising force and the young nun stumbled a few feet across the smoothly paved stones before she righted herself. She ran, her habit flowing, to the loose board just behind the meditation bench in the central patio. She lay on the stones, slipped the board away, then rolled as she had been taught into the coffinlike space. Then she pulled the board back

132

and snapped it into place with a *thunk*. There was a single nail hole in the board, and Lourdes put her eye to the board and peered out. She could see Mother Superior waiting by the gate, straight as a pine. A few moments later Sister Constanza, over three hundred pounds, waddled into view leading tottering old Father Diego to the gate.

"Open this fucking gate!" Salazar shouted from outside, and then Mother Superior said something to Sister Constanza and the fat nun shambled to the gate and started to unlock it. The old man seemed to be looking around for a place to sit, and Mother Superior took hold of his arm to bolster him. Then Constanza unlocked the gate and it was immediately pushed open by a swarthy, leering *agrarista* whose eyes darted hungrily around the convent patio. Salazar walked his satanic blood bay into the patio and the animal's hooves made a hollow sound on the polished stone. Behind him the other *agraristas* started to dismount. Mother Superior stepped forward to say something. Salazar leaned forward in the saddle to hear her, then he smiled as if what Mother Superior had said was mildly amusing, then he drew his revolver and shot her in the face.

Lourdes was so shocked that she pushed back from the nail hole and slammed the back of her head against the side of the compartment. She was dizzy and trembling so violently she could hear her legs bumping on the wood. Then there was a scream, then laughter and shouts, and when Lourdes looked out through the nail hole again she saw the swarthy *agrarista* holding up old Father Diego's decapitated head, a bloody machete in his other hand. The other *agraristas* had swarmed into the convent patio and several of them were ripping off Sister Constanza's tentlike habit. When her pendulous breasts and elephantine rolls of flesh were exposed to the sunlight the *agraristas* laughed and poked her fat body with the tips of their knives and soon Sister Constanza was smeared with wide swatches of her own blood, and then someone said, "Who wants to fuck this sow?" and since the others were already dragging the more desirable sisters down into the patio and pulling off their habits, no one wanted Constanza and a tall *agrarista* in hip boots grabbed her sweaty hair, pulled back her head and cut her throat. Constanza fell heavily and crawled forward as her lifeblood gushed out over the patio stones.

—◀◯▶—

IT WENT ON LIKE THAT ALL MORNING AND INTO THE AFTERNOON. THERE were twenty-seven Little Sisters of Charity in the convent, and in a few hours all had been raped and sodomized, even the eldest ones. In the afternoon there was a series of gunshots from the clinic adjacent to the convent. Lourdes held her breath in the "nun's hole" and cried silent tears and tried to pray, but her prayers were constantly interrupted by gunshots and screams. When night fell the plunderers lit torches and continued their fun. They got drunk on the convent wine, built a bonfire to burn icons and paintings, and gang-raped the naked young novitiates by the hellish flames. Sister Cleotilde was assaulted on the bench a few inches above Lourdes's hiding place by Lucifer himself—Severo Salazar.

Just after dawn the *agraristas* shot twelve of the older women, then tied the other fifteen together on a line and led them like dazed cattle through the front gate of the convent. The sated riders dozed in their saddles. Salazar on the red devil horse rode point, the swarthy *agrarista* in the rear, with a nun's cornet headpiece for a sombrero.

Lourdes remained in the nun's hole, motionless and silent, that whole day, awash in sweat and urine, and terrified they might return. When the night moon was high behind a scattering of clouds, Lourdes crawled out onto the blood-slicked patio. She wandered through the halls of the pillaged convent. Walls had been ripped out, floorboards torn up in the rapists' rush to find the hiding nuns. In the clinic adjacent to the convent the patients had been shot in their beds. One was a young wife about to deliver. Her *campesino* husband had been visiting her and he had been killed, too.

Lourdes stumbled out into the moonlight and stared numbly at the jumble of massacred nuns against the patio wall. She knelt by the bloody-mawed corpse that had been Mother Superior and began to pray.

In the morning Father Frank rode up to the open convent gate on a mule, followed by a score of believers who had joined him along the way from the Jesuit university in Guadalajara.

Frank looked around at the grisly scene, then slowly approached Lourdes, who was still kneeling and praying, her eyes tightly closed, her lips moving ardently, her thick wooden rosary clenched desperately. Frank knelt beside her and after a moment began to pray in a loud voice.

"Our Father, the Father of us all, and the Father of Your Son, Jesus Christ, the Savior of the world."

Lourdes stopped praying with a jolt, opened her eyes, and saw Frank for the first time.

"We beseech You, Father, to take unto You the souls of these poor sacrificed martyrs."

The others slowly approached the convent gates, their wide eyes darting about with fear and horror.

"Whose only crime was that they loved You, Father. Who were defiled and butchered because they had devoted their lives to You, our Father."

Frank raised his head and glared up at the wide robin's egg sky.

"And we swear, Father, to punish those who have done this. To wreak Your fury and vengeance upon Your enemies!

"We are Your soldiers in Christ! We are Your avenging fist in this unholy land!" Frank shouted at the sky. He was trembling. "We shall never rest until this blood has been revenged!"

Then Frank looked at Lourdes and she fainted and slumped over on the patio stones.

—◦—

QUINTANA TURNED IN HIS SADDLE AND POINTED OUT AT THE DUST OF almost two hundred riders approaching across the valley floor. Frank had already seen them. His eyes were wide.

"How many?"

Quintana shrugged. "Maybe a hundred and fifty, maybe two hundred."

"Women and children?"

"Only a few. These are *soldados*. They come to fight."

Frank's facial muscles danced with excitement. This was the army he'd been praying for.

"They've heard of me? They've come up here to join my rebellion?"

Quintana stared at him with something like amusement. "No, *padre*. They follow the *pistolero padre*. They follow your brother."

Again, Frank took Quintana to mean a brother priest.

"The sick padre?"

"*Sí.*"

Frank thought for a moment about what this meant to him. How he could bend it to his will.

"But someone heard of me? That's why you came here."

Quintana nodded. "*Sí.* We knew the *federales* wouldn't come up here."

"So, if this sick priest dies, these men will stay, right?"

Quintana shrugged. "I don't know. There is another priest, too. His name is Moreno."

Frank slapped the reins nervously. "But they don't follow him, do they?"

"No, they're with the gringo." He looked at Lourdes, who was still stealing glances at the red horse. "He killed the *agrarista* Salazar."

At the sound of the monster's name Lourdes took a sharp intake of breath and fingered her rosary nervously.

Rojas kicked his horse and moved forward. "Severo Salazar is dead?"

Quintana nodded. "In the plaza of Guadalajara. The gringo priest shot him." He looked at Lourdes. "I was there, right beside him, on the hanging scaffold."

"He's an American?" Frank was surprised. He had heard all the American priests had fled.

"If he killed Salazar, I can see why they follow him." Rojas spit as if he were trying to get rid of a foul taste.

"What's his name?" Frank asked. "I probably know him."

Quintana smiled to himself. "O'Rourke."

Frank considered the name, then shook his head slowly. "I don't think—"

"How are you called, *padre*?" Quintana asked suddenly. "What is your name?"

"I am Father Coyne."

"Ah," Quintana said slowly. "Coyne."

A score of *vaqueros* raced out from the approaching line. They galloped up and encircled the small party.

"Which one is the doctor?"

Frank's intention was to exert control from the beginning, as if it were his God-given right. "I am Father Francisco Co—"

"You didn't bring a doctor?" The *vaquero* asked of Quintana.

"There wasn't one," Quintana said. "How is he?"

The *vaquero* shook his head.

"The nun is a nurse," Quintana said. "She has medicines."

"He needs a doctor."

"We'll take him somewhere else," another horseman said, "where there is a doctor."

"Sister Lourdes is very qualified," Frank said, then added with emphasis, "We will handle this from now on."

The *vaquero* looked at Frank, then at Quintana, then back at Frank.

He was one of the first three, who had ridden up to the lean-to under the eucalyptus tree.

"You take responsibility for his life?" the *vaquero* challenged Frank. Quintana watched the priest closely. "Because if he dies—"

"Are you threatening a representative of Christ?" Frank shot back. "Because if you are, then you are no better than the godless *callistas.*"

The *vaquero* glared at Frank. Rojas nodded to his three sons and they gently touched the rowels of their spurs to their mounts and moved up around the buggy.

The *vaquero* looked to Quintana. "What do you think, Yaqui?"

Quintana looked out at the oxcart, coming on a hundred meters away, and the long line of horsemen stretched out behind. He turned back to the others. "Perhaps the gringo is meant to die. Perhaps he's already served his purpose by bringing us together." He looked at Frank and smiled that amused smile again. "But if he can be saved, Father Coyne will save him."

As THE OXCART AND THE BUGGY NEARED EACH OTHER, QUINTANA reined in the big red stallion beside Lourdes and whispered, "Watch, woman. This will be interesting."

Lourdes glanced at him timidly, and the Indian laughed.

"It's true . . ." she began softly. "That about . . . about Salazar?"

Quintana leaned over in his saddle and put one hand on the buggy seat behind Lourdes. "I saw it. With these eyes."

Frank reined in the buggy horse just as the oxcart pulled abreast. Beside the oxcart was an open carriage pulled by a matched set of thick-bodied white geldings, driven by a mestizo priest.

"You must be Father Moreno," Frank said as he stepped down from the buggy. "*Viva Cristo Rey*, Father." Frank started to move around the buggy horse to help down Lourdes, but Quintana was already there, holding up his outstretched arms. Lourdes hesitated but a moment, then rested her hands gingerly on Quintana's shoulders and jumped down. She took the doctor's bag from the buggy and moved quickly away from him.

"*Viva Cristo Rey*," the mestizo priest repeated as he tied up the carriage reins and stepped to the ground. "I am Father Moreno."

Frank was already moving toward the oxcart. The woman from the lean-to under the eucalyptus tree reached back and drew away the sheet they had propped up over the bed of the cart. The other women who had cared for the gringo priest had walked along beside the cart, and now they watched Lourdes come to the cart and climb in.

Frank came to the side of the cart and peered through the slats. The thin, sweating man half-sunken into the matted straw looked very sick. Frank looked away, down the long line of horsemen that stretched cavalrylike for a quarter of a mile. Here was his Catholic army. Here were his *cristeros*.

Quintana climbed up onto the oxcart and looked in at Tommy. Then he said to Frank, "Do you know this man?"

Frank pulled himself back from his thoughts and looked at Quintana. "What? Oh, no, I don't think—"

Frank looked back into the *carreta*. Lourdes was wiping the man's face with a cloth soaked in alcohol. Then she stopped and stared at the man a long time. She looked up at Frank and he saw the shock in her eyes. He heard Quintana chuckle. Frank pulled himself up on the cart to get a better look. The man *did* look familiar. He leaned over and stared in. For some reason Frank couldn't fathom, his scalp began to tingle. He felt confused. He looked up at Quintana and the Indian started to laugh. Then Frank understood. He recoiled as if from a rattlesnake and he lost his grip on the side of the cart and fell back into the dust.

◄◌►

WHEN FRANK WAS A TWO-AND-A-HALF-YEAR OLD TODDLER, BULLDOG went up to Sing Sing on a five-year lurch for strong-arm robbery and assaulting a policeman. For the rest of his life, Frank's earliest clear memory was of his mother sobbing uncontrollably under the vaulted ceilings of the courtroom.

On that day young Margaret Kelly Coyne became a prison widow. She was left with a pensive child and no family in America, and the hoodlum friends of Bulldog's who came around were only those who wanted to take Bulldog's place in her bed. Peggy sought refuge in the only other thing she knew—the local Roman Catholic Church.

Each dawn, after a hurried breakfast of lukewarm coffee and lumpy oatmeal, Peg would dress her son in the dark, shut the door on their miserable, rat-infested closet on Forty-seventh Street and hustle him four blocks over to the narrow little Church of the Sacred Heart. There, in the universal coolness of cathedral Catholicism,

Peggy would sit in her thin overcoat—summer and winter—and celebrate six, seven, and eight o'clock Masses. Frank, always a quiet and sedentary child, would stare wide-eyed for hours at the statues, the stained glass, the altar, the ritual. When kindly old Father Skelley—pastor at Sacred Heart since just after the Irish riots against Lincoln's draft laws—held up the chalice and intoned in Latin the liturgy of the Holy Eucharist, Frank could sense, even before he could communicate in words, the solemnity and drama of the defining moment of the service. Frank watched with fascination while the slick-haired, white-frocked young altar boys genuflected under the big plaster crucified Christ as they went about their duties. When they waved the smoking urn of incense Frank felt giddy from the scent; when they tingled the bells at the Offertory he was suffused with a delicious delight. He was like a child at a circus, and he wanted more than anything to do what those boys were doing.

Frank felt at home in the church—more at home than anywhere else. While Peggy prayed ardently he studied the desperate devotion of shawled women in the other pews, praying to put food in their children's mouths or for relief from beatings by their drunkard husbands. Frank felt the power of the faith well up in him. He understood instinctively—even at that age—the religion's purpose, and its eternal invincibility.

And there seemed to be a delicious *secrecy* to it all, shut off from the clamor of the crowded street outside, packed with jostling pedestrians, overladen horse wagons and carriages. In here there was a serenity and a safety. Frank and God were secure in here, encased in this stone fortress—for what were churches at their inception but battlements against pagan transgressors? Frank intuited this historical paranoia. He understood without instruction the need for protective architecture, the necessity of the church's *defense*.

PEGGY GOT INTO THE HABIT OF VISITING WITH FATHER SKELLEY IN HIS rectory after the last Mass of the morning. Father's French-Canadian housekeeper would serve coffee and cognac and cold ham sandwiches and Peggy and Skelley would reminisce about fair County Galway where they had both grown up, a half-century apart. Father would tousle Frank's hair affectionately and pour a tumbler of good Irish for Peggy and at some point Peggy would cry about her predicament and Skelley would stroke her hand and the Quebecois housekeeper would glare disapprovingly as she took away the china, and Frank realized he was witnessing some kind of strange, psychotherapeutic seduction that they thought him incapable of understanding.

Soon Frank took to leaving his mother and the priest talking intimately in the rectory, and wandering the church. Even at the age of three Frank could be depended on to act responsibly, so the little boy explored the whole place undisturbed. He stood before each Station of the Cross and inspected the workmanship of the gilt panels, the embossed suffering of the long-haired man carrying the timbers. He paused under the plaster likeness of Christ, broken, bleeding, yet somehow still lively in death, sprawled in Mary's arms. Frank sat in the first pew of the church and watched as old men and women of all ages slipped coins into the metal box under the votive candles—pennies mostly, an occasional nickel that clanged solidly—and then lit candles that flickered and sputtered in their little red and blue glasses.

Silent, unnoticed, he watched as the petitioners knelt and beseeched gods and saints to intercede on the behalf of loved ones. Some of them cried. Others moaned softly as they prayed. He was enthralled by their murmured prayers. They filled him with a palpable melancholia that bordered on rapture. Later, in catechism, Frank would learn about purgatory and salvation and crucifixion, but at this early age he only understood the sad devotion, the solemnity, the *faith*.

And he loved it.

WALKING HOME FROM CHURCH IN THE GLINTING AFTERNOON LIGHT, HIS mother laden with the wrapped packages of food the Canadian housekeeper had disapprovingly prepared, Frank would be near ecstasy. Weary, full of wonder, the small boy would fall instantly to sleep when Peggy put him to bed under the cheap, coarse blanket the Church had provided and his dreams were a cool, contemplative kaleidoscope of haloed saints, shadowed goddesses, crucified martyrs more content in death within their stone castle than anyone Frank observed in the world outside.

—◄○►—

THE DAY CAME, OF COURSE, WHEN THE FRENCH-CANADIAN church mouse carefully packed her cowhide suitcase and walked out of the Church of the Sacred Heart with her back properly straightened and her mouth a thin, grim frown. Then Peggy took her place as Skelley's housekeeper. Peggy's day began even earlier now—Father breakfasted at four-thirty—and Peggy carried her still sleeping son to the church. So Frank had the delight each morning of coming awake in a Sacred Heart pew, looking up into the docile eyes and extended arms of the Mother of God.

Peggy seemed to spend ever more time with Father Skelley. She cooked his meals, mended his priestly clothes, shined his shoes, swept and cleaned the rectory. To keep little Frank busy—his endless ruminations seemed to unsettle even his adoring mother—Peggy put him to work polishing the altar ornaments. The little boy sat on the stone floor in an alcove off the transept and dutifully rubbed the candlesticks with a soft chamois until the gold fairly *glowed.* The occasional afternoon worshipers, pausing in the empty church to admire the silent, industrious little boy at his work, would say to each other, "Look at what he's done with those wee fingers. What a good little lad." And her companion would reply, "Aye, and with his own father the devil incarnate." And then they would stare pointedly at the closed door of the rectory, look at each other and cluck. "And this one as old as Methuselah." Frank would pause in his task to gaze up at the old Irishwomen, trying to comprehend what they were saying. "And when the devil comes back, there'll be hell to pay, mark my words."

WHEN FRANK WAS OLD ENOUGH TO GO TO SCHOOL FATHER SKELLEY interceded with a nearby parish church—Sacred Heart had no teaching facilities and Peggy Coyne had no funds—and he was enrolled at St. Xavier's. Here, for the first time, Frank was torn from the cocoon woven by Peggy to protect her son—and, in truth, herself—from the harsh realities of turn-of-the-century New York, and catapulted into the wider, wilder society of parochial grammar school. The nuns were quickly won over—he rightfully saw in them a melding of his mother and Father Skelley and they correctly saw him for exactly what he was—a future priest. His good deportment, his attentiveness, his eagerness to volunteer for any task the nuns asked—whether chalkboard washing or illuminating the simple mystery of the Trinity to the rest of the class—all this won Frank instant approval with the wide-hatted Sisters. But much to Frank's confusion these very attributes branded him a pariah among his peers. Having never played or even associated with children his own age, Frank didn't understand that there was a very different standard of behavior among the young male offspring of saloon keepers and stevedores.

Frank was branded an ass-kisser, the sentence was continual, and the punishment was meted out by anyone, anytime, anywhere. The little boy ran home every day from St. Xavier's with bruised arms, bloody noses, tear-filled eyes, and no matter how often Peggy upbraided the Sisters or whispered in Father's Skelley's ear, she could not stop it. She could not protect him.

And then, when it seemed to Frank that life and God had betrayed him, when nothing could get worse, everything did.

Bulldog came home from the penitentiary, out on early parole.

Frank was almost eight, and already an outsider at St. Xavier's. Very soon he became an outsider at home as well. Bulldog came back from prison and swept into the tiny apartment like a storm, a storm with loud winds reeking of brew and cigars and semen. Immediately, Frank was banished from Peggy's bed where he had always slept and relegated to a hard, coarse cot in the hallway, where he lay awake all night listening to his mother moaning under Bulldog's pent-up passion.

The visits to kindly old Father Skelley ended abruptly. When Bulldog caught scent of the rumors circulating about his wife and the old priest, it was all Peggy could do to keep Bulldog from going over to shoot him. As it was, Frank heard for the first time his mother being beaten by his father. He lay in bed crying, jerking violently with each resounding blow. He heard Peggy sobbing, then later he heard her groaning with submission as the bedsprings creaked under his parents' weight.

Frank had learned sanctity and serenity. Now he understood sin and perdition.

SOON BULLDOG'S AMBITIONS AND PRISON CONNECTIONS SUCCEEDED IN moving the budding Coyne family—Peggy was almost immediately impregnated—into a larger flat off Tenth Avenue. Here the up-and-coming thief and strong-arm enforcer played host to a continuous parade of hard and hard-drinking young men who looked to Bulldog to channel their antisocial urges into profitability. Soon there were all-night parties, drunken gaieties with a one-eyed piano player pounding out Tin Pan Alley struts and Irish reels on the upright Bulldog had shanghaied from a delivery wagon. Tipsy women with powdered faces stumbled into Frank's bedroom off the kitchen and giggled when they saw the little boy staring out from under the covers. More than once, a woman would sit on the edge of the bed and feel under the covers for Frank's privates. Some of them would ask slurringly for a kiss, then push their tongues down Frank's throat. Another time a couple copulated standing against the locked door, never knowing that Frank watched them from the darkness at the other side of the room.

One night, about six months after Bulldog had come home, he went into the bedroom off the kitchen, lifted his sleeping son from the bed and carried him into the parlor. "Wake up, Frankie!" Bulldog grinned. "Wake up." Bulldog stood the little boy on the coffee table and announced to the grinning guests. "Lookit the little bastard! Ain't he grown while I was up at the Graybar Hotel!"

The celebrants laughed as Frank sleepily rubbed his eyes. He looked around in fear at all the distorted, whiskey-reddened faces, searching for his mother. He saw her leaning against a wall, a drink in her hand, a blank, drunken stare on her face. Frank was about to call out for her when Bulldog roughly mussed his hair and roared, "Give us a song, Frankie Boy! 'A Little Piece of Ireland'" Frank looked back at his father. The child's lower lip began to tremble, his eyes moistened.

"Here, you're scarin' 'im!" cried out Big Belly Mary, in her London-raised Cockney screech. " 'E's a delicate one!"

Bulldog turned back to his son and examined him carefully. "He ain't scared, are you, Frankie?" He looked closer. "And he sure as hell ain't delicate!"

The little boy raised his arms, beseeching his mother to rescue him. Peggy stared back, but didn't move. Bulldog misread his son's gesture.

"Lookit the little bastard!" Bulldog roared with pride. "The boyo wants to box!" Bulldog crouched down into a Jim Jeffries stance and gently flicked out his open left palm. It brushed Frankie's chin. "C'mon, c'mon! Fire back!"

It took a long moment, but slowly Frank's small face collapsed into a maelstrom of terror. His mouth became a yawning abyss and from deep within the child began a yowl of dread and dismay.

"Aw, Bull!" complained one of Bulldog's lieutenants. "You hurt him!"

Frank's wail grew in volume and intensity. Tears streaked from the corners of his tightly clenched eyes.

"Damn, Bulldog! Whatja do to him?!"

Bulldog looked at his son with disgust. "I didn't do nothing to him. I didn't hardly touch him!" Bulldog reached out and gripped Frank's arm. "C'mon, Frankie. Don't be a jenny."

At the clutch of his father's hand, Frank began to wail at an even more desperate pitch. He stood on the table, yowling with inconsolable, terrified sadness.

"Jesus!" a woman barked. "He sounds like a fuckin' train, he does!"

"What are you doin' to the boy, boss?"

Bulldog looked around the room with a challenging glare. "He's crying over nothing! I didn't do nothin' to him!" Bulldog fixed on Peggy, who was staring at her offspring with horrified rejection. "Peg! Come do something about this little pansy!"

Peggy reluctantly left the shelter of the wall and moved through the crowd. As she neared the little boy seemed to elevate toward her, his arms still upreached. Peggy stared at the crying child a moment, then picked him up in a gesture more of responsibility than response. Frank clutched at her, his wails unabating.

"What have you done to him?" Bulldog's accusing eyes shifted the blame to her. "You turned him into a bleeding fuckin' fop!"

Peggy was silent in her shame, but across the room someone called out, "Aw, he's all right, Bull!"

"He's just scared!"

"Looks like you got a priest in the family!" someone else offered, and then silenced quickly when Bulldog's head whipped around.

Then, as Peggy turned to carry Frank away, Bulldog pulled her back and slipped his hand between her and the boy's body and clutched her stomach. "I already put another one in the oven!" He grinned to the room as he shook Peggy's flat belly. "And this one's going to be another John L.!" The parlor resounded with relieved laughter.

"This one's going to be the spittin' image!" Bulldog rubbed Peg's stomach with vigor. Peggy smiled gratefully. The piano player started up again and the party resumed.

Little Frankie Coyne was forgotten.

IN THE BEDROOM OFF THE KITCHEN PEGGY DROPPED THE SOBBING BOY into his bed and angrily hissed, "You shut up! You just shut up!" All thoughts of Father Skelley and the Church of the Sacred Heart had been banished. Peggy Kelly Coyne was an opportunist, and right now opportunity ran thick and rich to the Bulldog. She wasn't going to let something like a weepy little boy spoil it for her.

Frank looked up at his mother through tear-drenched eyes and raised his arms to her for comforting. She slapped them away.

"You just stay in here and you stop crying!"

A woman's laughter rang out from the parlor and Peggy's head snapped to it, as if she had been issued a threat.

"Mama—" Frank managed through his gulping breaths. "Mama—"

"You just shut up!" Peggy barked, and then, for the first time, she struck her firstborn. She slapped him hard across his face. Frank's little hands flew to his burning cheek. His shock was so complete that for a moment he was as still as a photograph. The sobs took an eternity to come. Peggy straightened, looked down at him for only a moment longer, then quickly passed through the door, closing it soundly behind her.

The little boy buried his head in his pillow and screamed. He cried until the pillowcase was soaked and snotty. Then, in a frenzy of childish rage, he pounded the goose down with his small, clenched fists until his arms were leaden.

He finally fell asleep, sniffling and whimpering, the sound of the continuing party tolling sadly in his ears.

He was saying his Rosary.

—◇—

FROM THAT NIGHT ON, BULLDOG COYNE WAGED A WAR OF COLD cruelty against his son. His only communication with the boy was sharp rebukes, snide criticisms, disgusted shakes of his head. In a very short time, Frank learned to retreat into his tiny bedroom whenever his father entered the apartment. There, hunched over the apple crate he used as a desk, he assiduously pored over his Baltimore Catechism—studying the illustrations long before he read the text. Lost in the miracles and mysteries of boyhood Catholicism Frank felt safe and remote, and totally removed from the ever-present danger that was his father.

When the baby was born—a boy, Thomas Michael Coyne—both father and brother were relieved. Bulldog had a new son, and one— it was immediately evident—much more to his liking. And Frank was delivered from being the focus of his father's attention.

Tommy was a happy baby from the beginning . He would stare for hours up at the ceiling, giggling, clutching at his feet. He would kick off his covers and laugh as if he had stolen the Crown Jewels. Tickled, the baby would fairly guffaw as urine arced up from his tiny, rosebudlike penis. When he began to take his first few halting steps across the apartment, a fall would simply put a quizzical expression on his face. Then he would laugh as if it were all a great joke and immediately clamber to his feet and start again. If he hit his head on the corner of a piece of furniture, little Tommy's face would darken with consternation and he'd stare at the offending object as if committing an enemy's likeness to memory. Then he would rub his head thoughtfully and go on about his business. But there were no tears. Little Tommy seldom if ever cried. Bulldog found this to be a great relief and source of pride.

"Look at the little terrier!" Bulldog would crow to his assembled mob of hoodlums. "He don't get scared, he just gets mad!" Tommy would hear the deep male laughter and grin and look around in delight, as if nothing in the world could please him more than to be who and where he was at that very moment.

But the company Tommy sought out first, and most often, was that of his brother Frank. In fact, the first word the boy spoke, at the age of fourteen months, was a kind of "ank" squawk. Frank was in his room, on his knees, making an Act of Contrition when he heard a sound at the door. He turned to see his baby brother tottering in the doorway, smiling with joy that he'd found Frank. "Ank!" he exclaimed. "Ank! Ank!"

Frank's anger flared. He rose and strode quickly to punish Tommy for disturbing his prayers, but the child's happiness and love was so natural, so infectious, that Frank pulled up short, his hand raised and ready to strike.

"Ank!" Tommy was delighted that his big brother had noticed him. After a moment Frank lowered his hand, then said softly, "I'm praying to Jesus."

Tommy giggled, tottered in a few feet, then started to lose his balance. Frank reached out to steady him and he could feel Tommy's strong grip.

"Ank!"

Frank looked down at his baby brother's beaming smile and made a decision.

"Do you want to pray with me?" Frank took Tommy's hand and walked him slowly over to the bed. "I'll show you how."

Frank knelt by the side of the bed. "Like this."

Tommy laughed again and bounced up and down on his short fat legs. Frank said very solemnly, "Jesus lives in heaven. With Our

146

Father and the Holy Ghost and his Mother Mary." Tommy giggled,
then tried to kneel as Frank was doing. He squatted, then plopped
down heavily on his behind. His countenance darkened for a short
moment, then when Frank spoke again Tommy listened intently.

"Heaven is a real pretty place, with clouds and lambs and angels
and saints. . . ." Frank threw a look at the door, then whispered.
"It's not like around here at all."

Tommy was delighted at the conspiratorial tone. "Ank!"

Frank smiled down at his brother, then he said, "I've got a picture
of heaven. You wanna see?" Frank jumped up quickly and ran to
his apple crate desk. He came back with his catechism. He opened
the book and the frontispiece was a tinted wash rendering of the
Ascension. He looked at it reverently, then held the book before
Tommy's face. Tommy studied it with wide, interested eyes. Then
he looked at Frank.

"That's heaven," Frank breathed softly, as if it were a secret between the two of them. Then Frank nodded toward the door and
whispered, "They won't be there."

—◆◇◆—

As BULLDOG COYNE BEGAN TO MOVE UP IN THE HELL'S KITCHEN
hooligan hierarchy—loan-sharking, burglarizing riverfront warehouses, murdering for money—he began to develop richer tastes.
Custom-made suits, prime-cut-steak dinners in Broadway eateries,
and olive-skinned women. He discovered a penchant for Sicilians,
Neapolitans, Jewesses and light-complexioned mulattoes. It was a
secret weakness that the Irishman hid from his underlings and cro-
nies. But Peggy couldn't be fooled. At the first whiff of flowery
perfume on his tailored shirts, all Peg's instincts of self-preservation
began to howl like a hunting dog. Now the apartment on Tenth
Avenue reverberated with her accusations and condemnations. The
arguments were long and violent. One night, when Bulldog didn't
come home, while Tommy huddled in Frank's arms in their bedroom off the kitchen, Peg went through the cupboards and methodically began to break the entire Devonshire bone china set Bulldog
had recently brought home. She sat at the table with a bottle and
a glass and the china neatly stacked up beside her, and every few
minutes she would pick up a piece and fling it at the wall, screaming, "You fucking Paddy pig!"

When Bulldog arrived, alerted by a neighbor, he came through the door and ducked as a teapot shattered on the doorframe beside his head.

"You fuckin' bastard!" Peggy drunkenly flung herself at him, scratching at his eyes. Bulldog pushed her hard and she fell back onto the kitchen table and the table collapsed, sending china and whiskey bottle crashing to the floor. Peggy lay in the mess, sobbing. She looked up at Bulldog and choked out his boyhood name, "Aloysius—" and then she gulped once and vomited all down the front of her dressing gown.

Bulldog looked down at her in disgust. Then he stepped over her and paced the few feet through the kitchen into the boys' bedroom. He peered through the darkness at Tommy's empty crib, then saw the two pairs of frightened eyes shining whitely from Frank's side of the room.

Bulldog cursed silently and snatched up his younger son, giving Frank an accusatory glare that declared war over Tommy's soul. "What are you doin' with my Tom?" Frank shrank back from his father's rage and Bulldog whirled and walked out.

In the kitchen Peggy reached out and grabbed at Bulldog's passing leg. "Bull! Don't leave me!" With one arm Bulldog held Tommy high on his chest and with his other he swung in a wide backhand arc and slammed the back of his fist into Peggy's cheek. Her head snapped back and she went limp around his leg. Bulldog carefully extricated his pants from her fingers, then he grinned at Tommy.

"Let's get outta here and have us some fun, Tom." Tommy looked wide-eyed at his father's smiling lips, then down at his mother on the floor. Bulldog lifted Tommy's shirt and tickled the boy's fat belly. "Tommytumtum!" Bulldog playfully singsonged. The child giggled and rubbed his stomach. "Yeah, that's my boyo!" Bulldog unhurriedly walked out of the flat, leaving the door open behind him.

FRANK LAY IN HIS BED FOR SEVERAL MINUTES, LISTENING FOR ANY sound from the kitchen. Finally he got up and stood in the doorway. Peggy was still sprawled on the floor, amid the shards of broken china. Frank shut the hall door and locked it, then he went to the pantry and took out a loaf of bread and a crock of butter. He cut off a thick slice, buttered it, then sat in a chair, eating and watching Peggy. When he was almost finished Peggy moaned and tried to lift her head. Then she was still again. Frank put the rest of the bread back into the cupboard, then he knelt and uprighted the whiskey bottle. There was still a half-pint sloshing at the base. Frank put the whiskey on the cupboard, then he carefully picked up the larger fragments of china. He took a brush from under the sink and meticulously swept up the remaining dust and shards. He even reached under his mother and cleaned there.

When the kitchen was in order again, Frank wet a wash rag from the bucket by the sink and began to wipe away the puke from his mother's face. Peggy moaned again, and her eyes fluttered open. Her cheek was blue and swelling. She stared at her son, then she started to retch again.

Frank held her hair out of the puddle of puke on the floor, and Peggy choked out between heaves, "You're a good boy, Frankie. You're a—"

She was on her knees and elbows, her body wracked with violent thrusts every time she gagged and nothing came up.

"Please forgive me, Frank. I'm not a good mother!" She started to cry in huge gulps. "Please forgive me."

Frank wiped away the mess from her lips. And then he said, "Jesus forgives you."

—◄ ○ ►—

BULLDOG SET TOMMY ON THE BAR AND THE BROTHEL WHORES PRESSED around, oohing and aahing.

"Is he yours, Bull?"

"He's so beautiful!"

"Ah . . . bellissimo!"

They stood Tommy up on his fat legs and he giggled and took off his pants and ran up and down the bar holding his penis. The whores laughed until their tears rolled in rivulets down their cheeks and smudged their makeup.

Bulldog left Tommy in their care and went upstairs with a pair of Palermo sisters. When he came down in the morning Tommy was asleep cradled on the naked elephantine breasts of a big Sardinian country girl.

Later, the whorehouse cook made a big breakfast of chops and eggs and biscuits and Bulldog sat at one end of the table and the madam at the other and Tommy was passed along from the lap of one whore to the next, and each in turn kissed him and smoothed his hair and fed him tidbits from her plate.

Halfway through the meal there was a rustle at the front door and the colored doorman let in a trio of Sicilians. Bulldog stiffened when he recognized one of them as Broadway Joey Zanca. Zanca was a young up-and-comer in the growing Matranga mob, and the Matrangas had been earning a reputation for bloody ruthlessness all over Downtown. But Zanca was half-drunk in his tuxedo, and all he wanted, after a long night of booze and bright lights, was to continue his festivities into the next day.

Zanca and his two companions moved into the dining room, doffing their coats and hats. "Get us some breakfast, Rosalie," Zanca bellowed, taking in the dining room. His eyes fell on Bulldog.

"Hey, Irish!" Zanca cried jovially. "Whatcha doing in a wop whorehouse?"

Bulldog put down his knife and fork and said evenly, "Dagos got to be good for something."

The madam was immediately on her feet. She flew to Zanca, saying in guttural dialect, "Don Giuseppe, this is my place of business. This is where me and my girls make our living." Then she turned to Bulldog. "Mr. Bulldog, please. We don't want no trouble in here."

There was a tense moment, then Joe Zanca started to laugh. " 'Dagos got to be good for something,' hey, that's a good one. I gotta remember that one."

Zanca nodded toward the table and the madam quickly scooted three girls out of their chairs. She started to pick up the breakfast dishes as Zanca and the other two sat down.

"Feed us, Rosalie. First we eat, then we fuck!" The remaining whores giggled lasciviously. Zanca picked up a fork and started to eat sausage from a serving platter. "Bulldog . . . Bulldog . . ." He chewed while he thought. "I heard that name . . ." He smiled and shook his fork affirmatively, as if nodding. "Oh, yeah . . . Bulldog Coyne. You that Irishman almost beat a cop to death after he had you cuffed and shackled."

Bulldog was eating again. "I did a stretch at the Sing for it, too."

Zanca grinned around his sausage. "Fucking Irishmen. Always more balls than brains."

The whores got quiet and their eyes shot back and forth between the two men.

Bulldog had been cutting the meat from his chop bone. He stopped and looked at Zanca. He reached over and poured a pony glass of apricot brandy from the madam's cut-glass decanter. "Irish got more balls than brains, huh?" He held up the glass and looked at the golden liquid, then he smiled at Zanca. "I gotta drink to that."

Zanca laughed and reached for the brandy. "Whatcha gonna do?" The madam took the brandy decanter from his hand and poured one for him. "You all right, Coyne."

"You know, Joey. What they say about you is, you look like half-a-mick yourself."

Zanca had sandy brown hair and was a foot taller than his short, swarthy companions. Zanca chuckled. "Nah, it's just my *mamma mia* got off the boat before she had me. All that good ol' American milk made me grow big and strong." Now Zanca lifted his glass. "God bless America."

Bulldog's teeth curled back from his lips in a cynical grin that resembled a snarl. "God bless America." Both gangsters held their pony glasses up and a rich, throaty, threatening laugh rose up in both of them. Then Zanca saw Tommy.

"Hey, looka the kid."

Tommy was on a whore's lap, his eyes just above table level, examining the Sicilian.

"Whose kid?" Zanca looked up and down the table of whores.

"That's my son," Bulldog said.

"No kidding." Zanca rose and moved down the table. He nodded at a whore seated beside the one who was holding Tommy, and the woman quickly rose and held the chair for Zanca. "Ain't you starting going to cathouses a little early?" Zanca said to Tommy, and the others at the table chuckled.

Then Zanca said, "I got three of these little rug rats myself. How many you got?"

Bulldog chewed. "Just him."

"Well, get busy, Irish." He reached over and tousled Tommy's hair. The child's hair lent itself to touch. Then Zanca said to the boy, "You ever see one of these?" and he reached under his jacket and pulled out a sinister looking pistol.

Bull put down his fork and moved his hand toward the inside of his coat. The two darker Sicilians did the same. But Zanca held up his hand. "Take it easy, take it easy. I just want to see how the kid takes to it." He laid the gun on the tabletop. "They say that in Sicily, when a boy's about this age—What's his name?"

"Thomas."

"Hey, *Tomasino* . . ." Zanca positioned the weapon carefully on the tablecloth. "They say you put a gun in front of a male child, if he picks it up he's gonna be an assassin."

Tommy's eyes were already wide, examining the blue-black German automatic.

Bulldog relaxed. "And if he doesn't?"

Zanca shrugged, as if it were self-explanatory. "A priest."

The room grew quiet. All eyes were on Tommy. A servant girl entered the dining room laden with plates of food but the madam held up her hand and the girl stopped.

Tommy looked at the Luger a long time, then he looked at Zanca. "Whatcha gonna do, kid?"

Tommy leaned forward in the whore's lap and brought a tiny hand from below the table. Hesitantly, he reached out. The gun was cool and hard and oily smooth to his touch. Tommy looked around the table in awe. His father was watching closely.

Tommy gawked back at the weapon. Then he reached out with both his hands and traced his fingers over the cruel, Teutonic lines. He was fascinated. Without any more hesitation he fitted his small hands around the grip and lifted it.

The whores began to chatter prophetically in Sicilian dialect. Bulldog grinned widely. Then Tommy swung the gun around and pointed it at Zanca. The whores and the two other gangsters ducked.

"Hey, *hey!*" Zanca said, and reached for the Luger. Tommy didn't want to let go. Finally Zanca carefully extricated it from the boy's little fingers.

"An assassin," Bulldog said proudly. "Be careful, Giuseppi, someday he don't shoot *you*."

◄○►

ROJAS SENT HIS SONS INTO THE VALLEY BELOW TO BRING UP A HERD OF yearlings, and that night they slaughtered several and roasted them on huge spits set up in Sagrado Corazón's small, treeless plaza. The army of horsemen set up camp at the sloping edge of the pueblo, and a hundred small fires were built, and the hillside from a distance looked like a gathering of fireflies.

The women without men quickly paired up with *vaqueros* they found suitable, and the widows and older orphaned daughters from inside the pueblo walked out slowly among the dusty, hard-bitten men, and instant informal marriages were formed, sometimes by no more than a nod or a gestured invitation to lay one's blanket beside a fire. The remaining men reminded themselves that they were here to make war, for Christ, and waited for the meat to roast.

There was an electricity in the air, a sense of destiny—but also of trepidation. When some of the people in the pueblo began to set up stalls as if for a fiesta and a trio of mariachis started to play and sing at one end of the plaza, several of the men who had come all the way from Guadalajara walked over and told them to silence. "He needs quiet. He must recover," they said. "When he walks among us, then we'll celebrate."

In this way the story of what had happened in the square at Guadalajara spread quickly through the pueblo people, and when the moon rose the mestizo priest Moreno gathered them all in the plaza before the ruined church and led a Rosary for his recovery.

FROM THE SECOND-FLOOR BEDROOM WINDOW OF THE DISAPPEARED DR. Villanueva's house Frank surveyed with wonder the people kneeling in the stone plaza, holding candles, following the dark priest in prayer. He still could not believe what had happened today. His sense of reality was totally shaken. Frank had been in Mexico for seven years and he had seen cruelty and courage such as he had never imagined twentieth century man capable of, but he was stunned by what had he had found that afternoon in the oxcart.

Behind him Tommy shouted out again and Frank turned back to the room. Tommy was thrashing about naked in the doctor's big, ornate four-poster. The two nuns struggled to hold him down.

"No!" Tommy cried out. He was awash in his own sweat, boiling in feverish delirium. "Don't go in there!"

"Please, Father," Lourdes pleaded in English. "Just lie back."

"Da! Da!" Tommy shouted.

Frank felt eyes on him and turned to the door, where the Indian with the long, untamed hair sat backward on a chair, watching him. Quintana's anthracite eyes seemed to bore into him, to read his thoughts and examine his soul. It unsettled him. Frank stared back pointedly, meaning to intimidate, but the Yaqui didn't waver.

"*Noooo!*" Tommy shouted again, and then the fire within him seemed to flare out and he slumped back senseless against the drenched pillows.

"Help me," Lourdes said to Sister Manuela as she pulled at Tommy's arms to turn him over.

On a grand bureau against the wall the woman from the lean-to under the eucalyptus tree was heating a clay saucer over a candle. Frank looked at the Yaqui again, and then sheathed his emotions with a disapproving countenance.

"What is your name?" he asked of the woman.

The woman from the lean-to dropped her eyes at the priest's inquisitional tone. "Inmaculada Sánchez, Padre."

They had turned Tommy over in the bed. The suppurating bullet wound bulged with infection.

"What are you doing?" Frank asked Inmaculada Sánchez.

The woman didn't know what to say to the unkind gringo priest. She stood there motionless, her eyes downcast, the clay saucer hot in her fingers.

"What is that, Inmaculada? I'm waiting."

Lourdes was washing a scalpel in alcohol. "Father Frank, it's to draw out the poison."

Frank still fixed Inmaculada with a disapproving glare. "It's not pagan? It's not deviltry?"

Quintana, in his seat by the door, gave a cynical chuckle.

"No, señor," Lourdes said. "It's the old people's medicine, from the land."

Frank looked at the saucer with suspicion.

"Padre, if Inmaculada had not applied her poultice, then surely the father would have died." She looked at the scalpel, glistening with drops of alcohol, then at Tommy's buttocks. She took a deep breath.

Quintana rose from his chair. "Have you cut a man before?"

Lourdes shook her head. "I have assisted many doctors in operations . . . but I have never . . ." She swallowed and blanched.

Quintana pulled up a straw-wrapped jug of tequila from where it hung from a belt string and held it out to her. She started to shake her head again but Quintana sloshed the liquid around in the jug. "You need a steady hand to cut, woman."

She looked at Quintana and reached for the bottle. He took out the stopper before he gave it to her. He watched her throat work as she swallowed.

Frank saw him looking at Lourdes and frowned. Then he stepped to the bed. The sight of Tommy's blue-black flesh made him retch. He covered his mouth with his hand.

Lourdes took a breath, made a quick sign of the cross, then put the blade against the offense and made a quick, deep incision. The hot pus shot up over her arm.

—◄◦►—

FRANK WASHED OUT HIS MOUTH OVER A BASIN IN THE HALLWAY. Manuela was on her knees cleaning up his mess from the floor.

"I'm sorry, Sister . . ."

"It's nothing, Father."

Frank wiped his mouth and leaned his back against the wall. Directly across from him a small, ragged boy squatted by the bedroom door. Miguelito watched him through his one good eye, his crooked leg splayed out at an odd angle over the dark wood floor.

"You shouldn't be in here," Frank said weakly, then stopped when the bile began to rise again in his throat.

Miguelito made no effort to move. He tightened his arms around the leather-wrapped bundle he held like an infant and stared at Frank with curiosity.

Quintana stepped out of the bedroom. He frowned at the sight of the nun cleaning up the puke, then held out the jug of tequila to Frank.

"Sister," Frank ordered, "get me a glass."

"*Sí, padre.*" Manuela rose quickly and hurried away down the hall, wiping her hands on a cloth.

Frank swallowed, composed himself. Then he fixed Quintana with a scrutinizing eye.

"You were on the scaffold in the city? They were going to hang you, too?"

Quintana seemed amused by Frank's attempt to assert authority.

"*Sí*, they were going to hang me, too."

"You were the only man there who was not a priest. What was your offense?"

Quintana grinned. "They said I was wearing a religious medal. They said I killed the *agrarista* who ripped it off my neck. . . . But they were only using that as an excuse."

"You didn't kill the *agrarista?*"

"Oh, yes, I killed him. And I would do it again without hesitation. But you see, he had been sent to arrest me because they said I had deflowered the daughter of a *federal* alcalde."

"And had you?"

Quintana's grin widened. "And I would do it again, without hesitation."

"So, you ride into our pueblo like a hero for Christ, but in truth you are a seducer and a murderer."

Quintana cocked his head and inspected Frank with insolence. In

Mexico, only a priest or a politician would dare address a man in this manner.

"Then you were certainly in the right place with the right man, up there with my brother."

Sister Manuela hurried back down the hall with the glass.

—◄○►—

IN THE BEDROOM LOURDES WAS FINISHING CLEANING THE WOUND. SHE pressed a piece of gauze against Tommy's buttock, squeezing out the last of the infection. She bathed the area liberally with alcohol and then began to fashion a soft bandage. The woman from the lean-to under the eucalyptus tree stepped closer, the saucer of herbs in her hand.

"No, *señora*," Lourdes shook her head. "My way is better for now."

Inmaculada nodded. "*Sí*, Sister." She watched Lourdes deftly tape and tie the edges of the bandage.

"Sister, they're brothers, no?"

Lourdes shrugged. "Could it be any other way?"

Inmaculada shook her head with wonder. "Priest brothers . . . It must be a very sacred family."

She helped Lourdes turn Tommy on his side. They both looked at the thin, sickly face. "Will he die, *Madre?*"

"Not if God and I can help it."

Lourdes gently sponged the sweat from Tommy's forehead. "Is it true, *señora*, that he killed Severo Salazar?"

"I wasn't there, Sister, but they say he did. They all say he did." She leaned across the bed and whispered. "They say he was like an avenging angel. Like the right hand of God."

The two women looked at each other, and then at Tommy, and then they both crossed themselves.

"I was there," Quintana said from the doorway. "He killed Salazar all right." From behind Quintana a short form flashed by and scurried under the bed.

"What was that?" Lourdes knelt and grasped out for Miguelito. He hissed like a cat and bit at her. Lourdes snatched her hand back. "You evil little *gnomo!* Get out from under there!"

In the darkness under the bed, Miguelito backed away on his hands and knees.

156

"Suppose," Lourdes threatened angrily, reverting back to the hot-blooded young *mexicana* she was, "suppose I get a broom and beat you out of there."

There was a moment of silence, then from under the bed came, "Fuck you, you scar-face whore!"

Lourdes's mouth dropped open and she looked up at Quintana.

"It's no use," Quintana said. "He won't go away and they won't let me kill him. . . . He won't leave the gringo." He thought a moment. "I guess none of us can anymore."

—◀○▶—

THE *PLACITA* WAS ASLEEP WHEN THE WOMAN FROM THE LEAN-TO UNDER the big eucalyptus tree stepped out of the infirmary. All around the perimeter of the square the *cristeros* had bedded down against the adobe buildings, around the fountain, and in the collapsed church. A few candles had been left to burn down outside the infirmary, and Inmaculada took one and walked to the edge of the pueblo. There was an almost full moon, and the animals had been herded to a fairly level slope on the mountainside. A couple of *vaqueros* slept in their saddles as their mounts walked slowly around the herd.

A woman stood at the window of a whitewashed house and motioned for Inmaculada to approach. "Have you eaten, *hermana?*" There was a platter of roasted beef on the table behind her. She slapped a thick chunk of meat in an open tortilla, bathed it in thick chunky salsa, and then wrapped it and folded the ends. "I have coffee, too."

"*Gracias.*"

Inmaculada chewed slowly, realizing she hadn't eaten since they had broken camp that morning. The meat was stringy and strong. The woman handed a tin can of coffee through the window. "You're very generous," Inmaculada said.

"We must stick together, in defense of God," the woman replied. "*Viva Cristo Rey.*"

"Christ is King," Inmaculada repeated, raising the tin can in a toast.

"Things looked very bad, very bad," the woman said. "But now"—she nodded toward the infirmary—"with the *pistolero padre*, we will beat the nonbelievers." She grinned. "We'll beat them like

157

a neighbor's child." She looked at Inmaculada's thin blouse. "You've lost your coat?"

Inmaculada shrugged. "I left quickly. I had a blanket, but we used it for the priest."

"Wait," the woman at the window said, and then she came back with a rough woven serape. "Take this."

INMACULADA WALKED A HUNDRED YARDS DOWN THE MOUNTAIN, FOUND a patch of grass beside a rushing rivulet, and sat eating the taco and drinking the coffee. After a while a few dogs came sniffing by and Inmaculada threw a stone at them and they yelped and fled. She stretched out on the soft grass, wrapped the serape around her body and was soon fast asleep.

She awakened a half-hour later with the sound of soft prayers drifting up on the night wind. She clutched the serape around her and stepped carefully down the mountain. Before a small stone shrine the mestizo priest Moreno knelt in the moonlight and spoke to God.

"Our Lady, thank you for my life," Moreno said, looking up at the weathered Virgin. "I don't know why you saved me . . ." He dropped his eyes in thought. "I am no better a priest than those other two who died on the scaffold. Certainly no better a man."

Unseen, Inmaculada stepped closer.

"I have desires of the flesh, Our Lady. I hunger for the wetness of a woman. I have great fear." Moreno looked with pain at the image of the Virgin. "I'm afraid that I would commit a sacrilege, in order to save my life. I would have on that scaffold. I would have done anything, said anything . . ." Moreno shook his head slowly. "I wish only not to disgrace myself. Only not to defile the name of God. Give me the courage, Our Lady, give me just a dusting of the courage you have bestowed so generously on the *pistolero* priest, and I will die with honor, in your just cause."

Moreno crossed himself and bowed his head. He was motionless in the moonlight before the shrine and Inmaculada held her breath as she watched him.

When the priest rose he turned and saw her. She dropped her eyes.

"How is he, the gringo?" Moreno asked. "Does he live?"

"The nurse nun, the one with the face"—Inmaculada traced a finger down her cheek—"she stays with him and prays." Inmaculada shrugged. "She says she won't let him die."

Moreno nodded. The power of prayer.

"Where is your man?"

"I left him under a tree with the dogs." Inmaculada smiled. "He was worthless." She looked frankly at Moreno. "I am going to lay my serape over there, away from the pueblo."

Moreno returned her look.

"It'll be cold over there," he said finally.

"Yes, but I treasure my privacy."

"Yes." The priest nodded.

Inmaculada turned slowly and walked away into the darkness. Moreno glanced at the shrine, then crossed himself and followed her.

⎯⎯◇⎯⎯

WHEN TOMMY BEGAN TO RISE FROM THE DEPTHS OF THE NOTHINGNESS he had been drowning in he felt an ineffable weightiness. His limbs felt leaden. His breathing was labored. His very thoughts seemed heavy. His eyelids were so ponderous he couldn't open them. He knew it was daylight—he could feel the sun on his face, the lightness behind his closed eyes. He could hear animals in the distance. In the space of a few moments chickens clucked, a dog barked, from somewhere far away a cow bellowed. He heard a man say something in a foreign language and another man shout an answer. Children played and laughed. There were the intermittently rhythmic sounds of construction, of hammering, bricks falling, mortar being mixed.

For a long time Tommy didn't know where he was. Then he remembered. He remembered Hanrahan bleeding as he lay dying in a stone Christ's snow-covered, oversized hands. He remembered the Indian woman at the border crossing, running beside the train and whispering, *"Viva Cristo Rey!"* He remembered the rotting priest up in the eaves of a desecrated church and he remembered falling from the scaffold, the pigeons fluttering on the roof across the square—one was partially white—and the red-haired Mexican watching in the crowd. He remembered taking aim on the boss guinea on the big horse and he remembered the satisfaction he felt when the bastard bounced on the haunches of his horse.

Tommy opened his eyes and a nun was seated in a chair before an open window, looking out. For a moment Tommy thought there

159

was something wrong with his eyes. The nun's features seemed blurred, inexact. Then she turned her face from profile and looked at him and he saw it was a deformity. Her eyes widened when they met his and she rose quickly.

"Father. Father." Through her smile she was fighting back tears. "How do you feel?"

Tommy stared at her a moment, then he closed his eyes and the darkness enveloped him. When he opened them again it was night and a small boy who looked vaguely familiar was sitting on the bed playing with his nickel-plated automatics. The boy said something threatening in his little melodrama and made as if he were shooting the pistols. *"Pow! Pow!"* Then someone else in the room said something and the boy looked in that direction and Tommy's eyes followed his glance. The Indian from the jail cell was sitting on a bureau, his boots hanging down. He was smoking a cheroot and Tommy felt somehow comforted by the acrid odor, and by the sight of the Indian.

"Hey, gringo," the Indian said. "You live."

Then the boy moved quickly up the bed, offering the guns to Tommy. The boy had one cloudy eye, and Tommy remembered where he'd seen him. The boy said something and then Tommy closed his eyes.

They were still closed when Tommy heard his brother, Frank, shout out in Spanish, "No. The other direction. The other way!"

Tommy opened his eyes and Frank was leaning out of the window into the late morning sun, directing some unseen workers. He wore a long black priest's cassock. He looked older. There was movement in the corner of the room and Tommy turned his head and the young nun with the scarred face was folding a sheet with a squat, plain woman. The woman noticed that Tommy was awake and stopped. The young nun looked at her, then at Tommy, then she said to Frank, "Father?"

Frank leaned back into the room. He stared a long time at Tommy. Nobody in the room moved. Then Frank said, "You're still the luckiest Irishman in the world, Thomas."

Tommy managed a weak smile. He said something, but it died faintly on his lips. The nun moved quickly to bring him a glass of water. She lifted his head and dribbled a few drops into his mouth. Tommy swallowed painfully, and the nun rested his head back on the pillow. "Didn't expect to see me here, huh, Frank?" came out as a whispered croak.

Frank stepped closer to the bed. "Some have called it a miracle," he said with dry irony.

Tommy shook his head slowly. "But you know better, huh?"

Frank stared at his brother a long time. "I know that you'd only come here if you had nowhere else to go."

Tommy swallowed again. "Bulldog's dead."

"Yeah, he had to be." Frank's face was merciless and impassive. "Am I supposed to mourn? Am I supposed to pray for his immortal soul?" Frank looked around the room then. Lourdes's eyes were flicking between the brothers.

"Sister, would you and Inmaculada go tend to the other patients?" Frank said in Spanish.

"Yes, Father." Lourdes nodded to Inmaculada, and they grabbed up the unfolded linen. As they were going through the door, Lourdes said to Tommy. "God bless you, Father."

When they were gone Frank give a small, mirthless smile. "They think you're a priest."

"I figured that when they were hanging me."

Frank examined his brother's face. "Why did you come here? What'd you do, Al Capone? Kill a cop?"

Tommy managed a defiant smile. "They're cheaper by the dozen."

⟨○⟩

QUINTANA HAD BROUGHT A CHAIR UP TO THE FLAT ROOF OF THE cantina and sat in the sun, drinking pulque and watching them rebuild the church. It looked like hot work. Down in the *placita* Moreno was directing the workers. Lourdes and Inmaculada came out of the infirmary carrying baskets of soiled bed linen. Quintana remembered that the first time he'd seen the nun she'd been washing sheets. Lourdes hurried to Moreno and spoke to him excitedly. The mestizo priest nodded as he listened to her, but Quintana could see, even from up here, that he was looking at the woman from the lean-to under the eucalyptus tree. Then Lourdes and Inmaculada walked across the plaza toward the long corridor that led to where the pueblo walls parted and the land tilted downward toward the valley far below. Just before she disappeared into the corridor Inmaculada, trailing after Lourdes, turned and looked at Moreno one more time.

Quintana reached down for the clay jug of *pulque* at his feet and poured out a small cup of the viscous, milky liquid. Priests and nuns, in his experience, were no less human than anyone else. Just because they took a vow didn't mean they could always keep it. The fires of passion, the tyrannies of the flesh—these still coursed through their warm-blooded bodies. In fact, the seduction of nuns was a pursuit Quintana took particular pleasure in, no less so because he found it so easy. A young woman who has never been pursued, never been flattered, never been touched by the hand of a gentle, experienced lover—this young woman's vows of celibacy were as easily shucked as Quintana's own uncircumcised penis. For a night or, at least, a few hours.

The Yaqui had dozed off, his sombrero pulled down over his eyes, when Moreno came out onto the roof. The priest came over and looked at him. "You'll tire yourself, watching us work like this."

Quintana grinned under his sombrero. "Some need more sleep than others." His eyes rose to meet the priest's. "Some seem to need no sleep at all."

Moreno frowned. "You're drunk."

Quintana shrugged. "That's what happens when you drink *pulque* in the sun."

Moreno turned and looked down into the *placita*.

"The gringo . . . He lives."

"*Sí*, I hope."

"No, I mean he's awake. They're bringing him out into the plaza."

Quintana got up quickly and walked to the edge of the roof. Frank was directing four men as they carried Tommy's bed out into the sun. Miguelito ran crookedly alongside.

—◁○▷—

WITHIN A QUARTER HOUR THE PUEBLO HAD COME TO A STANDSTILL, and almost everyone—even the *charros* down the mountain—had gathered in the plaza to see the gringo warrior-priest. Some had never laid eyes on him, as there had been a steady trickle of refugees and *cristeros* up the mountain in the days Tommy had lain sweating and senseless. The legend—the *miracle*—of the *pistolero* priest was sweeping across the vast emptiness of the high plains, and the true believers were coming up to join him. They shuffled in a line by the disappeared doctor's big four-poster bed and the men nodded respectfully to Tommy, and some pledged to him their unwavering allegiance and their life's blood, and some of the women, crying, reached out to touch his form under the sheet and others knelt and crossed themselves and laid flowers and treasured rosaries in the bed and hurried away, too full of awe even to look directly at him.

Frank stood by the bed and watched this spectacle with an all-too-familiar resentment, but also with a stunned, growing realization of the power Tommy's myth had seized over the devout *alteños*.

Tommy lay there, trying to keep his head from swimming, trying to understand what the hell was happening. A new mother stepped up in line and offered her three-day-old infant. "Please, *padre*. Give him your blessing."

Tommy looked at the baby without comprehension, then up at Frank.

"Please, Father," the young mother pleaded. "Give him your faith. Give him your courage."

"What the hell does she want?"

Frank shook his head. "*Señora*, Father has been very ill and—"

The young woman quickly reached out and placed Tommy's slack-wristed hand on her baby's head. "Please . . ." Her eyes filled with tears.

After a brief moment Frank etched a perfunctory cross in the air. "Father gives his blessing, in the name of the Father, the Son—"

"Thank you!" she breathed gratefully, then quickly kissed Tommy's hand and moved away, lest somehow the blessing be taken back.

Frank looked after her, thinking that her kind of devotion was the stuff wars were won with.

At that moment Lourdes and Inmaculada reentered the pueblo. When Lourdes saw what was happening her imperfect face flushed with anger and she pushed roughly through the people.

"This is wrong!" she snapped at Frank. "He needs rest. And he shouldn't be around all these people! He—"

"Mind your tone, Sister," Frank said coldly. "Don't overstep your place."

Lourdes instantly looked at the ground. "*Sí, padre*. Please forgive my insolence. But this is not healthy for him."

Then, because he knew she was right, and because it served his purposes to establish himself as the conduit and gatekeeper to Tommy's glory, Frank addressed the plaza.

"The Father is tired. He needs rest and sunshine. He will be with you all later."

There was a moment of hesitation across the *placita*. Everyone wanted their moment with the hero of Guadalajara.

"He lives among us!" Frank shouted. "He is ours. He won't go anywhere."

Slowly the crowd started to disperse. Tommy looked around the plaza and said softly, "What the hell's happening here?"

—◁○▷—

A WEEK LATER TOMMY WAS SITTING WITH QUINTANA ON A BENCH against the cantina watching Miguelito play with a litter of puppies, when six horsemen in dark suits rode into the pueblo. They dismounted before the newly constructed church, and then one of the men saw Tommy and alerted the others to his presence.

"Six wise men," Quintana said. "Jesus only had three."

The six men approached them. One was older than the others, and had a full beard streaked with gray. "Are you the *pistolero* priest?" he asked Tommy in Spanish. Tommy stared at him.

"He wants to know if you are you," Quintana said.

One of the six was a gringo. He looked at Tommy and Tommy looked back. The gringo said something to the bearded man, and then the bearded man said in English, "You don't look like the right hand of God."

Quintana grinned. "Ah, *señor*, he's the right *fist* of God."

Frank stepped out of the church door and hurried quickly across the *placita*. "*Señores*. I have been eagerly awaiting your arrival." He held out his hand to the bearded man. "You've had a long journey. Please . . ." He indicated the building next to the church, which had been requisitioned as his rectory. "I have refreshments, food . . ."

The bearded man studied Tommy a little longer, then nodded to the others. Tommy recognized the American. He was one of the miners who had boarded the train at that mountain whistle-stop. The one the others called Gunny.

"This way, gentleman." Frank nodded sternly to Miguelito. "The boy will see to your animals."

As the party walked back across the *placita*, Gunny hung back. He stood before Tommy and grinned.

"I knew you wasn't no greaser."

Tommy leaned back against the cantina wall and stretched out his legs. He was still weak, but feeling stronger every day.

"On the train, remember? I asked you on the train if you was American, and you—"

"I remember you," Tommy said flatly.

Gunny's grinned widened. "But I didn't figure you for a priest. Not until they dragged you down the street in Gudala*horror*." He glanced at Quintana. "These fucking greasers, they're crazier than bedbugs, ain't they?"

Quintana was lighting a cheroot. He squinted coldly up at Gunny through the smoke.

Gunny held out his hand to Tommy. "John T. Gundersthaal. But everybody just calls me Gunny." Tommy ignored the hand until Gunny pulled it back. "Damn, you caused a lot of trouble back there."

"I was in the city, too," Quintana said. "Perhaps you remember me. Aureliano Quintana. But everyone just calls me greaser."

"Yeah, yeah," Gunny said to the Yaqui. "You was there, too. All the whores was crying because you were gonna hang."

Tommy chuckled then and Quintana smiled with him. "And did they celebrate when we escaped?" the Indian asked Gunny.

"The whole damn town celebrated. Except Terrazas and his *constitucionalistas*. They was madder than hell. They musta shot fifty people, tryin' to get somebody to tell 'em where you went. But you all disappeared like ghosts."

Quintana tapped some ash from his cigarillo. "Like angels, gringo. We flew away like angels."

Gunny inspected Tommy's face closely. "I know you from somewhere."

Tommy looked down. "You said yourself, you know me from the train."

"No . . . before that. You sure you ain't never been in New York?"

Tommy crossed his legs casually. "Tell me, Gunny. What's a miner doing up here? You figuring to find gold on this mountain?"

"No," Quintana said, "he's looking to mine blood."

Gunny frowned. Tommy turned to Quintana for an explanation.

"*Oye cómo va*," Quintana began, "Gunny here has government permits to ship mining equipment down from Texas. Only he don't put picks and shovels in the crates, he puts U.S. Army carbines, machine guns, maybe even some light artillery, eh, Gunny?" Gunny was glaring at him. "The permits get him past the American embargo, the *mordida* gets him over the border, and once he gets the guns down here to Jalisco, or over Guanajuato or Morelos . . . well, he don't have to look for the gold. The Mexicans just bring it to him."

"Don't they shoot you for that kind of thing down here?"

Quintana nodded. "In a heartbeat."

Tommy turned back to Gunny. "Sounds dangerous to me, Gunny. Sounds like bootlegging, only the product kills you quicker."

Gunny gave a tight smile as he wagged a finger at Quintana. "You one smart Indian. How'd you get so smart?"

"It's been done before. I done it myself."

Gunny let out a cynical little huff. "Never met a greaser who didn't ride with Zapata or run guns for Villa."

"Ah, Gunny . . . we are a clannish people."

Gunny's eyes traveled between the two of them. He had ridden into town in a group of powerful men and now these two were mocking him, challenging him, almost.

"I'll see you later. *Father.*"

He turned and strode quickly across the *placita* and toward the rectory where Moreno was holding open the door, waiting for him.

"He shows up in my life one more time," Tommy said softly, "and I'm going to have to kill him."

"We'll draw straws."

Gunny entered the rectory door and then turned back and looked across at them before he closed it.

"He's bad luck."

"*Sí, malo suerte.*"

"What?"

"*Malo suerte.* Bad luck." Quintana set the cheroot between his teeth and strode over to where the puppies played by the fountain. He picked one up by the scruff of its neck and it yelped. "*Cachorro.*"

"What?"

"*Cachorro.* 'Puppy.' " He set down the pup and pointed to the fountain. "*Agua.*"

"What the fuck are you doing?"

Quintana splashed the water. "*Agua. Este es agua.*"

Tommy watched as the Indian moved around the fountain to where Miguelito was watering the six horses. "*Caballos.*"

"I don't need to know that. I ain't hanging around here that long."

Quintana walked down the line of horses, touching each one as he named its color. *"Bayo, bayo, negro . . ."*

"I told you, I'm getting out of here."

Quintana paused and moved back toward him. "Yeah? Where you going?"

They looked at each other a long moment.

"I don't know why you're here, amigo. I don't know what sent you here, or what you're running from . . . But I do know you have no place to go." He pulled from its holster the big horse pistol he'd bought from another *cristero*. *"Pistola."* He spun the cylinder. *"Pistola."*

Tommy leaned back against the cantina wall and said. *"Pistola."*

—<O>—

LOURDES POURED COFFEE FOR THE MEN AROUND THE BIG ROSEWOOD table. Inmaculada and Manuela cleared away the plates. Gunny entered the room and took an empty chair.

"I know my Catholics in America, Don Enrique," Frank was saying to the bearded man. "They won't desert their Mexican brothers in their time of crisis."

The bearded man nodded thanks to Lourdes and sipped his coffee. He smiled up at Lourdes. "I was with your father in León just four days ago. He is very concerned about you. He wants you to come home."

"I'm where God wants me to be, uncle." She poured more cream into the cup, remembering how light he liked it. "How is he? How is Mother?"

The bearded man shrugged. "They're very concerned. After what happened at the convent . . ." He reached up and lovingly touched Lourdes's unblemished right cheek. "They were already getting ready for a Requiem."

"Father Francisco"—she nodded at Frank—"if he hadn't happened by . . ."

One of the dark-suited Mexicans had been listening to Frank with impatience. "It has been my experience that gringos don't consider us Catholic brothers at all. But more like, like"—he waved his hand—"like the animals we have blessed on Holy Saturday."

There was a murmur of agreement around the table.

"That's not the case, *señor*," Frank objected.

"I have never understood," said another, "how a man who speaks English can be a true Catholic." He looked around the table for confirmation of his insight. "Doesn't it seem very strange— *yanqui católicos?*"

Moreno, overcoming his innate shyness around such educated men, offered, "But where else can we turn? If the North Americans wish to help—"

"I become very suspicious whenever a gringo says he wishes to help a Mexican." The man was thin and wore a monocle. "Remember Huerta? Remember Madero?"

"Exactly. They love to sit up there and watch us slaughter each other."

"Then they can come in and pick at our corpses like condors."

"Just as they've always done."

"Señores," Frank pleaded, "the United States didn't start this war."

"No, the communists did!"

"The Bolsheviks."

The bearded man held up his hand and the table quieted. "Father Coyne, we were very impressed by the number of men we saw coming up the mountain. There must be two hundred, two hundred and fifty—"

"Over three hundred," Frank said proudly. "And three or four more ride in every day."

"They come for Father Tomás," Moreno said eagerly, then quieted when Frank shot him a quick look.

"For the *pistolero padre?*" Don Enrique said. "We've heard the stories of what happened in Guadalajara. Are they true?"

Lourdes circled the table, refilling the coffee cups. She could feel the gringo's blue eyes on her. Probing her body. Rudely examining her twisted face.

"I was there," Moreno said, avoiding Frank's glare. "They're true."

Lourdes had never been ashamed of her disfigurement—it was the way God had made her; it was the Virgin's tear streak down her face. Except once, when Tommy came out of his unconsciousness, when he first looked up at her. She saw his eyes trace over the slur of features on the left side of her face and she'd felt her body burn with shame and she'd quickly turned to show him the other side. To show him her beauty.

"Sister," one of the city horsemen said, and Lourdes came out of her reverie to see she'd overfilled his cup. The coffee was sloshing over into the saucer.

"Excuse me, *señor*," Lourdes murmured, ashamed of her thoughts. "I'll get you another."

"You have a small army," Don Enrique was saying. "But how long can you keep them?"

"They'll stay," Frank said. "They're true believers, and they've come to fight, and they—"

"What happens the first time you lead them into battle and the *federales* cut them down with machine guns? Or at the threshold of victory they run out of ammunition?"

Frank was silent.

"How long will they stay when you can't feed them anymore?"

Victoriano Rojas, at the table, kept his gaze steady. It was his beef that was feeding the pueblo's *cristeros*. He couldn't afford to do it forever.

"Their faith in God may have brought them here," Don Enrique pointed a sugar spoon at Frank, "but their faith in you to lead them, to provide for them—that will keep them."

Frank was humiliated by the older man's reprimand, but he kept his face impassive. "We were expecting help from the Catholic League. We were expecting help from you."

Don Enrique sat back in his chair and stirred his coffee with the tiny silver spoon. "Up here in the mountains you are cut off from what's happening down in the cities. Things are not going well."

"We have no support? That doesn't sound like the Mexican people I know."

"Oh, we have support. Here in Jalisco, in Guanajuato, Colima, everywhere. In the Federal District right under the President's nose. But the government controls the roads, the rail lines, the ports. The President's treasury prints the money. The President's agents control the borders. The President's spies watch the people . . ." Don Enrique waved his hand in a dismissive gesture.

"And the people are tired of war. Fifteen years of revolution has left them exhausted," said a studious-looking young Catholic intellectual, who would have been a boy in 1910 when the miner strikes began the revolt against Porfirio Díaz. "Calles knew exactly when to move against the Church."

Frank began to be uneasy. "What about international outrage? Doesn't the world know what's happening here?"

"The government denies everything." Don Enrique looked around the table before he spoke again. "Calles says the Bishop closed the churches in order to spark rebellion. They claim we're counterrevolutionaries."

"Precisely," said a man at the end of the table, a light-skinned patrician.

"Surely the Vatican will aid us."

"Rome is afraid of involving itself in Mexican politics. The Holy See thinks we're barbarous and unreliable."

"They've convinced the Pope to adopt a noninterventionist position."

"And Washington wants nothing to do with us. They're too afraid of the Catholics in their own country."

Lourdes and Inmaculada reentered the dining room carrying trays of flan. Lourdes glanced at Frank and saw the dismay hidden behind his mask and knew the proceedings were not going well. She traded quick looks with the mestizo priest.

"We are patriots, willing to fight and die for the true faith." Frank's voice began to rise. "Willing to sacrifice everything for our Catholic belief. I can't believe you're going to leave us out here to wither. I can't believe you don't have use for my *cristero* army!"

Don Enrique looked around the table. "Father, you have a ragtag battalion of undisciplined irregulars. Many of whom have never been out of these mountains. They're untrained, and worse—poorly armed." He paused. "We *will* put them to use. Night raids on small *federal* garrisons. The kidnapping and execution of *callista* officials up here in—"

"That's guerrilla terrorism!" Frank snapped. "I want to take my people down into their heartland. Into Guadalajara! I want to take them—"

"Father," Don Enrique said, as if he were talking to a child. "You will do as the League orders you to do. Without coordination, without central leadership, we have no hope of winning this war."

"Without audacity we have no hope! Without courage!"

The room was silent. Frank had challenged the older man's manhood, his *machismo*. And this from a foreigner, his collar notwithstanding.

But Don Enrique Hidalgo was a seasoned survivor of a score of battles, insurrections, mutinies and revolts. He had no need to prove himself yet again, and to a soft American Jesuit.

"First we'll properly arm ourselves," Don Enrique went on, as if Frank hadn't even spoken. "This man," he nodded at Gunny, "has access to modern U.S. Army rifles and automatic weapons, grenades, everything we need. He can deliver them right here to Jalisco. To the very edge of Los Altos. But they will cost."

Frank started to say something and the bearded Don Enrique quickly held up his hand. His visage was stern. He'd come up to Sagrado Corazón to give orders, not hear demands. "Whatever weapons your men receive, you will have to pay for them out of your own area's donations. This is how it will be everywhere, not just here." He lowered his hand. "I understand that this was not your parish. That you were a professor in the city. But *Señor* Rojas— you are Rojas?" Rojas nodded. "Rojas will accompany you around the countryside. *Alteños* are the most devoted Catholics in Mexico, so you should be very successful in your efforts."

"Devotion is one thing," Rojas said dryly. "Gold is another."

◄○►

THE NEXT MORNING FRANK AND MORENO CLIMBED INTO THE SURREY pulled by the matching white geldings and with Rojas and his three sons on horseback alongside they rode out of the pueblo and down the mountain.

Within minutes of Frank's departure a sense of release seemed to settle down upon the pueblo and there was a general relaxing, like the loosening of a fat man's belt. Battle-scarred men began to laugh and kick around a lifeless old ball. Women chattered like June birds over their chores, and indeed the exceptionally warm sun, together with the lack of authority, was like a false spring come to the mountaintop.

Quintana made a dummy of straw and a *federal* uniform jacket and he led Tommy—Miguelito always closely following—around the base of the pueblo wall to the rock-strewn back side of the mountain. There the Yaqui set the dummy on a stake and Tommy unwrapped his automatic .45s and together they practiced their shooting. Miguelito reeled around and giggled with delight every time Tommy fired off a rapid succession of pinpoint-accurate rounds. After a while they traded weapons and Quintana fired the automatics and Tommy shot off the Indian's big horse pistol and by the third reload Tommy could make the dummy dance with every roar of the massive revolver. When the scarecrowish flour-sack head exploded with a burst of grain there was a thunderous outburst of applause from behind them and they turned and looked up to see the back wall of the pueblo lined with the *pueblerinos,* watching from rooftops and the top of the wall as their warrior-priest displayed his prowess. Quintana grinned and Tommy walked away.

That night one of the leatherworkers in the pueblo presented Tommy with a hand-tooled gun belt and someone else gifted him with a big cavalry pistol much like Quintana's, and they draped belts of ammunition across his chest, his 45s in their familiar shoulder holsters, and he was so laden with iron he walked stiffly in his priestly skirt and the people laughed and slapped him on his back. Miguelito had adorned himself in the bullet-holed *federal* jacket and he lurched around the *placita* clutching at his chest as if he were being shot, shouting, "No more, *Padre Pistolero!* Don't shoot me again!" And the townspeople howled with laughter and felt confident their *Virgen* and their patron priest would protect them.

The next day, over Lourdes's strenuous objections, Tommy Gun Coyne rode a horse for the second time in his life—the first being when he galloped out of Guadalajara on Salazar's big red stallion, clutching Quintana's back. This time the mount was a gentle old mare and Tommy clung to the saddle, trying desperately not to show his terror as the swaybacked old nag carefully picked her way along the mountainside, and the Yaqui thought this was the funniest thing he'd ever seen, funnier even than the toothless old man in Matamoros who could collapse his face like an accordion.

"Be careful of your injury, Father Tomás!" Lourdes called out in genuine concern. And Tommy saw his opportunity to extricate himself with honor and shouted out to Quintana, "Get me off this damn thing!" And the Yaqui slapped his knees and guffawed and Tommy yanked out one of his .45s and held it to the mare's hammerhead.

"Goddamnit, get me off this thing or I'll blow its fucking head off!"

Quintana rolled in the dust and held his stomach and even Lourdes had to cover her mouth to hide her laughter.

THAT NIGHT THE *PLACITA* WAS FESTIVE AND ALIVE. GUITARISTS AND trumpeters played, and someone found the remnants of last year's Independence Day fireworks. The pueblo cheered as a rocket exploded in the night sky.

Tommy and Quintana strolled through the *pueblerinos,* and they were offered drinks of *pulque* and tequila, meats wrapped in tortillas, light pastries dusted in sugar. Men grinned as Tommy neared and nodded a respectful greeting. The women were more forward.

They pushed close and crossed themselves, or reached out to simply brush their fingers against Tommy's cassock. One young woman in a brocade jacket smiled warmly at him, then at the Indian. Her eyes were bright and piercing.

When they had crossed the *placita* Quintana turned and looked back at the milling, overcrowded plaza.

"I have to see about something."

Tommy nodded. "Yeah, I saw that something, too."

Quintana gave Tommy a strange smile. "Gringo, it's not like *I* have taken the vows."

Tommy shook his head. "Fucking greaseball."

Quintana sauntered away into the crowd, his back straight and his head held high with Mexican haughtiness. Tommy sat on the dusty steps of the infirmary and Miguelito hurried to sit beside him. Tommy looked down at the little urchin, so like the boys he'd seen by the hordes every day on the streets of New York.

"You think I forgot about you throwing those rocks at me—well, I haven't."

Miguelito didn't understand the words. He only knew Tommy was paying attention to him.

"I want to see you kill somebody," Miguelito said excitedly.

"You little shit." Tommy shook a finger at him. "If I'd had a clean shot at you that morning when I was up on that church—"

"Padre, when I grow up I want to be a priest just like you."

They carried on the conversation like this, neither of them knowing what the other was saying.

"A priest with a *pistola!*" Miguelito said eagerly.

"That's real brave, throwing rocks at men on their way to the executioner."

"Will you teach me how to shoot just like you, *padre*, please?"

Tommy saw the boy looking at the big .45 revolver on his hip, the one the townspeople had given him. Tommy pulled the gun from the worked-leather holster. "You like this, huh?"

Tommy spun the chamber on the long-barreled weapon. "The Father, the Son and the Holy Ghost." He tapped the cylinder. "And Matthew, Mark and Luke's in here, too, in case the Trinity don't stop 'em."

"Teach me to kill just like you did in the plaza in Guadalajara."

"You want to be a gangster, huh?"

Miguelito nodded, thinking Tommy was going to teach him to shoot.

"Well, any other place I would say it was a bad line of work,

173

but in this crazy fucking place seems like being a *priest* is the worst thing you can do. It'll get you killed quicker than anything."

"I want to be a *cristero pistolero* priest and kill *federales* like you do and stack them in the *placita* and—"

The door opened behind them and light spilled out. Lourdes looked down at them.

"Father." Her English was painted with a strange mélange of Spanish and Irish overtones, the Celtic picked up from the murdered Mother Superior. "May I get you something to drink?"

"Stay away from him, you black sow!" Miguelito hissed with malevolence. "You just want to fuck him!"

"You little bastard!" Lourdes hissed back in Spanish as she grabbed for his arm. "I've had enough of your blasphemy!" But the kid was quicker and jumped crookedly just out of her reach.

"Sister Vagina! Sister Vagina!" he taunted in a singsong, and then one of the *cristero* men in the *placita* cuffed him across the back of his head, saying, "Watch your mouth, you little *agrarista!*" Miguelito seemed shocked and pained, and rubbed his head a moment then shouted, "You ugly black whore! You just want his big dick in you!" and ran away into the crowd.

"What did he say?" Tommy asked.

Lourdes wouldn't meet Tommy's eyes. "He's a vulgar little heathen. I'm afraid his sudden conversion to our cause has less to do with Jesus than with you—and your guns."

Tommy shook his head. "This place is a madhouse. Shouldn't that kid be in school or something?"

"Actually, it was the schools that started this war."

Tommy looked up at her. "I don't under—"

"Article Three of the Constitution stipulates there will be no parochial schools. That's why the Bishop called the strike."

"The *Bishop* called a strike . . . This country is crazy."

Lourdes hesitated a moment, then she held the skirt of her habit and sat down beside him. More than a few eyes in the *placita* noticed this.

"We're not crazy, Father Tomás. We're Mexican."

"What the hell is that supposed to mean? Where I come from there's a whole lotta killing, but priests ain't number one on the list."

Lourdes smoothed her habit in a matronly gesture. "It's not only about the schools, it's about the land, the future of the country— and the past. In Mexico it's always about the past."

"They've killed priests here before?"

"Yes, they have. It's like an epidemic that breaks out every other

174

generation." The *placita* cheered as another firework rocket flared up and exploded over the pueblo. The colors seemed to reflect in the harsh whiteness of the coif framing Lourdes's face. Tommy looked again at the misshapen left side. The deformity was heightened by the light and shadows of the fireworks. "We are a nation born of rape; nurtured by vengeance . . . We're like a family with dark secrets. No one speaks of them, but everyone hates because of them."

"But priests—"

"They think the Church is the enemy, because we're always asked to come in and clean up afterwards. We have to console the people and convince them their blood and tears and sacrifice have a heavenly purpose." She looked out at the plaza. "The army doesn't keep order in Mexico, we do. That's what the *callistas* don't understand. And that's why the people come to hate us so."

Tommy examined her. "You almost sound like you belong on the other side, whatever side that is."

Lourdes thought a moment. "Jesus died for our sins, but sometimes, in Mexico, to be poor is a sin. One there is no redemption for."

"Then this whole thing is over money?"

Lourdes didn't answer him.

"I understand that . . . Fighting over money, that's something I know."

She asked him then, "Father Frank—he's your brother, isn't he?" When he didn't answer she said, "It can't be denied. Your faces reveal it."

Tommy nodded.

Lourdes smiled. "I knew it." Then, "You have other brothers and sisters?"

"Not that I know of."

At first she didn't understand, then comprehension crept over her face like a blush. "Father! You're making a joke! Your parents must be very proud to have two sons in the priesthood."

Tommy remembered Bulldog being chewed up by Hanrahan's bullets in the top floor of Gould's Department Store.

"Yeah . . ."

They had cleared one section of the *placita* and several couples had started to dance, circling around each other with grace and energy. Quintana was whirling with the woman in the brocade jacket. He was laughing.

"I don't know your name, Sister."

She looked away quickly. "Lourdes. Lourdes Hidalgo."

"Sister Lourdes," Tommy said simply. "So, how long have you been a nun, Sister Lourdes?"

"I took my final vows last fall, just before the troubles started." She looked back. "Until then I wasn't sure."

"But now you are?"

She smiled. "Yes . . . especially now."

"Why especially now?"

"Because now I know where I'm needed. Now I know what God wants me to do."

Tommy studied her a moment. "How old are you?"

"Eighteen."

"And at that age you know what the whole rest of your life should be?"

"I have seen things, Father . . . I have witnessed the devil at work." *And you killed him,* she thought to herself.

"Did you think you wouldn't get a husband because of—" Tommy suddenly silenced himself. Her hand started up toward her face, but she managed to stop it. "I have a husband," she said. "*Jesus Cristo,* and his Holy Church. You should understand that, Father."

"Yes . . . I didn't mean any disrespect, Sister."

"I know." She stood up. "I have to check on my patients." She started back into the infirmary. "Father, I didn't get you anything to drink."

He grinned. "You got any bootleg bourbon?"

"I don't think—"

"I was just kidding, Sister."

" 'Kidding'?"

"Joking . . ." He looked up at her. "I don't need anything."

She nodded and went through the door into the infirmary. Tommy looked back at the swirling dancers. Quintana and the girl in the brocade jacket had disappeared.

Then Tommy saw a form from the side of his eye and Miguelito slunk around the corner of the building. Tommy looked at the boy a moment, then patted the steps. "C'mon, siddown, kid. I'll tell you all about gangstering."

Miguelito grinned and limped over.

—◇—

THE NEXT AFTERNOON FRANK AND HIS GROUP RETURNED TO THE MOUN-tain. Frank was even more grim-faced than when he'd set out. He jumped down from the surrey and strode toward the church. He paused by the door and looked at Tommy, who was filing down the hammer on the big revolver.

"Be ready to go in the morning."

Tommy put down the pistol. "Go where?"

Frank's eyes flared. "Wherever the hell I say." Then he quickly passed into the infirmary.

Moreno explained it to Quintana, and Quintana in turn translated it to Tommy. Things had not gone well. The *hacendados*—the rich ranchers with their immense estates, who were all at least nominally Catholic and who would most benefit from the defense and preservation of the ancient church-rooted landowners' class system—had been impassive to Frank's impassioned pleas for contributions. These wealthy *alteños*—with their Parisian chandeliers, their English bone china, their Spanish governesses and Arabian stallions—had survived the most turbulent period of Mexico's history with their lifestyles intact, and they had survived by not aligning themselves with hungry young warlords and their grandiose ambitions. This Jesuit gringo priest was only another in a long parade of such men who had ridden up to their doors asking for some of their gold. And this one hadn't come with a loot-hungry army.

They had fed Frank and Moreno. They had brought their grandchildren and great-grandchildren to be confirmed and baptized. They had knelt and parodied the sacrament of Confession. They had celebrated Mass and taken Communion. And then they had patiently explained to Frank that the pittance they were tithing to him—though seemingly meager—was absolutely all they could spare in these tumultuous times.

And finally they had asked about this *pistolero padre* they had been hearing about. Did he really exist?

—◇—

THE DAY WAS SUN-FILLED AND COLD, AND TOMMY SAT BESIDE HIS brother in the surrey. Quintana and the Rojases rode their horses. Miguelito sat in the back, grinning broadly. He had screamed and refused to be left behind.

The brothers rode in silence for most of the morning, Tommy dozing in the gentle rhythmic sway of the surrey. The land was bleak and empty and Rojas rode point, leading them along an ancient etching of a path across the emptiness. They passed occasional *campesinos* in the windy nothingness, simple peasants who dropped to their knees in deference when they saw the priests. At one place, which seemed a crossroads in the middle of nowhere, a meaningless junction in the wilderness, a shrine had been overturned and smashed, and in its stead a human skull had been set on the crude stone pedestal. Quintana dismounted and stared at the skull with a strange smile.

"This is Terrazas's work. I hear he's made a vow to do this throughout Jalisco."

"Who's Terrazas?" Tommy asked.

"The one in the city who was going to hang us, *mi amigo.*"

"He's our enemy," Frank said. "And God's."

Quintana smashed the skull with his big pistol.

"I shoulda got him, too," Tommy said.

Frank nodded. "Yes, you should have."

They rode on. When Miguelito started to snore, curled up behind them, Frank asked, "What happened?"

"In New York?"

"Yes, in New York. The last time I saw you, you were the prince of the underworld. Hell's Kitchen's heir apparent."

It was the first time the brothers had spoken like this. Somehow the solitude, the vastness of the land, the sway of the surrey, brought them together—if only for now. Tommy shook his head. "All hell broke loose. . . . They killed everybody, the dagos . . . And the cops killed Da . . ."

"How'd you get away?"

"This priest at Sacred Heart, remember Sacred Heart—?"

Frank nodded. "I remember—" He thought of his mother and old Father Skelley behind the closed rectory door. "John O'Rourke, he's the pastor there now. I wrote him a few years ago."

"Right." Tommy thought of the strange Mexican stamps on the envelope. "Well, O'Rourke gave me sanctuary in the church. He wouldn't let 'em in. The Mayor come down, the Police Commissioner, didn't matter to O'Rourke."

"And in thanks you stole his clothes, his identity, and sneaked out the back."

Tommy turned to look at his brother. "Something like that." Then he said, "Ma's still alive. She was there."

Frank, holding the reins, said, "Peggy might have been there, but she's never been alive."

Tommy shook his head. "You were her favorite. She hates me."

178

Then, "She was talking about you like you were the Pope or something. Does she know what's happening down here?"

"I haven't written her since I went off to St. Bernard's."

"That was thirteen years ago."

Frank didn't answer.

"She always talked like you two kept in touch every—"

"She wrote me. I just didn't answer her."

"Never?"

"I didn't even open them."

"You just threw them away?"

"Burned them. I mean, what could have been in them that I wanted to know?"

They rode for a moment in silence. "I know you didn't give a damn about me and the Bulldog . . . But Ma—"

"She's a drunk and a whore. The world'll be better off when she's gone."

"That's our mother you're talkin' about."

Frank laughed. It was such an unusual occurrence that Quintana turned in the saddle to watch. After a moment, Tommy had to smile. Frank looked at him. "I can't believe you're here . . . It's very strange."

"Yes, it is."

"I thought I'd never see you again."

"No, you never *wanted* to see me again."

After a moment Frank said, "I certainly never thought I'd see you in a priest's cassock."

"See, all that time you was being good, I was being bad, and we wind up in the same place."

One of the white geldings arched its neck and bit at the other, for no apparent reason.

"You don't have any idea what you've landed yourself into, do you?"

Tommy thought about what Lourdes had said. "It's about the land, right? And the schools?"

"Where'd you hear that?"

"From—from Lourdes."

"*Sister* Lourdes," Frank reprimanded.

"Yes . . . Sister Lourdes."

The off gelding shook its head and Frank slapped the reins to remind it what it was about.

"What's happening in this country is like a primer on what's going to happen all over the world."

Tommy sat, waiting.

"What's the use," Frank said. "You don't understand anything east of Broadway."

"Goddamnit! Gimme a chance!"

Frank looked at him. "Okay. There was a revolution in a place called Russia—did you know that?"

"Yeah . . . yeah, I knew that."

"Well, it unleashed on the world unholy ideas. Ideas that are inimical to Christian thought and civilization. This conflict is a direct result—"

"But I thought they'd hung priests here before."

"Do you want to listen, or do you want to parrot what a teenage girl told you?"

"Well, it's her country, ain't it?"

A hawk circled in the dazzlingly blue sky above.

"These people—" Frank said finally, "these people are pawns in an international conspiracy, and they have no idea—" He shook his head. "And up here in Los Altos it's the best of them. In other states they're little better than serfs. They're superstitious, idolatrous, childish—"

"If you don't like them, why are you here?"

The hawk swooped in the distance and then rose with a scream and a rabbit.

Frank finally said, "What you're seeing here is a breakdown in the social order. The inmates have wrested control of the asylum." He frowned. "In one city I heard they've turned the churches into brothels. The so-called general expropriated all the artwork and set it up in his new commandeered mansion. All that he didn't sell to European dealers." His face showed his contempt. "And they call that sharing the wealth."

"From what I've seen, there ain't no wealth. Just a lot of dust."

—◄○►—

THEY TRAVELED UNTIL IT WAS TOO DARK TO SEE, THEN THEY SLEPT ON blankets on the ground. Just before midday the next day they rode into the adobe-walled hacienda of Adolfo Gómez. The compound was large and sprawling, almost a village unto itself. Pueblo Gómez. There were a couple of cars parked in the stone-hard dirt yard, and

Tommy, seeing them, realized how out of touch he'd been up on the mountain. It was like coming back from another century.

Don Adolfo stood on a pulpitlike tower on the roof and watched them approach. He was a thin, tall man with classic Castilian features—pale skin and a large scythe-blade nose

"Don Adolfo," Rojas called up to him. "If Mohammed won't go to the mountain"—he indicated the two priests—"we bring the mountain to Mohammed."

Gómez looked down at them from on high. His disapproving black eyes traveled slowly over Frank, lingered on Tommy, then rested on Quintana.

"The Yaqui stays outside," Gómez said finally.

As they dismounted Tommy turned to Quintana. "What's the deal?"

The Indian jumped from his saddle and led the big red bay over to the well fountain. "It's nothing. I'm staying out here with the boy."

"Why?"

"Go inside, Tomás," Quintana said. "You have business."

Tommy hesitated, and then Frank, entering the big house, turned to give him a look. "Stay out here with Quintana," Tommy said to Miguelito. "And don't get into any trouble."

Tommy followed his brother and the Rojas men through the big, brass hinged door. Miguelito, stricken to be separated from Tommy, looked around with alarm.

"You heard what he said," Quintana warned.

—◄〇►—

INSIDE THE HOUSE IT WAS ALL DARK, POLISHED WIDE-PLANK WOOD floors, overstuffed and ornate furniture, massive rococo gilt frames around pale Rubenesque European fantasies. The thick velvet curtains were drawn tightly—as if trying to keep out all Mexico—and the massive house was dim and cool. Adolfo Gómez's heels came down the curling narrow stairs with slow, authoritarian footfalls.

"Don Victoriano," he intoned, ignoring Frank and Tommy. "How is your family?"

Rojas indicated his three sons, who had entered behind him and were lined up against the wall, their hats in their hands.

"All healthy. And in these troubled times that's a blessing from God."

Gómez's family—wife, mother, brothers, sisters, in-laws, daughters, nephews, and nieces—were waiting in the parlor, arrayed in their best clothes. The men were somberly suited. The women wore their best lace, their necks craned stiffly in the high collars.

"How goes it out your way?" Gómez inquired, as his insolent eyes traversed between Frank and Tommy. There was a hint of derisive humor as they lingered on Tommy's weaponry.

"Don Adolfo, we are poised and ready to—" Frank began, but Gómez interrupted him, speaking to Rojas.

"Did you see any *agraristas* on the road?"

Frank tightened his lips in anger.

"None, Don Adolfo. They're terrified of Father Tomás."

Gómez stared impolitely at Tommy. "Really?"

Tommy stared back.

"Yes. Because of him the government stays out of the lean lands. They keep to the cities."

Señora Gómez moved forward then, and whispered something to her husband. Don Adolfo nodded, then said to Rojas, "We wish to celebrate Mass."

"That's why we've come," Frank said, determined to have the grandee address him directly. "To bring you Christ."

Gómez glared. "I would prefer not to have Him brought by a gringo."

Frank smiled. "Don Adolfo . . . I am Mexican."

Gómez gave a short, contemptuous laugh. Then he nodded at Tommy. "And him? He's Mexican, too?"

—◇—

ADOLFO GÓMEZ LED THEM THROUGH A LOCKED LATTICEWORK DOOR, down a narrow stairway, then he and his nephews pushed aside a false-front pantry that slid smoothly on wooden rollers and in the basement behind the false front was a full chapel, with seven rows of pews, an altar, even a short communion rail. There were more paintings of the style upstairs—depicting a very European Christ and Madonna.

Frank looked around in appreciation. "This is incredible, Don Adolfo."

Gómez nodded. "I am a cautious man. I trust no one but myself."

"And God?"

"Of course . . ."

Gómez pointed a finger at Frank. "You and the other priest will say Mass in here for my family. I will not allow religious services anywhere else on my land."

"But your people—"

"My people are greedy, opportunistic slackers who would like nothing better than to betray me to General Terrazas. If I hear of you priesting anywhere but in this room I'll have you hunted down and shot."

Frank stared hard at Gómez. "Someday this will all be over. And the Bishop will be interested to hear—"

"If you're about to threaten me, gringo, I would think better of it."

Frank held his words behind clenched teeth.

Gómez nodded to his family and they began to arrange themselves throughout the cramped pews. Frank said softly to Tommy, "Take off those guns. You're going to assist me."

Tommy was stricken. "Wait a minute, Frank. I can't do that."

"They want a show, we'll give them one. In fact, leave the guns on."

"Look, wearing this monkey suit is one thing. But it'd be wrong to—"

"I'm not going to argue with you," Frank hissed. "Just do what I tell you to do."

Frank opened his priest's bag—like the one Tommy had stolen from O'Rourke—and pulled out a pair of folded chasubles. He handed one to Tommy.

"You were an altar boy."

"For a week."

"It'll come back to you."

While Frank heard whispered confessions in a corner of the chapel, Tommy slipped the chasuble over his head and settled it around his gun butts. Don Adolfo watched him and snickered.

—◁○▷—

A YOUNG GIRL—IN DARK-SKINNED BLOSSOM—KEPT WALKING BACK and forth across Quintana's line of vision, carrying water from the well, bringing a horse bucket of oats for the red stallion, hanging peppers to dry in the shelter of the overhanging eaves. Quintana pretended not to look at her.

"Hey, Quintana?" Miguelito finally asked. "Do you know that bitch?"

The Yaqui was walking around the cars, inspecting them. "Where'd you learn to talk like that? Someday someone's going to kill you for your mouth."

Miguelito grinned. "Father Tomás will protect me."

"Ah," Quintana said with a wag of his head. "Maybe . . . but maybe he won't always be around when you need him."

A mechanic was leaning over the fender of the car, adjusting the carburetor.

"It would be better simply to watch your mouth. Hey, *hombre*," he said to the mechanic, "what kind of automobile is this?"

The mechanic took his time coming out from under the hood. He looked Quintana up and down. "Fuck you, Yaqui."

Quintana stared at the mechanic a moment, then said to the boy, "You see what I mean?"

"I OFFER THIS MASS FOR THE BUTCHERED MARTYRS OF GUADALAJARA," Frank was saying in Spanish to the assembled Gómez family. "May their blood and their sacrifice not have been in vain."

Tommy behind him whispered urgently. "I can't do this! I don't know any friggin' Latin!"

Frank turned to Tommy. "Just say what I tell you to say—"

"No! I can't—"

"Just repeat what I tell you!"

"I said I can't—"

"Just mumble!"

Before Tommy could refuse again Frank turned to the altar and said, *"In Nomine Patris, et Filii, et Spiritus Sancti." In the name of the Father, and of the Son, and of the Holy Ghost.* The Mass had begun. *"Introibo ad altare Dei." I will go to the altar of God.* Then from the side of his mouth he hissed, *"Ad Deum, qui laetificat juventutem meam." To God who is the source of my joy.*

Tommy hesitated and Frank shot him a hard look.

"Ad de—deum . . ."

"—qui laetificat—"
"—qui laetificat—"
Tommy fumbled over every syllable, but he didn't stop.

—◄○►—

QUINTANA LED MIGUELITO OVER TO A PLACE OUT OF THE SUN, UNDER THE overhang of the leathersmith's workshop.

"We'll sit down here. We'll stay over here."

"What's the matter?"

"Just sit down."

The mechanic left the two motor cars and walked over to where a group of *charros* were leaning against a wall. He said something to the men as he looked back at Quintana. The *charros* laughed.

"Motherfuckers," Quintana said softly.

Miguelito shaded his face and stared over at the *charros*. "Are you going to shoot them?"

"Look, just shut up, okay?"

"Why don't they like you, Quintana?"

"They don't like Yaquis, maybe . . ."

"Why?"

"They think they're better than I am. Look, Tomás told us to behave ourselves, and that's what we're going to do."

—◄○►—

"I WILL TAKE THE BREAD OF HEAVEN AND WILL CALL UPON THE NAME of the Lord."

Tommy, standing beside Frank, began to feel queasy.

Frank struck his breast in a rhythmic motion as he said, "Lord, I am not worthy that Thou should enter under my roof; but only say the word, and my soul shall be healed."

Frank broke a piece off the Communion wafer and slipped it between his lips.

"May the body of Our Lord Jesus Christ keep my soul unto life everlasting."

Frank reached into the ciborium and broke off another piece and held it out before Tommy's mouth. Tommy tightened his lips and glared at Frank. Frank glared back, his eyes indicating the watching Mexicans. Tommy slowly parted his lips and Frank slipped in the wafer.

Frank turned back to the altar and picked up the gold chalice, saying, "With high praises will I call upon the Lord, and I shall be saved from mine enemies."

Frank drank from the chalice. He patted the wine on his lips with his long narrow stole, then nodded at Tommy, indicating Tommy should accompany him with the paten. Frank stepped to the communion rail and said again, "May the Blood of our Lord Jesus Christ keep my soul unto life everlasting. Amen."

Gómez rose and helped to her feet an ancient old crone—obviously the matriarch of the clan. He led her to the rail and steadied her as she creakily engineered down to her knees. She crossed herself with a gnarled, twisted claw, laboriously inched her head back, and then pulled her painted lips back from her toothless gums. With her black lace and desiccated cheeks, her eyes clenched and her mouth gaping, she looked like nothing so much as a nestling crow, its beak wide and waiting to be fed. Tommy stared at her in horror.

As he looked down into the yawning maw that was the old lady's mouth he felt the queasiness rise up in him again. His legs felt leaden. The room seemed to be swallowed up by the old lady's abysmal craw. Tommy disappeared down her throat. He heard again the sounds of the big plaza of Guadalajara. Then he was there again, on the workman's scaffold in front of the cathedral. He felt a stirring of breeze caress his cheek; he saw the pigeons mating on the red tile roof across the square—the mottled-white male mounting the darker female; he felt the rough, hairy hemp prickling the tender flesh of his throat. Sunlight glinted off the polished chrome of a '22 Dodge. A thousand pairs of eyes were riveted on him. Then he felt the sole of the boot of the soldier behind him strike him in the small of his back and he left the scaffolding and the plaza of Guadalajara began to rise up before his eyes, and he knew he wasn't going to die. As he plummeted down toward the end of the hanging rope Tommy saw the pigeons rise up from the tile roof, their wings flapping; he saw the red-haired Mexican's mouth open in horror; he saw Salazar on the big red horse watch with pleasured fascination, his widened eyes following him down—and Tommy was detached. He was calm. He knew he wasn't going to die at the end of this rope. His neck wasn't going to snap; he wasn't going to strangle to death before the assembled throng—his tongue swelling in his mouth, mortal shit dribbling down his dancing pant leg. Tommy knew none of this was going to happen, and he was so amazed at this certainty that when his weight struck the end of the hanging rope and the weakened scaffolding collapsed and the plaza floor continued to rise up toward him and he plopped on the headless torso of the piggish priest, when Severo Salazar yanked him to his feet and then the *agrarista soldado* dragged him back up to the cathedral's parapet, the blank look of complete consternation on Tommy's face was not that he was alive, but that he had *known* he would be.

TOMMY'S HAND HOLDING THE FLAT GOLD PATEN UNDER FRANK'S host-filled ciborium began to tremble. It rattled against the base of the chalice.

"Tommy—?"

The ancient crone's eyes opened—her mouth still agape—and she stared at Tommy as his eyes rolled up into his eyelids and he reached out for the communion rail to steady himself.

THE DARK-SKINNED GIRL APPROACHED WITH A COVERED POT AND A basket. Her teeth were clean and white and she had pulled her blouse wider to expose her brown shoulders.

"*Hombre*," she said. "I thought maybe you and the boy might be hungry."

"*Gracias.*" Quintana took the pot from her hands and set it on the ground. She had covered the basket with two overturned plates, and under the plates were warm tortillas. "*Muchas gracias.*" Quintana handed one of the plates to Miguelito and began to ladle out a thick stew from the pot. It smelled piquant and tasty.

"Where are you from?" the girl asked. She couldn't have been more than sixteen.

"Up," Quintana said, nodding with his chin as he folded a tortilla. "Sagrado Corazón."

"Ah . . ." she said, "the stronghold . . ." An idea flared in her eyes. "And is that—"

"*Sí*, that's him. Father Tomás."

"The *pistolero padre*." Miguelito wolfed down the food.

The girl looked with reverence at the big house. "I have heard about him. They say he can kill a hundred *agraristas* with a single bullet."

Quintana grinned at the boy. "At least. Maybe two hundred."

The *charros* were still lounging against the wall. The girl threw a glance in their direction and then said, "After you leave here are you going back to Sagrado Corazón?"

Quintana thought as he chewed. "There may be other stops at other haciendas, but yes, we're going back there."

She said quickly, "Can I go with you?"

Quintana stopped chewing. He looked at the men against the wall. One of them had separated himself from the others and had walked out a few steps to better watch the girl. "Is one of them your man?"

"Not really," the girl said. Then, "He beats me. He hurts me. I've only been here three weeks. The *agraristas* killed my family."

Quintana looked at the girl, then he swirled a tortilla in the stew. "Do you think he's going to let you go without objection? A beautiful young girl like you?"

She leaned over closer to him. He could smell her. "I can please you," she said. "I know how to treat a man."

"Rosarita!" the *charro* shouted. "Get your ass back in the kitchen!"

"Take me with you!" the girl whispered in a rush, then turned and dashed back to the kitchen door.

The *charro* said something to the others against the wall and then he strode on toward Quintana. Quintana glanced up from his plate and said to the boy, "Go over by the well."

"No."

"Boy."

"No."

The *charro* was standing before them. He was tall and thick-shouldered, with a handlebar mustache and rough stubble on his cheeks. He stared down at Quintana as the Indian continued to unhurriedly eat his food. Then the *charro* looked over at the strangers' horses, where Miguelito had tied them.

"That red stallion you rode in on?"

Quintana didn't even look up.

"That's a lot of horse."

Quintana nodded. "Yes, it is."

The *charro* moved around so that his shadow fell upon Quintana. Quintana looked up.

"Let's go take a look at him."

"*Hombre*, I've already seen him."

"But I want to look at him."

"Then go look at him. I'm going to finish my stew."

—◀○▶—

ONE OF GÓMEZ'S DAUGHTERS HELD OUT A PONY GLASS OF BRANDY to Tommy. His hand was still trembling slightly as he reached out for it. He swallowed it all in one quick backward jerk of his head. It made his eyes water.

"Are you all right, Father?"

Tommy got the gist of what the Gómez girl was saying and nodded weakly. He was pale and unfocused.

Adolfo Gómez, sitting behind his massive, leather-topped desk, sputtered out a derisive chuckle. He thought Tommy was the funniest thing he'd ever seen.

"Get the good Father another brandy, Luisa María, in case he faints again." He looked at the males in his family and shook his head.

"*Padre Pistolero.*" He grinned, and his relatives were entertained.

"Don Adolfo," Frank said, moving on bluntly to his agenda. "The Church is relying on you. We have always been there for you *hacendados,* now we need you to be there for us. We'll fight this war for you, but we need your *pesos* to buy guns and bullets."

They were in Gómez's second-floor office. The women had been exiled to the parlor just outside the door. The Gómez men were aligned against the bookshelves and mounted Spanish tack. Rojas and his sons were behind Frank. Tommy was lost in a plush, pillowed chair.

Don Adolfo stared at Frank a moment. There was a rifle lying across his desk. A big-bore repeater with gold and silver inlay. It gleamed with polished newness.

"The Church has wealth beyond all conscience," Gómez said. "That's what your rebellion is all about—your refusal to part with a single *centavo.*"

Frank fought to contain his temper. "That's not true, Don Adolfo. And you know—"

"I know this." Gómez sat forward in his chair. "I know that if General Terrazas learns that I gave money to you in support of your rebellion, he'll come here with his *federales* and his *agrarista* bastards and they'll kill me and rape my daughters and burn my house and poison my wells and steal whatever there is left . . ." He eyes burned with anger. "There will be no more Gómez hacienda. And you, gringo, you will be somewhere else, hiding up on the mountain, or back in los Estados Unidos!"

"No, *señor*," Frank declared coldly. "This is my country now. I will stay here to fight the devil's attacks on the Lord and I will die here, if I have to, fighting for Mexico and Christ.

"Are you so naïve, Don Adolfo," he continued, "to think that the *callistas* will stop with the Church? Once they have wiped out the moral code we have given these savages—the only morality this land has ever known—then there'll be nothing to stop them from doing anything. How long do you think you'll keep your hacienda then? How safe will your daughters be then?"

Don Adolfo slowly opened a humidor on his desktop and withdrew a long, thick Cuban cigar. He cut off the end and examined it thoughtfully. "How long have you been in my country, *Padre Gringo*? Two years? Ten? A conquistador named Gómez came ashore with Hernán Cortés. That was four hundred years ago." He picked up a Taxco silver lighter, struck a flame and lit the cigar in a voluminous cloud of smoke. "Mexico *is* a revolution, interrupted by long periods of exhausted peace." He fixed Frank with a withering stare that pierced through the smoke. "How dare you preach to me about how to survive in my own land." He twirled the cigar in his fingers.

"I'll pay you a hundred *pesos* for the Mass . . . and you may water your horses. Then ride off my hacienda."

Gómez's daughter entered then with the second glass of brandy and touched Tommy's arm. He looked up but didn't take the liquor. He couldn't understand Don Adolfo's words but he was aware they were displeasing Frank. Tommy rose slowly from the chair and approached Don Adolfo's desk.

"Ah, the tender warrior." The grin returned to the *hacendado's* face. Tommy looked at him, then his eyes fell on the rifle lying on the desktop. "You like this, *padre*?" Gómez put the cigar between his teeth and lifted the weapon with two hands, as if it were a holy offering. "Here, get a feel for it." Gómez thought this was great fun.

Tommy took the weapon. He balanced it in his upturned palms.

"Heavy, eh, Father? It's English-made. It's for tigers." He winked at his relatives. "You ever hunt tigers?"

Tommy lifted the rifle to his shoulder and sighted at a point on the far wall. The Gómez men quickly parted and moved out of the way.

"You need these." Don Adolfo chuckled and held up a clip of large-caliber cartridges. They were as new and shiny as the rifle. "It doesn't work without these."

—◀◯▶—

THE TALL *CHARRO* MOVED AROUND THE RED STALLION, ADMIRING THE animal. He put his hand on the horse's flank and the stallion stamped his hoof in irritation.

"Where did you get such a horse, Yaqui?" he shouted.

"It was Severo Salazar's," Miguelito piped, and then was sorry when he saw Quintana's quick glare.

"Truly? Then I've heard of this stallion." The *charro* reached down to touch the red bay's black foreleg, and the animal bared its teeth and bit at him. The *charro* whipped his hand back just in time. "And how did you come by him?"

Quintana said nothing. He'd finished eating and wiped the last of the stew off the plate with the remaining fold of tortilla. The *charro* walked back to him.

"How much would you take for him?"

Quintana slowly shook his head. "He's not for sale."

"I'll give you . . . sixty pesos."

"I told you he's not for sale."

The big *charro* frowned.

"A hundred pesos. I'll give you a hundred pesos for him."

"Hombre, truly . . . He's not for sale. Not for a thousand."

The *charro* worked angrily at the end of his handlebar mustache. "Do you have a paper that says this horse is yours?"

Quintana put the plate down and stood up in a fluid Indian motion. The *charro* took a step back.

"I don't need a paper."

"How do I know you didn't steal it?"

"How can you steal a horse from a dead man?"

The *charro* shook his head. "I don't think the horse belongs to you."

"I don't give a fuck what you think."

He stopped twirling the tips of his mustache. Quintana waited. The tall *charro* said, "We shall see, Yaqui."

He turned and walked back toward his friends against the wall. Quintana thought he was a brave man to give his back like that. Brave and stupid.

"*Chico*," Quintana said quietly. "Go inside and find Tomás."

This time the boy didn't argue. He lurched quickly up to the kitchen door, just as the girl was coming out. She was carrying her belongings wrapped in a fringed shawl and she hadn't gotten far when the tall *charro* called out her name. She hesitated, looking at Quintana.

"Where do you think you're going?! Get back into the house!"

She glanced at the tall *charro,* then began to run.

"Rosarita!" he called out, then when she didn't stop he reached inside his jacket and came out with a pistol. She was reaching out to Quintana when he fired and the bullet entered her back and burst out through her right breast and she stumbled once and puked blood and went down.

—◦—

TOMMY HAD TAKEN THE CARTRIDGES FROM DON ADOLFO'S HAND AND expertly opened the breech and slipped them in. The *hacendado*'s smile faded just a little. Tommy slammed the breech and levered in a shell. Gómez glanced nervously around the room.

"Well, he has *held* a weapon before," he joked, but no one laughed.

That's when Miguelito's voice rang out from the parlor.

"Father Tomás! Father Tomás!"

"In here," Tommy called out in English and a moment later the boy rushed into the room, evading the women's grasping hands.

"*Padre,* Quintana!" the boy shouted and pointed to the balcony and at that moment the *charro*'s revolver barked.

—◦—

QUINTANA FELT FRAGMENTS OF THE BULLET KISS HIS EAR AND THE blood gushed from the young girl's mouth and she stumbled and fell and the Indian already had his big revolver in his hand and he shot the *charro* twice in his midsection and the tall man slammed back on his behind and looked down at the blood spurting from his belly and Quintana took quick steps toward him and when the big charro looked up Quintana shot him again in his face.

The girl had twisted as she fell and she lay faceup on the hard white ground—so hard-trodden it could have been laid stone or poured concrete—and the tall *charro* had slumped forward in death, forward and to the side, and his blood was spreading out like spilt wine. The friends of the dead *charro* had drawn their pistols and for a moment no one in the courtyard moved and then one of the dead man's comrades started to raise his weapon and the ground by his booted foot erupted in a geyser of hard stone pebbles.

Tommy stood on Don Adolfo's balcony, the muzzle of the big rifle smoking.

"No!" he shouted. "No!"

The *charros* looked up at him and then at Quintana and then at each other.

"Don't wait!" Quintana shouted. "Don't wait!"

There were four of them and they held their weapons down at their legs. One had a U.S. Army automatic.

Quintana took aim with his big horse pistol and cocked it and Tommy shouted, "No!" again and fired and the windshield of one of the motorcars exploded. And there was another brief second of suspended movement and then the man with the U.S. Army automatic quickly brought it up to aim and Quintana and Tommy fired simultaneously and the man came apart as he was thrown back against the whitewashed wall. Then before Quintana could even cock his revolver again Tommy had fired twice again and there were two more dead *charros* lying in the courtyard and the last one held up his hands and sank slowly to his knees, shouting up at the balcony, "*Por favor, padre!* Please don't kill me!"

Tommy turned from the balcony, and at his elbow stood a gawking, astounded Adolfo Gómez. The *hacendado* shrank back and Frank, seeing that, fairly snarled at Tommy, "Shoot him." Tommy looked at his brother and Frank's eyes danced with cold fury. "Shoot him!"

Tommy shoved Gómez and the tall man clattered back and plopped into his cowhide chair and Tommy raised the big English tiger gun and Gómez cringed like a woman—his hands whipping about in an attempt to ward off the bullets, and then when Tommy moved forward slowly and jabbed the muzzle of the rifle against his narrow chest Gómez was suddenly very still.

"Kill him," Frank said again. His voice was flat and final.

The Gómez males started to move forward and Frank said sharply to Rojas, *"Señor!"* and Rojas and his sons whipped out their pistols and pointed them at the unarmed Gómezes and Frank said, "Shoot them! Kill them all!"

Rojas hesitated, unsure if Frank was serious.

"No," Tommy said. "No!"

Don Adolfo was whimpering. Tommy looked back over his shoulder at Frank. "You don't have to kill them. Now he'll give you what you want."

Frank stared at Tommy a moment, then at Don Adolfo. Quintana's footsteps thundered through the parlor and he suddenly appeared in the doorway. He gawked around the room in disbelief.

"Jesus Cristo."

Then Frank leaned over the desk and slapped Gómez across the face.

—◄O►—

As they were riding out of the hacienda the dead *charros* were already being carried away by their women and friends. The girl still lay as she had fallen, looking blank-eyed up at the sun. Quintana reined in and stared at her.

Then he asked Tommy, "Do you have any money?"

Tommy shook his head.

"She has no family. If I don't pay someone to bury her they'll just drag her outside the walls for the wolves to take."

Tommy turned to Frank, who was sitting beside him, looking out with unfocused eyes.

"Frank."

Frank started. "What?"

"Gimme one of those coins."

Frank reached into the heavy money belt he now wore under his cassock and withdrew a gold fifty-peso piece. He handed it to Tommy and Tommy tossed it to Quintana.

"It's too much," the Yaqui said.

Frank was already staring out into the distance again, lost.

"I don't know," Tommy said. "Tell them to buy her a gravestone."

Quintana nodded, then spurred the stallion and rode over to the mechanic, who stepped back terrified when he saw the Indian was coming toward him.

Tommy, himself enveloped by inner turmoil, watched a moment, then turned to look at his brother. Frank was smiling to himself.

"What?" Tommy asked.

Frank came back from a long distance, then looked strangely at Tommy. "Do you believe in destiny?"

Tommy thought about this a long while, and when he was ready to answer Frank was looking away again. Tommy kept silent. Then Quintana rode back and said, "It's done. And they're going to dress her up nice, too."

Tommy nodded, then said to Frank, "Let's go."

After a moment Frank slapped the reins on the geldings' rumps and they rode out of the hacienda, Rojas and his sons closely clustered behind them.

—◁◯▷—

IN THE LATE AFTERNOON IT STARTED TO RAIN AND THE SKIES DARKENED and then the rain came down in drifting sheets and they stopped just before the early nightfall at a pig farmer's shanty and tethered the horses under canvas strung over the limbs of the scrubwood trees and they ate beans and tortillas and tomatoes by kerosene lamps under the shanty's overhang and watched the rain gush down from the eaves and later the seven men and the boy slept on the damp dusty floor and listened to the swine bumping their backs on the underside of the floorboards and in the gray morning it was still raining but much softer now, and Tommy stumbled out sleepily into the scrubwoods to urinate and as he was relieving himself on the sodden leaves he looked up to see a wraithlike apparition slip through the wet gnarled tree trunks fifty yards away and Tommy staggered backward, pissing on his shoes, and he fell into Quintana, who was just pulling himself out of his button fly, and they both got their feet tangled in the dead underbrush and toppled over.

"*Chinga, Tomás!* What are you doing, *hombre!*" Then he saw Tommy's face and said, "What is it?" Quintana pulled his big revolver and peered into the woods. "What?"

"I saw . . . something,"

"What?"

"I don't know . . . Something."

"What do you mean some—"

And at that moment the apparition appeared again, drifting through the trees.

"There!" Tommy pointed.

"It's a ghost!" Quintana said.

"You think?"

As they watched the creature looked back, saw them, and froze.

"We'll see." Quintana straight-armed the big horse pistol and was pulling the trigger when Tommy slammed his arm up. The bullet tore through the limbs above, sending down a shower of wet dead branches.

"What are you doing?" Quintana demanded.

"Let's find out what it is before we kill it!"

Quintana stared at Tommy in disbelief. "When did you start doing that?" He ignored the ghost, resting the weapon down against his leg. "What the hell's happening to you?"

"What do you mean?"

"What do I mean? *Hombre,* in this world you kill it or it kills you. You know that as good as I do." He was warming to his diatribe. "And yesterday at the Gómez hacienda, you shouldda shot when I told you to!"

"We might've got out of there without any more shooting! I mean, I go inside for a hour and you've got the whole guinea nation gunnin' for you!"

"If I don't kill that big bastard, you think he ain't gonna kill me, after he's already shot the girl?"

"So you're faulting me for tryin' to stop it there?"

"This is my country! Don't try and tell me what to do in my *own damn country!*" Quintana finished in a shout. They glared at each other as the others rushed up on them through the woods.

"*Qué pasa!*" Rojas said, out of breath.

Frank had a small pistol in his hand. Tommy gave his brother a quizzical look, then said, "We saw a ghost."

"What?"

"A ghost—"

Then Quintana shouted, "There!" and started to raise the gun again.

"No! *Señor!*" cried the pig farmer, whose name was Mariano, as he raised his hands. "*Son los albinos!*" he explained. "It's the albinos."

As they all watched, the seemingly translucent shape slipped behind the tree trunks and then just disappeared into the ground.

Frank fixed the pig farmer with a hard eye. "What kind of devilment is this?"

"No, is no devil, *padre*. It's *los indios albinos*."

As they walked through the trees toward where the apparition had disappeared, Mariano explained as best he could. The albinos had been living here in the woods when Mariano had arrived ten years before. He thought they had always lived here. At first they'd shied away from him, like wild animals, but he'd slowly won them over with plates of grain and canned fruit left at the entrance of their hovel.

"How many are there?" Frank asked. "A family?"

They would have to be related, Mariano said, but he could never figure out how. He didn't know if they were father and two daughters, or husband, wife and offspring. They knew little Spanish, and he couldn't understand their Indian dialect. Maybe you can talk to them, he said to Quintana.

IT WAS A LITTLE MORE THAN A MOUND OF STONES—MORE CELTIC THAN Indian—littered with the debris of a thousand autumns. Stuck in the wet rocks were snatches of ribbons that hung in the mist, tiny crosses made of animal bones, even sodden, sun-bleached photographs of Revolutionary generals—framed with garlands of wild weeds like icons of the Virgin. And on some of the stones there were older, ancient scrawlings—crude copies of pre-Columbian deities, exhortations to the sun. And there was an odor about the hovel—an odor of musty, frail humanity. An odor of oddity.

Frank sniffed at the air with repugnance. "This place is evil."

"No, *padre*." Mariano shook his head with decisiveness. "The old albino is a seer, a wizard. The poor people come from far away to have their fortunes revealed. . . . He told my woman she was going to die in childbirth and yes, she did." Mariano said this flatly, without involvement. A simple statement of fact.

Frank touched Mariano's shoulder. "Hombre, don't blaspheme. There is but the one True God."

"*Sí, padre*. And no other. But the old albino is a wizard, truly he is."

Frank smiled at Mariano as he would at a child, then he stooped and pushed aside the stiffened cowhide that covered the hovel's cavelike entrance. The smell was stronger in the warm air that rushed out. Frank looked back at Mariano and the pig farmer nodded, and Frank frowned and scrunched his shoulders and slipped in. Mariano held back the cowhide and Tommy and Quintana looked at each other, then entered the hovel.

Inside it was dim and rank. The Indian stink—not animal, yet not civilized—was choking. There was also the stench of age, of living flesh decaying, and over all, that redolence of strangeness.

In the darkness Tommy walked into his brother's back. They stood, their shoulders touching, hearing each other's breathing and the rustling of vague forms in the shadows.

Then Mariano struck a match and cupping it with his hand he lighted a kerosene lamp and adjusted the chimney and the hovel was suffused with a golden glow and seated on a pallet against the far wall was a pale skeleton of a man. He was naked, but his wrinkled ivory skin hung from his knobby frame as if it were clothing. His thin hair was white and long, and plastered to his skull with a greasy pomade. The skin on his pate was so pale that it shone between the streaks of hair like naked bone.

"His eyes," Quintana whispered behind the brothers. "Look at his eyes."

Frank leaned forward. "Merciful God . . ."

The old albino's eyes were milky with cataracts that covered both his lenses like thick spider webs. The old man was stone blind.

"Look closer," Quintana urged.

Frank took the lamp from Mariano's hand and held it higher. Behind the cloth-like cataracts a pinkish light seemed to glow; his sightless red irises moved like silhouettes behind a curtain.

"Fuck me, Molly," Tommy breathed.

"He can't see his hand before his face," Mariano said, "but he can see into eternity."

There were two half-naked crones shifting in the shadows, mewing like frightened animals, their alabaster skin stark and unhealthy in the hovel's gloom. So many "Spanish" in their lair at one time unnerved them.

Frank looked at them with distaste, then he moved his foot and his toe struck something on the earthen floor. He lowered the lantern and in the dirt before the old Indian's pallet was a well-worn grid of ancient markings scraped into the ground and outlined by streaks of dyes and in the magical grid were stones and shells and feathers and more animal bones like the ones outside. Frank glared down at the heathen altar.

The old albino said something to the albino women and one of them said something back in a strange, quaking voice.

"There, Yaqui"—Mariano turned to Quintana—"can you understand that? What tongue is that?"

Quintana listened closely as the old Indian said something else, this time more sharply, to the women. He shook his head. "It's not a true language. It's pieces of many . . . scraps . . . shit . . ." He eyed the old man with sympathy. "These people have lost their way. They have no language, no names, no home."

"No god." Frank kicked at the stones with disdain.

One of the ivory women left the shelter of the shadows and moved to the pallet. The old man reached out his flaccid arm and the woman helped him to his feet and held him up. Standing together, they seemed identical, except for the old man's shriveled chalk-dust penis.

The other woman approached Mariano. She was younger and pinker—the apparition they had seen out in the trees.

The woman said something to Mariano and the pig farmer nodded to Quintana and Quintana stepped closer and the woman said it again and Quintana answered back in still another Indian dialect and then nodded toward Frank. The woman spoke back to the old albino and the blind man took a faltering step forward.

"The old man says the women told him there is a holy man here," Quintana said. "The old man wants to meet him."

Frank frowned but didn't move and the old woman led the blind man forward and took his hand and slowly guided it to Frank's face. Frank flinched and started to turn away as the old albino's gnarled and dirty fingers touched his cheek, but the old Indian caught his chin and held it. Frank stared down into the eerie sightless white cataracts and watched the pink irises moving behind the clotted cloudiness as the old albino brought up his other hand and gently traced Frank's features. The old man paused, perplexed. At that moment Tommy moved and the old man heard the sound and his claw-like fingers struck out with shocking quickness and clutched Tommy's arm. Tommy was motionless as the old man turned to him and reached up. He sketched Tommy's features, then he stopped and started again, his fingers floating lightly over Tommy's face. Then he stopped and softly said something. Then the old man leaned forward against Tommy's chest and held on to him like a child.

"What—what's he doing?"

Quintana was looking at Tommy strangely.

"He says . . ." Quintana glanced at Frank. "He says you are the only holy man here."

There was a moment of stillness in the hovel, and then the old blind albino began to weep. He clung to Tommy's chest and tears slipped down from his milky eyes. Frank, watching this, became enraged.

"This place smells of pig shit and idolatry!" He kicked at the markings in the dirt, sending stones and bones scattering. The albino women evaporated back into the shadows.

"This place should be burned off the face of the earth!" and for a moment it seemed Frank would send the kerosene lamp crashing to the dirt floor. Then he whirled and walked out of the hovel. Everyone else stayed where they were and the old blind albino Indian sobbed into Tommy's chest and after a moment Tommy's arms came up and encircled the old man.

BULLDOG COYNE'S FAVORITE METHOD OF TORTURING HIS ELDEST SON was to send him to the rail yard to steal coal. The West Side rail line, on its way downtown, ran through the heart of Hell's Kitchen, and at the Sixtieth Street yard—a long thirteen blocks from the Coyne apartment—the neighborhood boys had fashioned a hidden entrance in the soot-blackened fence, and whenever the yard dicks were busy elsewhere across the tracks, bucketfuls, sackloads, and even wheelbarrows of coal were stolen from the mountain of coal chunks and hustled from the yard. But if the coal was free for the stealing, it had a price among the thieves. King of the Coal Mountain was Freight Train Shaughnessy. Freight Train was a squat, dirty urchin with a harelip and a hair-trigger temper, and he had come by his name when his old man had passed out drunk on the New York Central tracks and been cut in two by the 12:20 coming down from Harlem. Freight Train's mother had taken off for Pittsburgh with her lover the next day, leaving behind Freight Train and his two older sisters, both of whom immediately took to whoring. Freight Train had to fend for himself and he was exceedingly angry about this.

The first time Frank came into the yard he was terrified because he had never broken the law before. He was ten years old, and he worried for his immortal soul as he slipped through the fence and dashed across the oil-blackened rail yard and to the nearest hill of coal. He paused a moment, then realizing there was no way he was going to do this cleanly, he began to hurriedly scoop handfuls of coal chunks into the flour sack he had brought. The sack was only a third full when a quintet of dirty street children, lead by Freight Train, strutted out from behind the mountain of coal.

"Well, look what the cat brought in," one of boys said. Freight Train, mindful of his harelip, didn't speak much, but his eyes glowed with hatred.

"It's little Sister Asskiss," another kid said They fanned out around Frank in a classic posture of intimidation. Frank was already shaking. "I was in third grade with this little jenny-woman. He was the nuns' sissy pet."

Freight Train examined Frank with a demented anger and Frank stared back in disbelief. He was dumbfounded that someone so young, and someone he barely knew, could be so enraged with him.

"Wod chu 'tarin' at?" Freight Train lisped.

Frank couldn't look away. He couldn't speak. He was transfixed by the murderous rage in Freight Train's eyes.

The harelipped hoodlum took Frank's quiescence for challenge and punched him flush on his jaw. Frank literally didn't know what had hit him. He lay on the coal-dust-covered yard and looked up at the gray winter sky and the closing circle of children and he felt as if this were all happening to someone else.

"He's Bulldog Coyne's kid," said a runny-nosed kid in a thread-bare floppy cap.

"I don't tare who he ith." Freight Train pushed Frank with his hard-toed shoe. "Gotta pay me for my coal."

Frank rubbed the back of his hand across his face and it came away smeared scarlet. He stared at it in horror. "It's not your coal," he said, then looked up at Freight Train and wished he hadn't. Something that bore a passing relationship to a smile twisted across the boy's misshapen mouth. Freight Train dropped down on Frank and began to methodically pound him. The other children danced around and cheered. It only took a few seconds. Then they swarmed over Frank, ripping out his pockets, pulling off his shoes.

He stumbled home, dazed and sobbing, and when Bulldog saw him the big Irishman could hardly contain his pleasure. He manifested his joy by pointing an accusing finger at the boy and saying, "You little sally, you couldn't handle that harelip retard Shaughnessy?"

Frank stood before his father wiping the tears and snot from his face. "He says it costs two pennies to fill a sack."

Bulldog shook his head. "No son of mine is gonna pay for something every other kid in the neighborhood gets for free. That ain't how the Coynes operate." He glared at Frank with disgust. "Is this the way you take care of your family?"

Frank snuffled for breath and looked around the room in panic. Peggy stood in the kitchen cooking, a ladle in one hand, a drink in the other. She quickly averted her eyes. Tommy, almost six, watched from where he had been playing on the floor. His big eyes seemed to take in everything with silent comprehension.

"You're gonna go back there tomorrow, and you're gonna get us that coal, and you *ain't* gonna pay for it."

THE NEXT DAY FREIGHT TRAIN WATCHED JOYOUSLY AS FRANK CREPT through the hole in the rail-yard fence. That day, after he pummeled him, he filled Frank's mouth with coal dust and Frank spat and vomited all the way home. The next day he made a whimpering Frank kiss the glans of his penis while the other kids watched with fascination. When Frank came home an hour later, again without the sack of coal, Bulldog whipped him with the wide leather belt he used to wear when he was fresh off the boat, unloading cargo on the docks. Afterwards Frank lay in bed and sobbed violently. Tommy came in to him and tried to touch his brother's hand but Frank only howled as if he had been struck again. Tommy sat on the floor and stared at his brother mournfully.

IN THE MORNING, AFTER HE HAD ASSISTED AT MASS, FRANK ASKED THE priest if he could speak to him. He explained the situation, and then asked the priest what he should do. The priest, an officious young American from upstate New York, listened patiently and then explained that theft was a mortal sin and that Frank should make a formal confession and then never steal anything again. Frank, beginning to panic, asked what he should do about his father. The young cleric said that after the situation was completely explained to Frank's father everything would be all right. The young cleric was sure any good Catholic wouldn't want to place his own son's immortal soul in jeopardy. Frank sat back and stared at him. The priest rose and indicated with a conclusory nod that it was time for the altar boy to go. Frank walked woodenly toward the rectory door. That's when the young priest reminded Frank to pray for forgiveness and guidance.

*   *   *

SACRED HEART

FRANK KNELT IN THE FRONT PEW, HIS HANDS CLASPED TIGHTLY, HIS beseeching eyes upraised to the statue of the long-suffering Madonna standing pious guard over the bank of votive candles.

"Please, Mother Mary . . . I don't know what to do," the boy whispered, as if to a best friend. "Please help me . . . Please show me a way . . ."

A fat washerwoman lumbered down the center aisle of the otherwise vacated church. Her elephantine legs were swathed in ratty stockings, and her flesh bubbled out through the ruptures like half-cooked pork bursting out of sausage skins. Ignoring or not seeing Frank, she dropped her numerous sacks and bags at the base of the bank of candles, crossed herself, then dug out a small threadbare purse, jammed in her blunt fingers and pulled out a single penny. She slipped the penny into the slot and it made a small *chink* as it dropped down into the metal tube container. Then, as awkward as a camel settling down in the desert, the fat woman lowered herself down to one knee and began to pray. Within a few short minutes her voice began to rise in a mumbled keening as she prayed for someone's dead, suffering soul. But Frank didn't hear her moaning. All he could hear was the chink of that penny falling on others like it.

When the washerwoman was gone Frank waited a full half-hour before he slipped out of the pew and stole up to the bank of candles. He looked up at Mary, crossed himself, then knelt as if for prayer but instead reached under the candles and—as he had seen the priests do—unscrewed the base of the penny cylinder. Immediately coins spilled out into his hand and cascaded all over the marble floor. To Frank they sounded like tolling tenor bells as they struck in the church's echoey emptiness. He peered around in terror, then scrambled desperately after the coins. He crabbed about, this way and that, gathering up the nickels, dimes and pennies. Some of them had rolled all the way to the communion rail and beyond. As he was searching frantically for the last few coins the rectory door opened and the young American priest walked out talking to another, older priest. Frank pressed himself against the wall and held his breath. His pulse pounded in his ears. His throat constricted. His boyish chest silently heaved. The priests walked down the side aisle, talking animatedly, then they passed through the main entrance and into the street. They hadn't seen him.

Frank gathered up the few maverick coins, genuflected hastily, then ran out of the church.

—◄◯►—

HE HID THE COINS UNDER A LOOSE BOARD IN THEIR BEDROOM. EACH night, when he was sure Tommy was asleep, he would slide to the floor, slip under their bed, carefully pry up the floorboard and take a few pennies from his cache. Then he would kneel by the side of the bed and pray desperately for forgiveness and beg that he not die during that night with the black sin of stealing from God on his soul. The following day he would slip the pennies into Freight Train's grubby palm and sometimes the harelip would simply take the money and sometimes he would take the money and beat Frank anyway. There was no way of knowing, and no logic to any of it.

Bulldog would return home to the apartment from his mobster duties and whoring forays, take in the full coal bin, then glare at his elder son, who was usually bent over a book poring over the lives of Catholic martyrs or the histories of foreign lands. Bulldog understood that Frank had found a way to pay for the coal stolen from the rail yard, but studying the tortured face of the son he had rejected, he intuited that Frank was going through a personal hell much worse than any beating either he or Freight Train Shaughnessy could administer, and Bulldog was content with the knowledge that he had incited this torment.

—◄◯►—

TOMMY AWOKE EACH NIGHT TO HIS BROTHER'S TREMBLING FIDGETS. HE lay awake, knowing in a few minutes Frank would sneak from the bed, crawl under the mattress, and reach beneath the loosened floorboard to slip out a few of the many coins he had concealed there. Then Frank would bow his head and bury his face in his hands and Tommy could hear the whispered pleas as his big brother tried explain to his god that he was too afraid to fight Freight Train and too afraid of Bulldog to wipe this black sin from his soul. Sometimes in his prayers he cried. And Tommy, motionless and awake in the bed, listened to Frank and wished he could help his brother, whom he loved more than his own father.

SACRED HEART

—◄○►—

THIS WENT ON FOR OVER THREE YEARS. FRANK ROBBED THE VOTIVE BANK several more times. He became more proficient at it. He struck when the priests were at meal. He brought a small sack. He left some of the coins in the cylinder so as to avoid detection. But his shame and his pain didn't diminish. In fact, it grew along with his skill at thievery. He was a coward and a thief and a sinner and he wasn't worthy of Christ's love.

THE DAY CAME THAT BULLDOG, SEEING HIS ELDER SON WALKING OUT of the apartment door, was struck by a thought and said, "Take your wee brother with ye."

Frank was seized by fear and shame. "He . . . he'll get all dirty."

Bulldog spied the alarm in Frank's face and knew he had probed a nerve. He didn't know what transpired every day at the rail yard, but he could see Frank didn't want his little brother to witness it.

"Soap and water," Bulldog grunted. "Two cheapest things in the world. Take him with you." Frank's dismay filled him with triumph. Bulldog Coyne constantly chipped away at Tommy's love for his older brother, and the big Irishman gleefully intuited he had just broken through to the tender heart of Frank's vulnerability.

"Thomas—" Tommy was seated at the table, eating a piece of bread and apple butter. "Thomas, run get your coat. It's time you started paying your way around here." Bulldog's smile broadened. "Like your brother does."

Tommy jumped from the chair and ran quickly to the bedroom. Frank stared helplessly at his father, and then Tommy reappeared, pulling on his peacoat. He ran to his big brother and held out his hand.

—◄○►—

FREIGHT TRAIN GRINNED HIS MISSHAPEN GRIMACE WHEN HE SAW Frank's head and shoulders slip through the hole in the fence. The harelip had been saving up a dollar to give a Hell's Kitchen whore who had promised to take his virginity, and if he extorted a nickel off the little jenny he would have enough.

"Right on time," Freight said to his gang of urchins.

205

"Stay here," Frank whispered to his little brother at the fence. "Don't come in." Then he pushed his body through the opening and hurried across the blackened earth toward the mountain of coal.

"Thay!" Freight Train hollered. "You know youse gotta pay firth!"

Frank almost stumbled over his own feet as he changed direction and ran toward Freight Train. He hastily jammed the two copper pennies into the bigger boy's hand and started to turn away. Freight Train grabbed his arm and yanked him back.

"The prith hath gone up," Freight Train spit into Frank's face. "Ith a nickel now."

Frank panicked. "I—I didn't bring a nickel!"

"Then you don't get any coal."

A wave of petulant anger flooded over Frank's terror and he shouted, "That's not fair! You should have told me—"

Freight Train slammed his elbow into Frank's nose in a classic Hell's Kitchen argument stopper. Frank stumbled back and fell, blood streaming down the lower half of his face.

"Who the hell you think you are, stalking to me like that?" Freight Train fumed. "You little panthy, I'll pith in your mouth and make you drink it!"

To illustrate his point the harelip began to unbutton his filthy fly. The smaller children giggled in nervous anticipation. Freight Train stood straddled over Frank's face and stuck his fingers into his pants, rooting around. Frank threw up his hands to shield his face.

Then Freight Train felt something hit his back with a *thud*. Then again—*thud, thud*. He looked up and was surprised to see his gang of urchins backing away, their faces wearing looks of complete shock. *Thud*. Freight Train turned and Tommy stabbed the bloody penknife in his little hand through the harelip's cheek. Shaughnessy could feel the short blade pierce his face and plunge into his mouth and slice into his tongue. His mouth filled with blood and he started to gag. Tommy ripped out the point and stabbed him again in the face. He had to lunge up to reach the much taller boy. Freight Train cupped his hands under his mouth and the blood gushed out. He looked at Tommy in horror and as Tommy readied to cut him again the harelip tried to shout for mercy but it came out a choked gargle. Tommy slashed out and laid open Shaughnessy's nose. The bigger boy stumbled backward, holding his face together with his hands. He gave one terrified look at Tommy, then turned and ran away across the rail yard dripping blood. His filthy overcoat was soaked in back where Tommy had stabbed him several times.

The other children gaped at Tommy. He was younger and smaller than any of them, and yet he was their master.

Frank, still on his back on the cold black ground, could only look up at his little brother as if he had never seen him before. The viciousness of Tommy's attack, the total and complete disregard for anything except domination, the adultlike dedication to destruction—Frank was awed and dismayed. And he was frightened.

Tommy picked up the dropped coal sack and held it out to his beloved big brother. Frank could only stare at it.

—◄○►—

Spring came to Los Altos—hot and dry, and then the rains—*Las Aguas*. It rained all night sometimes, and in the mornings the great highland plateau was wet and misty and even laced with chill.

In the towns and villages that had been reconcentrated the people began to trickle back to their homes. The government made no move to stop them, hoping to defuse the Jalisco rebellion by ignoring it. *Federal* troops kept to the safety of the lowland cities and risked only sporadic patrols out into the countryside. It was a kind of phony war.

On the mountain called La Corona, in the pueblo of Sagrado Corazón, Frank watched with growing frustration as the *cristeros* began to depart, riding away in small groups, walking away down the mountainside. He went among those remaining, reminding them that this was a holy war, a war for Mexico's soul. He exhorted them to stay with him. He would lead them in the name of the Blessed Virgin against the infidels who would outlaw God. He sat with them around their campfires and ate their beans and tortillas and spoke to them of weapons that were at that very moment being smuggled through the American border blockade. Exceptional weapons. Modern American Winchesters and Springfields. U.S. Army machine guns. And grenades. With weapons like these and the might of God behind them, with their dedication and *huevos*, they could drive the federal government out of Jalisco. They could take Guadalajara. And after that, after that they could march through Guanajauto and Michoacán and ride victorious into the Capitol, as Zapata had done a decade before. They could be the vanguard of a new and glorious Mexico. A Mexico founded on the principles of Catholic responsibility and the rightness of Catholic social classes.

Frank moved through them with messianic fervor. He had a vision of what this country could be like, if everyone truly practiced the teachings of the Church. There was an order to things, a common sensibility, a destiny. He would lead them to that destiny.

The Mexicans listened respectfully and nodded their heads in agreement and in the morning another dozen would saddle up and follow the score that had slipped down the mountain during the night before.

Frank began to be alarmed.

ONE DAY, IN A DRIVING RAINSTORM, A TEENAGE BOY WALKED UP THE mountain, entered the battened-down pueblo and pounded on the church door asking for the whereabouts of Sister Lourdes Hidalgo.

Quintana, cuddled in bed with the wife of a *cristero* named Aragón who had left the pueblo with Frank to buy foodstuffs, was interrupted by the boy's shouts. He rose from the fiery-eyed *alteña's* hungry embrace and padded naked to the window. He threw open the shutters and peered down into the *placita* at the rain-soaked boy who was still hammering on the door.

"Come back to bed, man," the wife of Aragón purred. "I haven't finished with you."

Quintana smiled back at her. "And I haven't even started with you—" She sighed at that. "But for now, throw me my *pistola*." The small woman grinned and moved to fetch the Yaqui's big horse pistol from the floor beside the bed. She was small and chubby, with pert breasts and an apron of fat around her middle. Quintana grabbed her belly and shook it as he took the gun from her. The wife of Aragón giggled.

Quintana turned back to the window and raised the .45 revolver and aimed it down at the boy. "*Joven!*" he shouted. Juvenile. "If you continue to disturb this glorious afternoon"—he waved the gun barrel at the down-coming rain—"then I'll have no choice but to kill you." The Indian was in an expansive mood.

"I have to speak to Sister Lourdes Hidalgo," the boy shouted again, hunching his shoulders against the rain. "It's very important."

"It can't be as important as all that! Why don't you go around back to the church kitchen? They'll give you something to eat and when the rain lets up I'll go find her for you."

The boy turned back to the door and pounded his fist on the church wood. *"I am looking for Sister Lourdes—"*

The bullet struck the adobe an inch above the boy's head. He turned back angrily and shouted up at the window. "I've been walking for three days! I'm cold and hungry and wet! My feet hurt and my balls itch! And now I have to deal with an asshole like you?"

Quintana was impressed. The boy was impressive. "The priest isn't there. He's down in the valley!"

"There's only one priest? I heard there were three! Where are the other two?"

One priest—Moreno—would be enjoying this rain just as Quintana was. And Tommy? Quintana glanced at the naked woman at his side, a questioning look on his face. "What?" the wife of Aragón asked. Quintana stared at her a moment, then shook his head, answering his own questions.

"And besides," the boy shouted up, "I said I'm looking for Sister Lourdes Hi—"

"Yes, yes, I heard . . . What business do you have with the good sister?"

"I am her cousin. I've come all the way from León!"

Quintana studied the boy a moment longer. The rain continued to pour down.

"Wait there!" Quintana shouted. "I'll be right down!"

—≪O≫—

IN THE INFIRMARY THE RAIN SLUICED DOWN THE MISSING DOCTOR'S heavy leaded windows. The storm outside suffused the long narrow room with a churchlike dimness.

Tommy had been sitting watching Lourdes change the bandages of a five-year-old little girl whose left arm had been crushed under the wheels of a wagon. Lourdes had been forced to amputate. As Lourdes worked the little girl couldn't take her enormous brown eyes off Tommy.

"She's fascinated by you," Lourdes said.

"It's just that I'm a gringo."

209

"No." Lourdes wound the muslin around the little girl's sutured stump. She looked up, smiling at him. "It's because you're you."

Sister Manuela had entered the infirmary with an armload of clean linen. She plopped the sheets down on a bed and fixed Lourdes with a disapproving eye. Lourdes quickly looked back at her hands.

The little girl tugged on the sleeve of Lourdes's habit and when the young nun leaned over the little girl whispered something in her ear. Lourdes whispered something back, then they both looked at Tommy.

"What?"

"She's afraid she won't get into heaven. She thinks she will be ugly to God's eyes without her arm."

Tommy shrugged. "Tell her that's not true."

"She wants you to tell her."

Tommy started to shake his head. "Why—why does she—"

"Because you're Padre Pistolero. If *you* say God will love her, then she'll believe it."

Tommy looked at the little girl. She was clinging with her one small fist to Lourdes's sleeve. "Look, Sister, I can't—"

"If you don't tell her," Lourdes said with alarm, "you'll break her heart. Father Tomás, please."

After a moment Tommy pulled his chair closer. He started to reached out for the little girl, then stopped. "I don't—I don't—I've never been around kids much."

Lourdes tied up the ends of the bandage, picked up the little girl and settled her on Tommy's knee. He looked at the bandaged stump and quickly looked away. "What's her name?"

"Amalia."

Tommy gently brushed a few strands of straight black hair from the little girl's forehead. Lourdes watched Tommy's hand strokes with fascination, then glanced guiltily toward Manuela, who was making beds with an ambulatory patient at the other end of the long parlor.

"Amalia," Tommy said softly. *"Un nombre muy hermosa,"* he said in the halting pidgin Spanish he was beginning to pick up. "A very beautiful name. Very beautiful." He smiled at her. "And you, very beautiful."

The little girl shook her head. "Listen to me," Tommy said decisively. "You are very beautiful. Very, very beautiful. Very very very beautiful." The little girl's eyes widened in a universal feminine gesture. *Convince me, I want to believe you.* "And God loves you very much, just the way you are, exactly the way you are. Tell her that." Lourdes spoke softly and rapidly. The little girl started to smile, then her face grew thoughtful again. She wanted more. "Will you tell God to love me? He'll listen to you, Padre."

Lourdes told him what Amalia had said.

Tommy nodded. "Yes, of course. I'll tell God to love you very much. I'll speak to him personally." The little girl let her smile grow across her face. She slipped her one arm around Tommy's neck and buried her face in his shoulder. Lourdes felt herself warm with delight. Tommy reddened and smiled. Then Amalia turned and looked back at Lourdes. When Lourdes leaned forward to hear what the little girl wanted she reached out and touched her tiny fingers to the misshapen left side of Lourdes's face. Lourdes's hand started to whip up in embarrassment but she stopped herself. The little girl asked Tommy something and he didn't understand her. His eyes went to Lourdes and without looking back at him she said, "She wants you to speak to God for me, too, so I'll get into heaven as well." Tommy nodded and the girl asked him, "Is Sister beautiful in God's eyes, too?" And Tommy understood and said, "Sister is beautiful in anyone's eyes." Lourdes began to tremble and the little girl got a quizzical look on her face and Manuela on the other side of the room glared from over her half-made bed, and then there was a gunshot from outside, in the rain.

"That's Quintana's gat," Tommy said, rising.

—◄○►—

THE YOUNG MAN WAS NAKED, WRAPPED IN BLANKETS BEFORE THE kitchen fireplace, drinking a cup of tea laced with rum. Lourdes knelt before him and they spoke in whispers. Across the kitchen Quintana turned to Tommy and said, "What do you think it's about?"

Tommy shrugged. "I don't know. . . . Somebody in the family's sick or something?"

Quintana shook his head. "It's the war . . . It's about the war. . . ."

—◄○►—

IT WAS STILL RAINING WHEN FRANK AND HIS *CRISTERO* PLATOON returned that night with several canvas-covered wagons loaded with produce and provisions. In the morning the downpour had diminished to a steady drizzle and Lourdes left the room in the vanished Dr. Villanueva's house that served as an infirmary and trotted quickly across the *placita* to the rectory door. Her cousin was already there, waiting for her. They went in together.

Frank was eating breakfast alone at the long table. "Have you seen Father Moreno?" His brow was knitted with anger.

"No, Father. . . . Father, this is my cousin Alejandro."

Frank looked with suspicion at the young man. "Your cousin . . . ?"

"Yes, Alejandro is the son of my mother's brother. He's come all the way from León to tell you something."

Frank folded a tortilla and dabbed it at his eggs. "I'm waiting."

The youth hesitated. He was less impressive before a priest than before a naked Yaqui. Lourdes stepped closer to the table. "Father Francisco, Alejandro has been sent to tell you, my family has important information from the capital."

Frank stopped eating. "Sit down."

—◄○►—

AN HOUR LATER TOMMY WAS IN THE ROOM, FRANK WAS ANGRILY pacing the floor, and Lourdes and her cousin were staring silently at the wood grain of the table before them.

"What don't you understand?" Frank said sharply.

Tommy looked around the rectory. "Lourdes . . . Sister Lourdes has an uncle—?"

"My mother's brother," she said without looking up.

"Whose brother-in-law—"

"The brother of my uncle's wife."

"Who—"

"Ah!" Frank shouted and slammed his fist down on the table. "She has a relative who works for Calles! In the Ministry of Defense!"

Quintana stepped into the room. Frank glared at him. "This is a private conversation, hombre!"

Quintana smiled and leaned back against the door. "Then I won't let anybody in."

Frank shook his head and slumped into a chair. "There's a train leaving Guadalajara for Mexico City. A government train."

Tommy shrugged. "So?"

Quintana was digging for a cheroot. "Trains leave Guadalajara for Mexico every day."

Frank folded his hands together to contain his excitement. "This one is very special. . . . This one is going to carry fifty thousand gold pesos."

Tommy and Quintana immediately sought each other's eyes.

Frank opened his hands slowly, then clasped them again. "Do you know what those pesos would mean to our revolt? Can you imagine the weapons we could procure?" He lifted his eyes to his brother. "I could arm us like a true army. I could take all of Jalisco."

Tommy pulled out a chair and sat down. "When?"

Frank just stared in silence. Tommy looked to Lourdes. "When does the train leave for—"

"They won't tell me," Frank said quietly. "They won't tell me."

Lourdes moved her feet nervously. "My uncle's brother-in-law"—she glanced at Frank—"he will only speak to you. He will only talk to Padre Pistolero."

Frank rose and started to pace again. "It seems your fame has reached the capital." He couldn't conceal his envy. "You've become a legend."

Tommy was uncomfortable. "So . . ." he looked at Lourdes. "Have your uncle's brother—"

"Brother-in-law—"

"Whatever . . . Have him come up here and—"

"He can't do that!" Frank said sharply. "He's an assistant to the Minister of Defense. He can't just ride up here into the heart of the rebellion and—" Frank sputtered out in frustration.

"We have to go to him," Lourdes said reasonably. "To my family's home in León. That's the only way my uncle's brother-in-law will deal with us."

Tommy was confused. No one said anything for a moment.

"It might be a trap," Quintana said. "Have you considered that?"

Frank shook his head. "I don't think so."

"He's family," Lourdes said. "We are related."

"Everyone in this fucking country is related," Tommy said. "It doesn't stop 'em from killing each other." Tommy looked at his brother. "How many men do I take with me?"

Frank shook his head and said nothing, but Quintana understood. "You have to go alone."

"What?"

Frank wouldn't look at him. "You and Lourdes will travel together; you'll pass yourself off as a married couple. When you cross the state line into Guanajuato you'll be met by a car and—"

"Wait a minute! You want me to ride down there alone, with a nun! Do you know what they did to me the last time they had me?!"

"Yes, I—"

"They hung me!" Tommy shouted. "They fucking *hung* me! And they were gonna do it again!"

Frank's anger flared. "You think I want to send *you!* You think I don't want to go myself?!"

"Then go!"

"They want *you!*"

"As a man and wife," Lourdes offered, trying to defuse the situation. "As a bourgeois couple, we can get through the patrols outside the city. I know we can. León is my hometown. I can lead us—"

"No. Uh-uh. I'm not going to do it!"

"Tomás." Quintana arched his eyebrows. "Fifty thousand pesos . . . in gold . . ."

Tommy jabbed his finger at the Yaqui. "It's not you going down there!"

Quintana shrugged. "I'll go with you, amigo."

"Yes, good." Frank seized the moment. "Take him with you." He turned to Lourdes. "That would be good, wouldn't it?"

Lourdes thought a moment. "It would be better if there was an another woman, too. Two couples traveling together . . . They wouldn't suspect that."

"What other woman?"

"Well . . . Sister Manuela—"

"Aragón's wife," Quintana said quickly.

"Who?"

"*Señora Aragón?*" Lourdes said with suspicion.

"She's a good Catholic woman. She has killed many *callistas* . . ." Quintana was trying hard to keep the interest out of his voice. "I would trust her, and no other."

"Well . . ." Lourdes eyed the Yaqui. "Sister will be needed here, in the infirmary . . ."

"Good," Frank said. "Then it's settled."

Tommy looked around the room. "You're all crazy. I'm not going to do it."

They all looked at him, waiting.

SACRED HEART

---⋖○⋗---

THAT AFTERNOON THE WEATHER HAD TURNED BAD AGAIN AND THE white geldings stood in the driving rain with their heads down and their tails held low and Miguelito sat in the carriage seat of the landau beside Lourdes's cousin Alejandro. Rojas and his sons hunched in their saddles under the cantina overhang, water pouring from their sombreros.

In a second-floor room in the adobe building across from the rebuilt church Quintana was trying to get a full length view of himself in the tiny cracked mirror over the bureau. Finally he turned to Tommy and grinned. "How do I look, gringo?"

There had been a frantic search for suits to fit Padre Tomás and the Yaqui, and now Quintana was dressed in a brown four-button vested that had once been worn by the pueblo's Federal tax collector.

Tommy, in the trousers of an ill-fitting blue serge that had been hastily lengthened, was pulling on his shoulder holsters. He picked up the two nickel-plated automatics from the bed where he had carefully laid out all his weapons.

"Gringo!"

Tommy looked up as he cross-holstered the two .45s. "Tuck your hair under a hat. You look like a dago morphadyke."

Quintana chose a bowler from the dozen hats the people of the pueblo had collected. He held up his long black Indian hair and placed the bowler over it. He looked in the cracked mirror with distaste.

"*Now* I look like a *maricón.*"

Tommy was strapping on a big cavalry revolver.

"Tomás, you're supposed to be an American businessman."

Tommy drew the gun, holstered it, then reached for the blue serge suit coat.

"He's sending me to my death, do you know that?"

"Your brother?"

Tommy walked for the door.

"Yes. My brother."

---⋖○⋗---

FRANK WAS SEATED IN A RECTORY CHAIR. LOURDES WAS ON HER KNEES beside him. The rain pounded on the window panes.

215

"Father, I believe we can do this thing for the glory of Christ and the Virgin."

"Yes, my child . . ."

"But I've seen . . . I have seen the devil's evil."

"I know, Sister, I know . . ." Frank reached out and gently touched her shoulder. "You've witnessed so much in your few years."

Lourdes bowed her head. She was no longer in her habit, but a long-sleeved black dress, her hair covered by a lace veil. "I hope that when my time to die comes, I will be able to meet it with courage and grace."

Frank was silent. There was nothing to say.

"I want my soul to be cleansed of sin. I want to be able to spend eternity by the side of the Virgin."

"I have no doubt that there is a place in heaven reserved for you, Sister. So many of us here have been the recipient of your—"

"Father," Lourdes suddenly whispered, "sometimes . . . sometimes I doubt my vocation."

Frank was surprised. Lourdes had never evidenced any of the signs of dissatisfaction that he'd noted with contempt in many other young Mexican nuns. She didn't drink to excess, or steal from the Church to send back to her family, or gaze longingly at young men. She didn't constantly cry in her room, a sure sign of second thoughts about a life devoted to spiritual service.

"I don't know . . . I don't know if I'm fit to wear the veil."

Frank made a helpless gesture. "Sister Lourdes, we are in a war. We're struggling to save the Mexican Church. We're fighting for our very lives."

"It's not my life I fear for, Father. . . ."

She raised her head and Frank inspected her face, trying to understand her.

"It's my soul."

"Sister—"

"Father, I have lustful thoughts." There, it had been said. Frank sat back in his chair and his face darkened. Lourdes lowered her eyes and dropped her head. "Father, I am so ashamed. I am so—"

"As well you should be, Sister." Frank glared at her. "As well you should be. Did you take your vow of celibacy lightly?"

Her voice was a breath. ". . . No . . ."

"Are you not a bride of Christ?"

". . . Yes . . ."

"Did you not prostrate yourself on the floor of God's house and give your soul and your body to the Savior?"

Lourdes's lips trembled; she couldn't speak.

"Are you going to let your animal urges damn your immortal soul to the eternal fires of Hell?"

A tear coursed down her unblemished cheek and quivered on her chin.

Frank's countenance softened. He inspected Lourdes's downcast head. "Has someone been tempting you, Sister? Is it the Yaqui?"

She raised her tear-streaked face. "No, Father." She sobbed. "Father, my sin is even blacker than I've said." She gulped for breath, then cried out in a rush, "Father, please help me! I desire a priest!"

Frank didn't hesitate. He lashed out like a snake and slapped Lourdes across the deformed left side of her face. Lourdes fell back, clutching her cheek in horrified fright.

"How dare you!" Frank hissed. Lourdes shrank back across the dark wood of the floor as Frank leaned over her, stepped astraddle her. "How dare you blaspheme like this!"

"Oh, Father, I'm so sor—"

Frank raised his hand again and Lourdes hunched on the floor and covered her head with her arms.

"Pray for forgiveness, woman! Ask the Virgin to absolve you of your beastly lusts!"

Lourdes sobbed as she curled her body up into a ball on the polished planks. Then the rectory door opened and with a gust of windy rain Tommy entered and slammed the door behind him.

"What the hell's going on here?"

Frank raised himself from his crouch over Lourdes and glowered in Tommy's direction. His eyes were distant and unfocused, like the eyes of a man during sex.

"What are you doing to her?" Tommy moved quickly to Lourdes and, gripping her sleeved arms, began to lift her to her feet.

"No, no, no!" Lourdes cried in horror. She fought against Tommy's grip, tried to pull away.

"Leave her alone!" Frank shouted.

"No, *you* leave her alone!"

Lourdes ripped herself from Tommy's grasp and with a terrified look at Frank she ran to the door and out into the rain.

"What's wrong with you?" Tommy said. "What the hell—?"

Frank pointed an accusing finger at his brother. "Just do as you're told!"

"Fuck you!"

217

"You've been given a mission! A mission for God! For once in your life do something righteous! Something that big Irish drunkard didn't teach you to do!"

Tommy stared at his brother a long time, then he raised his own finger and said, "This isn't over."

"No, it isn't."

Tommy turned and walked out into the rain.

IN THE LANDAU CARRIAGE LOURDES SAT WITH HER VEIL PULLED DOWN and her face turned to the upholstery. Tommy strode splashing across the placita and pulled himself into the carriage. He sat beside her and Lourdes pushed closer to the carriage wall. Her shoulders shook as she silently cried.

Quintana took María Aragón's hand from her scowling husband and said, "*Señor*, I will look after her as if she were my own wife." Aragón stared hard at Quintana, at his woman's hand lightly resting in the Indian's, and his lips were a hard, tight line under his dripping sombrero. "No, truly, I will, man. Have no fear." He lead the wife of Aragón to the carriage and helped her in with great care, smiling and nodding back at her husband. Then Quintana got in behind her and shut the door.

Alejandro clucked and slapped the reins and the white geldings began to move and Rojas and his sons, with a score of other *cristeros*, fell in behind. Aragón hurriedly mounted up and joined them.

Inside the carriage Lourdes was still crying under her veil and the Yaqui looked at Tommy. "*Qué pasa?*"

Tommy said nothing and turned to look out the window of the landau and his eyes met Frank's, watching through the rain from the church door.

—◇—

THEY RODE TOGETHER UNTIL THE GRAY DAYLIGHT DROWNED IN THE west and then the *cristeros* lit kerosene-soaked torches and sat their horses in the downpour as Aragón leaned into the carriage and spoke in low, earnest tones to his wife for a long time. Rojas reined his horse around the other side of the carriage and said to Tommy, "Good luck, *padre*. Be careful."

"Take the boy back with you," Tommy said. "He won't want to go."

Then Aragón kissed his wife's cheek and gave smiling Quintana a hard look as he straightened in the saddle. Rojas reached up and plucked Miguelito from the driver's seat and spurred his mount, and as they disappeared into the rainy night Tommy could hear the lame boy's shouts.

—◄○►—

THEY ROLLED ALL THAT NIGHT AND IN THE MORNING THE DAWN KIND of bled through the gray wetness and Alejandro rested the horses in an ancient ramshackle barn that was home to a hundred feral cats that hissed down at them from the rafters and the acrid ammonia stench of their droppings was so strong that they left almost immediately and took shelter in a culvert under a stone bridge. They slept where they sat, and then Alejandro woke them warning that the culvert was filling fast and Tommy and Quintana helped him push the carriage out of the rushing, rising water and they started out again.

They stopped in late afternoon at a roadside inn just past the state border. Because of the storm they had seen no government troops whatsoever. There was an Oldsmobile sedan with tinted windows parked in the mud in front of the inn and the rain pounded off its roof. Helping Lourdes from the carriage Tommy put his hand on her waist and she shrank away in horror, almost falling into the sludge around their feet. Tommy grasped for her but she steadied herself on María Aragón's arm and quickly moved under the inn's overhang.

"What's wrong with her?" Quintana asked. She hadn't talked, or even lifted her veil, for the whole journey.

"I don't know," Tommy said. Then he asked, "What are you doing with the woman?" As soon as her husband had departed the wife of Aragon had snuggled into Quintana's arm, eventually falling asleep on his shoulder.

"Tend to your own business," the Yaqui said with a leer, "and I'll tend to mine."

Tommy clutched at Quintana's jacket and pulled him close in the rain. "This ain't no whorehouse jaunt! Remember what happened in Guadalajara?"

"Calm, gringo. Calm."

219

"We're here to get the gold. Don't be muckin' around!"

Tommy released Quintana's coat and strode through the mud toward the inn's door. Quintana glared darkly after him and muttered under his breath, "If you were not my friend, amigo . . ."

THE DINING ROOM OF THE INN WAS NEARLY EMPTY. THERE WERE A half-dozen *vaqueros* at the bar, and a table of men drinking in the middle of the room. In the far corner, under a crude Rivera-esque mural depicting the heroic victory over Maximilian's army, a young man in a dark suit rose from his table when he saw the two women—one sheathed by a veil—enter the dining room. The men in the inn all turned to inspect the women, then Tommy came in, Quintana right behind.

Tommy quickly took Lourdes's arm and when he felt her muscles tighten under his touch he rasped, "I'm supposed to be your husband." After a moment he felt her relax and he saw the young man at the corner table come out to meet them.

"*Señor, señora,*" the young man said, playing for the crowd. "With this storm, I was afraid your trip from the coast—"

"I think we made excellent time, considering," Lourdes said brightly, as she partially folded back her veil, keeping her left cheek shrouded. "You remember my husband, Mr. Johnson."

"*Señor* Johnson, of course. How have you been?"

"*Bueno,*" Tommy said animatedly. "*Muy bueno.*"

"And these are our business associates," Lourdes offered. "*Señor* and *Señora* Valesquez."

Quintana shook the young man's hand with what he imagined was *patrón*-like disdain. The young man quickly moved them back to the table.

"Sit down. I'll order some food."

"Let's get out of here," Tommy hissed. The men at the bar were watching them closely.

"It would look odd," Lourdes said softly. "The best way is to act naturally. We've just arrived after a long journey."

The young man pulled out a chair for her but she chose another, with her back to the room. She kept her left hand up at her veil, shielding her face.

When they were all seated the young man said softly, "Cousin, it's so good to see you. We were very concerned—"

"Yes, and you too, Esteban."

"But it's odd to see you out of your habit. It's . . . disconcerting."

"Yes," Lourdes dropped her eyes. "For me, too."

The waiter brought them a bottle of brandy and some glasses. He had a *callista* button on his collar and they talked of imaginary parties they had attended and phantom marriages being planned, and then when the waiter had gone away Esteban said he would drive them into Guanajuato and make a long loop on an unfinished government road and come into the city from the east, where there were fewer *federal* roadblocks.

"How is the city?"

Esteban shook his head. "It's madness. They thought they had discovered a priest last week, and they'd already shot the man before they realized he was only a Protestant *evangelista*. There was an apology to the American consul, but what good are apologies to a dead man?" He looked at Tommy. "This is he, eh?"

"Yes," Lourdes said softly. "This is the one."

"Can he really raise the dead? I've heard that he can."

"That's blasphemy, cousin," Lourdes snapped, then was quiet.

The innkeeper and the waiter brought out their meals, and they ate hungrily. After a while the men at the bar tired of snickering about the gringo and the *mexicana*, and they put on their slickers and went out into the rain. The table of drinkers followed them not long after. When they had finished eating Lourdes had Esteban ask the innkeeper where the toilets were, and then she and María Aragón went off together.

"I'll bring some food out to my brother," Esteban said, filling a plate with meat and tortillas. Alejandro had stayed with the carriage, to appear completely proper.

When they were alone, Quintana leaned over the table and said, "Did you understand what was said?"

"Some of it. . . .'"

"They shot a preacher in León last week."

Tommy nodded. "Let's do what we have to do and get the hell out."

"Damn right," Quintana said, as he had heard the Texans say so many times.

IN THE DRAFTY REAR ROOM THAT LED BACK TO THE PATIO OUTHOUSE María Aragón had unbuttoned her bodice down to her waist and was carefully powdering the tops of her girlish breasts, inspecting her handiwork by candlelight in a chipped, beveled mirror. Lourdes came in from the patio, droplets of rain shining on her lacework veil. She looked at María a moment, then began to readjust her own clothing. She looked in the mirror and their eyes locked in reflection.

"What?" María finally asked.

"*Señora . . .*" Lourdes said softly. "You are a married woman."

María didn't answer. She started to button up her dress front.

"What you're contemplating is a mortal sin."

María Aragón took out a small tin of lipstick, dipped in her pinkie and began to carefully finger-paint her full lips.

"Your husband is a good man. And I know you don't want to—"

"Sister, what my husband doesn't know won't hurt him."

Lourdes caught her breath with a sharp intake. "*Señora!*"

"Look, if the Good Lord didn't want me to fuck the Yaqui, He wouldn't have made him so beautiful."

Lourdes was shocked. She turned to face her straight on. "María, pray for forgiveness!"

"Listen, nun"—María stopped rouging her lips—"you serve God in your way, and I'll serve him in mine." She closed the tin with a snap. "If I am anything, I am a woman. I know how to please a man. That's why God put me on earth."

Lourdes started to speak and María stopped her. "God makes glorious men for me to please, and I pick out the best of them and give myself to them. The Yaqui is the finest I've ever seen." She cast a hard eye on Lourdes. "And don't act so high and mighty. You think we don't know how you yearn for the gringo?"

Lourdes was aghast. Her mouth hung open. She felt her whole body flush.

"The whole pueblo talks about it. You're like a puppy, chasing after him." María laughed, then her face grew lascivious. "They might have given you that nun's habit, but you're still a woman; you still get wet under here." She stuck her hand in the folds of Lourdes's skirt, pushing it between her legs. Lourdes shrank back. "And now you don't even have that black shroud on. With those silk drawers, you can really pretend you're his *esposa*." She leaned close and whispered, "You can dream about him hard inside of you!"

Lourdes took steps back in horror until her back struck the wall. There was a crucifix nailed there, and when she felt it dig into her back she jumped. María laughed. "There is God, little sister . . . and then there is *man!*"

She walked out of the dressing room, still laughing. Lourdes stood there, practically crouched in the corner. She raised her eyes to the crucifix, and after a moment desperately crossed herself.

SACRED HEART

—◄○►—

TEN KILOMETERS EAST OF LEÓN—AFTER THEY HAD MADE THE LONG detour around the city—they were stopped by a roadblock, the first they had seen. A sullen detachment of *federales*, waterlogged boys from drier climes, trying to stay out of the rain. After a desultory glance into the Oldsmobile they raised the barrier and waved them through without a word.

"If it all goes like that, it'll be good," Quintana said.

"Yeah." Tommy carefully lowered the hammer on the .45 in his hand, but kept it in his lap, under a blanket.

Lourdes and María sat opposite them—the Oldsmobile having once been used as a cab in Mexico City. Lourdes's veil was lowered again, and she hadn't spoken since they'd left the inn.

They had gone only a short distance farther when they saw pinpoints of light ahead of them, dancing eerily high through the rain. The Oldsmobile's headlights picked up the silhouettes of two columns of horsemen walking toward them on both sides of the road. Their wet slickers glistened in the car's lamps, and the firefly points of light were flashlights their officers were aiming at the car. On an unheard order the point men of both columns reined their horses toward each other, blocking the narrow, muddy road. The other riders came on around and behind, encircling them. Some of the riders were not in uniform.

"*Agraristas*," Quintana hissed with scorn as he reached for his big revolver.

"Esteban?" Lourdes said quickly.

"I'll handle it," her cousin said from behind the wheel.

Some of the soldiers had dismounted and were cursing about the mud on their boots. An *agrarista* leaned down from his saddle and squinted into the rain-speckled windows.

Under the blanket Tommy recocked the automatic and Lourdes reached over and put her hand on his. "*Calma*," she said. "*Calma*."

Esteban opened the window and hailed the approaching soldiers. "*Qué pasa, señores?*" A burly sergeant said without rancor, "Get out of the automobile." Esteban quickly slid from behind the wheel and stepped out into the mud.

"There are too many of them," Quintana said softly.

"Give me a *pistola*," María said, and after the briefest of moments the Yaqui pulled a .38 snub-nosed from his coat and slipped it to her.

"*Calma*," Lourdes said again.

Esteban was talking to the sergeant in the rain, and then another man dismounted. He had captain's bars on the shoulders of his raincoat. He stepped to the rear door and waited. Esteban kept talking to the sergeant and then the captain pointed to the rear door and said something but Esteban kept talking and then Lourdes leaned across Tommy and opened the door from the inside. The captain had to step back to allow it to open.

"Captain, what a terrible night," Lourdes said. The captain leaned down to look into the car's interior.

"My husband and I," Lourdes continued, "are on our way to León to catch a train for the *norte*. We're afraid the roads will wash out if we don't hurry."

The captain looked at her, then at Tommy, then at the others, then back at Tommy.

"My husband is an American businessman. We were investigating business opportunities on the coast and—"

"You came all the way from the coast?"

"*Sí*. From Nayarit."

"In this car?"

"No, *señor*. In a carriage most of the way."

The *agrarista* had dismounted and had pressed his face against the glass of the other door. His wide, coarse features were even more distorted. He tapped at the glass.

The captain studied them all again. "You saw no rebels along the way?"

"You mean counterrevolutionaries? No, Captain, thanks to you and heroic men like yourself."

The captain was suspicious. "If you came from Nayarit, why are you on the wrong side of the city?"

The *agrarista* yanked open the door and Tommy almost shot him then, but he waited.

"We were lost for a while, *Capitán*." Lourdes laughed. "The storm . . ."

The *agrarista* reeked of tequila and body stink. He leaned drunkenly into the car, ogling the two women.

The captain was staring at Quintana. "Who is this man? He is no American capitalist . . ."

"This man is my husband's bodyguard. He goes with him everywhere. And this is my sister." She took María's hand and clasped it tightly.

"I'd like to see your husband's passport."

The drunken *agrarista* looked at Quintana and laughed, showing rotted yellowed teeth. "A bodyguard?"

Quintana stared hard at the fat *agrarista.*

"Your husband's identity papers, *señora.*"

"Well, you see, *Capitán*, we had an accident in a culvert near the state line. Some of our luggage was washed away. If you wish you can accompany us into León and—"

"Will you please step out of the auto, *señora?*"

Lourdes hesitated. She began to be frightened.

"All of you, please, disembark from the car." The captain stood back and put one hand on the pistol at his waist. Esteban stopped talking for the first time since he'd stepped out of the Oldsmobile. Quintana looked at Tommy and with his eyes he said good-bye, gringo, and then he started to move and Tommy suddenly spoke up, in English, to Lourdes.

"Who is this man? Does he know who I am? Does he know who my friends are?"

Lourdes quickly replied, "I've tried to explain to him, but he won't listen."

Tommy looked at the captain with contempt. "What does he want, a bribe? What's his name? General Terrazas will be interested to know it."

"*Capitán*, my husband would like to know your name." But the captain was already staring at Tommy.

"Get his name. I'm sick of this behavior. The next time I speak to the President I'll be sure and tell him that . . . that . . . that . . . What the hell's this man's name?"

"*Capitán*, please. How are you called?"

The captain hesitated, then stepped forward and closed the Oldsmobile's door, saying, "We will accompany you to—"

"Goddamnit, what's his name?"

Just then the foul *agrarista* thrust his arm into the window and yanked Lourdes's veil from her face, exposing her disfigurement. He stared at it in fascination, and then, before even Tommy could react, Quintana had the muzzle of the horse pistol jammed into the *agrarista*'s meaty throat.

"No, no, *señor!*" The captain shouted, and then said in English to Tommy, "Please, mister. Tell your bodyguard not to shoot!"

Deliberately, Tommy put his hand on Quintana's arm. Then he said to the captain, "Sir, this is disgraceful! Is this the way you treat a visitor to your country? You insult my wife! You impede my journey!"

"No, mister, please!" The captain spoke sharply to the *agrarista*. "Sánchez, get back on your horse!"

The *agrarista*, even with the pistol in his throat, couldn't take his red eyes from Lourdes's blemish. *"Sánchez!"* the captain shouted. Quintana put his hand across the *agrarista*'s face and roughly pushed him from the car. He plopped on his ass in the mud.

"General Terrazas will hear of this!" Tommy said. "What *is* your name?"

"Señor," the captain pleaded, "please, I'm only trying to do my job." He quickly shut the door and moved back. He looked at Esteban and Lourdes's cousin quickly jumped back behind the wheel and started the engine. The captain shouted orders to his troopers and the horsemen spurred their mounts from the road. The Oldsmobile rolled forward slowly, and in a few short seconds the *federales* had been left behind in the downpour.

No one in the car spoke for a long time, and then Maria leaned forward in her seat and kissed Quintana deeply. Lourdes and Tommy just looked at each other.

–◄○►–

THE STREETS OF LEÓN WERE FLOODED. THE OLD, TWISTING COBBLESTONE byways the Spaniards had laid out hundreds of years before were awash with muddy water. The storm would not let up. The Oldsmobile sloshed slowly through hubcap-deep water and came to a stop before a garage. There was a corrugated metal door across the front of the garage and it unnerved Tommy. It filled him with dread and he didn't know why. Across the street from the garage was a small hotel and next to it a cinema showing Chaplin's *The Gold Rush*.

"This is it." Esteban nodded at the garage.

"I thought we were going to my father's house," Lourdes asked.

Esteban turned in the seat to look at her. "We must stop here first."

A man in working-class clothes came running around the side of the building, sloshing through the water-filled gutter. In the glare of the headlights he pulled apart the metal door and Tommy remembered that Matranga's warehouse on Thirty-eighth and Broadway had the same kind of corrugated iron door across the front of it. The truck with the snowplow claws had torn it apart. The man

226

swung open the big double doors and stepped aside, waving them in.

"Wait a minute." Tommy leaned forward and peered into the blackness of the garage. He thought he had seen something move in there.

"It's all right," Esteban said and turned back to the wheel. He put the car in gear and eased forward into the cavernous garage. Then the man stepped inside and pulled the doors shut behind him and the Oldsmobile was cast into total darkness. There was a long moment, and Tommy started to say, "There's something wrong—"

And then someone lit a candle and then someone else and then there were a hundred candles flickering and in the golden glow Tommy could see that the long, narrow garage was filled with people—men and women of all ages, children of all sizes—and the inside of the garage had been converted into a makeshift church. In the middle of the brick-walled, grease-stained corridor a board had been balanced between two stacks of tires and a clean white cloth laid over the board. An altar. And in the exact center, where the tabernacle should have been, sat a polished cherry-wood table radio.

"Jesus and Mary," Lourdes breathed, and then a small mustached man stepped to the Oldsmobile and opened the door. "Papa."

The concrete floor of the garage was damp, having been swept clean of flood waters only a few hours before. Lourdes stepped out and embraced her father, resting her head on his shoulder. *"Mi hija,"* he said softly. "My daughter. I prayed so diligently that the *Virgen* would protect you."

Lourdes tightened her hold on her father's neck. Over his shoulder she could see her mother and her uncle Don Enrique.

"Papa, she has been at my side always."

The small man stepped back from his daughter and inspected Tommy, who was just climbing from the car and looking around the garage. There were engine mounts hanging from overhead and harness rigging, from when it had been a stable.

"And this is the one?"

"Sí."

Don Enrique stepped forward. "Yes, this is the one."

Tommy looked at the cloth-covered board, and the hundred people staring at him. They had already started to edge closer, as if drawn by a magnet.

"What's . . . what's all this?"

"Padre," Lourdes's father, whose name was Don Hugo, extended

his hand. *"Padre,* we have been without God for too long now. We need His grace."

Tommy's eyes darted around the garage. He was becoming uneasy.

"We beg you to celebrate Mass with us," Don Hugo said.

Tommy looked at Don Hugo, then at Lourdes, then his head whirled as he sought out Quintana, but the Yaqui was gone.

—◁○▷—

QUINTANA AND MARÍA ARAGÓN SPLASHED HAND-IN-HAND ACROSS the water-logged street. With her other hand María held up her skirts.

"Ironed sheets," Quintana said with glee. "Perfumed pillows. French brandy!"

María squeezed his hand and laughed. "Maybe champagne! French champagne!"

They ran under the cinema marquee and on to the hotel's revolving door. They were laughing as they entered the lobby.

"I had champagne once, in Veracruz." Quintana's trousers were soaked to his knees. As they neared the reception desk he whispered into her ear, "I want to drink French champagne from your navel." The wife of Aragón giggled and across the lobby an American looked up from his newspaper and stared hard at them.

—◁○▷—

THE PEOPLE HAD BEGUN TO TOUCH TOMMY. TO REACH OUT AND softly take the cloth of his coat between their fingers and immediately release it, allowing others to move up in an ever-tightening circle of devotion.

"Please, my little angels," Don Hugo said to them. "Please. Give Father room to breathe." He turned to Tommy. "You'll have to pardon them, Father. It's been a year since they've seen a priest. Their souls hunger for salvation."

He took Tommy's arm and began to lead him to the cloth-covered board.

"Who . . . who are these people?"

"Family members. Old friends. Employees and their families. Parishioners. They have all heard of you, Father. "

"*Papacita*," Lourdes said, "why here, in a garage?"

"Why not, my daughter? Is it very different from a manger?" They approached the makeshift altar. "All our churches have been looted and padlocked. They shot the last priest in October. Everything has to be done in secret. There are spies everywhere."

"Don Hugo," Tommy said, "I can't say Mass. I didn't bring my— my things."

"Father, we have everything you need." Don Hugo gestured to the people and a woman moved forward, lifted her skirt, and carefully ripped out a chasuble that had been stitched in between her petticoats. In this manner, from a coat lining and between the layers of a crocheted shawl came a priest's maniple and stole. A long-hidden ciborium and gold chalice were produced from hiding places inside a big hollowed-out book and the interior of a globe.

"What about the Host, Papa? We can't say Mass without the Host."

"Ah . . ." Don Hugo smiled. He walked to the radio and turned it around on the clean white cloth. He snaked his hand in through the vacuum tubes and came out with a small metal case. A pyx.

"Father Luis hid this here before they killed him. He told us to save it for the time when the Church returned." He held it out to Tommy. "That time is now. That Church is you."

Tommy looked down at the silver case. He was afraid to touch it.

A FEW MOMENTS LATER TOMMY WAS SLOWLY VESTING BEFORE THE tire-stack altar. He slipped the stole around his neck and folded it over itself across his chest. Lourdes was standing close-by. Sensing his hesitation she stepped up and whispered. "Father Tomás, can I assist you?"

He looked at her and she saw the fear in his eyes. "What is it?"

"Sister, I can't do this."

She studied his face. He seemed truly stricken. "Father, I know the surroundings are profane, but these are good people."

"Sister—"

"They're good Catholics. They're risking their lives for the sacrament of the Mass."

"Lourdes, I can't say Mass."

"Father Tomás, I don't understand."

Tommy glanced around the candlelit garage. Every eye was upon him.

"Lourdes . . . I'm not—I'm not a priest."

She stared at him. For a long moment she tried to comprehend what he had said. He looked back at her, his eyes piercing and pleading. "I'm not a priest."

She shook her head slowly. "I don't understand. Of course you are."

"No," he whispered emphatically. "I'm not. I'm just a man."

She stared at him. "But why would—"

"I can't explain it now. Just believe me. I'm not a priest. *I can't say Mass for these people!*"

She slowly became aware that everyone was watching them. "But . . . but you must. They need you."

"How can I?"

"Just do it."

Tommy swallowed. "It would be a great sin."

"It would be a greater sin to deprive them of their faith."

"I . . . I don't know the Latin."

"I'll help you."

"*I can't!*"

"*You must!*"

"Sister . . . Sister . . ." Tommy turned away from the crowd, but there were more people behind the altar, only a few meters away. A young woman held her three year old son in her arms, the child's large dark eyes drinking in everything Tommy did. "Sister . . . I'm not even a good man . . ."

"Father—"

"Listen to me." Tommy turned to her and gripped her arm. She could feel his strong fingers through the lacy fabric. "I'm a . . . I'm a . . . I've committed great wrongs . . . Lourdes," he said desperately. "I've stolen . . . I've killed." He shook his head. "I've killed so many."

She felt she was hearing his confession. "Father, in war men sometimes do things they—"

"*I'm not your 'Father'!*" he hissed, and looking into his eyes, she finally understood what he was saying. Her hand flew to her mouth as she realized the fraud Frank and Tommy had perpetrated on her people. She took a step back.

And then, seeing the shame in Tommy's face, she gave him her absolution.

"It doesn't matter," she said with resolve. "They need God. And you can bring Him to them."

Lourdes turned to the people and loudly declared, "Because of the danger of the situation, Father will say an abbreviated Mass."

There was a quiet shuffling of feet throughout the crowd. These people hadn't come here, at risk of their lives, to have their religion tampered with. The attraction of Catholicism—its very value—was its ancient impregnability. Hadn't this very Mass been celebrated in the catacombs of Rome—another time when the Christian faith was a death sentence?

"Everyone will queue up for Communion, and at that time Father will give you spontaneous absolution—"

"My daughter," Don Hugo said. "We've never heard of such a Mass."

She blinked at her father. "It's a Mass they use in *los Estados Unidos*."

Don Hugo cocked his head. He looked at Tommy. "Are Americans in such a hurry they have to rush God?"

"Papa, please."

---◄○►---

THE WIFE OF ARAGÓN HAD A DESPERATE TWO-HANDED GRIP ON THE hand-carved headboard of the big dark four-poster. Her naked brown body was covered with a sheen of perspiration that gleamed like polish, and each time Quintana slammed into her from behind her buttocks shimmered with the impact.

"Is that good?" the Yaqui whispered hoarsely into her disarrayed hair that spilled down the bunching muscles in her back. "Is that what you need?"

"*Sí, hombre!*" she breathed urgently as she pushed back on him. "That's what I need!"

He reached around her and roughly molded his open palm across her bouncing belly, then up over her sweaty breasts. He captured one of her dark nipples, pulled and pinched it, and she caught her breath.

"Yes!" she gasped. "Fuck me."

María Aragón's unfocused eyes rolled back under her eyelids as her third orgasm started to build. She reached her hand back like a claw and dug her fingernails in his hard dark buttock and pulled him into her and he grabbed her hair and yanked her head back and there was a soft knocking on the door.

María didn't hear it. She was too lost in her passion, but Quintana had heard it, and though he continued thrusting into her, his intensity slackened.

"No!" she demanded. "Don't stop!"

Then he heard the knocking again, and he pushed her off his cock. Her face slammed down into the big goose-down pillow that muffled her furious curses and the Indian jumped from the bed and snatched his big revolver from its holster on the floor where it had been dropped in sexual frenzy. He cocked the hammer back and aimed the .45 at the hotel-room door.

María pushed her face up from the pillow and whipped around like an angry cat, ready to challenge the Yaqui on his manhood. "You son of a bit—"

She looked at the naked Indian, then at the big horse pistol, and immediately threw herself to the floor and came up with the little .38 he'd given her in the Oldsmobile. They exchanged glances and then there was again the soft tapping. Quintana moved quickly to stand beside the doorknob. He nodded at María to get behind the door. María flew across the rug and flattened herself against the wall. He touched the doorknob with his finger and she nodded and then they waited until the soft knocking started again and María grabbed out at the doorknob and pulled the door open and Quintana's hand struck out like a snake and caught the American's tie and dragged him into the room. He jammed the muzzle of the horse pistol into the American's chest, then stuck his head out of the door. There was no one else in the corridor. He kicked the door closed.

"Hey, hey, amigo." The American laughed nervously. "Go easy, go easy." He eyed their nakedness and grinned. "I'm sorry I disturbed you."

The wife of Aragón jabbed the little .38 against the gringo's temple and cocked it.

"Wait a minute! *Uno momento!*" The gringo put up his hands. "You know me!"

Quintana inspected the American's face. "The miner of blood. The gunrunner."

"Right! Right!" He tried to look around but María pushed his head back. "Gunny! Remember? Gunny."

"Tell me, Gunny"—Quintana leaned close—"Do you like to

watch two greasers fucking? Is that why you knocked on my door uninvited? Or are you looking to take our heads to Terrazas?"

"No! I—"

"You looking to sell our heads? You piece of shit!"

Gunny tried to shake his head but María, still flushed from the sex, held the pistol steady. "No, amigo. No!" Gunny made himself smile. "I want to show you something, that's all! I just want to show you something!"

Quintana glared in Gunny's face a moment longer, then he took his weapon from over the gringo's heart and threw it on the bed. He started to dress. María, still naked, didn't move.

"Tell her to uncock that *pistola*, amigo. Tell her I'm a friend."

Quintana said nothing.

"You don't trust him, do you?" María Aragón said in Spanish.

"Of course not."

"What does he want?"

"Whatever it is, it has to do with money. That's all this gringo cares about."

"That's all any of them care about," María said.

"Tomás?"

María shrugged. "Certainly, he is different. His brother, also. But as a general rule they are dogs."

The Yaqui pulled on his shirt and looked at the gringo.

"What do you have to show me?"

Gunny grinned. "You're gonna love this."

—◁○▷—

TOMMY MUMBLED, "TAKE THIS BREAD, FOR IT IS MY FLESH." He clumsily stuck the piece of wafer on Don Hugo's tongue. Don Hugo closed his mouth, looked at Tommy, looked at his daughter standing by Tommy's side assisting him in this extraordinary ceremony, then looked back at Tommy. He rose from his knees and walked away. Don Enrique, Lourdes's bearded uncle, stepped into his place and knelt before Tommy, bowing his head. All the others were strung out behind, waiting their turn at salvation. "Take this bread, for it is My Flesh."

In the end, for the last few, there was no Host left, just a few crumbs, and Tommy finally had to simply press his finger to the people's tongues and mutter a few sounds in ersatz Latin. Then all had been served Communion and Tommy felt drained, spent. He stared dumbly around the musty garage and barely heard the thunder that rumbled over the roof. His hands shook.

"Tomás," Lourdes whispered, and then when he didn't respond, "Tomás!"

He came back as if from a far place. "What?"

"Are you all right?"

He studied her face so long she blushed with confusion. "I don't know," he said finally.

Don Hugo and his brother Don Enrique approached them. "The man you must see is waiting in the back." Don Hugo nodded his head at the far end of the garage. The people were already starting to disperse, slipping out the front door in twos and threes. The makeshift altar had been dismantled, the radio stuffed away.

There was a door half-hidden behind a curtain of hanging chains and rotted tack, then a truncated flight of stairs up to a cramped little room that smelled, incongruously, of gasoline and horses. A small youngish man in octagonal spectacles sat nervously gripping a briefcase across his stomach as if he expected it to shield him from danger. His eyes flew back and forth between the two Hidalgo brothers as they entered, then they fixed on Tommy. Lourdes stood behind him.

"What took so long?" the anxious man said. "I've been in here for an hour."

"First things first," Don Hugo said.

"*Padre*," Don Enrique said to Tommy. "This man is my wife's brother-in-law. You don't need to know his name."

The smallish man eyed Tommy through his lenses.

"Is this the one?" the man said.

"*Sí.*"

"I will speak to him alone."

Don Hugo looked at Don Enrique. Then they slipped past Lourdes and down the stairs. Lourdes turned to leave and Tommy caught her hand.

"She stays," Tommy said.

"No." The smallish man shook his head.

"Yes," Tommy insisted. "My Spanish is not so good."

The man considered this. "We will speak English." Lourdes nodded and left, closing the door behind her.

When they were alone the man nodded to a chair, indicating Tommy should sit. He did. The man leaned forward in his chair, his elbows on his knees, his hands still gripping the attaché. "You are the priest they speak of? The gringo who cannot be killed?"

After a moment Tommy nodded.

The man's eyes drank in Tommy as if he were a religious icon. "They say you fear nothing. In the capital they sing about you in the streets."

Tommy shrugged, waiting.

"You understand, I risk my life to come here. If I were discovered, they will brand me as a traitor. They would throw my family out into the streets. They would torture and kill me."

The man seemed to expect a reply, some kind of validation.

"It's no more or no less than the rest of us," Tommy said. "We do what we do for God."

The man nodded silently, looking at Tommy. Then he said in a rush, "On the twenty-first of this month a train will leave Guadalajara for Mexico City. It will carry civilian passengers, mostly government officials and their families, and as well several troop cars. There will be machine guns mounted on the boxcar roofs."

"What time will it leave Guadalajara?"

The smallish man shrugged. Train schedules in Mexico were a fluid thing. "It's of no importance the time. Your spies will tell you of its progress."

"Of course."

"On this train there will be an armored car, and in this armored car, guarded by an elite escort of Terrazas's *agrarista* guards, will be one hundred thousand gold pesos, maybe more."

"Will Terrazas be on the train?"

"It isn't planned."

"A hundred thousand pesos? I was told fifty thousand."

The bespectacled little man shook his head. "Maybe even more. It's taxes collected from Jaliscans, bound for Mexico City to pay for the war against the *cristeros*."

Tommy looked at him, expecting more. "Is that it?"

"That's all I know. Only a handful of us in the capital are aware of this train. They've kept it very secretive."

"Good. You've helped the cause greatly. God bless you, *señor*."

Tommy started to rise, but the man took one hand from his briefcase and tugged him back down. "Father?"

"Yes?" Tommy had what he had come for. Now he wanted to get out of the city.

"Father, please hear my confession." The little man slumped

down to his knees with a hollow bump. He let his attaché slip to the floor. "Please, Father."

Tommy stared at him. If he'd already committed blasphemy in the celebration of the Mass, what was the difference if he heard this man's confession? "Quickly, señor. These are dangerous times. Are you sorry for all your sins?"

The little bureaucrat gave a slight nod. "Oh, yes . . ."

"Then don't do them again."

Tommy again rose to leave but the man rasped, "Father, don't go! I must get some things off my soul, please."

"I forgive you, in the name of Father, the Son, and . . ." Tommy suddenly felt a sense of foreboding, like the one he'd felt when he first came to Mexico. "You are absolved."

Tommy pulled his sleeve out of the man's grasp.

"Father," the little man begged, "in the name of the Virgin, hear my confession."

"Then do it, man," Tommy snapped. "I don't have all fucking night."

The man blinked up at Tommy a moment, then he whispered, "Father, I have betrayed my friends. I've informed on members of my own family." He started to cry. "I was afraid, Father! They said the only way to prove my loyalty was to give them names. Others in the government who met for secret worship." He crumpled over and sobbed, "I've caused many people to die. Many of my fellow Catholics. People I loved."

Tommy looked down at the little man in disgust. Above all else— more than coppers, more than Sicilians—Tommy Gun Coyne had hated informers. The little man reached out and gripped Tommy's leg. He choked out, "Father, I'm so afraid!" He raised his tear-streaked face. "I don't want to burn in hell!"

Tommy thought about killing the stool pigeon then. He had strapped on his pistols after the Mass, and he thought about shooting the man now. The garage would muffle most of the sound. And after he had explained what the man had told him, no cristero would judge him. A snitch was always a liability, forever and ever, anywhere in the world.

"Please, Father!" the little man moaned. "Please."

Tommy sat down slowly. The little bureaucrat gulped for air between his sobs. Tommy stared down at him.

"Father . . ."

Tommy reached under his coat and withdrew one of his shiny automatic .45s. He looked at it. So did the little man. Tommy realized his weapons were the only thing left from his life in New York. "You have committed very grave sins, *señor.*"

The little man's eyes widened behind his octagonal lens.

"You understand, I can only give you absolution if you are truly, truly sorry for your actions."

The little man nodded slowly.

Tommy pulled back the slide on the top of the pistol, readying it. The little bureaucrat's mouth dropped open.

"Are you truly, truly sorry?"

The little man nodded more quickly.

"Of course, a true repentance would mean you would never inform on anyone ever again." Tommy looked at him. "That would mean you were heartily sorry."

"I am," the man whispered, but it was more of a plea. "I am so sorry."

"Because if I give you absolution for these putrid sins, and you repeat them, then I would be forced to seek you out." Tommy loosely raised the gun. "I would be forced to take God's own revenge." Tommy leaned forward and, his face only inches from the bureaucrat's, whispered, "And as you know, I cannot be killed. My vengeance is immortal."

The little man was shaking.

"Do you repent from your transgressions?"

"Ye—yes, Father."

"You are heartily sorry?"

"Oh, yes, yes . . ."

"And you will never do them again?"

"Never. *Never!*"

"Then I forgive you."

"Oh, thank you Fa—"

Tommy raised the .45 and touched the muzzle against the man's temple. "In the name of the Father." The bureaucrat froze as still as a hunted rabbit. His eyes slowly closed because he knew this devil priest was going to kill him. After what seemed like an eternity Tommy took the barrel away from the man's forehead. It left an imprint in his flesh. The little man in the octagonal glasses was just about to breathe again when Tommy shoved the gun into the man's gut. "And of the Son." The little man shook like a leaf in a wind. Tommy next jabbed the automatic into the man's right breast. "And of the Holy Ghost." Slowly Tommy dragged the muzzle across his breast and stopped when it was just over the little bureaucrat's heart. He cocked the weapon. The man—his eyes still clamped closed—gave a little jolt at the metallic intake of breath. Then Tommy softly said, "Amen." The man began to whimper uncontrollably. He was going to die. After a while Tommy took the weapon from over the man's heart and stood up. The bureaucrat opened his eyes. He couldn't believe he was still alive.

"Go," Tommy said. "Go, and sin no more."

The little man tried to get to his feet but there was difficulty. Tommy helped him up. "Go home," Tommy said.

"Yes! Yes, Father." He tried to pick up his briefcase but he couldn't get a purchase. Finally Tommy lifted it and set it in his arms. "Remember me," Tommy hissed, like a serpent. The little man rushed for the door.

"And remember—!" Tommy said. The little man stopped short, his eyes wide as he looked back.

Tommy stared at him a long time, then said softly, more to himself than to the bureaucrat. "None are without guilt, señor. None of us."

The little man nodded, then fumbled the door open and fled with his forgiveness and his life.

—◀○▶—

GUNNY OPENED THE DOOR TO HIS HOTEL ROOM AND STEPPED BACK, indicating Quintana should enter. Quintana, now fully clothed, shook his head and Gunny grinned and walked through the door.

"I don't know why you don't trust me, amigo. I'm going to make you a very wealthy man."

Quintana said nothing as he shut and locked the door. Gunny walked to the table beside his bed and picked up a newspaper. He held out the paper to Quintana.

"I picked this up in the Capital last week. It's six months old." Gunny's eyes danced with excitement. Quintana slowly took the newspaper.

It was an American weekly. The Yaqui was not as comfortable reading English as he was in conversation, but the fat, scrolled Victorian title jumped out at him: *Police Gazette*. Below that was a grainy photograph of Tommy, glaring coldly at the camera. Quintana immediately identified it as a police mug shot. He looked up at Gunny.

"Go 'head, amigo. And hold on to your hat."

Quintana slowly read the top headline: *"The Most Wanted Man in America!"* And then, *"Cop Killer Coyne! $25,000 Reward."*

"He ain't no priest at all!" Gunny said gleefully. "I knew I'd seen him before. He was pointed out to me once in Jim Jeffries' bar. That son of a bitch"—Gunny tapped the newspaper—"is a fucking mick gangster. Him and his old man used to run everything west of Broadway. Most ruthless fucking mob in the city!"

Quintana carefully read the rest of the story, which covered the whole front page. "Massacre . . . multiple murderer . . . armed and dangerous . . . sought church sanctuary . . ."

"He's on the lam down here, hiding out behind that collar." Gunny shook his head and laughed. "Damned strange time and place to pick to be a priest, but damn—" He tapped the paper again. "That's twenty-five thousand dollars, amigo. *Dolares!* Not pesos." He grinned. "That's a lot of money to split up between two good amigos, eh?"

Quintana stopped reading and looked at Gunny. "You've told no one else about this?"

"Hell, no." He leered at Quintana. "This is between you and me . . ." His eyes sharpened like knives. "Where is he? Still back there on the mountain?"

Quintana grinned back. "No. He's here in the city. He rode in with me."

Gunny slapped his palms in delight. "Fuck! That's lucky, amigo. That's real lucky!" Gunny started to pace the rug in excitement. "When I looked up and saw you walk into the lobby downstairs, I knew the cards were coming my way." He stopped. "How many we need to take him, you think? The stories I've heard, I think maybe a half-dozen *vaqueros.*"

The Yaqui shook his head. "I can do it by myself."

"You really think so?"

"No problema. He trusts me. I can come up behind him."

Gunny's face pinched in thought. "I don't know. I was there in Guadalajara when—"

"I was there, too, amigo." Quintana looked down at the *Gazette.* "Maybe once he was dangerous, but not anymore." He chuckled. "He's gotten soft. He's gotten religion."

"How you gonna grab him? The reward don't say nothing about 'dead or alive,' so I figure, he's gotta be in working condition."

"That's not what we need to talk about, amigo." Quintana sat on the edge of the bed and sprawled back. "What we got to talk about is the split."

Gunny looked at him, his brain functions almost visible. "Okay, okay . . . The way I see it—"

"It's fifty-fifty, or it's nothing."

"Now, wait a minute—"

"I'm taking the chances. I'm the one delivering the goods."

"You're delivering them to me. I gotta transport them all the way to the border and across. Only a gringo could do that."

"You're not taking him anywhere without me, amigo. He's worth too much to let out of my sight."

Gunny thought a moment, then said, "All right, fifty-fifty. It's a deal." He held out his hand. Quintana stared at it. Gunny pulled back his hand.

"You don't trust me, amigo." He feigned insult, but it was so crude it was comical.

"What's to stop you," Quintana said, "from cheating me out of my half once we get him across the border? Gringo laws don't apply to greasers."

Gunny was about to offer the Indian his word, but thought better of it. "I'll put it in writing. I'll draw up a fucking contract. Whaddaya say?"

Quintana studied the American's face as he considered this. "We both sign it?"

"Right, right." Gunny hurried to a tiny writing table in the corner. "We'll both sign it. We'll make it all legal." Pulling out the minuscule drawers, he located a few dusty sheets of paper. "Here we go." Gunny sat down, plucked out his pen from his coat pocket, unscrewed the cap, and began to dictate to himself as he wrote. "To Whom It May Concern . . . This is a contract verifying that—"

Quintana rose slowly from the bed, slipped his hand behind his back and withdrew his blade from its belt sheath. He moved toward Gunny.

"—the reward for the capture and return of Thomas Coyne . . . alias Tommy Gun Coyne—"

Gunny heard the Indian coming up behind him and said, "Here, you can watch over my shoulder as I write it down and then—"

"No thanks," Quintana said and grabbed Gunny's hair, yanked his head back and slit his throat. The blood spurted all over the desktop. For a moment Gunny stared at the spraying red flow without understanding, then he rose from the chair and turned to the Yaqui. His face was a mask of terror.

Quintana stepped back and wiped the blade on the bedspread. Gunny watched him, then he started to stumble toward the door.

Quintana stuck out his leg and Gunny fell over it, landing hard on the rug.

"*Shhhhh*—" the Indian said. "Be quiet, Gunny."

Gunny started to crawl toward the door, pushing the rug into mounds before him. His blood geysered out and spattered on the dark wood floor. Quintana sat on the edge of the bed and put his foot on the American's back, holding him down.

"Gunny, you ever have a friend?"

Gunny clutched out at the rug, but he was already weakening.

"I mean, not just a guy you drink with, or steal with, but a true friend."

Gunny desperately tried to raise himself to his knees, but Quintana leaned his weight on his leg and Gunny flattened with a sickening whoosh. The blood was spreading. "You use the word 'amigo' a lot, but do you even know what it means? I don't think so. . . ."

"Help me," Gunny pleaded stupidly.

"Tomás is my friend. Gunny, he's the truest friend I've ever had." Gunny began to gurgle as he lost consciousness. Quintana pressed down harder with his boot. "And I believe he will lead me to God."

─◄○►─

TOMMY CAME OUT INTO THE DARKENED GARAGE AND DON HUGO and Don Enrique were waiting for him, with Lourdes and Esteban. The little bureaucrat had gone. There was no one else now. Thunder boomed above.

"*Padre*," Don Hugo said, then embraced Tommy warmly. "You are a very brave and godly man. We need more like you in these Satanic times." Lourdes said nothing, but she felt proud despite her ponderous secret.

"We must go now," bearded Don Enrique said. "When the rains stop the police will come out to enforce the curfew. Esteban will drive you back to your carriage." He put his hands on Tommy's shoulders. "The information you have is of momentous importance. You must return safely to Sagrado Corazón, so be very, very cautious."

Tommy nodded and the big bearded man embraced him. "Go with God," Don Enrique whispered in his ear. "And protect my niece."

When the two Hidalgo brothers had slipped through the door and out into the rain Esteban said, "We can't stay here much longer. It's too dangerous."

Lourdes looked at Tommy and Tommy said, "We won't leave without Quintana. We'll wait for him to come back."

The rainwater on the garage roof had accumulated and was starting to find seams in the boarding and seep through, pouring down in gentle sheets.

"Then let's wait in the car," Esteban said. "At least it'll be dry."

Esteban got behind the wheel and Tommy and Lourdes sat in the back. Lourdes looked at Tommy. The torment on his face was gone now and he seemed at peace, lost in his thoughts. *He's not a priest*, Lourdes allowed herself to realize. She studied his face in profile. *Was he any more a man now?* she asked herself. *Did she desire him any more than she had when she thought he was a priest? No. She wanted him now as she had always wanted him.* Lourdes waited to feel the heat of her shame burn her face but it didn't come. She was surprised at her own brazenness.

Tommy turned then and looked at her. He saw her eyes devouring him. *"Qué te pasa?"* he asked in well-accented Spanish and she burst out in laughter. Esteban turned in his seat and looked at her, then looked away.

"It's nothing," she said, smiling. "You are becoming Mexican, that's all."

"You don't hate me for what I've done?"

She glanced at the back of her cousin's head. "No. I could not hate you. Don't you know that?"

"I've committed blasphemy. I've—"

"You've given my people hope. Didn't you see how they looked at you tonight? How grateful they were?"

"But it's all a fraud. It's not real. *I'm* not real."

Esteban's neck muscles seemed to tense. Lourdes reached over and took Tommy's hand to quiet him. Then Esteban turned and looked back through the Oldsmobile's back window.

"Did you hear something?"

Then he looked down at their entwined hands and someone fired a pistol through the right front window and the interior of the car was filled with glass and blood and bits of flesh as the left side of Esteban's face exploded and he was slammed back against his door. Lourdes screamed and Tommy reached for his weapons but the doors were already yanked open and a rifle jammed into his chest. Tommy froze and looked up into a leering fat brown face. The *agrarista* from the roadblock. Sánchez laughed evilly and Tommy could smell the tequila stink. Then a dozen hands reached in and pulled them from the car.

━◁○▷━

THE WIFE OF ARAGÓN WAS JUST BUTTONING UP THE BODICE OF HER silken dress when Quintana came through the door.

"What did that fucking gringo want?" Her lovemaking interrupted, María Aragón was cross.

Quintana quickly began to pull on the rest of his clothes—vest, tie, coat. "We have to get out of here."

That's when María noticed his bloody footprints leading from the door. She stared at them.

━◁○▷━

THEY HAD TOMMY DOWN ON THE WET GARAGE FLOOR AND THEY were kicking him. Sánchez leaned against the car—Esteban's body sprawled halfway through the yanked-open door—and gleefully twirled Tommy's automatics.

"I knew I'd seen that face before." He leered over at Lourdes, who was being held from behind by an *agrarista* who kept grinding his groin into her buttocks. "That beautiful face." He traced the muzzle of one of the automatics down his left cheek. He laughed then, and walked to her. "You don't remember me, do you, bitch?" Lourdes was terrified, but she had already given her death to God. She glared haughtily at the drunken *agrarista*. "I used to work for your father, cleaning out his fucking stables," Sánchez said. "I remember the day you were born. All the wailing and crying." He reached up to touch her deformity and when Lourdes tried to turn her face away the *agrarista* behind her yanked her head still. Sánchez ran his dirty thumbnail down the slur of flesh. "I watched you grow up. The little princess. The little bitch princess."

The other *agraristas* were still kicking Tommy and Sánchez turned to them and shouted, "Enough!" The *agraristas* stopped. They were breathless and excited. "Drink," Sánchez said. "We have all night."

He turned back to Lourdes. "And I believe that is a very special gringo. I believe that's the famous *Padre Pistolero*."

"*Ayyy*," one of the men said. "Terrazas will make us all colonels!" There was laughter, and a bottle was passed around.

"I watched you grow up." He looked down at the dress covering her breasts. "I watched your tits come in . . . and come in and come in." There was a great burst of manly laughter. "We used to jerk off in the stable, watching you through your bedroom window. You didn't know that, did you? You never felt our eyes on you?" Lourdes looked at him with disgust overlying her fear. The bottle was handed to Sánchez and he took a long pull. His eyes glowed with heat. "And then when we heard you were to become a nun, *ay yi yi*, what a fucking waste we all thought. That wonderful body, and only the pig priests get to see it." He caught her chin then, in a viselike grip, and poured tequila down her throat. Then he tossed the empty bottle to the floor and Lourdes coughed and choked. "Well, that's all changed, bitch." He took a two-handed grip on the fabric of her dress and ripped down viciously. Lourdes's young, heavy breasts popped out of the rended material and the *agraristas* got very quiet, like a wolf pack spotting a lamb.

"Fuck," Sánchez breathed, looking down at her youth and womanliness. He caught one of her breasts in his thick-fingered hand and squeezed. Lourdes tried to pray but she couldn't block out the roughness of his calluses. Sánchez grinned, and keeping his eyes on Lourdes's face, he ducked his head and noisily sucked her nipple into his mouth.

One of the *agraristas* stuck his hand in his leather pants and began to masturbate. Tommy was trying to get to his knees.

Sánchez caught Lourdes's nipple between his yellowed teeth and bit down. Lourdes shouted out in spite of herself, and the men laughed again. He took his mouth from her flesh and said, "I have an idea! Let's watch the pig priest fuck Christ's whore!"

The men were too aroused for such ironic subtlety. "*Jefe*, let us have her! Fuck the priest!"

"We will all have her," Sánchez shouted. "But first, I want to see them do what they do on the altar. The Fucking Sacrament." He glared around at the circle of men in the dark garage, lighted only by the kerosene lamps the *agraristas* had lit. "Get her naked."

They pounced on Lourdes as dogs would on a hare, ripping her garments away in shreds like skin torn from bloody meat. They grabbed at her breasts, clutched at her buttocks, jammed their fingers into her wetness. After a few seconds Sánchez had to wade into them, pulling them off her. "Get off! Get back! I want to see the priest fuck her! Get off!" The band of men stumbled back, their muttering like growls, surly at being interrupted in their pleasure. One of them angrily kicked Tommy in the ribs.

"I said enough!" Sánchez glared around at them, then he looked at Lourdes and his face filled with carnal rapture. She stood naked before them, shivering with fear and humiliation, finally terrified beyond all faith or fortitude. Her trembling, supple body fairly glowed in the lamplight. Her dark, closely shorn hair made the fullness of her breasts and hips even more provocative.

Sánchez grinned. "Bring her her Christ, for her to fuck."

They pulled Tommy to his feet and dragged him before Lourdes. He was bruised and bleeding but, having gained his footing, he ripped out of their grasp. Sánchez shoved the muzzle of Tommy's own .45 against his skull and Tommy quieted. Sánchez leaned against him and rasped in his ear. "Look at her." Lourdes raised her eyes and locked them with Tommy's. "Look at those tits. Look at that bush." Sánchez's eyes drank her in. "Don't you want to fuck her, Father?"

"Go fuck your mother," Tommy said in an even tone.

Sánchez and the others laughed. "Ah, this one has faith," Sánchez said. "He's not afraid to die. But he's afraid to fuck!"

They all laughed again, then Sánchez said, "Hey, maybe he's already had her!"

"No." An *agrarista* held up a finger. "I dug around inside her. This filly's unbroken." The *agrarista* sniffed his finger and they all laughed once more.

"Ah, *padre*," Sánchez grinned. "You can fuck the *Virgen*, just like you always wanted to." He nodded to an *agrarista* standing behind Lourdes and the man put his boot in her naked back and shoved her forward. Tommy caught her to keep her from falling and she was in his arms, her breasts mashed against his chest. The *agraristas* watched with hungry eyes.

We are going to die, Lourdes thought and knew that somehow he could hear her. He held her close to comfort her, and she whispered her thoughts into his neck, *I love you, Tomás. God forgive me, but I love you.*

"Look at the little doves." Sánchez smirked. Then his face darkened. "But we want to see more. *Padre,* take out your Bishop's staff, we want to see her suck it."

The *agraristas* nudged each other. This was going to be a good show. Someone uncorked another bottle.

245

"Take out your prick, gringo," Sánchez said again. When Tommy didn't respond Sánchez nodded to his men and they reached in and pulled them apart. Tommy lashed out with a right that sent one of the *agraristas* to the garage floor, and then Sánchez put the automatic to Lourdes's head and cocked it. Everyone watched carefully. Sánchez pushed her to her knees and looking at Tommy said, "Take out your fucking cock or I'll blow this whore's head off."

Tommy looked down at Lourdes—her close-cut nun's hair, her heavy bruised breasts, her young fleshy body—and he was washed with that feeling again, that insane certainty that all was well. He began to unbutton his fly and then the garage became a hellish maelstrom of gunfire. Three *agraristas* went down immediately and then there was another series of flashes from the shadows of the garage and Sánchez's left shoulder erupted in an explosion of blood and bone. Tommy snatched up the fallen .45 and threw his body over Lourdes and twisted around just in time to fire at two men taking aim on him. One man dropped to his knees and Tommy shot him again and then the other one fell and the wife of Aragón was behind him, holding the little .38.

"*Quintana!*" Tommy shouted, then someone fired and María Aragón made a sound like the wind being knocked out of her and Quintana's big horse pistol barked again in rapid succession as she crumpled. Tommy saw in the flashes an *agrarista* running toward the door and he fired at the fleeing figure and when he turned again he realized he was standing and he didn't know where Lourdes was.

"Gringo?" Quintana said as he came slowly out of the shadows.

"Did we get them all?"

"I don't know."

"Where's Lourdes? I don't know where Lourdes is." All but one of the kerosene lamps had been knocked over in the melee and it flickered weakly in a corner, throwing a soft circle of light on the sprawled bodies. Quintana knelt over the wife of Aragón and slipped his hand under her head. She was dead.

"I'm sorry, María. You were much woman." He kissed her lips and lowered her back to the garage floor.

They were suddenly bathed in harsh light and whirled to face the flashlight and the torch fell to the concrete floor and clattered and a moment later Sánchez pitched forward, glassy-eyed. Tommy rose and went to Lourdes, still naked, shaking uncontrollably, a bloody dagger in her two-fisted grip. He held her tightly and after the briefest of moments Quintana said, "We have to go. We have to get out of here."

—◄○►—

THE OLDSMOBILE WAS BULLET-RIDDEN AND USELESS, AND THEY TOOK to the rainy predawn streets in clothes and slickers taken from the dead *agraristas,* Lourdes masquerading as a boy, a hat pulled down over her face. She wanted to go to her father's house but Quintana said it was too dangerous and Tommy just wanted to flee. On the edge of the city Quintana pounded on the door of a riding stable until the proprietor got out of his tack room bed to open the stable door with a lamp in one hand and a pistol in the other. He peered at them suspiciously through the slackening rain and Quintana showed him some coins and the stable master let him in alone and when the Yaqui saw President Calles's photograph on the tack room wall he slit the proprietor's throat as he had Gunny's and they saddled quickly and rode out over the proprietor's body and when the rain finally stopped and the sun broke through in the east they were already ten kilometers from the city. Quintana said they weren't going back to the roadhouse, so they kept to the outlands.

They rode hard that day and night and the next, and then Tommy's horse collapsed and they walked to the next hamlet and bought two mules and another horse for twice their value from a German-immigrant farmer who spoke almost no Spanish and who knew better than to look them straight in the face. They took turns sleeping in the saddle, and finally, when they reached the rise up to Los Altos country, they saw Federal patrols on the ridge line and hid a full day in the barn of a family Lourdes knew to be loyal to Christ. At dusk they rode out on fresh mounts and two days later they saw a dozen men riding down on them, holding their rifles above their heads. It was Rojas and his three sons and his *vaqueros.* The husband of María Aragón was with them. When Aragón saw that his young wife was not with them he reined in next to Quintana.

"*Señor,*" Quintana said, "I promised you I would protect your María, but God had other plans. I am sorry."

Aragón, who had known he would never see his wife again when he rode over the ridge and saw she wasn't with them, slumped in the saddle.

"She died a martyr's death," Lourdes said. *"Señor,* she was a saint."

Rojas said they must get back to the stronghold. The *federales* had intensified their patrols. They had attacked another band of *cristeros* in the town of San Julian to the east and there had been a pitched battle in the streets. Many of Sagrado Corazón's men had left to join that band, over Frank's furious objections. They wanted to fight.

As they rode over the lean, hard lands Rojas told them there had been new *agrarista* atrocities. A priest had been found hiding in the brambles of a dry riverbed, and he had been crucified on a rude cross wrapped in kerosene-soaked burlap and then the cross had been set afire. The *agraristas* had made the residents of the nearest pueblo watch him burn. In another town the *agrarista jefe* had promised coins and candy to any child who informed on a parent witnessed in secret prayer. Several did, and the parents were summarily shot. The children ate their chocolate as they watched the executions. These children, Rojas said, are demons and they must not be allowed to live.

—◅◦▻—

THEY RODE DOWN A NARROW CANYON, STAYING HIDDEN AS MUCH AS possible, and as they climbed up out of the canyon, on a solitary hillock to the north a dense flock of ravens were feeding on two bodies propped up on crossed sapling racks. As they came upon the bodies—blackened by the sun, covered by the jostling, digging iridescent black birds—Rojas gave out a small *ah.*

"It's the priest Moreno, and his woman."

Quintana's mouth tightened as he realized the rotting cadaver, its eye sockets empty and blackened with dried blood, was the woman from the lean-to under the eucalyptus tree. He wheeled his horse toward the racks and shouted. The ravens rose like a fluttering of black devils, screaming their frustration. The bodies were rank. Their hands and feet had been severed. Theirs had not been easy deaths. Quintana covered his nose with his hand and shouted, "They say we Yaquis are savages, and they do this!"

"What were they doing out here alone?" Tommy asked of Rojas, and the *alteño* looked back at his sons, then said, "They were driven out by your brother."

"Why? Didn't Frank know the *agraristas* were riding?"

Rojas didn't speak.

"Of course, he knew!" Tommy yelled. "Why did he do this?"

Lourdes knew. "They had sinned," she said softly.

Tommy looked at her. "What do you mean?"

"Your brother caught them together on the ground, making love," Rojas finally admitted. "He banished them from the pueblo."

Tommy's face darkened with anger and he jumped down from the saddle. He went to Quintana and said, "Give me your knife." The Yaqui dismounted and they began to cut the bodies down from the sapling racks.

—◀○▶—

MIGUELITO SAW THEM FIRST. HE HAD SAT EVERY DAY, PERCHED ON the highest palisade, squinting down the mountain, scanning the empty flatlands below. There were sentries, too, ordered there by Frank, who grew ever more fearful of a *federal* attack, but the sentries got bored and rolled cigarettes and drowsed in the sun. When Miguelito clambered to his feet and called out, "There! There!" and pointed to the dust cloud slowly moving up the mountain the sentries stood erect and nervously fingered their weapons. Some of the *pueblerinos* came to the edge of the mountain and shading their eyes peered down with concern at the distant riders.

But Miguelito knew. Within seconds his one good eye had picked up a trait in one of the faraway specks—an angle, a movement— and the boy whooped with delight and jumped crookedly from palisade to roof and back again. He lurched down three flights of stone steps and flapped like a broken-winged bird across the *placita* and into the church. He jumped onto the bell rope and lifted his uneven legs from the floor and the bell began to toll crazily, then he raced back across the plaza and down the mountainside road in a hopping, skipping lope.

When he neared the horsemen Miguelito pulled up short and stared. Tommy rode lead, with his face covered with a cloth. Then came Lourdes, Quintana and the others, all masked the same way. The last rider in the queue led two packhorses on a long tether. Miguelito took hold of Tommy's stirrup strap and walked along beside, looking back at the two foul-smelling, slicker-wrapped bundles tied across the backs of the packhorses.

They rode slowly into a very different pueblo than they had left

249

only ten days before. Many of the *cristeros* who had come up to the mountain to follow Tommy, to fight for Christ with the *pistolero padre*, had departed, leaving to join other bands. They had been replaced by a coterie of flat-eyed brigands with dead expressions on their wolfish faces. Tommy reined in and stared around at them.

"Who the hell are they?"

Quintana crossed his leg over his saddle horn and dug out a cheroot. "Deserters, probably. Renegades. *Bandidos*."

"What the hell are they doing here?"

Quintana struck a match and pulled down his bandanna. "It's my guess, they've come for the gold."

Victoriano Rojas kicked his mount and came up abreast of them. "Father Francisco has promised them a hundred pesos apiece, when we take the train."

"They know about the train? He told them about the train?"

Rojas spit before he spoke. "When you didn't return from León the people were dispirited. He had to replace the soldiers who departed."

Tommy shook his head. "With these?"

Frank came out of his rectory door, stumbling slightly as he stepped across the threshold. Tommy realized with a jolt that his brother had been drinking.

"Father Tomás," Frank said with cold irony, slurring his words. "Everyone thought they had gotten you." He gave a short, bitter laugh. "But I knew better. I knew you'd be back. You can't be killed. You're a fucking angel."

Frank turned his cold eyes on Lourdes. "Sister. Maybe it's time you got out of those trousers and back into your habit. I wouldn't want you to get confused."

Lourdes dropped her eyes. "Yes, Father." She dismounted.

"And what's that hellish stink?"

Tommy dismounted then, too, and the others followed his lead. "We found Father Moreno out there. They'd torn him apart."

Frank looked at the pack animals. "Moreno and his whore?" He watched Lourdes as she hurried into the infirmary house. "You should have left them where you found him."

"We brought them back to bury them."

"Not in my cemetery."

"He's a priest," Tommy said evenly. "He'll rest in consecrated ground."

Frank's eyes narrowed, then he laughed derisively. "Don't forget who you are."

Tommy got very still and Quintana stood away from his horse, waiting. Then Tommy said so only his brother could hear, "No, *you* don't forget who I am."

Frank was furious. He glanced around at his *bandoleros.* "Father Tomás. Could I speak to you in the church, please?"

Inside the church that still smelled of new adobe, Frank slammed the doors and whirled on his brother. "Don't you ever talk to me like that in front of—"

Before he could finish Tommy had clutched Frank's cassock and shoved him back against the freshly hewn door. It was the first time in their lives Tommy had ever been violent toward his older brother. "In front of who, those killers you went out and bought? You finally got your own mob, Frank?"

Frank tore at Tommy's grip. "Let go of me!"

"Moreno was loyal to you! Hell, the man and I stood on the gallows together!"

"He was a fornicator! He broke his priestly vows!"

"And you sent him out to his death!"

"He was fucking on the ground like a dog! He was an abomination, and I won't tolerate that!"

"Who the hell are you to tolerate or not?! This is Mexico! Moreno was a Mexican!"

Frank finally pulled out of Tommy's grip. "Do you know what these people did before we brought them salvation? They ripped out each other's hearts!" Frank's eyes blazed with zeal and tequila. "The Princes of the Church must be beyond reproach! We have to set an example!"

Tommy studied his brother's face. "You're bugs. And you're drunk."

"How dare you preach to me, *Father* Thomas!" Frank's face filled with rage. "Tell me, *Father* Thomas, how many men have you killed with your own hands? How many begged you for mercy?" He moved toward Tommy. "And you enjoyed it, didn't you, Tommy Gun?! You felt like God Himself!"

Tommy hit his brother then, but at the last second he pulled the punch and Frank fell back against a pew and righted himself and in a fury launched himself back at Tommy. Tommy simply stepped out of Frank's path and let his momentum carry him against the church wall. Frank's feet got drunkenly entangled and he slammed hard to the floor.

Tommy stood over him and said with a brogue, "Ah, the apple of Peggy Coyne's eye . . . And didn't she tipple a wee bit herself?"

"I'll kill you!" Frank shouted and scrambled to get up, but Tommy put his foot on Frank's chest and held him down. Frank struggled ineffectually, like a beetle on its back. "You son of a bitch!"

"If you want that train, Frankie Boy, you better do like I say."

Frank stilled. "You know when it's leaving for the capital?"

Tommy looked down at him. "Moreno gets a Catholic burial in the cemetery. The woman, too. And you give the eulogy."

After a moment Frank nodded.

"And you leave Lourdes alone. Or I'll kill you."

—◦—

WHEN FRANK WAS ACCEPTED BY THE JESUITS IN GUADALAJARA HIS counselor in the seminary, Father Donahue, instructed him to travel to New York City and say good-bye to his family. Frank had been at St. Bernard's for five years. He had excelled in languages, showed a predilection for theology, and was passionate, if intransigent, about politics. Father Donahue felt that Frank would be a reliable, though stolid, asset to the Society of Jesus, but he was uncomfortable with the young man's refusal to talk about his childhood and the nosy old Galway cleric was aware of the stacks of unopened letters from Peggy that Frank kept under his bed. He knew that Frank hadn't even invited his parents to his ordination, something almost unthinkable in Irish America. Donahue always instructed his departing seminarians to say good-bye to their families. It served two purposes. First, it closed a door on the young Jesuit's past life, reinforcing the credo that from henceforth his life belonged to Christ, the Church, and the Society, not necessarily in that order. And the saying of farewells gave the young priest and his family an opportunity to heal old wounds, if healings were called for.

On the train to the city Frank was so filled with apprehension that even the constant adoration afforded him by his fellow Catholic passengers failed to lift his spirits. Walking the fifteen blocks from Grand Central to his mother's apartment on Twelfth Avenue he looked about at the gritty, crowded streets of Hell's Kitchen with wonder and distaste. He'd been cloistered away upstate for almost five years. He'd forgotten how ugly and alive the old neighborhood was. Surveying the streets he realized he'd passed through his childhood among these people with so little effect that not a single human being recognized him. He was a stranger here, as he had ever been.

Frank stood for an hour across the street from Peggy's apartment house, staring up at the grimy windows of the fourth floor walk-up. Finally he traversed the street through the crowded traffic and entered the building. The hallways smelled of cabbage and disinfectant. Frank recalled the odor without affection. Outside Peggy's door he didn't know whether to knock. He tried the door and it was unlocked.

Peggy was dead drunk, passed out on her rumpled, soiled sheets. Frank stood over her and watched her snore, insensate. There was a quart of bootleg on the floor beside the bed.

Frank sat at the scarred kitchen table and didn't know what to do. He could see his mother through the alcove. On the stove was an iron skillet. Peggy had burned something black in it.

Frank noticed an open composition notebook on the table, of the type used by children. He recognized Peggy's surprisingly exact Irish-parochial-school script. How could he not? The hundreds of unread letters under his bed were all addressed in the same hand. Peggy had started yet another letter to him. Since he had never opened even a single envelope, his eye, out of natural curiosity, scanned the page. Peggy was writing to tell him, yet again, how proud she was of him. Father Donahue had sent a letter congratulating her on Frank's acceptance to the University of Guadalajara, and she scribbled on and on about how she'd always known he'd make her proud, he was the only Coyne ever amounted to anything, and his success was the answer to her endless prayers. Then she began to recount various little stories of the neighborhood: a Sardinian family had tried to move in down the block, but the people in the building had thrown their belongings into the street; Rohena Reilly's husband Jerry had gotten a job driving for a rich Protestant family; unspeakable rumors were circulating again about that slattern Joséphine McCarthy and her big dim-witted son—someone was going to *have* to say something to nice Father O'Rourke at Sacred Heart, this could not be allowed to go on. Reading the letter—the first from his mother he'd ever read—he was struck that she made no allusion to the fact that he'd never answered her hundreds of others. It was as if just being able to write Frank and tell him the minutiae of her lonely life was enough. She didn't expect Frank to involve himself.

Just then Peggy started to retch. Lurching up from her pillow she flung her upper body over the side of the mattress and her hands grasped out blindly under the bed. She yanked out a chamber pot and puked into it. Frank stood up. He was repulsed. As he watched Peggy wiped her mouth with the sheet, then turned over and started snoring again. She hadn't seen him or known he was there. Frank walked out.

ON FORTY-SEVENTH AND TENTH A CROWD HAD GATHERED. TWO TEAM-sters were fighting, rolling around on the streetcar tracks. Their wagons had collided in the intersection, locking wheels, and obviously each man blamed the other. Frank stood in the doorway of a butcher shop and watched with fascination, along with the others. The observation of violence was always riveting to Frank. It had been ever since that day he'd witnessed little Tommy drive a penknife through Freight Train Shaughnessy's cheek.

The wagoneers were biting each other's ears, gouging each other's eyes, throwing wild roundhouse punches, and then a touring car drove up and a man leapt out. He was already on the two fighters before Frank realized it was his father. Bulldog pulled the two men to their feet and held them by their collars, shaking them like disobedient dogs. The crowd tittered. Bulldog grinned at the crowd, then suddenly slammed the two men's heads together with such ferocity that the crack of skull on skull was like a gunshot. The two men crumpled as if their spines were severed and the crowd roared. Bulldog left the two teamsters sprawled in the street and climbed back into the touring car. That's when Frank saw Tommy sitting in the touring car. His little brother had changed so much in the years Frank had been away that he needed a few moments to be certain. Tommy was now a slim, muscular young man, with a coldly handsome face, hair combed straight back from his forehead and his body encased in a tight-waisted, tailored double-breasted suit. He had become a gangster like his father, and he looked born to the role, which, of course, he was. There were three heavily made-up young women in the touring car with Tommy and when Bulldog climbed back in one of them—raven-haired with amber-hued skin— kissed him on his mouth. Tommy sat with a girl cuddled in each arm and when the touring car—chauffeured by an ebony man in a top hat—passed by Frank could see that one of the girls was rubbing the back of his neck. Everyone in the car was laughing.

Frank walked the streets of Hell's Kitchen in a daze. The love and camaraderie he'd just witnessed between his father and brother filled him with an overwhelming melancholy. They were *friends*, he thought, stunned, as a cold autumn wind whistled down between the tenements. He'd always known his father hated him, and he had reciprocated that revulsion. And he'd never doubted that Bull-dog adored Tommy—his younger brother's popularity was a law of nature, like gravity or sunrise. But to see them like that, out whoring together on a Friday afternoon, made Frank's rejection by his father seem just as universal.

Frank wandered until he found he was standing before a church. Sacred Heart, the small, narrow stone church his mother used to bring him to when he was still a toddler. The place where he fell in love with Catholicism. Frank entered and sat in the back pew and watched as a priest celebrated Mass for a handful of Irish cleaning women. Nothing much had changed at Sacred Heart. He recognized the priest in the chasuble. It was John O'Rourke, the father mentioned in Peggy's unfinished letter.

Frank felt himself calm in the reassuring familiarity of Sacred Heart. If the afternoon had reminded him of how painful his father had made his childhood, worshiping in this old stone church had renewed the memory of how he had survived that suffering, and showed the way he could survive it still. Once again, as he had when he was a small boy, Frank Coyne gave his life to his Savior. He would seek refuge in his faith, serve it with complete devotion, and defend it with all his being, here in Hell's Kitchen, or in Mexico where he was being sent.

For a moment, during the elevation of the Host, Father O'Rourke's eyes met Frank's across the narrow dimness of the center aisle. Frank would visit with him after Mass.

Book III

The Train

THEY WERE LIKE DANCING DOLLS—THE LITTLE GIRLS IN THEIR colorful swirling skirts, the boys in dazzling white *campesino* uniform, with the only color their bronze faces and the red or blue kerchiefs knotted at their throats. They moved around and between each other with the precision of a childlike clockwork. The boys kept their hands clasped behind them, in the small of their stiffly held backs, and their feet flashed in polished shoes purchased only that morning. Every once in a while one of them would gave out a high-pitched Indian yip over the lively music. The little girls batted their eyes and flounced their skirts in exaggerated imitation of femininity.

"They are our future," General Terrazas said proudly. "They are the Mexico of tomorrow. Look at them." He turned to the others seated at the long row of rough plank tables. "Without class. Without shame. Without superstition. Their potential is limitless. As is Mexico's."

Muñoz, the Spanish doctor, was seated beside him. "It's just what they're doing in the Russian Soviet, *mi general*. A nation without caste, without subjugation, without religion. A nation like that can become whatever it wants."

The English journalist put down his glass of punch. "Dr. Muñoz, isn't it true that though the peasants of the Russian Union publicly denounce their Orthodox Church, in secret they are as pious as ever?"

"Mr. Lancaster, the poisonous tree of Christianity was planted in Eastern Europe over a thousand years ago. It will be a while before every diseased root is pulled up."

259

They were seated in the cobblestone courtyard of what was formerly the Little Sisters of Charity convent. The nunnery had been transformed into a public school and today was its dedication day. General Terrazas and his staff had been asked to attend, and the Spaniard—who was tutoring the general's sons—had accompanied him, along with the Englishman, who was sending almost daily dispatches back to London. The patio was decorated with colored streamers and *piñatas* and there was a crude mural dedicated to the Revolution covering one wall.

"The Catholic Church, " Muñoz continued, "has only had four centuries here in Mexico. It won't be so difficult to throw off its shackles."

The Indian general Hernández snorted. "Yes, it only took us three hundred years to get rid of the Spanish." Hernández never tired of needling the young doctor.

"Religion is a tool of oppression," Terrazas said, watching the dancing children. "That's its purpose, and it has no other. You eliminate the oppressors and their instruments reveal themselves for what they are. When the Revolution succeeded the Church's days were numbered."

The guitarists closed the song on a joyously strummed chord as the little girls shook their voluminous skirts and the boys stamped their heels in an exultant final gesture. The parents and the teachers and government officials applauded loudly. As the children ran out of the courtyard a mannish woman teacher introduced a male student who began to recite a long poem about a great victory.

"General," Lancaster began, "what do you make of the rumors that President Calles is bowing to international pressure? That he intends to rescind the Articles and declare an amnesty for the Catholics?"

Terrazas waved his hand in dismissal. "I never listen to rumors, *Señor* Lancaster. Besides, the government didn't start this war, the Church did. And their fanatical lackeys will never agree to a cease-fire. That would mean they'd have to abide by the law, and they'll never agree to it. That's why they have to be driven from Mexico."

"By 'fanatical,' do you mean clerics like the Irish-American Father Frank?"

Terrazas's face darkened. "A foreigner priest! His very presence in this country is a violation of Mexican law." He smiled again. "But from what my spies tell me he is dissolving in alcohol, like all those pigs do eventually."

"What about Padre Pistolero?"

No one but Lancaster dared to mention Tommy to Terrazas, and even the journalist carefully picked his opportunities. Ever since

Guadalajara Terrazas had been possessed by a terror of the gunfighter-priest, and though the general tried to hide it everyone around him knew. Terrazas didn't think Tommy could be killed. He'd hung him, shot at him, had him hunted like a fox, and the priest seemed only to grow stronger. He remembered when, on the scaffolding in front of the cathedral, after having killed Severo Salazar with the dead lieutenant's pistol, the *pistolero* priest had pointed it across the plaza at the balcony where Terrazas was standing. The general had pulled his sons down, and he was fearful for them. Those things he had just seen should not have happened, and they could only have happened if the *pistolero* priest was somehow more than human. If he had divine aid.

Everyone at the table looked at Terrazas, watched him. He took a long time in answering.

"That man is an outlaw, nothing more. Before this war is over his body will be dragged into the plaza at Guadalajara and I will hang it from the cathedral belfry."

"The people love him. Even the government troops speak of him in awe."

Terrazas forced himself to smile. "Mexicans love bandits, it's part of our culture. The shadowy desperado galloping through the moonlight, that sort of thing. It's why Villa was able to always raise another army. . . ." Terrazas looked around. "But when this devil priest's body lies in the plaza, they will forget him and find another to venerate. That, too, is part of our culture."

The boy had finished his heroic poem. There was a smattering of applause and then the new school principal stepped into the center of the courtyard and addressed the gathering.

"We are so proud today," he began, smiling. "Proud of our children, proud of our school, proud of our country and of our federal government—" He was a chubby, intense young man, and he had studied oratory. "And proud of that hero of the Revolution, the man responsible for our new school, the man who has been charged with defeating the counterrevolutionary forces here in Jalisco . . . *Compañeros y compañeras*, we are proud that General José María Terrazas has traveled out from Guadalajara to honor us with his presence on this momentous day!"

There was an honest outburst of applause. These were people devoted to the ascendancy of secular society and the dissolution of the Roman Church's power in Mexico—politically, socially and spiritually.

Terrazas stood up and acknowledged the applause, then started to sit down. "Please, *General,*" the young principal said, "please, honor us with a few words." It was an act. The principal had been instructed to ask Terrazas to address the gathering.

Terrazas rose to the warm applause. "My countrymen. My fellow *constitutionalistas.* We are gathered here to watch the dawning of a new day. A new day for Jalisco and for all of Mexico. This"—he gestured around the courtyard—"this beautiful new school was once an academy for harlots." He delivered this in a moderate tone but the words struck them, and their faces grew serious. "A bordello to provide whores for those silk-robed, gold-encrusted parasites who ordered us to address them as 'Father.' "

Through the open gates of the former nunnery several autos and carriages were visible, arriving outside. Terrazas, still speaking, watched as a score of men and women got out of the vehicles.

"In this institution where our children used to learn fear and superstition and subservience—"

The *federal* guards halted them at the gate and the sergeant looked back at Terrazas.

"—now they will be taught to be free and fraternal and revolutionary. Sergeant, let those people enter. They have come to celebrate the opening of the school."

The sergeant stepped out of their way and the people filed into the courtyard and lined up against the convent walls. They wore grim, accusing faces. A man with a full beard stood in the forefront.

"This school is the first of the reclaimed Roman properties to be converted into an institution of real learning. But there will be others—many, many others."

There was a murmur going through the courtyard. A tension. Terrazas glanced at his staff. Hernández was saying something to him.

"What?"

Hernández stood, his eyes on the bearded man, and said, "That's Enrique Hidalgo."

Terrazas had heard of the "lion of León." One of most powerful of the bourgeois Catholics. A former high-ranking official in the now-outlawed Catholic League. Terrazas glared at Don Enrique and Don Enrique glared back.

"*Señor* Hidalgo." Terrazas refused to address him with the respectful *Don.* "Have you come to celebrate this great day with us?"

Don Enrique strode slowly forward, his eyes carefully moving over the faces of all present. The principal's ebullience had drained and he was left pale. Sometimes, in the dark of the moon, Catholic night riders would come for the government teachers and dawn would find their mutilated bodies in the town plaza. Everyone there knew they were being noted.

Don Enrique stopped a few feet before Terraza's table. "We have not come to celebrate, Terrazas, but to mourn."

"Of course you have. You've come to grieve the death of your counterfeit faith." Terrazas looked around, expecting laughter at his joke, but the people were silent, alert.

"No, we've come to mourn our daughters who were murdered in this courtyard. Butchered on your orders."

"That's shit," Terrazas said, and his bodyguards tightened their grips on their weapons.

"Every one of these Jaliscans"—Don Enrique pointed at those behind him—"had to bury the tortured, violated body of a loved one."

"The inhabitants of all Church properties had been warned to vacate. The women who were here were whores and outlaws!"

"Daughters! Sisters! Aunts! Nieces!"

"Harlots!"

Don Enrique jabbed his finger at Terrazas. "Their deaths are on your head! And their souls will never rest until they are avenged!"

Terrazas gave a shout and his troops raised their weapons. The teachers screamed and scrambled for cover under the tables but Don Enrique didn't flinch. Slowly he turned his back on the soldiers and walked out of the convent. The others followed him. Terrazas thought about giving the order to fire, but he didn't want the massacre witnessed by the English journalist. Finally the interlopers climbed into their cars and carriages and rolled away. One of them stuck his fisted arm into the air and shouted, *"Viva Cristo Rey!"* There were a score of echoing shouts, and then someone called out, *"Viva Padre Pistolero!"*

THAT NIGHT TERRAZAS WALKED THE HALLS OF THE MAGNIFICENT mansion he had expropriated from a wealthy Guadalajara priest. The priest had been aged and feeble, and being the only surviving male of his patrician bloodline, he had come back to the family manse to die.

"Perfecto," Terrazas had grinned, then he'd shot the old man between his eyes. He had declared the house Church property, and therefore forfeit. He'd moved in immediately.

Terrazas checked on his two sons. Antonio was sleeping soundly, his arms wrapped around a pillow. Terrazas grinned proudly. He knew his elder son was fucking four of the five housemaids. He was probably dreaming of a tryst with one of them as he slept. Across the hall, lost in the big brass bed, Paco tossed fitfully in his twisted sheets. The General sat on the edge of the mattress and watched the boy battle his dragons. This son was chubby and thick, but his father knew his was the more turbulent soul. He was the thinker, the true revolutionary, and Terrazas loved him because he saw himself in Paco. Terrazas leaned back against the brass-work frame and thought again, as he had thought uncountable times, that his sons were growing up very differently than he had. The General had been born indigent and unwanted, the illegitimate offspring of an ugly *mestizo* woman in a tiny pueblo on the state border between Aguascalientes and Zacatecas. The woman had seven other bastard children, from three different fathers, and Terrazas's earliest memory was of being taunted by his half-siblings that he was the son of the village priest. Whenever his mother heard the taunts she would anger and chase the others away, but she *slapped* Terrazas. It taught him that he was a shame, and he became ashamed. His father never spoke directly to him, and while all his brothers and sisters were baptized and confirmed by the priest, he refused to acknowledge Terrazas's existence. When Terrazas was ten, a *federal* cavalry unit bivouacked near the pueblo and when the regiment pulled out the next morning the unwanted little boy was riding in the cook-wagon. He had been in the Army ever since. And ever since he had loathed priests and all their ilk.

DOWNSTAIRS, IN THE MURDERED CLERIC'S OPULENTLY APPOINTED office, Terrazas sat behind the massive German desk and considered the coming day. Tomorrow he was sending a train to the capital with over a hundred thousand pesos—money he had confiscated from Jalisco's rich Catholics, and from the sale of *cristero* haciendas and Church properties and artworks. The European dealers were breathless for the ancient paintings and gold altarpieces, and while many if not most of the generals and government officials lined their personal pockets with the proceeds from this rich mother lode, Terrazas was scrupulous in his government accounting. He felt strongly that the insurrectionists' ill-gotten gold should be used to finance the struggle against them. The vengeful justice of it all appealed greatly. But Terrazas was concerned. This war was far from won. Mexican rebellion was a hard fire to put out—he'd learned that in the long bloody years of the Revolution. And the Catholics had the power of fanaticism. They had secret societies and mystical ritual; they imbued their gullible legions with promises of martyr-dom, of eternal salvation, of everlasting happiness in heaven. They were no better than the Moors of Arabia.

Terrazas angrily poured himself a snifter of brandy. He was always incensed when he considered the massive fraud the Church had per-petrated on his beloved Mexicans. Confronted with Aztec culture, the Spanish priests had destroyed the biggest library in the world. Since they were too ignorant to decipher the hieroglyphics, the books had to be demonic. They had usurped local gods, supplanting them with their ridiculous fictions of saints; they had used their horror stories of fire and brimstone to emasculate and control a proud and indepen-dent race of warriors, traders and craftsmen. They had forced upon the conquered an insipid, bloodless creed whose totems were a sex-less corpse and an unfucked mother. Terrazas shook his head in dis-gust. *Why couldn't his paisanos see through it all? Didn't they know the future had no place for these ancient, foreign myths?*

As he sipped his brandy Terrazas thought about what the En-glishman had talked about. The rumors of an amnesty had been circulating for months. The expelled bishops in their silk skirts were running like frantic women to all the cities of the world—Rome, London, Madrid, but especially Washington and New York—telling their sanctimonious lies, warning of the end of Western Civilization, weaving lurid tales of pagan butchery and godless humanism. The Church was a worldwide spiderweb, with hundreds of millions of followers on every continent. Its wealth was uncountable. It could bring to bear immense pressure on a struggling postrevolutionary government like Mexico's. There had been talk of a secret com-pact—a "gentlemen's agreement"; the Catholics would accept the validity of the Constitution if the Articles that dealt specifically with the Church and its properties were not enforced. Terrazas knew that such an unholy accord was unthinkable. The Church must be broken, now and forever. No quarter could be given. If the snake was allowed to live it would surely grow again its poison fangs.

Terrazas opened the desk drawer and took out several sheaves of the dead priest's imported writing paper. He slowly, carefully began to draft a letter to the President. Slowly, because he had learned to read and write as a man and it was arduous for him, and carefully, because of the importance of the words he was writ-ing. The President must be made to understand the direness of the situation here in Jalisco, the danger that all the advances of the Revolution could be lost because of a few thousand recalcitrant counterrevolutionists—*vaqueros,* really—cowboys who measured their manhood by their independence, their purity of blood, the number of women they seduced. And by the depth of their Catholicism.

And because of a devil of a murderous American priest who the people believed had been sent by God Himself.

Terrazas would have the letter delivered to the President by his own sons, to drive home the importance of the words. To illustrate that they were struggling for Mexico's future.

He would send his boys on the train.

—◄○►—

TOMMY KNEW IT WAS GOING TO BE A BAD DAY ALMOST FROM THE BEGIN-ning. They had planned to pull up a length of rail track at a water-tank crossing, but just after dawn a warning was shouted and everyone jumped down into a gully and watched as a biplane flew over low. It could have been a government spotter, or a rich gringo, or anybody, but they couldn't take the chance. Frank made the decision that the train would be blown as it passed this point. There was a copper mine a short ride away and Quintana was about to gallop out on his big red stallion when a convoy of four automobiles drove up to the crossing. The cars were packed with government officials from the neighboring pueblo and their families, on their way to Guadalajara. The *alcalde*—the mayor—stood up in the lead car and he knew instantly they had all made a grave error. The men were dragged from the cars, stood up against the base of the water tank and unceremoniously shot. Water poured through the bullet holes and splashed down on their bodies as their women keened. Tommy looked at Quintana, and the Yaqui in his saddle shrugged. "It's our custom."

Then the newer men, the *bandoleros*, began to drag the young women, some only twelve and thirteen, into the gully and Frank shouted, "No!" The *jefe* of the *bandoleros*—a light-eyed and scarred cutthroat named Cota—glared at Frank and then stepped back.

"We are not debauchers," Frank said. "We are Christ's soldiers."

"Don Francisco," Cota said, "we can't keep these people and we can't send them away."

Frank looked at the wailing women and said, "Execute them."

Tommy shouted, "Frank, what the hell are you doing?" but Cota had already cut a little girl's throat and was reaching for another.

266

Tommy grabbed for a weapon but suddenly he was surrounded by *bandolero* muzzles. They had encircled Quintana, too. Tommy looked at his brother, then at Quintana. "Is this your custom, too?" He found Rojas's eyes behind the *bandoleros* and shouted again, "Is this your custom, too?" Rojas looked away.

"It's the Christian thing to do," Frank said, then nodded to Cota and the females and children were murdered and thrown into the tall grass of the gully. Tommy stumbled to the edge of the gully and stared down at their bodies. Quintana spurred the red stallion over to Tommy, leaned down in the saddle and said softly to him, "The gold, *mi amigo*. We get the gold and we leave this business behind. Fuck these bastards."

Tommy raised his face and the Indian was stunned by the sadness he saw there. Tommy seemed inconsolable.

"The train," Quintana hissed. "Think only of the train." Then he raked the stallion with his spurs and the animal screamed and leapt forward and Quintana galloped away.

Tommy climbed down into the gully and walked among the dead. The ground was spongy with their blood. He stooped and took a little boy into his arms. The child was wearing a white shirt and black suit, as if he had dressed for his own funeral. "God," Tommy said softly, without realizing what he was doing, "this little boy did nothing wrong. He's innocent. I don't understand why you allowed this to happen, but I hope this little boy . . . I hope this little boy . . ." He stopped then, not knowing what he hoped for the slain little boy. He went to the next corpse, a girl of sixteen, who at the moment of death had tried to shield her mother with her body. Tommy said, "This young woman died a hero's death. She had more courage than any man here." Then without irony he said, "Please protect her." In this manner Tommy went to each of the victims, mumbling a few words that their deaths would not go unremarked. At one point he looked up and Frank was watching him from above. The brothers' eyes locked for a moment, then Tommy went on doing what he was doing. Frank turned away.

Miguelito rode up on a small white jenny mule and looked around frantically. Then he saw Tommy climbing out of the gully. Miguelito stared. Tommy's clothes were stained with blood, his eyes were dulled. With the rising sun at his back it looked as if Tommy were climbing a stairway up out of hell.

"*Padre Tomás!*" Miguelito shouted and kicked his bare heels into the little jenny's flanks. "*Padre!* I am here!"

Tommy seemed to come back from a distant place. His eyes focused on the boy on the mule.

"What are you doing here?"

"I followed you! I am *cristero!*" Miguelito grinned and held up an ancient, rusted pistol. "I stole this fucking mule and I—"

Tommy yanked Miguelito from the back of the jenny and dragged him to the edge of the gully. "Look! Look!" He held Miguelito's head so the boy couldn't look away. "See that? That's what we're doing today! Is that what you want to be part of?"

"*Padre*—"

"And we might all wind up like that! *You* might end up like them!"

"*Padre*—"

Tommy lifted the boy and roughly settled him back on the little mule. "*Padre Tomás!*" Tommy slapped the animal hard on its rump and the startled jenny began to trot away.

"Get away from here!" Tommy shouted. "Go home!"

That's when he heard the rifles, and a moment after the train.

THE BIG RED BAY WAS GALLOPING FULL OUT, RUNNING ON THE WIND, its powerful legs pumping, its tail straight out behind it bannerlike, its chest mottled with the white foam of exertion. Quintana hunched over the horse's withers in a Yaqui crouch, his long black hair whipping. Bullets zinged all around him, throwing up small tufts of red dirt as they struck the ground and the canyon wall. He had ridden hard to the copper mine, killed four guards, stolen the dynamite, then on the way back he had followed the train tracks down into a long canyon with steep walls and then suddenly the train came up on him from behind.

The troops riding on the roofs of the boxcars started firing at him as soon as they saw him and some of the soldiers thought they recognized the horse as Severo Salazar's devil red and speculated that the Yaqui was the one from the incident at the plaza. A lieutenant, realizing that the horseman was trapped between the train and the canyon walls, suggested a gamble and the riflemen each in turn threw a month's pay into a hat and took his shot, but the stallion was a champion and the Indian an integral part of the animal and so they kept missing.

In Yaqui Quintana shouted in the stallion's ear, "Run, Brother! Run!" and the big bay's shoulders pistoned its long legs and its hooves seemed to thunder on air and in jest and in salute the train engineer blew the train's whistle and the stallion seemed somehow to gallop even harder and the engineer kept the train's speed down so he could watch the hunt.

Behind the two boxcars were three passenger cars—two salon cars and a Pullman sleeper—and the well-dressed people rushed to the window and laughed and cheered every time a bullet ricocheted off a rock close to the racing Indian. This was great sport.

Then the lieutenant on the boxcar saw that the canyon floor was rising, was leveling out onto the mesa and he ordered his riflemen to fire a volley before the Yaqui got away, but then the sergeant of the sandbagged machine gun on the roof of the next boxcar shouted out that his men should be given a chance and the lieutenant thought it would be interesting to see what a machine gun could do to the galloping animal and he shouted back fine, but do a good job and don't let the Yaqui bastard get away.

The sergeant ordered his machine gunner to hurry and the gunner yanked back the toggle bolt and swung the barrel around and sought for the horse in his sight. The train was coming up out of the canyon and onto the mesa and the Indian had already started to veer off and the sergeant cursed the machine gunner and told him to fire and then the machine gunner had the Yaqui dead in his sights and was starting to squeeze the trigger when the train was struck by a barrage of small-arms fire and the machine gunner was lifted up from his place behind his weapon and flung lifeless through the air.

Frank's army of *cristero* light cavalry was already in a dead run on both sides of the tracks, so that when the train climbed out of the canyon it was immediately surrounded by a hundred firing horsemen. Before the startled engineer could get the locomotive up to speed a score of *vaqueros* had already leapt from their mounts and onto the train. The soldiers on the boxcars fired down and picked off half of them. Those *cristeros* who managed to cling to the side of the Pullmans were clubbed by the soldiers inside the boxcars and they tumbled under the steel wheels and were torn apart. Two *cristeros* managed to get into one of the lounge cars and they were immediately shot down by the civilian officials inside.

The machine-gun nest on the first boxcar was still inoperative, but there was another sandbagged weapon on the roof of the caboose and it chattered a withering hail of rounds into the galloping horsemen. Horses exploded like ripe fruit. Others plunged shrieking, sending their riders slamming to the hard ground.

Quintana galloped beside a parlor car, firing his horse pistol into the windows. He saw a fat man spurt blood and heard a woman begin to wail and Quintana gave out a yipping Yaqui howl that was part savage and part animal and in the midst of all the fighting the Indian remembered his grandfather going out to track down a wolf who had taken a child, painting his body with a thousand white crosses so Christ could protect him from the wolf's spirit.

The big red bay stumbled and caught himself and Quintana realized the mighty beast was finally tiring, and he remembered he had the dynamite in his saddlebags, and at that a moment the slain *alcalde*'s car bumped up abreast of him. Tommy was behind the wheel.

"You got the dynamite?" Tommy shouted.

"Yeah!"

"Jump in!"

Quintana hesitated, then someone fired from the parlor car and one of the auto's headlights flew off.

"Fucking jump!"

Quintana reached back and yanked up the saddle pouch, slapped it over his shoulder; then he leapt up into a crouch on the seat of his saddle, pushed himself off and landed with a *thunk* on the open car's trunk. He shouted with glee, then his grin faded as he started to slip off behind. Tommy grabbed back and caught the saddlebag; Quintana clutched the other end and rolled around, back and forth, over the trunk.

"Stop messing around!" Tommy shouted back at him.

Quintana's boots were bumping over the ground. He lunged up and managed to get a heel on the bumper. He shot Tommy a dark look, then clambered over the trunk and into the seat as more bullets zinged around them.

"We gotta stop the train!" Tommy yelled.

"The gold?" Quintana shouted back, and when Tommy didn't answer he shouted again, "We get the gold and we get the hell out of here! This place has gone crazy!"

Tommy looked at him and then nodded. Then a bullet zinged between them and crashed through the windshield. Tommy jerked on the steering wheel and the car swerved around a stand of cactus.

"*Bueno*," Quintana said and began to dig into the saddlebags. He pulled out a stick of dynamite.

"Cut the fuse short!"

Quintana unsheathed his killing blade and sawed off half the length.

"Shorter!"

He halved it again.

"No, shorter!"

"It'll blow up in my fucking hands!"

"Listen to me, I know what I'm talking about."

Quintana leaned down under the dashboard and struck a match.

"I used to blow up speaks every other week!" Tommy shouted. "If you leave the fuse that long—"

The flame caught and the fuse started to sputter. Quintana stood up in the seat and flung the stick of dynamite like a knife. It tumbled end over end and then disappeared, landing on the top of a boxcar.

Quintana gave out a victory shout. Then the dynamite came flying back. It landed right in front of the car and Tommy yanked the wheel and the car swerved away and a moment later the ground behind them erupted.

"—that can happen!" Tommy shouted.

Quintana looked at him, shaken. Tommy's mouth tightened into a grim line and he raced the car up to the head of the train. "We gotta blow the engine!" he shouted. "Here, take the wheel!" Tommy let go of the wheel and began to climb into the backseat.

Quintana had no choice. He jumped behind the steering wheel and only then shouted, "I don't know how to drive a car!"

"Then it's time to learn!"

Tommy dug out a handful of dynamite sticks. Using the knife he cut all the fuses almost flush with the ends. Quintana, glancing back, widened his eyes and crossed himself. *"Jesús y María."*

Tommy twisted the short fuses, then tied all the stray ends together into one long length then wrapped the length around the pack.

"You're going to blow up all of Jalisco!"

Tommy looked up. The locomotive was just ahead of them. The riflemen on the boxcars were busy with the *cristeros* attacking on the other side of the track. "Faster! Get closer!"

"What are you going to do?"

"Just get fucking closer!"

Quintana spun the wheel and the automobile almost went under the churning iron drivers before he straightened out, and at that moment Tommy leapt onto the side of a boxcar and hung there, his cassock whipping out behind him. Quintana fought the automobile and kept looking back. Tommy edged along the side of the boxcar until he reached the coupler, then danced across the coupler and grabbed hold of the coal tender's steel ladder. He was about to pull himself onto the tender's deck when the boxcar door behind him rolled open and a *federal* stuck out a rifle and took aim at

271

Tommy's back. Quintana had been driving with one hand and he raised the other and fired three times with the big horse pistol and the *federal* rolled out of the boxcar and slipped under the train.

Tommy pulled himself up onto the deck of the coal tender and looking back he could see the nine cars of the train stretched out behind him. The soldiers were in a furious gun battle with the *cristeros* who were losing ground on the train. No one was looking forward. Tommy turned back and looked down. The fireman and the engineer had their heads down and they were shoveling coal at a demonic pace. Tommy humped his body, stuck the pack of dynamite under his arm and yanked out Quintana's matches. He struck one and it immediately went out. He struck another and it too blew out. He was digging for another match when a shadow fell across his face and he jerked back just as the fireman's shovel slashed through the air where his head had been and clanged off the tender deck.

"Fuck your mother!" the fireman said when he saw the pack of dynamite. He raised the long-handled shovel again and before Tommy could draw a weapon he slammed it down like an ax and Tommy shifted his weight and the blade of the shovel tore a crease in his shoulder. Tommy cried out, then saw that the rend in his cassock was smoking. The shovel blade was glowing from the heat of the firebox. Tommy grasped out and caught the shovel at its hilt. He felt the heat sear his hand and fingers but ignoring the pain he shoved the packet of dynamite against the blade. The fuse immediately began to sputter. Then Tommy tossed the dynamite forward into the locomotive, where it landed on the iron floor and skidded to a corner.

Tommy and the fireman looked into each other's eyes, then Tommy jumped to his feet and leapt back onto the following boxcar and started running. He was past the machine gun nest on the second car before any of the *federales*—all facing out and back—saw him. Tommy kept running and jumping from one car to the next and was on the first of the lounge cars when the morning exploded.

A trooper on the front boxcar had risen and taken aim on Tommy's back. He was squeezing the trigger when the dynamite blew. The blast ruptured the steam boiler, and a moment later the locomotive exploded in a thunderclap of twisted steel and sizzling water. The trooper disintegrated, as did the boxcar he was standing on. The next boxcar burst into flames. As the blast roiled over the lounge cars, all their windows blew out as one. The back draft dragged out a stout woman as if she were a rag doll.

The *alcalde*'s car flipped over and landed running backward until it plowed its back bumper into a thick growth of agave. Quintana covered his head with his arms as the scalding drops of water rained down over the plain.

The rail cars began to fold into themselves like playing cards as Tommy, still trying to outrun the explosion, tore across their roofs toward the caboose. The blast lifted up the Pullman under him and he was thrown through the air as the last four cars jumped the track and furrowed through the red earth. The trailing *cristeros* reined in and watched as their warrior-priest flew like a black angel and came down rolling on the soft, sandy embankment. The four renegade train cars were still clawing up the earth, and then the last boxcar and the caboose lashed around and snapped their couplings and turned on their sides in a rising cloud of dust. Then, as suddenly as it had started, all was still. Chunks of metal and a mist of boiling water fell from the sky.

Quintana slowly lifted his head from under his arms. He couldn't believe he was still alive. Then he called out, "Tomás!"

He pried himself from behind the steering wheel and jumped to the ground. As he sprinted toward the wrecked train the *cristeros* rode up shouting *"Viva Cristo Rey!"* and "Death to the Infidels!"

Quintana slowed as he neared the train. The carnage was incredible. Bodies and bloody body parts were scattered everywhere. There was a slowly rising moaning from inside the wrecked cars. "Tomás!" Quintana cried out again as he ran among the dead and maimed. A soldier staggered to his feet and gawked about through dazed eyes. A *bandolero* galloped up and lopped off his head with a saber. Other *cristeros* were walking about shooting anyone who moved.

Quintana scampered over the half-buried mound of metal that had once been a rail car and jumped down to the other side of the tracks. *"Gringo!"* Quintana scanned up and down the wreckage but he couldn't see Tommy's black cassock. Then he heard Tommy's voice behind him. "What have I done?"

Quintana spun in the dust and Tommy stood looking at the devastation. He held his seared right hand across his chest and his left shoulder was dark with blood where the shovel blade had sliced his flesh. "Dear God, what have I done?"

Quintana ran to him. "Tomás, are you all right?"

Tommy stared at him without comprehension. "Dear God . . ."

Quintana quickly sized up Tommy's wounds. "You have survived," he said simply. Then, "We have to find the gold."

*   *   *

273

THE BAGGAGE CAR HAD BEEN CONVERTED INTO AN ARMORED ROLLING treasury, but the extra plating had buckled in the wreck and both the doors had sprung off and skittered away like stones. Gold coins were slowly spilling out of the ruptured seams. Quintana stuck in his head and saw that the bags of pesos, the cases of gold chalices and altarpieces—all had slammed to one end of the car, crushing the four-man honor guard. Their blood was leaking through the coins. A *bandolero* was stuffing the bloodstained pesos into his shirt. He saw Quintana and he giggled. Then the baggage car echoed with a sharp gunshot and the *bandolero* pitched forward. Frank stood in the other doorway, the little pistol in his hand smoking.

"This gold is for the struggle," Frank said to him, as if he could read Quintana's thoughts. "This is Christ's gold."

Quintana stared at him and said nothing.

BY THE TIME TOMMY STUMBLED AROUND TO THE OTHER SIDE OF THE wreckage, all the soldiers had been executed and the surviving civilians had been gathered into a terrified herd. Trapped inside the wreckage the wounded and injured could be heard whimpering, begging for help.

Tommy saw a man crouched over a naked corpse. As he got closer the man looked up at him. It was the husband of María Aragón. His chest and arms were black with blood. He held in one hand a butcher's knife and in the other the corpse's severed genitals. As Tommy looked on Aragón crammed the organs into the corpse's yawning mouth. Then he moved to another body and began to hack away at its clothes.

"God's vengeance is a terrible thing," Frank said. He was watching Tommy. Cota and his *bandolero* bodyguards were around him.

Tommy stared about in a stupor.

A *bandolero* uncorked a clay jug and took a drink. Cota pointed to Frank and the *bandolero* offered the jug to the priest. Frank took a drink and wiped his mouth with the back of his hand. He smiled.

One of the *cristeros* guarding the quaking civilians had discovered an old enemy. He shouted his name and the man came forward slowly. The *cristero* grabbed him and dragged him from the pack. The civilian's wife screamed and tried to pull the man back.

"What have we done?" Tommy mumbled.

"What have we done?" Frank laughed. "What have we done?" He looked around at his escort. "We've stuck it up their ass, that's what we've done." Cota and the *bandoleros* laughed.

The *cristero* pushed the civilian to his knees, stepped back and pointed his pistol down at his head. The man's wife threw herself between them and the *cristero* shot her. The civilian took his wife in his arms and bawled and the *cristero* shot him, too.

"Frank," Tommy said. "You have to stop this."

Frank looked at him. "It's war. These things happen."

Tommy shook his head. "It's enough." He looked around. "It's too much."

One of the civilians began to shout out in English. "I'm an English journalist! I'm a noncombatant!"

Frank nodded to Cota. "Bring me that man."

Tommy moved closer to his brother. "Frank, please."

When he came back with Lancaster, Cota said, "There's a doctor, too. A Spaniard."

Lancaster was soiled and had a bleeding cut over his left eye. He had been shaken to his core, but he still understood the power of the press. "I'm a journalist . . . I can write . . . I want to write a story about . . . all this . . . About what happened today." He waved his hand weakly. "This . . . I've never experienced anything like this."

Frank stared at Lancaster a moment, then turned his eyes to Cota. "A doctor?"

"*Sí*. He's trying to stop their bleeding."

Lancaster asked, "Are you Padre Pistolero?"

Frank coldly inspected the Englishman. "Get me the doctor," he said to Cota.

"Frank," Tommy said, "let these people live. For the love of Christ."

Frank smiled bitterly at his brother. "When did you start caring about Christ's love?"

Lancaster turned to Tommy. "*You're* Padre Pistolero." He kept looking between them. "Are you two . . . brothers?"

Cota came up roughly leading Muñoz.

"He's young," Frank said.

Cota grinned, showing a mouthful of rotted teeth. "*Comunista*."

Muñoz was shaking with fear. One of his eyeglass lenses was cracked.

"Why were you on that train, Doctor?"

Muñoz was so frightened he couldn't speak. His jaws worked but nothing came out. Cota laughed. "*Maricón*."

Frank slapped Muñoz then, knocking his glasses askew. "Answer me, communist."

"I'm—I'm just a doctor."

Rojas called from a distant ridge. "Father Tomás!"

Tommy shaded his eyes with his hands.

"Father Tomás, come quickly!"

Tommy took a few steps toward the ridge.

"Quickly, Father!"

Tommy was filled with dread. He started to trot to the ridge.

"What kind of doctor?"

"A sur—surgeon."

Lancaster moved closer to Frank. "He's Terrazas's personal physician."

Frank's eyes narrowed at the mention of the name. "Is that true?"

Muñoz swallowed. "*Sí.*"

Lancaster saw an opportunity. "He's a political tutor to Terrazas's sons."

Frank looked toward the train. "Terrazas's sons?"

"Yes," Lancaster said. "They're over there."

TOMMY SCRAMBLED UP THE RIDGE AND WHEN HE SAW THE SPRAWLED WHITE mule he knew what he was going to find. Quintana was in a *campesino* stoop over Miguelito's inert body. He looked up at Tommy and shook his head. Tommy slumped down to his knees. "He's dead?"

"I can't find a wound," Quintana said, "but . . ." He shrugged.

"I saw him riding behind us," Rojas said. "I tried to send him away, but then we had to fight." Rojas and his three sons had survived the attack on the train. The plain was studded with the bodies of *cristeros* who had not.

The boy's death was overwhelming for Tommy. It was the final stone in a landslide of horrors that had engulfed him and bore him down. Tommy dragged Miguelito's body from under the mule mare's outstretched neck and took him in his arms. He began to rock back and forth on his knees. Quintana and Rojas looked at each other.

"WHERE ARE THEY?" FRANK DEMANDED. THEY HAD WALKED TO THE cowering crowd of civilians. "Which ones?" Lancaster pushed in and the people parted, and Terrazas's sons were hiding in the center. "There," Lancaster said. "Those two."

The *bandoleros* pounced on the boys and dragged them out and threw them to their knees before Frank. The younger boy—the chubby one—was crying.

Frank looked down at them and smiled.

*   *   *

Cota was pushing Muñoz ahead of him. He pushed him down into a ravine and then started to unlace his leather trousers. He gave the terrified young doctor his rotted-tooth grin. "I never had a Spaniard," Cota said, "or a *comunista*." And then Quintana jumped down into the ravine and took Muñoz's arm.

"We need the doctor."

Cota's face darkened. "He's mine. You can't have him."

Quintana put the big horse pistol in the *bandolero*'s face and cocked back the hammer. "Don't fuck with me, Cota."

After a moment Cota relaxed. "Take him. He's just a Spanish faggot, is all." But his glare evidenced his disappointment.

Frank pointed to a young woman in the herd of civilians. "You! Come here!"

The woman hesitated, then slowly stepped forward.

"I want you to watch this, and report everything you see to General Terrazas. Do you understand?"

The young woman nodded with uncertainty. Frank leaned down and said to the quaking boys, "How are you two called?"

The older boy raised his trembling head and said, "Antonio."

"Antonio." Frank seemed to consider this, then he looked to the other one. "And you?"

The fat little boy began to sob uncontrollably.

"Come. Don't be frightened. What's your name, boy?"

His eyes were squeezed shut but the tears slipped down the rounded curves of his face. Frank shook his head and made a tsking sound with his tongue behind his teeth. Then he asked the first one, "What's his name?"

Antonio glanced at his brother and then back at the priest above him. "Fr—Francisco."

"Hey," Frank said with delight. "We have the same name, you and I."

The boy was leaning so far over his brow was touching the ground.

"Paco, Paco, Paco," Frank said. "Don't be frightened. Nothing is going to happen to you. But I want you to do something for me. I want you to make an Act of Contrition."

The two boys were motionless. The only sound was Francisco's uncontrollable crying.

"Now repeat after me. Oh, my God . . ."

Antonio said, "Oh, my God . . ." then looked at his brother, who hadn't spoken.

"Paco," Frank admonished, "you're not cooperating. Now say it. Oh, my God, I am heartily sorry for having offended Thee—"

The chubby little boy wrapped his arms around himself, as if that would protect him.

In one movement Frank drew the small pistol from his cassock and fired into the dirt. "Say it, you little bastard! Say it!" The *bandoleros* laughed and nudged each other. The boy had soiled himself. Then the boy looked up at Frank and through his tears shook his head.

"What a brave little man," Frank said. "What a brave little *callista*." Then Frank put the pistol to the top of Antonio's head and looked at Paco. "Say it."

The little boy squeezed himself as if he were in great pain and then he nodded.

"Oh, my God, I am heartily sorry . . ."

The two boys repeated the words.

MUÑOZ SAID, "I THINK IT'S HIS HEAD. I THINK THE MULE FELL AND he crushed something in his head."

Tommy had been reluctant to release the boy, but Quintana had gently said, "Amigo, let the doctor look at him," then had taken Miguelito from his arms and settled him on the saddle blanket Rojas had laid on the ground.

"Is he—is he going to die?"

Muñoz raised the boy's eyelids, examined his eyes. "I think so." He looked at Tommy. "I think so."

"If he dies, you die," Quintana said flatly, and Muñoz nodded numbly. He expected no less.

The gold had been loaded onto pack animals. The bodies of the *cristeros* killed in the attack had been wrapped in blankets and slickers and slung across their mounts. They would be taken back to Sagrado Corazón for burial. The wounded were lifted into their saddles. Some had to be tied on.

The spotter biplane flew over again, then banked and came back. This time the *cristeros* fired up at it and the plane didn't return. Rojas leapt into his saddle and galloped the two hundred meters down the slope to where Frank was standing over the two boys.

"Padre, we must ride. The plane will report us. They'll be coming." Rojas wheeled his horse and raced back up the slope.

Frank looked down at the boys and said, "Go join the others." They looked up at him in disbelief. "Go!" The two Terrazas boys quickly got to their feet and ran back to the other civilians. The young woman Frank had picked out started to walk away, too, and Frank said, "No, you stay. And tell Terrazas everything you saw here today."

The woman stopped and looked around her in uncertainty.

"Cota!" Frank called out and the *bandolero* came to him.

"*Sí, mi patrón?*"

"Where's the bottle?"

Cota grinned and produced the clay jug. Frank took a drink and saw Lancaster approaching.

"Father, Father, I'd like to come with you."

Frank looked at Cota and then back at the Englishman. "You want to ride with us?"

"Yes," Lancaster said eagerly. "I could wire dispatches from your base camp, or use messengers, or homing pigeons." He stepped closer. "Father, it would make a wonderful story. People will read about you all over the world. You and Padre Pistolero."

Frank took another swallow. He smiled and offered Lancaster the clay jug. "Have a drink." Lancaster grinned and took the clay jug and lifted it to his lips and Frank fired the small pistol through the base of the jug and it shattered in an eruption of tequila and blood and Lancaster was on his back writhing on the ground and Frank aimed the pistol and shot him again. Lancaster was still. The young woman from the crowd stepped back, thinking she was next, but Frank looked at Cota and said, "Kill them all but her."

MUÑOZ HAD RIPPED UP A DEAD MAN'S SHIRT AND CRUDELY BANDAGED Tommy's seared hand and torn shoulder, and Tommy lifted himself painfully onto a horse while Rojas held the reins and then Quintana handed the comatose boy up to him. Tommy cradled Miguelito in his arms and then the shooting started down by the train. They looked down from the slope at Cota's *bandoleros* firing rifles and pistols into the civilians lined up before the derailed train. The people toppled over. Some began to climb over each other in their panic to escape. Others clambered through the paneless windows into the train, but the *bandoleros* reloaded and fired into the rail cars.

"Sweet Jesus," Tommy breathed.

"Your brother," Rojas said sadly, "your brother has developed a taste for blood." He looked at Tommy. "He can't satisfy himself."

Tommy knew that Rojas was right. Frank couldn't get enough of killing.

Within a few minutes none of the civilians were left standing and there were flames licking up inside the rail cars. Some of the rounds had ignited the kerosene from the shattered lamps. Someone inside one of the cars was screaming. Still the *bandoleros* fired on.

A few minutes later they all rode out, heading back to Los Altos. There was a thick black funnel of smoke rising up to the clear blue skies. The seats were burning. The young woman watched them disappear across the plains.

—◁ ○ ▷—

THE WOMEN OF SAGRADO CORAZÓN WAITED ON THE MOUNTAINSIDE for their men to return, and Lourdes waited with them. There was a strong wind blowing and she held down the whipping folds of her habit and her squinting eyes scanned the plain below.

"You shouldn't worry, Sister," said the squat woman to her right. "Nothing will happen to yours, he cannot be killed."

Lourdes felt the heat of shame rise to her face. Her passion for Father Tomás was the pueblo's open secret.

"It's my Carlos I am concerned about," the squat woman said. "He's not immortal like your priest."

Swallowing her embarrassment, Lourdes found her voice. "I pray that God allows all our men to return."

The squat woman slowly shook her head. "God might allow it, but the *callistas* won't."

Lourdes knew that the woman was speaking the truth, but she also knew that Tommy was not immortal, that he wasn't even a priest. He was only a man, and Lourdes's anxiety for his return was not that of a nun for her pastor, but of a woman for her desired. Even though she was disquieted for his safety, ever since Tommy had revealed to her in León that he was only pretending to be a priest Lourdes had felt as though chains had been torn from around her heart. Her desire for Tommy might still be a mortal sin—after all, *she* wasn't just masquerading as a nun—but at least now she knew she wasn't tempting Tommy to break his vows.

Lourdes felt a cold wave of uncertainty wash over her. She didn't know if she was tempting Tommy at all. He'd never tried to hold her or touch her. She couldn't remember him even *looking* at her with hunger. And the thought that Tommy didn't desire her was more intolerable than the repudiation of any vow made on a cold cathedral floor. She shivered.

"Sister Lourdes." Lourdes jumped at Manuela's rebuking voice.

Sister Manuela had come down the mountainside, descending with difficulty because of her increasing girth. She'd pushed through the women, elbowing them aside from behind, and when her eyes fell on Lourdes they turned hard and disapproving.

"Sister," Manuela said in a low flat voice, "your patients need you."

Lourdes dropped his eyes. "*Sí,* Sister." She turned to look once more out at the plains below, shading her eyes with her hand.

"Sister Lourdes!" Manuela hissed. "Remember yourself!"

Lourdes glanced around at the other women to see if they'd witnessed her shame. Manuela took her arm and started to lead her up to the pueblo.

"You are a young girl," Manuela said. "And these are barbaric times. But remember what happened to Father Moreno and his concubine. We must be above reproach at all—"

A shout went up from the women. "They're here! They're returning!"

Lourdes whirled with a cry. "Thank God!"

The women were running down the mountain. Manuela clutched at Lourdes's arm but the young woman glared back with wild eyes and tore away. She hiked up the folds of her habit and ran after the others.

"Tomás! Tomás!"

LOURDES RACED PAST THE OLDER WOMEN AND DIDN'T SLOW UNTIL she reached the head of the column. The riders' faces were grim under their sombreros. They were leading the packhorses with their motionless burdens. Lourdes stared at the dead slung over the backs of the animals and then she desperately scanned the long column riding slowly up the mountain. She caught a glimpse of a black cassock and ran along the line of horsemen and then the priest was there before her and she blurted out breathlessly, "Tomás!" But it was Frank, surrounded by his escort of murderers. He looked down at her with cold, raptorial eyes, and Lourdes felt naked and transparent before him. Then Frank's kestrel gaze moved on, as if he had rejected her as suitable prey, and as he rode by Lourdes saw that the hem of his cassock had stiffened with dried blood.

She moved down the line, calling, "Father Tomás? Where's Father

Tomás?" She was gripped by terror. He was not, after all, immortal. "Father Tomás?"

A *cristero* leaned out in his saddle and pointed to the rear of the column. Lourdes wanted to ask more but she was afraid. She took a few steps, then stood there and let the riders pass her. There was keening up and down the column as some of the women Lourdes had waited with discovered their husbands slung facedown over their horses. Then she saw him and whispered, "Thank you, God."

He was holding Miguelito in his arms, cradling him gently as if to cushion him from his mount's movements.

"Tomás." Lourdes smiled as she fought back tears of relief. "Tomás. Welcome back."

"He's hurt," Tommy said. "He's hurt bad."

He doesn't know how I love him, Lourdes thought. "What—what is it?"

"It's not a bullet. Mule fell on him." Tommy nodded to the rider just behind him in the column. "We have a doctor."

Lourdes glanced back. "Good. Good." She searched Tommy's face. He seemed as distant and removed as his brother, but the two had traveled to very different destinations.

"We have to save him," Tommy said, and his eyes connected with hers for the first time.

Lourdes felt a surge of female protectiveness well up in her. *He needed her.* "We will. We will . . . Are you unharmed, Tomás?"

Tommy didn't seem to hear her. "We can't let him die." He looked down at the boy in his arms and his mount moved past her. Lourdes watched after him until the next horseman came abreast of her. Muñoz was staring up at the mountaintop pueblo. For him it was the heart of darkness and Catholic ignorance, the lair of the idolatrous Mexican beast.

"Doctor, I'm a nurse."

Muñoz managed to pull his eyes from the mountain. He looked down at her. "You're a nun."

"Little Sisters of Charity." She realized he didn't know what she was talking about. "We're a nursing order."

Muñoz was afraid to say more. He knew if he gave anyone offense his life was forfeit.

"We've needed a doctor for so long," Lourdes said. "You are a blessing from God."

"He's a communist. He doesn't believe in God's blessings." Quintana was just behind, on the blood bay. "We captured him."

Lourdes walked beside the Yaqui. "What happened? What happened at the train?'

Quintana was smoking a cheroot. "Evil. Evil happened." She waited, wanting more, and then Quintana exhaled and said, "The priest has curdled. He's gone bad."

She knew he didn't mean Tommy.

---<o>---

TOMMY CARRIED MIGUELITO UP TO THE SECOND FLOOR OF THE infirmary and laid him in the same bed he himself had almost died in, all those months before. Lourdes and Manuela quickly eased the boy out of his clothes and Muñoz gave him a quick visual examination. One half of his torso was deeply bruised, the purplish color running up one side of his throat. There was a trickle of blood from his left ear. Muñoz probed his flesh with long, aristocratic fingers.

"I can't feel any broken bones. I wish I had my stethoscope." Lourdes reached under the bed and produced Dr. Villanueva's valise.

"This was our doctor's, but he fled. He never came back. We don't know what happened to him." Muñoz glanced up at the photos of the refugee physician and his family mounted on the wall. He wondered if his friends in Guadalajara would be soon saying much the same about him. *He took a train to the capital one day and disappeared. We don't know what happened to him.* He opened the valise and looked inside. There was a heavy silver cross on top of the medical instruments. He lifted it out carefully and laid it on the bed, making sure not to look anyone in the eye. Then he took out the stethoscope.

As Muñoz listened to Miguelito's chest Tommy stood by the side of the bed and watched closely. "Can you save him?"

"I don't know." He glanced at the scowling Indian, seated on the floor. "I—I don't know what's wrong with him."

Muñoz continued to listen to the crippled boy's frail brown chest. "His breathing is labored. . . . His heart is weak. . . ." Muñoz had studied medicine to please his father. His own passion had been the pursuit of politics. Right now he wished he'd paid more attention in the surgery.

The Spaniard took the stethoscope from his ears. He looked at the young nun and Lourdes stepped closer. Together they gently turned the boy over. Muñoz probed his fingers in the boy's back, up to his skull. He felt a swelling in the cranial region. He teased it with his fingertips, and he didn't know what to do.

"What is it?" Tommy asked.

"There's a concussion . . . I think the brain's swollen." He dug in Villanueva's bag, but it was for show. He didn't know what he was looking for.

"We could put wet compresses on the area," Lourdes offered. "Maybe it would bring down the swelling."

"Yes, yes." Muñoz turned back and from across the room Quintana's eyes bored into him. "Yes."

—◀○▶—

TWENTY-SEVEN CRISTEROS HAD BEEN KILLED IN THE ATTACK ON the train—the machine-gun fire had been deadly. Another four of the two-score wounded had died in the saddle on the ride back to the pueblo. Their bodies were buried that afternoon in a communal grave in the mountainside cemetery, their lifeless flesh wrapped in bleached gunnysack and covered with an eternal ghostly blanket of quicklime as their grieving women wailed graveside. For their martyred souls there would be a requiem in the morning. Four of Frank's hired bandoleros had died too, but no one cried at their passing.

Of the eighteen wounded still alive, jamming the rooms and corridors of the infirmary, seven were critical and Muñoz and Lourdes and Manuela worked frantically all day and into the dusk. Twisted hunks of lead were dug from shattered bones, punctured lungs, shredded muscle. Three arms and two legs were amputated—one unlucky cristero lost one of each. By dusk the physician and the two nuns were bathed with blood, bone-weary as they rushed to save lives.

Lourdes had seen immediately that the Spaniard was unfamiliar with this kind of desperate doctoring. She led him through the first few furious bloody battles, and then Muñoz took over. His training came rushing back, and the dire circumstances of the situation didn't give him time for introspection or self-doubt. He barked orders and Lourdes worked beside him, his right hand. He cut and dug and sawed and sutured, and by the time the moon had risen they'd not lost a single patient.

SACRED HEART

—◁○▷—

Tommy wouldn't leave the boy's bedside. He sat in a high-backed chair and held Miguelito's hand, as the little urchin had held his in the oxcart coming up the mountain. Quintana stayed in his place on the floor, his legs crossed Yaqui fashion. His breathing was slowed and measured. He seemed almost trance-like.

Muñoz and Lourdes came into the room. When the doctor saw Miguelito, his weary face grew sharp with concern. The boy had gone very pale—a sickly shade of gray-green—and he looked drained of life.

"Is he all right?" Tommy asked. Muñoz felt the boy's throat for his pulse. There was a feathery throb under his fingertips, and it was faltering. He raised the boy's eyelids and examined his eyes. "He's going to be all right, isn't he?"

Muñoz looked at Lourdes and Lourdes came around the bed and took Miguelito's hand from Tommy's and tried to lift him from the chair but he stopped her. "Wait a minute!"

Lourdes was crying. She wanted to be strong for Tommy but she was tired and she had started to cry.

"Please, Tomás. Come with me out into the plaza." She brought him to his feet and began to lead him from the room. Tommy pulled back. "Tomás, please." Finally he let her lead him away.

Muñoz never took his eyes from Miguelito as he said, "*Señor*, if you still intend to kill me . . ."—he breathed deeply—"then do it now. Because this boy will die before the sun rises."

Quintana didn't move for a long time. Then he slowly rose and walked from the room.

In the plaza Lourdes tried to lead Tommy away from the infirmary but he wouldn't go. "Tomás, we've done all that we can do. It's up to God now."

The people of the pueblo had waited around in the plaza for their priest-general to tell them what to do, to give them direction, but Frank had immediately disappeared into his rectory on his return and hadn't come out since. *Bandolero* sentries leaned outside his door, their rifle butts propped on their hips, keeping everyone out. The *cristeros*, having risked death in the taking of the train, resented this display of arrogance and aloofness.

And the train attack itself was the topic of much dark discussion. The mission, it was roundly agreed, had been ill-planned and badly executed, resulting in the extremely heavy casualties. If Padre Pistolero hadn't exhibited his customary valor in his incredible dynamiting of the steam engine—which no one found surprising—the attack would have failed and all the *cristero* deaths would have been in vain. True, there had been unforeseen complications—the spotter plane, the early arrival of the train—these could only be labeled Acts of God. But their faith in their military and spiritual leader had been shaken.

And then there were the atrocities—the killing of the civilian officials, the massacre of the children from the automobiles. The *cristeros* were hard, vengeful men who had no qualms about exterminating their enemies, but they had witnessed Frank taking great pleasure in his bloodletting, in his terrorization of the Terrazas boys. They remarked about the stench of burning flesh and the women's screams and they shook their heads at the memory. This behavior seemed more satanic than priestly, and it concerned them. They felt their cause had lost some of its moral high ground. For the first time in a long time, there was discussion about Frank's *foreignness*. Maybe, it was said, he delighted so in the spilling of Mexican blood because he felt it was worth *less*.

So when Lourdes led Tommy out of the infirmary and into the *placita*, where there should have been a victory celebration, there was instead indecision and grief, and disgruntled sullenness.

"We've done all we can do, Tomás. It's in God's hands now." She took his arm to draw him away. Though she had been assisting Dr. Muñoz without pause all day and part of the night, she shook off her own weariness and was concerned that Tommy looked so tired. She didn't think he'd eaten since he'd ridden in with the others that morning. She wanted to feed him and put him to bed. She wanted to care for him.

"Lourdes?"

"Yes, Tomás?"

"I want to ask God to help . . ." He looked at her. "I want . . . I want to pray for Miguelito, but I don't . . . I don't know how. Will you help me?"

Lourdes felt a flash of irritation. She didn't want to pray and she didn't want him to pray. She wanted to be with him, alone.

"Of course, Tomás, but—"

Tommy knelt where he stood on the rough plaza stones. Lourdes glanced around. Everyone was looking at him. She gathered her habit folds and knelt beside him. Tommy was looking up at the second-story infirmary windows, as if God were housed there and not in the church a few doors away. He put his hands together as he had when he was a child, the way his big brother *Ank* had shown him. After a moment he glanced sideways at Lourdes.

"What do I do?"

The irony of a man in a priest's cassock asking how to pray was not lost on her. "Just talk to God. Just tell God how you feel." She was amazed at how resentful she felt of Tommy's newfound religiosity. She liked it better when he wanted to talk to *her*.

"Will He listen to me?"

Lourdes didn't know what to say. God's favor for Tommy was so obvious, so immutable, that she was shocked he wasn't aware of it.

"Tomás," Lourdes said a little testily. "Just say to God what you want to say. He will hear you."

The people in the plaza had begun to drift closer. They were curious about what their hero-priest was doing.

Tommy looked back up at the infirmary windows. Then he swallowed and softly said, "God." The plaza quickly quieted, people nudging each other.

"God . . . I'm not here asking for myself. I know better than that." He dropped his eyes as if in shame, then lifted them again. "But I just want to say, you gave that boy up there in that room a shitty deal, right from the first card. Miguelito never had a Chinaman's chance in this world . . ."

The women, hearing Miguelito's name, realized Tommy was praying for the boy's life. Many of them had a motherly fondness for the profane little orphan. They took turns feeding him from their cooking pots. They nursed him when he caught colds, and gave him castaway clothes to wear, as poor as they were.

"I mean, you made him lame and half-blind. *You* did that. And God only knows"—he paused, realizing he was *talking* to God, who only knew—"where his folks are . . . And anyway, they threw him away as soon as they got him . . ."

Lourdes, her head bowed, sneaked a quick look at Tommy. This was like no prayer she had ever heard.

"It ain't right . . . It just isn't right." He searched for words to match his thoughts. "All right, the little bastard threw rocks at us, and cursed us that day on the gallows . . . but he just didn't know any better . . ."

A woman came and knelt behind Tommy, then another and another. Then the whole plaza slipped to their knees, almost in unison. They didn't comprehend the English, but they understood Tommy's emotion.

"He came up here with us. He's been like . . . like my own kid, sometimes . . . like a little brother . . ." Tommy breathed deeply. "All he wanted to do was be one of us. To fight in your name. And now he's dying. . . . God, I'm asking you to save this kid. Give him the chance you screwed him out of before. Make it right. . . . Give him another chance. . . . Please, God, don't let him die. You can do that . . ."

After a long moment Lourdes softly said, "Amen."

◄○►

FRANK WAS COUNTING OUT THE GOLD PESO COINS ON THE RECTORY table, then marking the sums down in a ledger. The table glittered.

"*Patron,* come see this." Cota stood at the window, looking out at the plaza.

"I'm busy," Frank said, carefully aligning a column of coins. "What is it?"

"It's the other priest. He's praying out there."

Frank lost his count. An expression of annoyance pinched his face. He rose carefully so as not to disturb the gold and went to the window. Through the flawed panes of glass he saw Tommy kneeling in the middle of the plaza, Sister Lourdes beside him. Tommy was surrounded by the pueblo women. Some of them had lighted candles and they flickered in the night wind. Frank stared a moment, his face growing darker, then he turned away. He sat behind the table again and slowly extracted a bottle from among the stacks of pesos and poured himself a drink. Then the door to the plaza opened and one of the sentries stuck in his head.

"The Yaqui . . ." the sentry said, looking to Cota.

"Let him in," Frank said, and swallowed a gulp of tequila.

The *bandolero* stepped away from the door and Quintana entered, eating a tamale. He held the unwrapped corn husk in his open palm and ate the filling with the fingers of his other hand. Cota stared hard at him but Quintana ignored him and stood before Frank, the gold-laden table between them.

"They told me you wanted to see me?" Quintana looked around and Frank nodded at Cota and with a tight, grim set to his mouth the *bandolero* pulled a chair from the wall and set it behind Quintana. The Indian sat down and propped a boot up on the table, jarring several stacks of coins into an avalanche of gold. Frank was about to lunge for them when he caught himself. Quintana grinned, showing a mouth full of cornmeal, and Frank methodically rebuilt the golden pillars as he spoke.

"I have a business proposition."

Quintana said nothing, taking another clump of tamale in his fingertips as he chewed what he had in his mouth. Then Frank smiled. "You know, hombre, I can't figure you out."

Quintana shrugged, giving away nothing.

"You're not *alteño*. You don't give a damn about the Church. You don't give a damn about anything, as near as I can observe. Yet you fight beside us, you risk your life repeatedly . . . Why?"

Quintana popped the last of the cornmeal into his mouth and carefully ran his finger up and down the corn husk, getting every bit.

"I am," Quintana said in English, "a victim of circumstance." He grinned again. "I heard that once in Texas, and that's what I am. A victim of circumstance."

Frank laughed at that, at the English, and then he poured a glass of tequila and set it on the table before the Yaqui. The Indian looked at it, and then sucked his finger.

"Why aren't you out there with my brother," Frank said with a cold smile, "at his prayer meeting?"

"I was hungry." Quintana picked up the glass and swallowed the tequila in one deep gulp.

"My brother the priest," Frank snickered. "A leopard can't change his spots."

Quintana considered this, as if it had been on his mind lately, as if it were the most portentous thing he had ever considered. "Maybe that's true, but I saw this book once, this little *negrita* in Beaumont had. There was this picture of a lion in Africa, and the lion cub in Africa when it is born, it *has* spots. Then later it looses the spots and becomes a lion. So maybe a leopard can't change, but a lion can."

Frank stared at him. Then he poured himself a drink. As he was about to set the bottle down Quintana tapped his own glass with his grease-stained finger and Frank poured again.

"The American gunrunner, Gundersthaal, has disappeared."

Quintana sipped his tequila. His face showed nothing.

Frank looked away as if seeing something in the distance. "I can't depend on Don Enrique and his Catholic League any longer. I can't depend on the Archbishop. I can't depend on the Church." He looked at the pillars of gold before him. "I have made my own contacts. There are powerful Catholics in California who will help us procure arms. We can avoid the Texas border blockade."

"California doesn't have a border?"

"California has a coast."

"Ah . . ."

"Arms stolen from the Presidio can be smuggled onto a ship in San Francisco Bay, then transferred to a Mexican fishing boat anchored off Los Angeles. That's where the money will change hands." He indicated the gold before him. "That's where I need you."

Quintana nodded, understanding. Frank needed a gun to protect the money.

"Let me ask you something." Quintana leaned his elbows on the table and the coins shimmered. "What's to stop me from taking all your gold and never looking back?"

Frank smiled. "Cota'll go with you."

Quintana looked over at the *bandolero* and the scar-faced man glared at him. The Yaqui already was thinking of how he would kill him.

—◁○▷—

TOMMY FELL ASLEEP WHERE HE KNELT, AND IN HIS SLEEP HE LAY DOWN on the plaza stones. Lourdes covered him with a blanket and was looking down at him when Manuela came out of the infirmary and gave her a disapproving glare. The young nun left him reluctantly and followed Manuela inside. Some of the people in the plaza dispersed to their homes, but many threw blankets and slept where they were.

At gray dawn Tommy awoke before anyone else and picked his way through the sleeping mounds to the fountain to drink and wash his face. Leaning over the water, he looked up and saw Muñoz staring down at him from the second-floor infirmary window.

TOMMY WAS TAKING VILLANUEVA'S STAIRS TWO AT A TIME WHEN Muñoz met him at the top. The young Spaniard was afraid. "I did all I could, *señor*." Tommy pushed past him and entered the bedroom. Miguelito, in the middle of the bed, looked much smaller in death. Tommy slumped into a chair and stared at him.

"He passed in the night. The mule must have broken something when—"

Quintana entered the room then, and the Spaniard shut his mouth. Quintana looked at the dead boy and then at Tommy.

Muñoz, terrified, began to wrap the body in the bed sheets, as if he would be in less danger if he got the body out of sight. When Muñoz had Miguelito shrouded he started to lift his small body and Tommy said, "Leave him alone."

THE PEOPLE OF SAGRADO CORAZÓN AWOKE TO THE GRIM VIEW OF Tommy slowly carrying Miguelito's sheet-wrapped corpse across the plaza. They arose in silence, clutching their blankets in the dawn chill, as Tommy picked his way through them. God had failed their hero-priest. His prayers had gone unheeded. Father *Tomás* was not infallible after all.

A man and woman who lived in a house that fronted on the *placita* brought out a cedar chest they had hurriedly emptied and the woman lined the chest with a length of brocaded curtain and Tommy slipped in Miguelito's body. It fit perfectly. Tommy sat on the edge of the fountain and covered his face with his hands. The *cristeros* watched him and felt his despair, and it inflamed their own. Their faith was shaken—their faith in their cause, their faith in him, and their faith in God.

—◀◯▶—

QUINTANA WENT OUT THE BACK DOOR OF THE INFIRMARY AND WALKED down a narrow alley to the open back door of a stable. Inside, a short barrel-chested man was pumping a bellows. He watched as the Yaqui walked to a stall and looked in at the red stallion.

"You rode him hard, *hombre*," the blacksmith said. "Another animal would have been ruined."

Quintana looked at the horse and the horse looked back. In the Yaqui manner, Quintana would never deign to stroke his horse, or feed it from his hand, or even give it a name. He respected the animal too much for that, and the bay seemed to understand this.

"I want him reshoed."

The blacksmith stopped his pumping and picked up a glowing piece of iron with a huge pair of tongs.

"You're planning a long ride? He needs a few more days."

The smithy began to beat at the piece of iron with a hammer, fashioning a door hinge. The stable echoed with the pounding of metal on metal. Then Quintana saw through the open stable doors the passing funeral procession. He left the stall and stepped outside and watched.

Frank led the way, reading from a missal. He took very slow, measured steps, and Quintana knew he had stayed up all night drinking and counting his gold. Quintana knew he was drunk. Frank was flanked by a quartet of altar boys. One carried a cross on a long staff. Beside him a taller boy bore a rough, artless rendering of the Virgin of Guadeloupe that stiffened in the morning breeze. The two children behind swung urns of smoking incense. Then two *cristeros* bore the cedar-chest coffin on their shoulders. Tommy and the nuns followed right behind. Passing, Tommy turned his head to Quintana and the Yaqui saw the desolation and dismay in his eyes. *He's lost himself,* Quintana thought. *He's like those albinos in the forest. He's caught between worlds and part of none.*

The blacksmith came and stood beside Quintana. "Why aren't you with them, hombre? I thought the gringo was your friend?"

Tommy dropped his eyes then and looked down at the ground as he trod woodenly behind the coffin.

"A man has to take care of himself . . ." Quintana spat. "Besides, I'm not one of these people. I'm Yaqui. . . . Why aren't you with them?"

The smithy settled his sledgehammer on his shoulder. "I have no religion and no politics. . . . I don't see the use in either."

THE GRIEVING WIDOWS WALKED BEHIND THE NUNS. SOME OF THE more affluent had dressed themselves in mourning black. The others wore only their sorrow. The rest of the people brought up the rear. A rider on horseback carried a *cristero* flag—the Mexican tricolor with an image of the *Virgen* at its center—tied to the barrel of a carbine and flapping in the wind. Beside him walked a small dark-haired boy blowing an Jaliscan dirge on a cornet. The boy's father was one of the *cristeros* buried yesterday in the mass grave, and tears down ran his cheeks as they puffed with his playing. The whole pueblo had turned out. It was as if along with Miguelito they were burying their innocence.

THE PROCESSION LEFT THE WINDING, SHELTERED STREETS OF THE PUEBLO and came out onto the openness of the mountainside. There was a chill in the air and the wind had picked up. They followed a rock-strewn trail curving around the mountain and there, on a level area behind the high rear walls of the town, was the graveyard.

The *agraristas* had desecrated the cemetery when they'd raided the town. The crosses had been smashed and the headstones overturned, and though the people of Sagrado Corazón had done their best to restore it, the graveyard still had a ravaged look. It reflected the *cristeros'* present mood.

They set the cedar chest on the ground beside the long furrowed row of raw red dirt that had been thrown over the newly buried *cristeros*. The train attack didn't feel like a victory, indeed, it seemed like the movement's nadir. At the end of the covered trench was a hastily dug hole—smallish, but large enough to bury an adolescent.

Frank took an aspergillum from an altar boy and drunkenly flicked around holy water. The effort made him stagger. The Mexicans glared at him. This was their *raza* they were eulogizing, and they expected more respect. And then they looked at Tommy. His head hung in defeat, and they hated him for it.

"In war," Frank began to speak, "there are deaths. Blood must be shed"—he slurred the word—"in the eternal battle between good and evil." He swayed on his feet and caught himself. "We are engaged in just such a struggle, and so"—he took a step up onto the mound of the freshly dug grave dirt and blearily scanned the crowd—"we will by necessity have our casualties. In the grand scheme of things they hardly matter." The *cristeros* looked around at each other. This man took their deaths lightly. "What *is* important is to ensure that these brave men, these brave men and this poor crippled boy, did not give their lives in vain—"

Frank took a step and as the mound of dirt settled under his weight he overcorrected and lost his footing, fell heavily on his back and slid down into the open grave. The people in the cemetery gasped, but no one moved forward to help him. It had happened so quickly and besides the priest's actions were too shameful and disgusting. They were embarrassed for him.

Tommy glanced at Lourdes, whose mouth hung open in shock. He felt the mourners' mood turn ugly around him, and he was about to hurry forward to the open grave when the sound of laughter floated across the cemetery. It took a moment before Tommy could pinpoint the source and when he did he felt disgraced. His brother was in the grave, laughing. Tommy rushed to kneel at the lip of the hole and Frank lay on his back looking up to the wide blue sky. He had a silver flask in his hand and he poured tequila into his mouth and laughed again.

A wave of resentment and anger passed through the *cristeros* like a ripple of wind, and there was general grumbling and shifting of boots. This kind of behavior could not be tolerated, even from their priest. "This is disgraceful!" someone shouted out.

"Maybe if he likes it in there so much," another said, "we can help him to spend eternity there."

Rojas and his sons, on horseback, traded looks. Their allegiance had always been to Frank, but some things could not be tolerated.

Tommy reached down and grabbed Frank's cassock and started to pull him up. "What the hell are you doing?"

Frank punched at Tommy's face and snarled, "Get your fucking hands off me!"

Tommy glanced around. "Frank, you can't do this!"

Frank's voice was a low venomous hiss. "Don't you ever tell me what I can or cannot do. . . . Don't you ever—"

And that's when they heard it.

A cry. A weak, waking call. "Father Tomás . . . Father Tomás . . ."

Tommy raised his eyes and they met Lourdes's, staring back at him. Her face had drained of color. She had heard it, too. And she knew where it came from. Tommy looked back at Frank then, and from the cedar-chest coffin Miguelito's voice called out again, "Father Tomás," and as Tommy watched, Frank fainted. His eyes rolled up behind his eyelids and he slumped back into the grave.

A woman screamed and then another and another, and all around the cemetery people dropped to their knees and crossed themselves. A babel of prayers erupted, and then silenced instantly when the voice called out again. "Padre Pistolero, get me out of here!" And then in the endless stillness that followed Tommy rose and went to the cedar chest and looked at Lourdes again and then knelt beside the coffin and slowly raised the lid and Miguelito's shroud-wrapped form sat up. There was pandemonium throughout the cemetery again until Tommy raised his hand and everyone held their breath, and then he pulled the bed sheet from Miguelito's face and the boy smiled at him. "What the fuck are you doing to me?" Miguelito asked, and someone screamed, "It's a miracle! He can raise the dead!"

"God's favorite!"

"He's a saint!"

Tommy lifted the boy from the cedar-chest coffin and cradled him in his arms and smiled down at him.

"Lazarus!"

"Un milagro! Un milagro!"

"It's a miracle!"

The women rose as one and rushed to Tommy. They knelt at his feet and kissed the hem of his cassock and kissed his shoes and wiped the tears from their eyes and caressed his hands and touched his face and Tommy was so stunned he could only stand there and let them worship him. They begged him for his blessing. They beseeched him for his favor. They pleaded that he heal their ills, forgive their sins, protect their husbands and sons. A few women even began to dig desperately with their hands at the communal grave, in the belief their miraculous priest could restore life to their dead beloved. The *cristero* men had to drag them away again and again before their hysteria subsided.

Practical-minded Manuela jumped into the grave and tried to lift out Frank.

"Sister!" the stout woman snapped. "Help me!"

Lourdes was staring dumbly at the adoration of Tommy. She felt he had been torn away from her. She had been vying with God for Tommy's soul, and God had decided to show her the immense error of her arrogance.

"Sister!"

Lourdes started out of her thoughts, then hurried to help. As they were pulling him from the grave Frank came back to consciousness. He opened his eyes and saw his army, his parishioners, his pueblo, idolizing his brother. His face filled with rage and he threw off the nuns' hands and clawed himself out of the grave. Standing erect, he sought Tommy's eyes but there were too many worshipers surrounding him. Frank stalked out of the cemetery.

TOMMY FELT HE WAS DROWNING HE WAS SO SUBMERGED IN THE *pueblerinos.* A hundred hands stroked his face, his hands, every inch of his exposed flesh. In their rapture they tugged at his cassock and it began to tear in a dozen places. They touched the cross dangling from his belt cord with such faith that he felt the imprint pressed against his groin.

"*Padre! Padre!*" Miguelito cried out in fear, and Tommy looked down at the boy and remembered he was holding him.

"Are you all right?" Tommy shouted to be heard over the sea of prayers.

"What's happening?"

"How do you feel?"

The boy's fear subsided at the sound of his hero's voice. "I'm hungry!"

Rojas and his sons carefully reined their mounts into the crowd and Rojas held out his hand to Tommy. "*Padre,* jump up behind me!"

"No, take the boy!"

Rojas stared at the resurrected boy and his face showed his trepidation.

"Take him!" Tommy shouted and fairly threw Miguelito up into the *alteño's* arms. Rojas backed his horse out of the crowd and it closed again around Tommy.

"Saint Thomas!"

"He's a prophet!"

"Father, can you see my mother in Heaven?"

"Can you see the *Virgen?*"

Tommy didn't try to push them away. He didn't resist. He gave himself over to them and began to be swept up by the flood of faithful, borne along like an offering from hand to hand. He went limp, his arms outstretched in involuntary mimicry of the Savior, and he was raised up as they would an adored icon, his eyes wide and empty and skyward, and then the crowd closed over him like thrusting carrion birds and he was immersed in his believers.

A gunshot reverberated over the graveyard. The people, those that weren't already on their knees, hunched down and quieted.

Quintana stood on a tomb, his horse pistol in hand. "You're killing him! Get back away from him!" The Yaqui's eyes fixed on the boy in Rojas's arms as the *alteño* rode by.

The people hesitated, resistant. They were reluctant to give up their idol. They clutched to their breasts torn-away swatches of his cassock, strands of his hair. They touched their brows with fingernails red with his blood. Quintana fired again, shattering a clay flower vase, and they scuttled away like humped-over beasts, preliterate idolators from an earlier millennium.

Tommy lay on the consecrated ground, torn and stunned. Quintana jumped down from the tomb and stood between him and the others.

"Get up." There was an edge of anger in Quintana's voice. "Get up, Tomás." Tommy staggered slowly to his feet. He tottered there, much as Frank had done only minutes before.

"Get back to the pueblo," Quintana said. "This can't go on. Get back to the church."

But when Tommy took a faltering step it was not in the direction of the pueblo but farther out around the mountain.

"*Tomás!*"

Tommy didn't seem to hear him. He limped slowly across the graveyard, moving right through the people—who now parted before him, crossing themselves—and out the other end of the cemetery.

*　　*　　*

SACRED HEART

THERE WAS A MASSIVE OUTCROPPING OF ROCKS ON THE BACK SIDE OF the mountain, just under the high ramparts that guarded the rear of the pueblo. It was said that before the Spanish came the Indians of the mountain, cleansed and purified by the summit's springs, would hold ceremonies here to thank their gods for life's struggle. When the priests arrived with their soldiers they witnessed these pagan rituals and anathematized the rocks, calling them the Devil's Throne. Soon the Indians were extinct and the rocks were known only as a place of evil and romantic danger to the descendants of the Europeans who settled there. Naturally, the Devil's Throne became a place of moonlight trysts for the pueblo's secret lovers.

Tommy slowly descended the well-worn path to the outcropping and sat down heavily. The plains below him stretched out endlessly to the east, the mountains of Guanajuato on the horizon. Tommy brought up his shaking hands and covered his face. His limbs felt leaden, weary beyond all comprehension. Just the act of raising his arms was an enormous effort. He sat there, on the Devil's Throne, in the blowing wind, on the edge of nothingness, and the people who had followed him from the graveyard began to congregate on the mountainside. They found level spots among the rocks and pebbles and knelt and prayed. Behind Tommy, above and below and all around, keeping a respectful distance, the faithful knelt and prayed and watched him closely. They expected more miracles. They expected to see the *Virgen*. They already had their Christ.

THE MORNING SUN MOVED OVERHEAD AND BECAME HIGH NOON AND then the shadows lengthened into afternoon and still Tommy didn't move. A woman—thinking Padre Tomás must be hungry by now, and hoping to win a blessing—brought a dish of tortillas and approached warily. She edged within a few meters then shyly set the dish down on the ground and dashed back to her kneeling place. Others, chagrined they hadn't thought of it themselves, rushed back to the pueblo and hurried back with their own dishes. Soon the slope behind Tommy was studded with plates. Each woman brought her own specialty—stew, beans, corn pudding—much more food than Tommy could ever have consumed, even if he hadn't ignored it all. At that seamless point in time the food ceased being gifts and became offerings—oblations to a demigod, devotions to a saint. By the second day of Tommy's vigil the people were bringing small renderings of Christ, pictures of the Virgin, bowls of blessed beads and locks of hair. The Devil's Throne had become a sacred shrine. By the third and last day, the devotees were leaving treasured family heirlooms—golden rings, small worked objects of Taxco silver, earrings of Indian turquoise—but on that first day they brought only food, and when the sun set, blankets and serapes.

When Lourdes came out to the outcropping just after dark the people had lit candles and when the strong southerly wind blew them out they relit them and cradled them with their bodies. From a distance the Devil's Throne looked like a fiesta of lights.

"Tomás, how long are you going to stay out here?"

He was staring out at the dark abyss below. In the night nothing was visible on the plains below except the eyes of darting animals reflecting the candles' light.

"Tomás?" When he didn't answer, when he didn't even acknowledge that he'd heard her, she shivered, and not from the wind. She felt, even as the fire of her own desire grew, something inside him dying, going out. She hesitated, then picked up one of the blankets stacked on the rocks—the people were too timid to cover him themselves—and laid it around his shoulders. As she drew it around his chest and knotted the corners she whispered, "I love you, Tomás." She looked into his eyes and there was nothing, only emptiness. She stayed a moment longer, then went back past the praying people and up to the pueblo.

⸺⟨○⟩⸺

QUINTANA HAD BUILT A ROARING FIRE IN THE BRAZIER IN THE *PLACITA*, and he was sitting in a chair, drinking pulque and staring into the flames. The plaza was empty. Everyone was out on the back of the mountain. Then Muñoz stepped out of the infirmary and saw the Indian. He approached warily, reluctant to enter the circle of light.

"Come, *comunista*." The Yaqui poured pulque into a bowl and held it out. "Have a drink."

The Spaniard eyed him with suspicion. Quintana gave a short, bitter laugh. "Come on, I'm not going to kill you. I have no killing left in me." He looked up at the night sky. "Just like him."

Muñoz took a few steps closer then hesitated, in the manner of an anxious dog. Quintana shook the bowl, and the Spaniard walked the last few strides and took it. He looked at the thick milky liquid, then said, "He was dead."

The Yaqui sighed and said simply, "*Ay yi yi . . .*"

"You saw him. He was dead, was he not?"

The Indian shrugged.

"No, I examined him. There was no pulse, no respiration. . . . The boy was dead."

Quintana looked up at the physician. The Spaniard thought that the Indian seemed very tired.

"You think I *wanted* to pronounce him dead? I wanted desperately for him to live, desperately . . ." He took a quick drink of pulque then, and grimaced. "But he was dead."

"Ah . . . but he lives now, doesn't he?"

Muñoz turned slowly and looked up at the lighted infirmary window where he knew Miguelito to be.

"How can that be?" he asked softly.

Quintana leaned back in his chair and looked at the fire. "Just another unwanted little brown boy. Mexico grows them like ears of corn. Why make such a fuss over a little crippled orphan?"

Muñoz sat down quickly on a bench by the brazier. "I've tried to think of how I could have made such . . . such an error. I thought, maybe a coma, or some kind of trance. Sometimes a blow on the head can produce these things. . . ." He turned slowly and stared, like the Yaqui, into the flames. "But . . . the boy was dead. He was truly dead." His pleading eyes wanted an answer. "How can that be?"

Quintana smiled softly and shook his head. "You are not Mexican. You can't understand."

"Understand what?"

"The magic, *hombre.* The mystery."

"There is no magic. There has to be an explanation."

Quintana settled his chair back on the stones and stirred the fire with a blackened branch. The myriad sparks blew away on the wind. "Sometimes I think an educated man is like a blind man. Once" He held up the gnarled, smoking stick. "Once in Chihuahua I saw a wolf bitch suckle a baby. The baby had crawled away from the pueblo, and a week later they found it in with a litter of wolf cubs, and when the mother lifted the baby from the wolf bitch's teat, the bitch licked the baby's behind." Quintana pointed a two-fingered *V* at his own eyes. "This I saw myself when I was just a boy. And two summers after that we were crossing the desert in Sonora and we ran out of water, and a rainbow appeared where there was no rain, and at the end of that rainbow the rocks sweated pure springwater and we licked the rocks and saved ourselves. I can taste that water still." He dug in his pocket for a cheroot and stuck it between his teeth. "In the big plaza in Guadalajara I saw a man they could not hang. I think you saw it, too, Spanish. And this morning I saw a dead boy rise out of his coffin and demand chocolate. You saw that, too."

"There is an explanation," Muñoz said hollowly.

"Sí, there is God's hand in all these things."

"No, I can't believe that."

Quintana lit the cigarillo with the end of the burning stick. "A man who doesn't believe his own eyes, that man is a fool."

Muñoz stared at him, then said, "It's . . . it's impossible. . . ."

Quintana exhaled, and the smoke disappeared on the wind. "The boy was dead, you said so yourself."

"He was dead."

"Then explain it otherwise."

Muñoz slowly shook his head. "I can't."

Lourdes entered the plaza, her head down, and hurried across toward the church.

"God can do whatever he wants," Quintana said softly, watching her. "He can give life, or take it. Give a man a friend, or take him away. If you struggle with God, you are sure to lose." He stuck out his chin, indicating. "Just ask her."

Muñoz looked up, just as Lourdes entered the church.

⸺◁◯▷⸺

COTA WATCHED FRANK POUR HIMSELF YET ANOTHER DRINK, SLOSHING tequila all over the gold pesos. The priest was unshaven and disheveled. He hadn't stopped drinking since he'd returned from the graveyard. He was slumped back sullenly in his ornate high-backed chair, glaring red-eyed over his empire of coins, and he drank constantly. Cota had never seen a man fall apart so rapidly, even a priest.

Frank raised the glass to his lips, paused, and made a toast. "To merciful God," he muttered in English. "And his bastard son." Then he gave a short ugly laugh. Frank had been talking to himself since early afternoon. Cota didn't understand the words, but the whole thing made him nervous.

Frank's flat, pitiless eyes fell then on Cota, and they seemed to

300

see him for the first time. "Cota, my friend. Just the man I wanted to see." He reached for another dirty glass, upsetting several stacks of pesos. The coins rolled off the table and bounced across the floor. Frank didn't seem to notice. "Have a drink with me."

The *bandolero* cautiously approached the wide table.

"Sit down, *mi compadre*," Frank offered, nodding at the chair Quintana had sat in the night before. Cota grinned nervously at the chair, but didn't sit. He picked up the drink Frank had poured him and held it up. *"Viva Cristo Rey,"* he toasted, and Frank glared at him and Cota didn't know what he'd done wrong.

"Here," Frank said, and angrily pushed a stack of coins at the *bandolero*. Cota had to jump to catch the collapsing pesos as they tumbled off the edge of the table. "Here! Here!" Cota's two hands overflowed and the coins pinged off the dark plank floor.

"What's this for, *mi patrón?*" Cota laughed as he grasped the pesos to his belly.

"I want you to kill him," Frank said hoarsely and Cota, looking into his own rancor and remembering last night's meeting with Quintana, nodded in agreement. "With pleasure, *patrón*. I was thinking the best place would be on the boat . . ." Then he saw Frank slowly shaking his head. "Not the Yaqui?"

"I want him off the face of the earth," Frank breathed. "I want him dead. Kill him."

Cota suddenly understood and he stared at Frank and Frank's dead eyes stared back. The *bandolero* said firmly, "No, *patrón*," and leaned over the table and dropped the pesos.

"It's not enough?" Frank said bitterly. "How much is one man's life worth? Here!" He shoved more stacks at Cota.

"Patrón, no."

"Yes!" Frank shouted and with his arm swept half the table clean. The coins clattered and skittered across the floor. "Yes!" The *bandolero* stepped back, shaking his head.

"I will not."

Frank slumped back into his chair and reached for the tequila. He laughed acidly. "You too think he's a saint." He gulped from the bottle. "He's not. Believe me, he's not."

"No, *patrón*, it's not that." Cota didn't want to lose Frank's favor. "I would kill anyone for you."

Frank had upended the bottle and was choking down the fiery liquid. He yanked it from his lips and the tequila gushed down his chin. "Then kill him!"

Cota raised his hands in a pleading gesture. *"Patrón*, they would tear me to pieces." He stepped forward. "The people love him. They worship him. If I am to kill him, it can't be in Sagrado—"

He stopped then because Frank had dropped his face into his hands. Cota wondered if the gringo priest was crying. He sat down slowly in the chair. "*Patrón . . . Patrón . . .*"

After a long moment Frank raised his head and stared at the *bandolero* through glazed eyes.

"*Patrón*, tell me . . ." Cota leaned forward. "He's your brother, is he not?" Even for the murderous bandit this was remarkable.

Frank suddenly gave a quick sob as if a massive pain had pierced his breast. Then he cut off the tears with a gulp from the bottle. When he turned back to Cota his face was cold and remorseless again. "What if he is?"

Cota was searching for something to say when Frank went on. "Cain and Abel, you know the story?"

"Of course, *patrón*. The sons of Adam. The brothers—" Then the Mexican quickly shut off his words.

"The parable of the good son and his evil brother." In his drunkenness Frank's brow knitted with concentration. "In jealousy Cain slew his virtuous brother Abel and God condemned him to live out his life in the wilderness. Cut off from the company of other men. Condemned. Damned by God."

"*Sí, patrón.*"

"But we're not told the whole story, don't you see? We're not told of the pressures Cain must've felt his whole life. His disappointment, his pain." The sudden sob again. "Always trying to do the right thing, to win God's favor, but always coming up short to Abel." He sneered. "Abel, to whom everything came so easily. God's little favorite." He fixed Cota with a questioning glare. "You see?"

Cota thought to himself that anything he said would be wrong.

"It was a trick, don't you see? Another one of God's ugly little tricks."

—◄○►—

MUÑOZ SLIPPED IN THROUGH THE DOOR AND CLOSED IT BEHIND HIM. The church was dark and somehow colder than outside, in the wind. The only light was from a single taper flickering in an alcove.

The young Spaniard took a step forward into the golden gloom of the still new-smelling church and stopped, staring forward. Affixed to the wall above the altar was a naïve crucifix, and as his eyes adjusted to the dimness the primitive crucified Christ seemed to hover in the shadows. Muñoz stared wide-eyed, and then there was a sound from one corner of the church and Muñoz squinted and made out the nun, seated in a pew.

He assumed she was praying. The doctor hadn't entered a church since he was a boy of nine and he had a quaint perception that anyone inside a church would be engaged in the futile superstition of prayer. She was slumped over, not kneeling, but seated on the rough bench, her head bowed. Muñoz approached her slowly, put out his hand to touch her, hesitated, then laid his palm on her shoulder.

"Sister," he began, and Lourdes fairly jumped away from his hand. As she whipped up her head he could see she'd been crying. Her misshapen cheek was streaked with tears. Sometimes it seemed to Muñoz that every other Mexican he saw was in some way deformed.

"What do you want?" Lourdes barked, and her attitude shocked him. Working feverishly beside him yesterday in the infirmary the young nun had been diligent and deferential to the physician. Now her face was pinched and angry. She hadn't expected to be disturbed.

"Sister, I'm sorry, but—"

"I'm not your sister, *comunista*," Lourdes hissed. "What are you doing in here?"

Muñoz again felt he was a foolish lamb who had wandered into a lion's den. He faltered for his words. "I wanted to ask you . . ."

"Yes?"

"I wanted to ask you about . . . the boy. . . ."

Lourdes glared up at him.

"You were with me when I examined him. He had no pulse . . . he wasn't breathing . . ."

She said nothing. She wasn't going to give him any help.

"Do you think . . . Is it possible . . ." The Spaniard glanced nervously at the phantom Savior. "Did I make a misdiagnosis? Did I make a mistake? Could the boy have still been alive?"

Lourdes gave the doctor a look of scornful pity.

"Of course, you made a mistake," she snapped.

"I did?" He was surprised at her certainty.

"You must have, because if you didn't and the boy was dead then he's a miracle worker. He can raise the dead. Then he's not like other men." And neither of them wanted to believe that. Lourdes looked away, lost in her thoughts.

"You made a grievous mistake."

—◄○►—

BY AFTERNOON OF THE SECOND DAY OF TOMMY'S CONTEMPLATION the people of the pueblo had begun to inch on their knees—as they had done for centuries at the basilica in Guadaloupe Hidalgo—from the pueblo church to the cemetery, site of the miracle, then on around the back of the mountain to Tommy's precipice aerie. As they snailed along—one knee dragged forward, then another—they dutifully clutched rosaries and rhythmically recited their chaplets of Hail Marys and Our Fathers in a mantric monotone murmur. The mountainside hummed like a beehive, and the rough stones of the trail wore away the fabric over their knees and the penitents left blood-streaked trails behind them.

Quintana came up the path, stepping around the votaries, and walked out beside Tommy on the Devil's Throne. Tommy hadn't moved. He sat where he had sat for over twenty-four hours, looking out at nothing. The blanket Lourdes had tied around him had slipped from his back. His arms were folded over his chest and his hands gripped his shoulders.

"Hey, amigo. Don't you have to shit or something?"

Quintana walked around to the edge of the overlook and turned to face Tommy. But Tommy's eyes, though gazing out, were seeing inward.

"You're scaring me, gringo." The Yaqui searched the American's face for a remnant of his friend. "What are you doing out here?"

When Tommy didn't answer Quintana sat on a rock and pulled out a cheroot. "Amigo, why don't we take that gold and get the hell out of here?" He squinted at Tommy as he torched the cigarillo. "We don't belong here, you and me," he said softly. "You and me, we're men with a price on our heads. With those pesos we can buy new names, new lives, we can go anywhere in the world. Buenos Aires, Madrid, Paris." The long-haired Indian grinned. "I hear the women in Paris are something special, amigo. *Chingado,* all night long." He made the pumping action with his fist, but when Tommy didn't respond he stopped. "Don't you ever want to go fucking again, gringo?" His face filled with concern as he examined his friend. Then he stood up and looked out across the empty brown plains below. "Okay, we leave the gold." He turned back to Tommy. "It's bad luck anyway. We just take off riding and we don't stop until we reach an ocean, what do you say? We take a boat to Havana. I hear there is need for men with our talents "—he touched his holstered weapon—" in Havana. Or Maracaibo, or even Africa. We'll raise hell and *chingado* all night long, until the bullet with our name on it finds us, what do you say?"

He sat down again and studied Tommy for a long time. He looked for a response, an explanation, a refusal, but there was nothing. Tommy sat as if in a trance, his unseeing eyes remained fixed on the distant sky. Then Quintana rose and walked away, saying, "You scare me, gringo."

—◄O►—

TOMMY WAS THINKING OF JIMMY DILLON. JIMMY WAS A BIG, DUMB enforcer in Bulldog's mob, and whenever he tried to do something on his own he always got pinched. The last time he got arrested he was holding up a Chink laundry on Bayard Street. As he ran outside there were two cops waiting there for him. They practically walked him from the door of the laundry into the black mariah, Dillon was that stupid. And at 100 Center Street the coppers pummeled him pitilessly for two days—Tommy later heard that Jackie Hanrahan had orchestrated the beatings and assigned shifts—until Jimmy began to give up information about the Coyne Mob. They wrote down everything Jimmy said and had him make his mark and then they *released him back onto the streets.* The big, dumb mick went home to his wife and kids, ate a huge serving of cabbage and pig's feet, plopped into bed and went to sleep. Later that night Hanrahan sold the whole package—transcript, signed statement, confessions, everything—to Bulldog for seven thousand dollars and Bulldog called Jimmy and said be waiting outside on the stoop. Tommy couldn't believe Dillon would be so stupid as to just be standing there, on the stoop, his coat turned up against the March thunderstorm—a cow awaiting slaughter. They took him to a warehouse by the docks at the foot of West Fifty-fourth and Jimmy D. didn't suspect a thing until Bulldog put on the heavy leather apron. Then Bulldog's rage boiled up and spilled over, his face enraged and reddened, and he went at Dillon with a hatchet. When the walls were splattered with blood and poor Jimmy lay moaning on the warehouse floor Bulldog pulled a short, sharp blade from a sheath stitched into the butcher's apron and held it out to Tommy. "Cut out his fuckin' stoolie tongue!" Tommy stared at the knife but didn't move to take it and Bulldog jumped at him, shrieking, "You don't have the stomach for it, Tommy Boy?" His father's face was inches from his, quivering in fury, wild-eyed with bloodlust.

"If you're enjoying yourself so much, Da, then you do it."

"Damned right I will," Bulldog sneered and dropped down over Jimmy Dillon's head. Jimmy started to scream. "If you're such a fucking jenny-woman," Bulldog spat back at Tommy, "maybe you oughtta wear skirts like your sissy brother!" Suddenly Jimmy's screams became a horrifying gurgle. Bulldog stood up, the grisly trophy in his dripping hand. "Now, let's see if he stool pigeons on anyone again."

Jimmy was puking up a thick crimson goo. His face was so bloody only his pathetically pained eyes were visible. He looked up at Tommy and gargled something and Tommy pulled one of his automatics and shot him twice in his chest.

Bulldog glared at Tommy and said, "Ye have a soft heart, Thomas. I suggest you rid yourself of it."

THEY THREW JIMMY DILLON'S BODY OFF THE DOCK INTO THE RIVER AND somehow it got hung up in the pilings and three days later it bobbed to the surface right where they'd dumped it. When Bulldog was told the coppers were pulling up Jimmy's body he made Tommy accompany him down to the wharf. There were a score of people gathered at the end of the pier. Hanrahan was there with the other dicks, a few onlookers, and Dillion's wife and six kids. The clothes had been washed from Jimmy's corpse and the hatchet slashes had bubbled out white and swollen—like boiled egg out of a cracked shell—and the fish and the crabs had gotten at the wounds, and at his eyes and his ruined mouth. Dillon's woman stared grim and silent, clutching her dirty children around her, as tears flowed down her face. Bulldog went to her then, expressed his regrets at her husband's death, promised to find out who was responsible, and offered her a handful of twenties. She glared at him—she knew he had murdered her big dumb ox of a husband— but in the end she had to think of her children and take the money. When Bulldog turned back to him, Tommy saw that his father was relishing the moment.

*   *   *

TOMMY REMEMBERED AN ITALIAN WAITRESS AT CARUSO'S SPAGHETTI House, on Mulberry Street. She walked out of the kitchen laden with plates of linguini and clams, laughing as she shouted back over her shoulder to someone in the kitchen, and the two bullets struck her one in the abdomen and the other in her breast and she was thrown back against the kitchen door and the plates of linguini clattered to the floor.

Tommy had walked in from the street, his hat pulled down over his face. It was one of his first "hired-out" killings—commissioned by the Matrangas, in fact; they wanted to use an Irishman to deflect suspicion. Fat Sally was seated by himself, eating pasta, and it looked like it was going to be an easy drop, but then Tommy, nervous and unseasoned, had let his eyes linger on Fat Sally too long, and when he looked away Fat Sally, strands of spaghetti hanging from his mouth had started to rise and go for his gun, and Tommy had to shoot him from across the restaurant and the two slugs tore through Fat Sally's soft body and killed the waitress.

The newspapers said she had two kids, three and five.

AND THAT MADE TOMMY REMEMBER FLINTY MCGUINTY. IT WAS FIVE in the morning and Bulldog watched from the car as Tommy ran to the front windows of Flinty's barroom, punched out the glass, then tossed in the dynamite. It was only going to be a warning, just a little terror to convince Flinty to tap Coyne brew, but the coppers dug out seven bodies. Flinty, his wife, and their brood of five. They had been evicted from their flat and were sleeping in the barroom that night.

Though no one was ever arrested for the McGuinty slaughter, the neighborhood knew who'd bombed the place, and it added to the sanguineous legend of the Coynes. *These people will do anything.*

AS THE SUN ROSE OVER HIS RIGHT SHOULDER ON THE THIRD DAY THE faces of the dead kept bobbing to the surface of Tommy's memory, the way Jimmy Dillon's bloated, slashed and fed-upon corpse had floated to the top of the brown Hudson. Little Mo Rabinowitz begging for his life on knees, invoking the name of Jesus, as if that were a trump card to be played with Irishmen about to kill you. Cullen Doyle running down Forty-second Street slamming into walls, then getting up and flailing forward again as they pumped rounds into him from behind. Jackie Hanrahan, cradled in the over-sized arms of the snow-covered Christ, looking down at the hole in his gut. "Fuck me, Molly." Severo Salazar bouncing back on the rump of the big red stallion as the bullet from the scaffolding above tore down into him. The train passengers keening and wailing in the sizzling, still moment after the explosion.

So many people. So much suffering, Tommy thought as he gripped his arms and rocked back and forth on the rock. *How can You forgive me? How can You ever forgive me?*

—◦—

WHEN THE SUN BEGAN TO DIE IN THE WEST ON THAT THIRD DAY, FRANK stumbled out of the rectory and, with Cota beside him to give occasional support, staggered across the plaza. Quintana, in the blacksmith's stable watching the smithy shoe the red stallion, glanced up and saw them pass.

The Devil's Throne was lighted by hundreds of glowing candles. There was no wind this late afternoon and the flames burned tall and strong and bathed the mountainside in a pale yellow glow. By the time Frank reached the rock outcropping the cold, high air had cleared his head and straightened his gait, but the contempt on his face lengthened as he stepped around the praying worshipers and out onto the precipice.

"What do you think you're doing?" he sneered at his brother. He moved around him, glared in his face. "You might trick these primitives, but I know you, remember? I know who you are." He leaned forward until he was fairly spitting in Tommy's face. "You're Bulldog Coyne's favorite boy. You're a gangster and a murderer and a thief. Just like he was." His voice became a clenched-teeth whisper. "And now you're a blasphemer as well. And you'll burn in hell for it."

When Tommy didn't respond Frank straightened and shouted at the worshiping devotees, "This man is not a saint! He's not Christ!" There was a momentary break in the hum of prayers, the way cicadas will suddenly silence for a few seconds on a summer night, then the mountainside went back to its devotions. "He can't work miracles! He can't raise the dead!" Frank's face reddened with anger. "He's not even a priest! He's a charlatan! *He's nothing!*"

They ignored him and continued praying.

"He's nothing!" Frank shrieked, and then in hatred Frank slapped

308

Tommy hard with the back of his hand. The whole mountainside seemed to gasp for breath, and then the people rose as one. *"He's nothing!"* Frank pulled back his hand to strike again and Quintana stepped up and put his horse pistol against Frank's skull and cocked back the hammer.

"Touch him again and I'll blow your fucking brains out."

Then Cota pointed his revolver at the Yaqui and for a moment there was complete stillness. No one on the mountainside moved. Then there was the sound of great heaving sobs. Quintana was watching Frank's eyes, looking for a movement that would tell him that Cota was preparing to fire, but Frank turned to the sound of the weeping and Quintana followed his gaze and Tommy was sobbing. He gripped himself tightly, rocked back and forth on his stony perch and cried like an inconsolable child.

Quintana brought down the horse pistol and leaning over said softly to his friend, "Gringo, don't do this." The people began to shuffle forward, thinking the tears were part of the on going miracles that had chosen to visit their mountaintop.

"Catch Padre's tears! They will heal sickness!" a man shouted.

"They are like the tears of the Virgin!"

Quintana put his hand on Tommy's shoulder and gripped it tightly. "Hombre, this is unmanly. Don't do this."

Tommy raised his tear-streaked face and looked at the Yaqui—the first time his eyes had focused on anything since Miguelito's resurrection—and the Indian saw two deep maelstroms of grief and sorrow and regret. The enormity of the pain in Tommy's eyes caused the Indian to take a step back and stare in fear.

And then Lourdes came out of the crowd and put her arms around Tommy and lifted him to his feet.

"Come with me, Tomás," she whispered, and he looked at her without comprehension through his tears and she firmly gripped his arm and began to lead him protectively through the *pueblerinos* who surged forward and started to claw at the ground where they hoped Tommy's teardrops had fallen. Quintana stepped away quickly but Frank was almost swept off the cliff before Cota pulled him back to safety.

—◁O▷—

LOURDES SPOKE QUIETLY, CONTINUALLY, AND URGENTLY AS SHE LEAD him across the deserted *placita*. "You are going to be all right. You just need to rest." She looked at him. "I'll take care of you."

Tommy struggled to speak through his flowing tears. "So much blood—" he choked out. "So much— How can He forgive me?"

"It's all right, Tomás. I'll take care of you."

Muñoz was sitting in what had been Villanueva's parlor, poring through the disappeared doctor's medical books. He was trying to find an explanation for his misdiagnosis of the dead boy. The boy who wasn't dead. He looked up when the infirmary door opened and saw Lourdes helping the priest into the foyer. He sat up in fear at the appearance of the miracle worker, and when Lourdes shot him a dark glare Muñoz looked away. He was relieved when they moved on down the hall.

Lourdes led Tommy to her small room in the back—it had once been the playroom of the Villanueva children—and closed the door behind them.

"I can't take it back," Tommy cried in despair. "I would, but I can't!"

"*Shhhh—*" Lourdes comforted as she sat Tommy down on the edge of her narrow bed. "*Shhhh—*"

She began to unbutton his torn soutane, whispering to him, "You just need to rest. You can sleep here, in my bed."

"I would bring them *all* back to life if I could!" She gently pulled his arms from the cassock's sleeves. He looked up at her. "Please believe me."

His chest was bare and she lightly touched the muscles in his shoulder. His wounds from the train attack were scabbed over. "I'll wipe you in alcohol," she said huskily. "I'll bathe you."

When he was naked she carefully laid him back in the bed and looked down at him.

"I would die to bring them back," Tommy's sobs increased. "I would die—"

She kissed his chest then. A single light touching of lips to flesh.

"So much blood on my soul," Tommy cried. "I'll never be clean . . ."

Her kisses moved up his chest to his throat, then through the stubble of beard on his jaw. His cheeks were wet with his tears, and she licked the salty dampness with the tip of her tongue.

"Lourdes . . ." It was as if Tommy finally began to realize what she was doing. "Lourdes . . . don't . . ."

She kissed him then, sliding her tongue between his teeth as she crawled on top of him. His mouth tasted of tears and staleness and it was wonderful. She felt the contours of his body molded against her own and an electric thrill coursed through her. Her body seemed to open like a blossoming flower. She reached back and fumbled with the buttons at the back of her neck but her hands were shaking with desire and after a moment she gave a furious shout and ripped open the back of her habit and yanked it over her head, dragging off her pinned-on veil and exposing her dark, close-cropped hair. She tore at the laces of her sleeveless chemise and her heavy young breasts fell out into view.

"Jesus," Tommy gasped and then Lourdes cupped her breasts in her two hands and guided them into Tommy's face. Her dark, protuberant nipples brushed against his lips and she felt him begin to harden under her flanks. Instinctually she began to undulate against him, flesh to flesh, and as he hardened and lengthened she reached down and tugged at the waist string of her pantaloons, then dragged them down over her buttocks and she felt him throbbing against her vagina. She looked in his eyes and whispered, "I love you, Tomás. You are *mine!*" and on the last word she slammed down her hips, impaling herself on him. She cried out at the sharp pain, but then she felt him inside of her and the heat of her desire flashed over her body and she slammed down again and again, shouting with each plunge. "Mine! Mine! You're *mine!*"

SISTER MANUELA STOOD OUTSIDE THE CLOSED DOOR AND LISTENED openmouthed. She had heard the sounds of copulation as she descended the stairs from the patients' rooms. She knew instantly where the cries of passion were coming from, and she also knew who Lourdes had in her room. Manuela, always on the vigil for the incubation of the Devil's lust among her sisterhood, had suspected from their first meeting that the young sister would someday renounce her vows and enjoy the pleasures of a man. The girl was just too young, too beautiful—even with the disfigurement—too desirable and too strong-willed. And then also the girl was well-born, and Manuela being the daughter of a *campesino* had a natural resentment of the rich. The squat, fattening nun knew without question that had she come into this world Lourdes Hidalgo de Gutierrez instead of as herself, she would never have chosen the veil.

Manuela walked away from the door with her face mirroring the conflicting emotions of judgment, satisfaction, and not a little jealousy. In the foyer she looked up to see the communist doctor sitting in a chair, a medical book open on his lap, staring back at her. He too could hear the sounds of copulation, and he was as shocked as Manuela. Hearing the fucking then seeing the *comunista*—the nun considered this a very bad omen and crossed herself quickly and went out into the plaza.

—◄○►—

LOURDES LAY BESIDE TOMMY, WATCHING HIM SLEEP. EMOTIONALLY, physically, and sexually spent, he had fallen asleep—Lourdes gently kissing his face—almost immediately after she climbed off him. Now she reached up and traced her fingers across his jawline, down his rib cage—*he's too thin*—and into the damp hairs around his penis. She touched him lightly, caressed the soft ridge around his glans, and his flesh stirred and she snatched her hand back with surprise. She stared at his penis in wonder—the recent source of so much pain and pleasure—and knew she wanted to feel it inside her again and again.

She rose from the bed and padded to her habit thrown in passion to the floor. Holding the ripped, useless garment in her hand, she knew she would never put it on again. As she stood there contemplating her future a flood of hymenal blood and semen coursed down her thighs and she jammed the garment between her legs to catch the flow.

—◄○►—

MIGUELITO AWOKE IN THE HOUR BEFORE DAWN AND SLIPPED FROM HIS bed. The other patients were all still asleep, and neither of the nuns were around. The boy tiptoed down the hall, stole a pair of *huaraches* from under a wounded *cristero's* bed and trod softly down the stairs. He spotted the physician asleep in a chair in the parlor and wondered who he was. Miguelito had seen the Spaniard for the last three days, staring oddly at him from the doorway, afraid to approach. Before that, before opening his eyes to a single shaft of light leaking through the lid of the cedar chest in the cemetery, there was only the blackness. Before the blackness, the last thing the boy remembered was kicking the jenny mule with his bare heels and riding beside the speeding train.

312

Miguelito silently lifted a comforter from the armchair across from the Spaniard and slipped through the front door, closing it soundlessly behind him. Around the dying fire in the brazier *cristeros* and their women slept under mounds of blankets. The plaza was still and chill and Miguelito wrapped the comforter around his body and stepped carefully in the oversized huaraches across the sleepers to the brazier. There was a kettle of beans hung over the embers, and a plate with a few greasy, half-eaten beef ribs. He poured some of the beans into the plate and stealthily crept away, as careful of his footsteps as only the crippled can be. Miguelito was used to stealing food. It was how he'd fed himself his entire short life. And though the *pueblerinos* had been bringing him treats ever since he'd come out of the blackness, he felt more fulfilled stealing his own breakfast. He felt safer.

Miguelito scrambled up to the church's humble bell tower and sat on the ledge and began to gnaw at a beef rib. He liked to come up here to eat. It was the only time in his existence he felt above everyone else. When he was just finishing the third rib the boy looked up and stopped chewing. The horizon to the east was lightening, turning a glowing blue. His eyes narrowed to slits and he stared down the mountain. He shaded his face with his hands, then suddenly his eyes widened and alarmed. He threw down the plate and leapt on the bell rope and as the bell started to clang he screamed, *"Terrazas! Terrazas!"*

—◄○►—

THE FIRST FEW SOLDIERS WHO GALLOPED INTO THE PLAZA WERE PULLED down by the pueblo women. Inspired by the miracles of the mountaintop, they were furies, throwing themselves under the horses' hooves, stabbing at the animals' bellies, slicing at the *federales'* legs. When this first vanguard of overeager troopers was brought down they were set upon and hacked to pieces with knives and hatchets, and when the second wave of cavalrymen thundered up the mountain road and through the entrance to the pueblo the *cristeros* had gotten to their weapons and a furious gun battle ensued. The *federales* hurtled around the plaza fountain, firing at anything and everything. The *cristeros* ran beside them, shooting them from their saddles. Some riders veered off, clattered down narrow side streets and alleys, and were fired upon from windows and doorways.

313

Tommy rushed out into the plaza from the infirmary, just as Frank came through the door of the rectory. The brothers' eyes met, and it was as if each were a stranger to the other, and then a *federal* galloped across the plaza and his horse splashed through the fountain and Frank raised his hand and fired the small revolver and the *federal's* horse screamed and crumpled into the fountain water, blood spurting from its eye, and then as the rider struggled under the plunging animal Frank stepped up and shot the rider. Then he looked at his brother again.

"Padre! Padre!"

Miguelito dodged the riders and terrified horses galloping around the plaza and hopped toward Tommy, clutching Tommy's holstered automatics in his arms. "Padre!"

A cavalryman with a lance shouted something furious and unintelligible and leveled the lance at the scrambling boy and raked his mount with the rowels of his spurs.

"Chico!" Tommy shouted. "Watch out!"

The boy kept coming, thinking only of delivering the weapons to the man who could do something with them, and Tommy ran in front of the galloping horse waving his arms and shouting. The animal shied and stumbled and Tommy made a grab for the shaft of the lance and pushed the cavalryman from his saddle. The cavalryman landed hard and rolled.

"Padre!"

Miguelito thrust the guns at Tommy and Tommy took the weapons and looked down at them.

"Padre, qué té pasa? Kill him!"

The cavalryman had stumbled to his feet and was drawing a knife from the top of his polished boots.

"Padre, kill him!"

Tommy started to unholster his .45, as he had thousands of times before during his violent life, but then he stopped. He stared down at the gun in his hand, then over to his brother by the fountain. Frank stood with his small-caliber pistol held at his thigh. He was watching the unfolding drama with iniquitous detachment.

"Shoot him!" Miguelito shrieked to Tommy.

The cavalryman started toward the priest who had unhorsed him, the knifepoint held down to rip upward and eviscerate, but Tommy didn't take the .45 from its holster.

"Padre!"

The cavalryman smiled as he understood what was happening. This priest was not going to protect himself, and the other didn't seem to care. The *federal* thought this was humorous and provocative, and as he accelerated toward Tommy he let out a primordial killing yell.

"*Shoot him!*" Miguelito was bouncing up and down on his sound leg as riders galloped past. "*Padre!*"

Then a shot rang out and the cavalryman stumbled and slid to his knees. He pressed his hands over the wound in his side, but the blood poured in rivulets through his fingers and down his ribs.

Quintana picked up the knife where it had fallen from the cavalryman's hand and jammed it into the trooper's chest. In his other hand he held the smoking horse pistol. The Yaqui looked at Tommy, then his eyes dropped to the still-holstered automatic.

Frank was gone.

—◁○▷—

FRANK RAN TO THE PUEBLO GATE AND STARTED SHOUTING INSTRUCTIONS to the *cristeros* as he hurriedly reloaded his pistol. The government soldiers had been driven out of the pueblo and now they were regrouping down the mountainside, just out of range. Frank ordered the mountain road to be barricaded at the entrance to the pueblo and the *pueblerinos* dragged carts, doors, paving stones, even items of furniture into the breech and stacked them in a rushed panic. Government sharpshooters had taken cover in the brambles and a woman beside Frank suddenly slumped and fell at his feet. The *cristeros* who had been camped outside the pueblo walls were being tortured and their screams died on the morning breeze like distant bird calls. Then a bugle sounded attack.

"They're coming back!" Rojas shouted. He and his sons had positioned themselves behind the barricade, with fifty other *cristeros*, and now they fingered their rifles and took aim on the forward riders of the regiment of cavalry that thundered up the mountain road.

Frank slapped his cylinder back into his pistol and watched the line of horsemen surge up the mountainside. He held his *pistola* tightly and shouted, "Don't fire until I give the order!"

The riders were whipping their mounts. An officer pounded forward, his saber held high. A *cristero* down the line emptied his weapon in a flurry of gunfire and Frank ordered, "Wait! Wait until I give the word!"

315

Frank carefully took aim, as Cota had instructed him, on the officer's midsection and slowly squeezed the trigger. The officer dropped the saber and slumped forward over his horse's neck and then slipped from the saddle and was trampled under the following hooves.

"*Fire!*" Frank shouted, and it seemed as if the entire front line of horsemen crumpled under the *cristero's* precision marksmanship. Men and animals shrieked. Horses foundered in a tangle of deadly thrashing legs. Then the wave of riders following galloped over the dead and, unable to turn their mounts, slammed into the barricade, knocking askew portions of the wall. Some of the horses tried to climb the jumbled barricade. They clambered for purchase with pumping hooves as their riders beat them and screamed at them and the succeeding horsemen crushed them from behind. Then a section of the barricade collapsed and a score of *federales* tore through the breach.

Quintana, running in from the plaza, fired pistols in both hands and four of the galloping *federales* flew from their saddles. He turned and shot another in his back.

Frank was reloading and he glanced through a bed frame and saw a soldier take aim through the barricade and fire and Rojas shouted and sat down and then the soldier saw Frank and was turning his weapon on him when Frank shot him in his face. Frank knelt by Rojas. There was blood spurting from the rancher's throat. Frank squeezed the wound closed and shouted at the sons of Rojas, who were helping to close up the breach in the barricade.

TOMMY CARRIED ANOTHER BLEEDING *CRISTERO* INTO THE INFIRMARY. The hallways were jammed with the wounded and dying, and the Spaniard Muñoz was soaked with blood as he frantically clamped arteries and fashioned crude tourniquets. Lourdes, working beside the physician, looked up at her lover expecting him to acknowledge her, but he wouldn't meet her eyes. She wore a man's trousers and shirt and her head was bare. There had been no time for consideration. When the shooting started she'd grabbed at any garments in the Villanueva closets, and there had been no pause since for anyone to remark.

Tommy laid the *cristero* on the bloody wood floor beside a mortally wounded *cristero,* and the dying man weakly said, "Father, hear my confession," and Tommy wouldn't look at the man and hurried back out into the plaza. Miguelito waited for him outside the door, thrusting up the holstered automatics he had picked up after Tommy'd dropped them on the plaza stones.

"*Padre,* they need you, listen!" The battle at the barricade was still raging, just out of sight of the *placita.*

Tommy stuck his arms under the armpits of a bloodied man and began to drag him toward the infirmary, the unconscious man's heels bouncing on the plaza stones.

"*Padre!*" Miguelito cried in alarm. "Without you they'll kill us all!"

Tommy didn't respond to the boy, he was intent on getting the bleeding man into the infirmary. Then Cota grabbed his arm and said, "That's a *callista,* asshole."

Tommy hadn't noticed the man he was dragging was a *federal.* He hesitated, then continued to pull him toward the infirmary door.

"I told you that man is a *federal!*" Cota said. "Let him die!"

When Tommy didn't respond Cota stepped forward and shot the soldier in the heart. Tommy stumbled backward and fell under the man's weight. He held the soldier's body in his arms and buried his face in the dead man's shoulder.

"You have become a woman, priest," Cota said. "A useless woman."

Tommy laid the soldier gently on the plaza stones and rose to his feet. A *cristero* staggered into the plaza, blinded by blood from a head wound, and Tommy ran to him and put the man's arm around his shoulder. "It's going to be all right, amigo. You're going to be okay."

Just then a mighty shout of exultation rose from the direction of the barricade. The attack had been repulsed.

Tommy led the wounded *cristero* into the infirmary and Lourdes rose quickly from a patient and came to them.

"Thank you, *padre,*" the blinded *cristero* said. He had recognized Tommy's voice. "You are truly a saint."

Lourdes took the *cristero's* arm and was going to say something to Tommy, but he walked past her and knelt by the dying man who had wanted confession. "*Señor,* if you wish to make your Confession, I'll hear—" Tommy stopped. The *alteño's* dead blue eyes stared up at him. Tommy had missed the opportunity. After a long regretful moment he reached down and shut the dead man's eyes.

And then the three Rojas sons bustled their bleeding father into the infirmary.

*   *   *

317

F RANK WAS EUPHORIC WITH THE HEAT OF VICTORY. I T WAS A FEELING he'd never had before. He paraded up and down behind the barricade, gesturing with his pistol as he shouted out, "We stopped them! We stopped them cold!"

Quintana was reloading his big horse pistol and now he had other revolvers, taken from dead cavalrymen, lined under his belt around his waist. "We stopped them this time, but they'll be back again."

Frank was not going to let his triumph be diminished. "And we'll stop them again!"

The Yaqui stuck the horse pistol into its holster and took another from under his belt. His chest was crisscrossed with bandoleers. "Terrazas has a whole regiment down there. He has eight men to your one."

Frank's voice was sure and defiant. "This *pueblo* is impregnable. We have food, fresh water—"

"But how much ammunition?" Quintana held up a bullet. "And how many people? Look around you."

Dead *cristeros* lay everywhere. Weeping women were stripping their men's bodies of gun belts and bandoleers and buckling them around themselves.

"These people will fight to the last man."

"They may have to."

Cota came up then with his *bandoleros*. "*Patrōn*, we have prisoners."

Frank waved his pistol in dismissal. "You know what to do with them."

"They asked for you, *patrón*."

T HE SOLDIERS WERE LINED UP AGAINST THE WALL OF THE CHURCH. There were seven of them, three wounded, and one had to be held up by his *compadres*. Frank glared at them as he and Cota approached. He fixed his eyes on the highest-ranking man—a sergeant. "You expect mercy, *callista*? And our dead lie everywhere?"

"No, *padre*," the sergeant said, "we know we're going to die. We accept that."

"Then what?"

"*Padre*, we're soldiers, but we're also good Catholics. We beg you to forgive us our sins before we have to stand before God."

Frank looked at the sergeant, then at the other six soldiers. "You took up arms against the Church. You don't deserve its blessing."

The sergeant's face filled with fear. "Father, please." He sank to his knees. "We were only following the orders of our officers. Let us die with our souls clean."

Frank sneered down at the soldier. "You want my blessing, apostate?" He pressed his pistol against the sergeant's brow and rasped, "Burn in hell," and then he blew out the man's brains.

Walking away he said over his shoulder, "All of you are damned for eternity." He nodded at Cota and the *bandoleros* opened fire and the *federales* slumped back against the church wall.

INSIDE THE INFIRMARY MUÑOZ WAS WORKING DESPERATELY TO staunch the blood that spurted from Rojas's throat. Then the Spaniard realized the rancher was going to die, and Rojas saw the realization in the doctor's eyes. He reached up and grabbed the physician's vest. "Get me the priest!" He raised his head and glared around at his sons. "The priest!" One of the Rojas sons started toward the door, shouting, "Father Francisco! Father Fran—"

"No!" Rojas gurgled. "The other!"

Tommy was just carrying in another wounded *cristero,* and the Rojas boy took his arm and brought him to where his father lay on the floor. Tommy knelt and Rojas grabbed his hand and clutched it in a death grip.

"Do—do you have any sins you wish to confess?"

"No time. There's no time." He gripped Tommy's hand with urgency. "Speak to God for me." And then he died and Tommy felt, as his hand relaxed, the rancher's soul ebb away. With his free hand Tommy etched a sign of the cross and the youngest Rojas son began to cry and when Tommy looked up he saw Frank standing in the foyer, glaring at him.

Then someone out in the plaza shouted, "They're coming in under a white flag!"

—◦—

"YOU ARE ALL *MARICÓNS!*" TERRAZAS SCREAMED AT HIS ARMY. "You're all cock-sucking cowards!" He was riding up and down his line of troops on a black Arabian. "You have no heart, no courage, no balls!"

General Portillo de Vásquez turned to the Indian general Hernán-

319

dez beside him and said, "Does he always speak to his troops in this manner? No wonder he's been so ineffective." Portillo de Vásquez had been sent out from the capital to evaluate Terrazas. After the initial rush of reconcentration and the purge of the clergy, the military ruler of highland Jalisco had seemed, in the estimation of the President's advisers, to content himself with opening new schools in expropriated Church properties, executing individual *hacendados*, and sending almost daily communiqués to Mexico City advising how best to combat the Church's perfidious power. But Terrazas hardly ever left Guadalajara City. He appeared to be afraid of the Los Altos highlands he had been assigned to subdue. It was whispered he was terrified of a local phantom priest—a priest who supposedly couldn't be killed. Portillo de Vásquez had been in Guadalajara three days, trying to convince Terrazas of the importance of a speedy resolution to the *cristiada*, when the young woman was brought in, starved and sun-baked, and told her eyewitness account of the train attack.

"A handful of rebels!" Terrazas shouted. "And half of them women! You should be filled with shame!" He wheeled the Arabian and trotted down the line in the other direction. "Are you frightened of the priests? Are you frightened of the *pistolero* priest? You should be more afraid of me!"

Portillo de Vásquez shook his head in disapproval. This was not the way to inspire a victory.

"Because I will shoot any man who runs, any man who retreats, any man who does not fight to his last breath! This pueblo will be taken, and we shall wipe it off this mountaintop, or the foxes will feast tonight on our intestines!"

The Indian Hernández said softly to Portillo de Vásquez, "He wasn't always like this. It's the loss of his sons."

The day before yesterday Terrazas had knelt over the blackened, twisted bodies of his two boys and openly wept as the entire regiment watched. The acrid stink of the smoldering train ruins still hung in the air, although the train was now only gray ash and sooted iron wheels. The young woman, who had been spared to do just that, stood beside the general and softly recounted how the gringo priest had forced Antonio and Paco to pray before he executed them.

"We shall sleep tonight with their bodies under our feet," Terrazas screamed now on the mountainside, "or we shall never sleep again!"

Portillo de Vásquez stepped out of the line of horsemen and

strode purposefully toward the approaching general. Terrazas reined in, and Portillo de Vásquez noted the unbuttoned collar, the stubble of beard, the madness in the man's eyes.

"*Mi general*," Portillo de Vásquez said evenly, "we may indeed all die, trying to take such a formidable redoubt."

Terrazas looked up at the pueblo. "So be it."

Portillo de Vásquez shook his head again. "General, wasn't the massacre at the train bad enough?" He nodded toward the regiment. "Do we have to waste everyone's sons?"

Terrazas glared down at him with such malevolence that Portillo de Vásquez wondered if the man was going to shoot him. Then Terrazas said, "General, do you have sons?"

"Yes, five."

"Then you must understand."

"I understand that as an officer in the Army of Mexico I have responsibilities to my President, my uniform, and the men I command—and those responsibilities supersede my personal emotions."

"Then, sir, you are a man of straw," Terrazas said bitterly. "And your words are as worthless as chaff in the wind."

Portillo de Vásquez was growing impatient with this lunatic. "Watch your mouth, *señor*. I am the President's personal emissary."

Then the shout came from the rear. The line of troops parted slowly and a trio of men on horseback walked through flying a white flag. The lead rider—Don Enrique—even had a white sheet draped over the pommel of his saddle.

Terrazas yanked on his reins and spur-raked the black Arabian and the animal wheeled and galloped down on the three horsemen. Terrazas rode a complete circle around them before he reined in.

"Hidalgo, you're an even bigger fool than I thought. You will never leave this mountain alive."

Don Enrique pulled an envelope from his suit coat. "President Calles gave this to me two days ago, in the capital. It's for you." He held it out for the General, but Terrazas didn't take it. "The president and the Bishop have come to terms. The Church strike is over. On Sunday morning Mass will be celebrated in churches all over Mexico. The Bishop has directed all Catholics to lay down their arms."

Portillo de Vásquez was approaching. "I was with the President a week ago, he said nothing to me about a cease-fire."

"The attack on the train changed everything," Don Enrique said. "The news of the massacre is known all over the world. The Bishop was under pressure from Rome, and the President is afraid the rebellion might spread."

Portillo de Vásquez took the envelope and opened it. He began to read the letter.

"How do I know this isn't just another Catholic trick?" Terrazas was watching the President's man read the missive. "Maybe you're trying to save this pueblo from destruction."

Don Enrique held a steady gaze on Terrazas. "It seems to me, General, this pueblo is in no immediate danger. It seems to me—"

Portillo de Vásquez looked up from the letter and said, "This is the President's signature. This is authentic."

Terrazas's eyes blazed. "Maybe this papist has convinced you, but I can't be fooled so easily."

One of the men with Don Enrique pulled a newspaper from his pocket. "Perhaps this will persuade you, *General.*" The paper was from the capital, three days before. The headline read, *"Amnestia!"* A nearby trooper saw the headline and shouted out, "It's over! The war's over!" And the cry went up along the line and hats were tossed and rifles fired off in celebration.

Terrazas furiously pointed up at the mountaintop and shouted at Portillo de Vásquez. "Those people up there are in open rebellion against the Republic of Mexico. They've already killed fifty of my men. I won't let them go unpunished!"

Don Enrique and Portillo de Vásquez exchanged looks, and then Portillo de Vásquez said, "General Terrazas, the war is over. Our President decrees it."

Then Don Enrique said, "I'll ride up and inform Father Francisco of the Bishop's dictum. There need be no more bloodshed."

—◇—

FRANK CLAMBERED TO THE TOP OF THE BARRICADE AND WATCHED through field glasses the three horsemen approaching. The white banner flapped in the strong wind and the sheet draped over the lead rider's saddle pommel filled and emptied with each new gust.

"Father Frank," Don Enrique called up as he reined in a short distance from the barricade. "I bring you news from the Bishop."

Frank had recognized the horseman almost immediately, but he'd given no order to clear a path through the barricade. Instead, Frank accusingly asked, "Why did Terrazas let you through? How have you betrayed us?"

Don Enrique was taken aback by the priest's tone, and by his appearance. He was not the same man Don Enrique had met all those months ago.

"It's a directive from the Bishop. He's made a peace with the President."

Frank smiled coldly. "So you *have* betrayed us."

Don Enrique walked his horse up to the barricade, directly under where Frank stood.

"Father, I am a representative of the Bishop of Mexico and the Catholic League, and so my words come through a clear channel all the way from Rome. The strike is ended. The rebellion is over. *Cristeros* are laying down their guns all over the country. Mass will celebrated again this Sunday."

Frank glowered. "At what price, *señor*? At what ungodly price?"

"We have a peace—"

"A peace at any cost? Have you sold our Mother Church to men like Terrazas, to be relegated to a social afterthought, to be plundered and—"

"There will be concessions, of course. There are in any truce. But the Church will survive."

"How can you be so sure?"

"The Church has always survived. It can't be eradicated by despots or governments." He paused, and then said, "Or even by wicked clergy. The Church will be here long after you and I are gone, Father."

Frank shook his head. "This was my worse fear. Betrayal from within."

Don Enrique was growing angry. "It was your butchery at the train that cemented this truce! You behaved like a madman! The Bishop had no choice!!" Then Don Enrique, in a quieter tone, said, "There must be no more killing. No more bloodletting."

"Blood washes clean, *señor*! I don't care how much blood I have to spill to protect—"

"*Sí, padre!* You have no compunctions about spilling Mexican blood! Need I remind you, *padre*, that this is a Mexican war. And we have found a Mexican solution." Don Enrique straightened in his saddle. "And you, *señor*, are a foreigner. Maybe that's why it's so easy for you to see us die!"

Frank stared down at Don Enrique a long moment, and then without speaking he raised his arm and shot the bearded man with his pistol. It was such an unexpected and outrageous act that the *cristeros* behind the barricade were shocked speechless. They gawked at their priest-general and the old foreboding came over them. This could not end well—shooting a Catholic comrade under a white flag.

"He was a traitor to our cause!" Frank shouted. "He tried to surrender us to the *callistas!* But we'll never surrender! We'll stand firm, with faith and resolve, and they'll never drive us from this mountain."

The *cristeros* looked around at each other with uncertainty.

"And our stand will ignite a fire that will inflame the whole country!"

—◄○►—

WHEN DON ENRIQUE'S *COMPADRES* BROUGHT HIS BODY BACK ACROSS HIS saddle, Terrazas glared at Portillo de Vásquez and said, "You see what animals these people are? They even murder their own! You expect me to just ride away."

Portillo de Vásquez grimly watched the body-laden horse walk by. Then he gestured with the President's letter, which he still held in his hand. "It makes no difference. We have our orders."

Terrazas looked up at the pueblo.

"General," Portillo de Vásquez said, "we're going to leave these people to strangle on their own bile." When Terrazas didn't reply he said, "They're nothing. Now they've even ostracized themselves from their fellow Catholics. They'll shrivel and die like a bud cut from a vine. We don't need to conquer them, they've defeated themselves."

Terrazas wouldn't take his eyes from the mountaintop.

"*Mi general*—" the President's man started to say.

"No," Terrazas said firmly. He turned his eyes on the President's man. "I cannot."

Portillo de Vásquez sighed and shook his head. "General Terrazas, I order you to lead your regiment from this mountain. If you ignore my command, I'll consider you in revolt and you'll be summarily shot. I beg you to reconsider your—"

Terrazas spurred the black Arabian and galloped down the line away from Portillo de Vásquez. Then he reined in and surveyed the hundreds of men.

"They say the war is over! They say the rebels up there are our countrymen again! Our *paisanos*." He had a quirt looped around his wrist and he slapped his saddle with it. "I say *no!* I say I can never make peace with those who have tortured and murdered those whom I loved above all others. I can never forgive those who have torn out my very heart!" He pranced the Arabian slowly up and down the line. "How many of you have suffered from their pious savagery? How many of you have had members of your family butchered by those black pigs, as I have?!"

Portillo de Vásquez had mounted a horse and he galloped down the line, shouting to the regiment. "Your President and your country orders you to discontinue this offensive, and to return to Guadalajara!"

"How many of you cannot forget?"

"Do you wish to die on this mountain, acting in disobedience of your government?"

"How many of you can *never* forget?"

"I order you to turn about and begin an orderly retreat!"

"I won't leave this mountain until that pueblo is swept away!" Terrazas roared. He drew his saber with a savage flourish and held it high. "Who hungers for *cristero* blood, as I do?"

The *agraristas* moved first. Fifty strong, they rode out of the line as one and gathered behind Terrazas. This was no surprise; even in a peace, these men were marked for eventual death. Then an equal number of cavalrymen left their positions up and down the formation and fell into a loose column at Terrazas's right flank. He looked back at them and said, "One of us for each of them. So be it."

Portillo de Vásquez said, "God help you, General." Then he raised his hand and began to lead the rest of the regiment down the mountain road. The Indian Hernández rode with him, without looking back.

—◀○▶—

TOMMY WENT TO EACH OF THE WOUNDED MEN LYING IN BEDS AND sprawled on the infirmary floor, speaking a few words of encouragement, of succor. Some of the critically wounded asked him to hear their confessions and Tommy consented, slowly nodding his head as the men purged themselves of their litany of lusts and transgressions. Then several of them asked for Extreme Unction—

325

the sacrament of the last rites—and Tommy mumbled something cryptic and Latin-sounding and told the dying men and women they were ready to be judged by God. He had done just such for a gut-shot woman—her five children gathered around her—when he looked up into Quintana's black eyes, watching.

"What?"

"Your brother has completely lost his mind. He just killed the *patrón* from the Catholic League, the one with the beard."

Lourdes dropped a pan of bloody instruments. "My uncle? He killed my Uncle Enrique!"

"And now he's tearing down the barricade."

She turned to a wounded *cristero* bleeding onto an armchair and yanked away the rifle the man still held in his hands.

"Lourdes!" Tommy shouted.

"He must be stopped!" She levered a shell into the breech and ran for the front door.

—◄○►—

FRANK HAD WATCHED THROUGH HIS FIELD GLASSES AS TERRAZAS AND the other Mexican general raced back and forth before the long column of horsemen. At first he was confused, and then when the other general began to lead away the regiment down the mountain Frank thought it was a trick, that they were going to try and come around behind the mountain and scale the walls. But he watched them make their way down the road, and then he understood. Terrazas didn't want a peace, either. Frank smiled, and then his smile faded and he did a quick count of the *agraristas* and *soldados* who remained with Terrazas, and he smiled again.

"Pull down the barricade!" he shouted back over his shoulder. The *cristeros* looked at each other and didn't move. They thought they had misheard their priest. Frank lowered the field glasses and glowered at them. "Do it! Tear it down!"

"*Padre*—" A *cristero* humbly stepped forward. "*Padre*, but then Terrazas will ride right into the pueblo!"

"Do what I tell you!" Frank screamed in fury, and then when the *cristeros* didn't move he looked to Cota, at his side. Cota cocked his pistol and said, "Pull down the barricade!"

Reluctantly, under the *bandoleros'* guns the *cristeros* began to dis-

326

mantle the barricade. When the job was almost completed Lourdes ran up with the rifle, Tommy and Quintana right behind.

"You bastard!" she shrieked. "You murdered my uncle!"

Frank looked her up and down with cold scorn. Her head was bare. Her dark, closely shorn hair was plastered down with perspiration. Her shirt and pants had stiffened with dried *cristero* blood. "Sister Lourdes, how you've changed," he said with dripping sarcasm. "Now you look like exactly what you are." Then with a venomous hiss. *"A whore crawled up out of hell."*

She raised the rifle and was pulling the trigger when Tommy stepped up and reached around her and jerked the rifle barrel skyward. The bullet sped harmlessly toward the clouds, and Cota aimed his pistol at Lourdes and Tommy shouted, "No!" Cota looked to his *patrón*.

Frank smiled at the sight of Tommy's arms around Lourdes. It seemed to give him some kind of bitter satisfaction. "I'll deal with your sacrilege later, Sister." His eyes found Tommy's. "It comes as no surprise."

Tommy nodded toward the dismantled barricade. "Are you crazy? Terrazas will be all over this pueblo as soon as he sees—"

"Exactly! That's precisely what I want!" Frank's face glowed with messianic vengeance. "He may ride in here, but he'll never ride out!"

Tommy felt an eerie sense of having experienced this all before. Bulldog in the snow on the last night of his life, impervious to anything but his own desire to wipe out the Matrangas. Tommy had warned his father that they were walking into an ambush but the mobster had been so blinded by his avarice, ambition, and animus that he had driven himself to his death, a victim of his own pertinacity. And seeing Frank like this, Tommy realized with a jolt something he had known all his life but had never acknowledged to himself. His brother was the one most like their father.

"His army's deserted him!" Frank was shouting. "He's undermanned! If I can lure him inside the pueblo I won't let him get away."

"Why'd you murder my uncle?" Lourdes shrieked as she struggled against Tommy's grip.

"Enrique Hidalgo was a traitor!" Frank angrily gestured down the mountain. "He brokered an unholy pact with the devil!"

"A pact?" Tommy looked around. "You mean, there's a truce?"

"Not on this mountain there isn't!" Frank said, and then a *cristero* on a rooftop shouted, "They're coming!" and before the *cristeros* could find shelter Terrazas's cavalry battalion of *agraristas* and vengeful troopers thundered through the pueblo gate, some hurtling the remaining carts and furniture, but the mass of horsemen rode right down on the scattering *cristeros,* trampling them under their mounts' hooves.

Cota was killed instantly, and without a hesitation Lourdes shoved the muzzle of her rifle into his killer's side and pulled the trigger and the *agrarista* flew from his saddle. Then a cavalryman darted toward her and she was struck by the beast's shoulder and tumbled across the hard-beaten ground.

"Lourdes!" Tommy shouted and started for her. Then Terrazas himself galloped through the pueblo gate and down the long corridor that led to the plaza. He leaned out in the saddle and hacked his saber at Tommy and when he realized he'd missed his target he reined in hard and was trying to turn the little black Arabian in the stampede of charging horsemen and then Frank screamed, *"Terrazas!"* Frank was standing on the side of an overturned cart and he held his pistol stiff-armed before him and Terrazas looked back at Tommy and then slammed his spurs into the Arabian's haunches and the little animal shrieked in protest and bounded forward. Frank smiled as Terrazas bore down on him and then Frank steadied his weapon and pulled the trigger and then when nothing happened his smile faded and then Terrazas was on him and with a triumphant shout thrust his saber deep into Frank's chest. As the Mexican swept by he twisted the blade in Frank's trunk, sawing and tearing, and when he yanked back the saber blood geysered from Frank's mouth and poured out the gaping wound in his chest. Frank fell heavily backwards off the cart.

"Frank! Frank!" Tommy ran along the wall of the corridor and an *agrarista* separated from the charging column and aimed his rifle and Tommy heard the bullet sing past just over his head and then Tommy was at the cart and he ducked down under and Frank looked at him dully. His mouth was red and his chin dripped blood and he stared at the gaping wound in his chest. His heart and lungs were visible, pumping. "Oh, God," Frank breathed and then Tommy gathered up his brother in his arms. When he started to stand Terrazas was back again and hacked at them with his saber. Tommy fell back and the blade sliced through the wood of the cart and Terrazas shouted in frustration and then Tommy had his brother and was running down a narrow alley that veered off at a right angle from the corridor. He turned into an even closer alley and suddenly the battle in the corridor was muffled and distant.

Tommy kicked open a door and carried his brother through the doorway and they were inside the church.

Tommy laid Frank in the chancel under the wood-and-plaster altar, and they both were covered with Frank's blood, blood that pooled out over the stone-and-adobe floor. Frank's eyes closed and for a moment Tommy thought his brother had died, and then he opened his eyes and stared glassily up at the altar and the crude wooden crucifix and he gasped, "Oh, God ..."

Tommy ripped away the altar cloth, sending chalice and altar-pieces clattering. He frantically wadded the cloth and pressed it over Frank's gaping chest wound, but then he saw the blood sluicing out from Frank's back and he knew that Terrazas's saber had delivered a mortal wound. He gaped at the spreading pool of blood and suddenly wrapped his arms around Frank and clutched him close.

"Frank!" Tommy wailed. "Frank!"

"Oh, Jesus," Frank rasped. He felt himself dying.

"Frank!" Tommy was sobbing. "I don't know where the doctor is!"

Frank didn't respond, and Tommy didn't move except to hold his brother closer.

Then Frank whispered into his brother's ear, "Tommy."

"Don't die, Frank!" *You're my big brother.*

"Tommy . . . I'm scared . . ."

Tommy wept and gently rocked his brother in his arms.

". . . I'm afraid to die . . ."

"Aw, Frank . . ."

Frank's cheek was lying on Tommy's shoulder and his eyes were uplifted to the wooden cross and the simple Christ painting over the altar.

"I turned my face from God," Frank breathed into Tommy's ear. "I betrayed my vows . . ."

"Frank, Frank, no . . ."

"I betrayed my Savior . . ." Frank coughed and a thick clot of blood slipped down his chin. "Tommy . . . I'm afraid to face God . . ."

Tommy sobbed and held his dying brother.

"Help me . . ."

"Frank—I can't! I wish I could, but I can't!"

"Yes . . . you can . . ." Frank rested his lips in Tommy's ear, as if he were about to share the deepest of secrets, and almost inaudibly whispered, "Bless me, Father, for I have sinned . . ."

Tommy shook his head and the tears streamed from the corners of his eyes.

"Please, Father, grant me absolution . . ." Frank whispered in a labored rasp. "Make me ready to meet my Christ . . ."

A long anguished wail came up out of Tommy's chest and echoed off the church walls. *"I can't! I can't!"*

"Please, Father, I beg you . . ."

"Frank, you know I can't! I'm not a priest!"

"Yes . . ." Frank rested his cheek against his brother's. "Yes, you can. *You're* the priest. God's chosen you. He loves you, Tommy. He always has. . . ." He coughed up more blood. "That's why I hated you so much. . . . Forgive me . . . Please forgive me . . ."

Sobbing, Tommy ran his fingers through his brother's hair, as if he could somehow hold back his death.

"I'm a murderer . . ." Frank breathed, ". . . and a thief and . . . a blasphemer . . . and . . . and . . . Tommy, hurry! God will listen to you, and I'm so scared—"

Tommy felt his brother start to relax, to slip into death, and he pressed his cheek against Frank's and choked out, "You are forgiven . . ." and then Frank slumped against him and Tommy knew he was gone. He tightly held Frank's supple yet lifeless corpse for a long moment—the muffled shouts and screams and gunfire of the battle raging just outside the thick church walls—and then laid him down on the chancel floor and said, "God, please accept my brother's soul." He etched a cross in the air. "He made mistakes, but who the hell doesn't?" It was then that he saw the pistol still clutched in Frank's death grip—the pistol that hadn't fired. Tommy pried it from his brother's fingers, then examined the cylinder. The pistol was fully loaded—six unspent cartridges. There was no earthly reason it hadn't fired when Frank pulled the trigger on Terrazas.

The church door burst open and a headless *cristero* body fell in. Then Terrazas on the black Arabian clattered into the church. He saw Tommy rising from beside the dead priest's body—the pistol in his hand—and the Mexican let out a killing shout, raised his bloody saber, and sunk his rowels into his mount.

BOOK IV

The Cardinal

THE BAND WAS PLAYING AN INTERESTING MELODY, ONE THAT the Cardinal seemed to have been hearing everywhere lately. Lilting, bittersweet, and evocative, it riveted him each time he heard it. The Cardinal turned to the woman seated next to him—an Italian journalist named Julianna Occhipinti—and said, "What's the name of that song?"

The journalist smiled at the Cardinal and leaned over to answer, showing him the tops of her full, globular breasts. She had been doing that all evening. She seemed to be one of those women who loved to show priests what they weren't supposed to have. The fact that she was forty years the Cardinal's junior only seemed to inflame her temptress fantasies.

"It's called 'The Fool on the Hill,' " she said with a sly, mysterious glow in her eyes. The woman imbued the most mundane comments with a salacious subtext.

The blond man seated to the Cardinal's left at the banquet table tugged at the Cardinal's sleeve and when he turned the man spoke loudly into his ear. "It's by the Beatles! They're a rock band from Britain!"

Across the table Father Galvan frowned. The young Mexican priest had been assigned to shepherd and chaperon the Vatican's representative during his visit to the city, and he knew the long-haired Swiss photographer was annoying the elderly cleric.

"Have you heard of them?" the photographer shouted.

The Cardinal smoothed his napkin, indicating he thought the

question and the questioner were ridiculous. "Of course. Everyone's heard of them."

"*Señor*," Father Galvan said to the Swiss, "the Cardinal's hearing is perfect. You don't have to shout."

"Oh . . ." the photographer said, then turned to the Cardinal and in a louder voice said, "I'm sorry, *Cardinale!* Please excuse me!"

The waiters arrived with their *ceviche* salads and began to distribute them among the diners. It was a banquet for the international press, in town to report on the XIX Olympiad, beginning in just over a week, and as a courtesy to the Vatican the Cardinal—who sometimes wrote articles for the American Catholic intellectual community—had been invited to attend.

The Cardinal looked at the salad before him and felt his stomach turn over. He tasted the bile in the back of his throat and grimaced. Father Galvan watched his charge with concern. That morning, when he'd arrived at the Cardinal's hotel room, the man had been on his knees before the toilet, vomiting up blood. Then he had calmly wiped his mouth with a towel, risen with the younger cleric's aid, and washed his face, saying, "Father, don't ever grow old."

"Is this what I think it is?" Julianna Occhipinti asked, holding up a piece of something on a fork.

"Calamari," said an Australian television personality who had been trying to flirt with the Italian all night. "Squid. They eat their fish raw in Mexico."

"Oh, my God," Occhipinti put down her fork. "Cardinal, would you like to dance?" The orchestra was playing a forties swing ballad. Not waiting for an answer the journalist was already rising, holding out her hand. The Cardinal was only too happy to escape the plate before him. He allowed Julianna to help him push back his chair and standing, he turned to the Swiss and said in an overloud voice, " 'All the Way,' by Frank Sinatra . . . Ever hear of him?" And then as the table erupted in laughter, the Cardinal took Julianna's hand and they walked together out onto the dance floor.

Slipping into the Cardinal's arms, Julianna said, "Seeing you like this, it's hard to imagine that you're a Cardinal." Both the Cardinal and Father Galvan were dressed in black business suits. She leered, "I keep picturing you in your red silk." Then, "Are you incognito because you're planning an assignation?"

He looked down at her and said, "*Signorina*, please desist from these advances. Even if I wanted to lose my celibacy, I'm too old to do anything about it. And you're too—*mature*—to be playing the coquette."

That silenced her. It was like being chastised by her father. "Before I left Rome," the Cardinal continued, "I was given strict instructions on how to dress and behave in this country. The Mexican government is very touchy about the Church and its influence."

"So you don't wear your collar and oversexed women like myself get to make fools of themselves." They were dancing slowly past the bandstand. The Cardinal said, "I haven't danced for—it must be fifty years."

She smiled sweetly, truly touched. "Well, you haven't lost a step. You're as graceful as a swan."

He looked down at her with skepticism and they both laughed. "*Signorina*, I hope you plan to go to confession tomorrow."

The band segued seamlessly into another ancient ballad, and they continued dancing. "How long have you lived in Italy, *Cardinale*?"

"Almost ten years now."

"You came in with John the Twenty-third?"

"Yes ... We had met years ago, and he remembered me."

"Yes, he liked Americans."

"You knew the man?"

"I interviewed him once, one of my very first. I was so scared I was shaking, and he was so charming, so charismatic, he put me at ease immediately. And I applauded what he was doing with the Church. There was a wind of change blowing through Vatican City. It felt like the Catholic Church was finally becoming a Christian church. It was as if, after twenty years of Pope Pius, it was finally entering the twentieth century."

The Cardinal smiled. "Yes. It was a wonderful time."

"But that all changed when the great man died."

The Cardinal didn't reply.

"Now the dour, reactionary Paul the Sixth is Pope, and the shutters have once more been secured against those winds of change."

The Cardinal cocked his head to one side. "You *are* a writer."

"What I don't understand, Your Eminence, is how you managed to stay on in Rome, with the change of regimes."

The Cardinal's laugh was colored with bitterness. "They made me a tour guide ... a maitre d'." He could see she was puzzled. "When wealthy American Catholics come to the Vatican, I show them around. I point out the obvious—the Sistine Chapel, St. Peter's Basilica, the catacombs. I orchestrate *ooohs* and *ahhhs* from the Topeka Knights of Columbus, and of course their pious families. I feed them *capellini* at Rome's best restaurants, just before they reach for their checkbooks."

She inspected his face with true interest. "You don't sound happy...."

The Cardinal looked back at her with a trace of scorn. It was such a typically female thing to say. "I'm an old man, *signorina*. I've seen too much. Life holds no more pleasant surprises for me, I fear."

"And I fear you didn't join the priesthood to be a tour guide."

Just then the band slipped into an ersatz rock n' roll beat, and the dancers around them began to gyrate spasmodically. The Cardinal stared around and Julianna broke into laughter. "I think our dance is over, Your Eminence."

As they were walking back toward their table the ballroom was suddenly awash in glare and from outside came the vibrating, percussive thump of a helicopter motor. A copter's searchlight panned back and forth outside the floor-to-ceiling glass doors and as it slipped over the diners and dancers their faces were momentarily caught staring back into the beam like figures frozen in the flare of a flashbulb.

"What on earth is that?" Julianna said. Everyone was hurrying to the glass doors and the men got them open and they stepped out onto the balconies and looked down at the immense expanse of the *Plaza de las Tres Culturas* six stories below. From a side street by the ancient church Santiago Tletelolco thousands of students were marching into the plaza, chanting, "We don't want the Olympics! We want a revolution! We don't want the Olympics! We want a revolution!"

A Chilean newspaperman elbowed his way between Julianna and the Cardinal and surveyed the plaza below. "This is bad," the small man said. "This is very, very bad!"

"What's happening?" the Cardinal shouted at Julianna.

"The students have been demonstrating for months!" she shouted back. "They're using the Olympics as an opportunity to communicate their displeasure to the world!"

"Hippies and drug addicts!" the Chilean spat out. "The dregs of society."

"Really?" Julianna's eyes flashed with fury; she was aroused by the excitement below. "This is happening all over the world! Can they all be the dregs of society?"

"It may be happening all over the world, but when it happens in Mexico—" The little Chilean shook his head. "President Díaz Ordaz won't allow this to go on! Especially during the Olympics!"

"What are they demonstrating about?" the Cardinal asked.

"Nothing!" the Chilean barked.

"Everything!" Julianna shouted back.

Another river of protesters flowed into the plaza from a different street, and these were rhythmically shouting, "Mexico! Liberty! Mexico! Liberty!" In the middle of the plaza was a cordoned-off pre-Columbian ruin, and the leaders of the demonstration scaled the battlements, turned back to the crowd and thrust up their hands, their fingers in the international *V* for victory sign, which in this decade signified "peace." The crowd roared so loudly the walls of the Nonoalco-Tletelolco housing unit—in which the banquet was being held—seemed to shake, then the plaza become very silent and one by one the student leaders mounted the pre-Hispanic ruins and addressed the crowd.

"Where are they from?" the Cardinal asked Julianna. The long-haired Swiss photographer had pushed through to the balcony.

"They're from the University," said the man at the Cardinal's right. The Cardinal saw that it was his waiter, still in his white jacket. "And the National Polytechnic Institute. Those boys are the sons of workers. My son attended Poly."

"Then, you approve of this?"

"I don't approve of the long hair, or the drugs, or the short skirts—but, Your Eminence,"—and by the way the man addressed him the Cardinal knew the waiter was a devout Catholic—"this country cannot go on this way. The President and his crew, we call them Ali Baba and his forty thieves. The people have nothing, and each year they have less."

"The rich get richer," Julianna said, "and the poor get poorer."

"*Sí, señora,*" the waiter nodded. "Exactly. And now the President invites the world to his big Olympics party, while the Mexican people have nothing to eat."

Father Galvan had spotted the Cardinal and was pushing through the crowd on the balcony. "Your Eminence, I couldn't find you!"

"Father Galvan," the Cardinal said, "tell me, what's your opinion on all this?"

"Your Eminence, I think we should leave immediately." Galvan didn't want any harm to come to the Cardinal while under his protection.

"No, I mean the demonstration. This is your country."

Galvan looked at the huge gathering below, as if noticing it for the first time. He listened to the speaker shout of liberty and economic opportunity and an end to the paternalistic one-party system.

"I don't know." He looked at the Cardinal. "First, I'd have to know what my Church would say."

"First," the Cardinal said, "I would want to know what my Christ would say."

From across the plaza a smaller group of demonstrators marched into the square.

"You're a Cardinal," the Chilean said, "and you talk like that? That must be heresy."

"No," Julianna smiled, "it's rekindled idealism."

As the newer arrivals approached the ruins a great shout went up from the crowd. These men were older, thicker, and clad in dusty working-class suits of toil.

"The railroad workers!" the waiter exulted. "They've come to join the students!" He pulled off his jacket and began to untie his apron as he pushed back through the reporters on the balcony, hurrying to join the crowd in the plaza.

"This is very, very bad," the Chilean said, and then he too turned and wedged his way off the balcony.

"Your Eminence, I beg you, please come back inside." Galvan had only one thing on his mind—the safety of his charge.

The leader of the workers had climbed onto the ruins and he began to address the crowd. While he was speaking, on the balcony two floors below student leaders appeared and hurried to set up lights and a speaking platform to be ready to take over as soon as the union leader was through. Julianna and the Cardinal—and everyone else on the balcony—leaned over and watched with interest. Then the leader of the workers concluded to a great roar and the student demonstrators on the balcony below started up the chanting again. "Get the army out of our universities!" and *"Libertad! Mexico! Libertad! Mexico!"* and "Olympics, no! Mexico, yes!" and the crowd joined in and began to clap their hands in rhythm with the chants, and then the helicopter reemerged out of the night sky and swooped down over the plaza and the crowd raged at the chopper and shook their fists and as their heads turned with the aircraft they saw the government troop transports entering the other end of the plaza, and then the Army jeeps with their mounted heavy-caliber machine guns rolled into sight and the crowd in the plaza got very quiet and in the silence everyone in the plaza could hear the sounds of hundreds of tanks and half-tracks lumbering into place in the streets all around the plaza, and the students knew they were surrounded.

"Don't provoke them!" shouted a student leader with a scarf tied across his brow. "Don't give them a reason to shoot us!"

The soldiers—*granaderos*, in dark green combat uniforms—were jumping from the transport tailgates and forming irregular lines behind the machine gun jeeps. The Cardinal glanced up at the roofs of the buildings directly across the plaza and his eyes narrowed and the helicopter pilot made another pass and flashed its search-light over the rooftops and the Cardinal said, "There are men with rifles on the top of those buildings."

"And in the chopper, too," Julianna replied, and the Cardinal saw the muzzle of the rifle in silhouette against the searchlight.

"They're coordinating their movements," the Cardinal said.

"They're going to attack?" Julianna cried in disbelief.

"Never!" said the long-haired Swiss photographer. He had read-ied his camera and was clicking rapid shots of the demonstrators, the *granaderos*, the chopper. "They wouldn't dare, not with all of us witnessing!" Then the helicopter came back for another slow pass and it hovered over the plaza just opposite them and the pilot slowly turned the searchlight on the balcony and they all squinted back into the blinding glare and the chopper was so close Julianna's wrap was blown from her shoulders.

"Your Eminence!" Galvan shouted over the backwash. "We should leave this building now!"

Three green flares arced up from the helicopter and a moment later there were short percussive pops, like firecrackers, all over the plaza.

"Are those shots?" Julianna screamed. Then the Swiss photogra-pher was lifted from his feet and tossed back on the people behind him and blood poured from a hole in his chest, and Julianna shrieked and then Father Galvan had hold of the Cardinal's jacket and was pushing him through the panicking crowd, pulling him off the balcony.

"Let go of me!" the Cardinal raged, but the screaming, shoving crush of people propelled them forward as it scrambled to escape the death in the plaza. The Cardinal heard Julianna shout out for help once more, and then he and Galvan were swept back into the ballroom.

The young priest had a tight grip on the Cardinal's arm and with his free hand was pushing people out of the way.

"Take your hands off me!" the Cardinal shouted into Galvan's face, and the priest shouted back, "No! Your Eminence, you are the guest of the Archbishop! Please do as I say!"

The stampeding crowd fairly carried them into the corridor and down the stairwell. People from the lower floors flowed into the jostling, fleeing current, and then on the second floor the crowd jerked to a halt as a student with a bush of hair staggered up the steps and collapsed. He had been shot in his back. The river of people parted and flowed around him, and a pair of women stooped to help but they were trampled by those behind.

"We can't just leave him there!" the Cardinal begged the priest.

"Yes, we can!" Galvan propelled the Cardinal down the stairs. "We have to get out of here!"

On the ground floor the crowd rushed for the back doors, but they had been padlocked, and then everyone ran toward the entrance from the plaza. Galvan pulled the Cardinal through another door and they were in a narrow empty hallway and they could hear gunshots and screams from the crowd who had run toward the plaza. The young priest hurried the old man along the hallway and then angled him off into an office and as the Cardinal watched Galvan broke the lock on a window and then climbed through and helped the Cardinal out. They were in one of the streets than led from the plaza like spokes on a wheel, and there were students running away from the shooting and then three half-tracks at the next intersection turned their searchlights on the street and the students and the clerics were caught in the harsh artificial glare and the *granaderos* came running from that direction, throwing long, cartoonish shadows. It had started to rain and the raindrops slanted through the searchlight beams like pellets.

"Get against the wall!" the soldiers shouted. They were carrying rifles and truncheons and they hit a teenage boy who tried to push through them and they kept hitting him until he lay motionless in the street. A young-looking man in hippie garb, with a beard and a loose Afro, came down the line pointing out demonstrators who were then dragged off toward the half-tracks. He wore a white glove on his right hand and as he came abreast of Galvan and the Cardinal the young priest stepped out and said, "This is a mistake. This man is a Cardinal in the Roman Catholic Church."

The undercover agent glared at Galvan. "Don't speak unless I ask you a question."

"But he's a Cardinal, and I'm responsible for—"

One of the soldiers beside the undercover agent slammed the butt of his rifle into Galvan's knee and the priest cried out and started to crumple. The Cardinal caught him and held him up. "God is watching you," he said to the undercover agent. Another *granadero* raised his tape-wrapped stick to hit the old man but the agent saw something in the Cardinal's eyes and he reached up and stopped the blow.

"Who are you?"

The Cardinal looked back steadily at the plainclothesman. "I'm not Judas."

"He's a Cardinal!" Galvan gasped out. "And I'm a priest!"

The security man closely inspected them. The shooting in the plaza seemed to intensify. "Then what are you doing here, with these revolutionaries?"

"We were at a banquet!" the young priest blurted. "We were eating!"

There was a disturbance down the line and they all turned to it. A demonstrator was shouting into another undercover cop's face and as they watched the cop raised his hand and shot the demonstrator in the chest. The boy flopped as he lay on the ground and the cop stood over him and shot him again. Then some of the students—thinking they were all going to be executed—bolted from the wall and ran back toward the plaza. The *granaderos*—rural, working-class young men with an instinctive envy of everything urban and educated—broke into a sprint and ran after them. There was deadly confusion in the street and the half-tracks started rumbling forward and all the students dashed toward the plaza. The undercover agent who had been questioning the Cardinal shouted for the demonstrators to halt and then a half-track machine gun began to chatter and a row of glass storefronts shattered and several students slumped to the street and didn't move. A heavy girl in faded jeans and a fatigue jacket tried to lift her wounded companion and cried out for help. The Cardinal rushed to her and together they hoisted the youth between them and the fat girl shouted, "The old church! We have to get him to the old church!"

A few soldiers had been cut down by the half-tracks' machine guns, and the undercover agents and the Army officers ran back toward the glaring searchlights, waving their hands, and in the absence of any kind of order the Cardinal and the heavy girl dragged the wounded boy into the plaza.

If the street had been bedlam, the plaza was hell. The unseen sharpshooters, high on the roofs of the modernistic buildings, were still sending an almost continuous hail of high-powered rifle fire down into the plaza. The dead lay everywhere, getting wet in the rain. The living lay among them, covering their heads with their hands and screaming, "No more! No more! Please no more!"

They carried the slumping boy around the edge of the prone crowd. A tank lumbered into the plaza and they ran behind it just as the machine gunner let loose with a long burst. Scores of people rose then and ran for the big wooden church door. Across the plaza a building had caught fire from the rounds fired into it and the smoke poured out the broken windows. The machine gun chattered again, and the keening rose to a desperate pitch.

The Cardinal and the fat girl got the wounded boy to the church entrance, where hundreds of people were huddled against the centuries-old wall. "There's a convent!" the heavy girl shouted. "The nuns will let us in!"

She pushed through to the door—dragging the Cardinal and the youth with her—and then she balled her fist and pounded on the church door, shouting, "Let us in. They're murdering us!"

The others started banging then, wailing, "Let us in! In the name of God, let us in!"

The machine gun was firing again, and the rooftop riflemen had never stopped. The big girl let go of her companion then and beat on the door with both fists. The Cardinal couldn't hold the youth's weight and as he bent to lay him down he saw the boy had died. Then a fusillade of rifle fire hit the crush of people by the church and the Cardinal saw the fat girl slide down the door. Someone pulled him down, and he lay with the others and covered his head and screamed over and over, "Stop! Stop! Stop!"

—◁○▷—

THE CARDINAL SAT ON THE COUCH, SMELLING HIS OWN CLOTHES. THE stench of sweat and fear seemed to be soaked into the fabric. He wondered if he'd have to throw them away. There was a pack of cigarettes on the low coffee table before him, and he shook one out. His hands were trembling. As he fumbled for a match Galvan picked up the table lighter and lit a flame. The Cardinal leaned forward, looked up at the bandage over the young priest's eye and said again, "Father, I'm sorry if my actions—"

"I don't blame you, Your Eminence." But his tone of voice told the Cardinal that he did.

Just then the door to the Archbishop's office opened and the Archbishop's secretary and gatekeeper Monsignor Zamorano came out and moved quickly to sit across from the Cardinal.

"Your Eminence, words cannot convey the Archbishop's dismay over what happened to you last night."

The Cardinal shook his head. "It was unbelievable."

"The Archbishop hopes you understand last night was not representative of our country, not at all."

The Cardinal suddenly realized the Archbishop wasn't going to see him.

"I had hoped to speak to him in person."

The Monsignor frowned with regret. "The Archbishop really wanted to talk with you, too, but I'm afraid he was called away on Church business early this morning."

The Cardinal knew the Monsignor was lying. He glanced at the Archbishop's closed door, and then looked back at the Monsignor.

"I would think, after what happened last night, that the Archbishop would be petitioning the government for a thorough investigation."

Monsignor Zamorano took a moment to answer, registering a silent rebuke to the Cardinal. "The government has already issued a statement. A riot was started by communist agitators from the University. Bombs were hurled. Molotov cocktails—"

"That's not what happened at all!"

Zamorano waited a beat, and then went on. "Police officers were attacked. The Chief feared the riot would spread so he called in the Army."

"Those are lies."

"Unfortunately, the demonstrators were well armed but not well trained. In firing at the police they killed a number of their own, as well as soldiers and police." The Monsignor pulled a piece of paper from his pocket. "Twenty-seven were killed and a few more wounded—"

"Twenty-seven!" the Cardinal slumped back in the sofa. "I saw hundreds of dead; some as young as ten or eleven. They didn't have a chance! It was a bloodbath! A government massacre!"

Monsignor Zamorano stared at him. "I'm afraid you're mistaken, Your Eminence."

"There were scores of foreign reporters at that banquet. They saw what I saw."

Zamorano smiled again with feigned regret. "Ah, Your Eminence. The story the world wants to see and read about is the 1968 Olympics. And that's what the journalists will give them. What happened last night in Tlatelolco will hardly rate a sidebar in their morning

343

papers, and by the time the torch is lighted to begin the games, the world will have forgotten."

The Cardinal knew the Mexican was right, and it infuriated him. He started to rise. "Not if I have anything to say about it!"

"Your Eminence, please sit down," the Monsignor said, but it was more a command than a plea. "Please." He made a placating gesture with his hand, motioning for the old man to sit back down. The Cardinal slowly sat.

"Your Eminence, let me explain something to you. Mexico is titularly an overwhelmingly Catholic country, but there is a deep, almost nationalistic anticlerical strain in my people. Even Mexicans who practice our faith—shall I say religiously—would be incensed if they thought any of our clergy were engaging in antigovernment protests."

"Engaging?! They were shooting at me! They were shooting at everybody!"

"Bloody civil wars have been fought here," Zamorano went on, "over just this issue. And many years ago a détente was reached, an unwritten agreement. We don't criticize the government, and they don't harry us."

"Monsignor," the Cardinal said quietly, as if speaking to a madman, "they were butchering your countrymen last night. He was there. He saw." He pointed at Father Galvan, but the young priest looked away. "Doesn't that mean anything to you?"

"Once again, the majority of those involved were communists and rabble-rousers, and—"

"That's a lie!" the Cardinal shouted. "Aw, this is ridiculous." He pushed himself to his feet and strode for the door, saying, "I am not without friends in Vatican City and—"

"Yes, you are," the Monsignor shot back, and the Cardinal stopped, his hand on the doorknob, and turned back. "You've been a maverick and rules breaker everywhere the Church has sent you," the Monsignor said. "And now you're a lame-duck Cardinal. A holdover from Pope John's liberalistic meanderings. You didn't think they sent you on this meaningless assignment because you're admired, did you?"

After a while the Cardinal let his hand slip from the doorknob. He walked slowly back to the couch and sat down, not looking at Zamorano.

"The Mayor, the President, and Chief of Police are all very interested in why, in the midst of all this left-wing unrest, a representative of the Church—a Cardinal, in fact—was implicated, arrested and jailed in a murderous communist attack on our Army. You have to understand, there are some young priests who misguidedly espouse a very radical, very seditious, very heretical Catholicism. They bring suspicion on all of us."

The Archbishop's secretary took off his eyeglasses and began to wipe them with a cloth from his pocket.

"I've managed to convince the government that it was all a regrettable accident, that you were a victim of circumstance. So"—he cleaned his glasses methodically, pausing to hold them up to the light from the window—"it will be as if you were never there. It would be best for all concerned that you speak to no one, no journalists, no students, no foreigners, no one, about your experiences last night. And the Archbishop has determined that it would also be best if you went on a tour of our beautiful country. His Grace has provided an automobile for your convenience. It will be roomy and quite comfortable, I assure you."

"You're getting rid of me...." the Cardinal said in a low tone.

Zamorano put his glasses back over his eyes. "Father Galvan will be your driver. You'll visit San Miguel de Allende, Guadalajara, the Jalisco highlands. Do you know, some of our churches are almost as old as those in Europe?" Monsignor Zamorano looked to the young priest then, and Galvan walked to the door and opened it, then stepped back from the door.

The old man slowly got up again and walked heavily to the door, defeated. At the threshold he stopped and turned back to Zamorano.

"Last night, as they were shooting us, we pounded on the church doors. We pounded and pounded, but no one ever opened them.... Were you inside?"

The Monsignor's flat black eyes showed no emotion, but there was a barely perceptible tightening of flesh around his mouth.

"Good day, Your Eminence."

"Good-bye, Monsignor."

—◄○►—

IT WAS A FORGOTTEN HIGHWAY CROSSROADS, A SMALL CLUSTER OF working-class restaurants and bars, a grocery store, and a Pemex gas station on an intersection of crumbling blacktop routes, bypassed by population and progress. The only distinctive thing about the crossroads was a giant, towering eucalyptus tree. Its tendrils of long,

345

dusty leaves shimmered in the lazy midday breeze. Its pale gray trunk was stained with the passings of a hundred years of men.

The four-door Mexican-built unadorned Ford pulled off the highway and bounced over the gravel of the Pemex station and came to a stop in front of the single pump. Galvan opened the door and got out from behind the steering wheel, a young man in a black suit and an open-collared white shirt. Clerics were prohibited by Mexican law from appearing anywhere in public in ecclesiastical garb. The Pemex attendant—young, thick, mustachioed, in a grease-streaked company shirt—came out to fill up the tank. He looked at the Federal District license plate, then at the bandage over Galvan's eye.

Galvan came around to the passenger side and leaned down. The Cardinal was staring forward. He had hardly looked at or spoken to the young priest during their week-long tour, and hadn't said a word since they'd left Guadalajara this morning. Galvan tapped lightly on the glass, and after a moment the Cardinal turned to him, stared blankly, then rolled down the window.

"Are you hungry, Your Eminence?" Galvan asked. "We could get something here."

The Cardinal's eyes went to the humble establishment the priest was indicating. "It doesn't look like much," Galvan said. "If you'd rather we find a more appropriate—"

The Cardinal opened the door and stepped out of the car. He strode woodenly across the hard-beaten dirt and gravel and entered the restaurant.

Inside there were only four tables, bare of any covering. The Cardinal sat at one and looked down at his hands. He had been in a deep depression ever since they'd left Mexico City. Ever since the Night of Sorrow, as they were calling it on the Ford's radio.

A wide-hipped waitress came from behind the counter with a basket of tortillas and put them on the table, along with a knife, fork and paper napkin. Suspecting him for a foreigner, she nodded at the blackboard menu hung on the wall. The old man nodded back. Then Galvan came into the restaurant and sat across the table from him. The young man glanced at the Cardinal, but the old cleric was looking at his hands again. Galvan twisted in his seat and read the menu, then ordered *albóndigas* soup and enchiladas for the both of them.

They sat in silence until the food came, and then the Cardinal stared down at his meatball soup without eating.

"Your Eminence, aren't you hungry? Don't you feel all right?" This morning he'd again heard the old man choking up blood in the adjoining hotel room. The Cardinal took up his spoon and ladled some soup into his mouth. After a moment Father Galvan began to eat. Neither of them spoke. When their enchiladas were ready in the open kitchen, the waitress got up from her chair where she had been reading a newspaper and picked up the plates with straw pot holders and brought them to the two men. As she returned to her seat near the kitchen, the Pemex attendant came into the restaurant and went to sit with her. He spoke softly to her, looking at Galvan. The Cardinal dawdled over his food, but the young priest ate well. When Galvan was half finished his enchiladas the Pemex attendant rose and walked to their table.

"Excuse me, *padre.*"

Galvan looked up. "Of course." He put down his fork and reached for his wallet.

"No, no, *señor.* Not the petrol. I wanted to ask you . . ." He was looking at the bandage over Galvan's eye. "I saw your license plate. You're from Mexico?" he asked, meaning Mexico City.

Galvan glanced at the Cardinal, who was staring at him.

"Yes."

The attendant pointed shyly at the bandage. "Were you . . . were you at Tlatelolco?"

Galvan didn't look at the Cardinal again as he said, "Yes, I was."

"You were?" the attendant said, then turned to the waitress. "I told you." The waitress quickly approached the table. "You were there, Father? At Tlatelolco? Did they do that to you?"

Galvan nodded. "Yes, they did." The Cardinal got up as quickly as his aged body would allow him and walked out of the restaurant.

HE SAT IN THE CAR, HATING THE YOUNG PRIEST, HATING THE CHURCH, HATing himself. What had occurred inside the restaurant had happened several times on their trip. Simple people—workers, *campesinos,* hotel maids—somehow intuiting they had been in the Plaza of the Three Cultures when the innocents were slaughtered, and wanting to hear a firsthand account. And each time Galvan would allow himself to be seduced into retelling the horror of the Night of Sorrows; each time embellishing his eagerness to protect the young students; each time exaggerating his bravery and devotion, and with each telling the Cardinal grew to despise the priest and the priesthood more and more.

The old man must have fallen asleep, because he woke with a start, feeling eyes on him. Arrayed around the car were a dozen people—inhabitants of the crossroads. Galvan was standing by the door of the restaurant, talking to the attendant, the waitress, and the woman who had been cooking in the kitchen.

"*Señor* . . ."

The Cardinal turned to look into the face of a thin, incredibly wrinkled, old man in his late seventies—the same age as the Cardinal himself.

"*Señor*," the old *campesino* said, taking off his battered straw sombrero in respect, "they said you were there. At Tlatelolco."

The Cardinal nodded. "*Sí*, I was there."

The old *campesino* said, "They're killing us again."

The Cardinal didn't know what to say. He and the old *campesino* stared at each other for a long time, gazing into the reflections of their respective long lives etched on the lined faces and bent bodies, then the old *campesino* stepped back and a small, very pale little boy—his eyes at the Cardinal's shoulder—appeared in the Ford's window. He was so light he was pinkish, so white the Cardinal was disconcerted. The boy wore a woven Mexican sweater with the hood pulled over his head and a scarred pair of reflector sunglasses. The Cardinal was noticing the tufts of longish white hair peeking out from under the sweater hood when the boy took a step closer to the car and put his hand on the window frame. His fingers were milky white, and his nails ghostly. Then the boy took off his glasses and the Cardinal could see the reddish irises—the blood vessels of the eye reflecting the midday sun with a total absence of coloration. The boy was an albino.

"You are *norteamericano*?" The boy's voice was eerie only in that it was so normal, yet the Cardinal felt the hair on the back of his neck tingle.

"Yes. At least, I used to be."

The boy's eldritch eyes traversed over the Cardinal's face, then he said, "Are you going to Sagrado Corazón?" It was a child's voice, but it possessed an inexplicable authority. Again the Cardinal felt his skin prickle.

"I don't think—No, it's not on our itinerary. We're returning to the capital soon, so I don't think we'll be able to—"

"You should go to Sagrado Corazón," the boy interrupted. "There's a man there who wants to see you. He used to be American, too."

The Cardinal experienced a strange sensation then, a brief detachment from all he'd ever known or lived through, an ephemeral disconnection from reality.

"Once there were miracles in that pueblo," the albino boy said. "Everyone knows it."

The driver's door opened and the Cardinal started and whirled his head to the sound. Galvan was sliding behind the wheel and when the Cardinal quickly looked back the boy was gone. He scanned all the crossroads people, but the boy wasn't there. Galvan started the motor, put the car in gear and started to pull out. The Cardinal twisted in the car seat, looking back at the crossroads. The boy had seemed to disappear. Then he saw the weathered old *campesino* sitting on a bench under the eucalyptus tree. The old man was watching him.

The Cardinal turned back and sat there, wondering about what he had just experienced. Galvan glanced over at him. He knew why the Cardinal had walked out of the restaurant. He knew he disgusted the old cleric.

"Is there anything wrong, Your Eminence?"

The Cardinal didn't speak for a long time, and then he said, "Are you familiar with a place called Sagrado Corazón?"

The young priest shrugged. "It's a small town on a mountaintop. Totally off the beaten path. I think I visited once when I was a boy."

"We're not going there, are we?"

"There's nothing there to see, Your Eminence. Just a town. On the top of a mountain. In Los Altos."

Neither said anything for a few minutes, then the Cardinal spoke, "I'd like to go."

"Your Eminence, Monsignor Zamorano charted a very detailed tour. I think it would be better if—"

"I'd like to go there."

The young priest said nothing more, and they both knew his silence was acquiescence. They drove for a while, and then Galvan said, "There must be a hotel of some sort there."

The Cardinal turned to him. "What does 'Sagrado Corazón' mean?"

"It means—well, it means 'Sacred Heart' . . ."

The Cardinal nodded and looked forward, out the windshield at the rising land. "That's what I thought."

—◇—

THEY DROVE ALL THAT DAY, AND JUST AFTER NIGHTFALL GALVAN negotiated a turn off the two lane highway onto a hard red-dirt road and they rode until after midnight. The Cardinal had long since dozed off and Galvan pulled onto a clear area just off the road and both men slept in their seats and just before dawn Galvan was awakened by a gentle jostling, and he opened his eyes to see a large form rubbing against the Ford's left fender. He turned on the headlights and a large brown and white cow was scratching herself against the car. A herd had come up and, grazing lazily, had surrounded the four-door sedan. Galvan tapped the horn and the animals slowly ambled away. The young priest bumped the Ford back onto the road and kept his speed down, watching for other animals. He glanced over at the Cardinal, but the old man had slept through the encounter.

THERE WAS NO ACTUAL SUNRISE. THE SKY HAD CLOUDED DURING THE night and the east simply *blued* out of the darkness. A few raindrops fell, but not enough to activate the windshield wipers. The Cardinal awakened with a coughing fit, and Galvan wondered if he should stop the car, if the old man was going to cough up blood again this morning, but the Cardinal seemed to be able to suppress whatever was ailing him, and then out of the distant misty flatness the mountain called La Corona emerged in the dark blueness.

"At the top of that mountain," the priest said, "is Sagrado Corazón."

WHEN THEY REACHED THE BASE OF THE MOUNTAIN THERE WAS A SMALL farmer's market—selling fruits and vegetables, fresh milk—and a ramshackle collection of roadside stands that dealt in secondhand tools, recycled auto parts, and utilitarian craftworks—heavy cowhide gloves, cheap sombreros, tire-tread-soled huaraches. This was a place that sprang into being not for tourists but for locals only, and the small size of the stands said that no one slept here. They all went up the mountain at night.

Galvan bought coffee and unglazed Mexican pastries at just such a stand and brought the breakfasts back to the car, where the Cardinal was standing beside it.

"Stretch your legs, Your Eminence?"

The young priest didn't expect much morning banter. He knew what the old man thought of him, so he was surprised when the Cardinal said, "Look at that, Father."

Stuck between two tiny stands vending chiles and eggplant, there was an even tinier kiosk selling religious items—wood-and-glass-bead rosaries, drawings of Jesus, the requisite card-sized poly-chrome renderings of the Virgin of Guadalupe. But hung from a sagging cord, held in place by homemade clothespins, were dozens of small photographic representations of the mountain before them.

"Is there a shrine on this mountain?"

"In Sagrado Corazón?" Galvan shook his head. "No, not that I've heard of."

There were two middle-aged peasant women at the kiosk, spending a few precious pesos on one of the photographs. They could be no nationality but Mexican, but they were not *mestizo*. One's hair was dark blond, the other's a reddish brown. After buying their photos they picked up the several straw carryalls at their feet and started up the mountain road.

"We should probably give them a ride," Father Galvan said idly around a mouthful of pastry, and then the Cardinal walked across his line of vision on his way to the kiosk. Galvan joined him just as the old cleric was laying a one-hundred-peso note on the cracked counter.

"No, Father." The man behind the counter smiled. "It's free. I don't want to take your money." He had recognized their black suits and white open-collared shirts.

"It's all right, young man." The Cardinal left the bill on the counter and walked back to the Ford, studying the photograph in his hand.

JUST BEYOND THE CLUSTER OF STANDS A WORK CREW WAS DIGGING A ditch. As the Ford approached, a man in overalls and a baseball cap stepped from behind a stack of sewer pipes and waved his hand.

"Yes?" Galvan asked after he braked the car.

The man in the baseball cap looked at the two men, at their clothing, and he grinned. "Father," he said to Galvan, "the foreman said he doesn't need me today. I was hoping I could get a ride home." He nodded up the hill.

"Get in, *señor*," Galvan said.

The man in the baseball cap jumped into the backseat. He was a gregarious, affable man and he leaned over the seat and offered his hand to the Cardinal, in a very American gesture. "My name is Claudio Nuñez de Rojas. Are you from Arizona, Father?"

The Cardinal was startled. "No, no, I'm not."

"I worked in Arizona for fourteen years as a *bracero*, picking crop." He grinned sheepishly. "But then I drank too much, and the *jefe*, he said I had become unreliable." He chuckled. "The man was right, I had." He shrugged. "I like the Budweiser too much. Have you ever been before to my town?"

"Sagrado Corazón?" the Cardinal said. "No, I haven't."

"It's a good town. My grandfather was a Rojas, and he was a big *hacendado* around here. Then he died a hero of the *cristiada*."

"Did he?" Galvan said, looking into the rearview. "God bless his soul."

"Mr. Nuñez," the Cardinal said, holding up the little photograph, "were there ever any miraculous occurrences in your town?"

"Miraculous occurrences—? Ah, you mean the miracles. *Sí*, Father. During the *cristiada*."

Galvan was still watching him in the mirror. "I've never heard of any miracles in Sagrado Corazón. Does the Church recognize them? Have they been investigated and authenticated?"

"Oh, I don't know about that, Father. It's a local thing. It belongs only to our pueblo. And around." With his forefinger he drew a circle by the side of his head, indicating the surrounding area.

Just then the Cardinal said sharply, "Stop!" and Galvan stepped on the brake. Fifty yards before them, at the side of the mountain road, the two women from the icon stand were kneeling by the side of the road, praying up to the mountain. Galvan inched up the Ford parallel to them. The women's eyes were closed, their lips moved continuously as they fingered their rosaries, then one woman reached down and without any interruption of her prayers, slid forward the pad under her right knee, then under her left. A moment later the woman beside her did the same. They must have carried the pads up the hill in their woven straw carryalls.

The Cardinal stared at the two peasant women. It seemed as if he hadn't seen faith like that in decades. Or maybe it was that he hadn't felt it in himself. And again that mysterious dislocation came over him—that same eerie separation from his own existence—that he had felt looking into the albino's eyes.

"Where—" the Cardinal said softly, "—where are they going?"

"To the graveyard," Nuñez said, "and then to Father Tomás's Vigil."

" 'Father Tomás's Vigil'?" Galvan's brow knitted with puzzlement. "What's that?"

Nuñez waited a moment before he spoke, he had suddenly turned reticent. "It's a place on the other side of the mountain. Just a bunch of big rocks." Then he became loquacious again. "It won't do any good to offer these good women a ride. They'd just refuse it. They must have a sick husband, or a son in prison, or maybe even a dead loved one in hell. It must be very serious, because it will take them a day and a half, maybe two, without sleep. They carry fruit and tortillas in their bags. You see, they hope that by praying up the mountain in this way, they can win God's favor. Or maybe they've promised a saint that—"

"I think, *señor*," Galvan said icily, "that we understand the Act of Supplication."

Galvan's tone was so reproving that Nuñez silenced, and after a while sat back in his seat.

THE TOWN HAD ONCE BEEN CONTAINED WITHIN ITS HIGH, WHITE-washed walls, but now it spilled down the sides of the mountain crest. As human habitation is inexplicably apt to do, one section had grown much more than the other, and there was a sprawling, slope-hugging hodgepodge of small, neat one-family homes, some of them two-storied, some with ornamental ironwork and Spanish-style lights. A rare gentle slope of the mountain had been leveled and a small soccer field etched in the dirt, and a baseball diamond. The road was lined with the usual mix of bars, shops, restaurants, markets—all clustered in with the people's homes. There was pov-erty—after all, this *was* Mexico—but the children weren't naked or undernourished. There wasn't a continuous display of desperation as there seemed to be in other parts of the country, and even the stray dogs weren't as rib-boned skinny.

"That's my house there," Nuñez said, pointing out a small con-crete block house slathered with garish blue paint—an alcoholic's house. "But I'll ride with you to the Mayor's office." Nuñez smiled as if he knew a secret. "The *alcalde* is a very interesting man. They call him Mayor Milagro."

The Cardinal looked back at Nuñez. " '*Milagro*'? Isn't that Spanish for—for—"

The smile under the Dodger cap widened. "*Sí, padre.* For miracle."

THEY PASSED THROUGH THE WALLS INTO THE "OLD PUEBLO." HERE the buildings were close on each other—newer little lean-to cottages built up against aged adobe structures. It seemed every possible construction space had been utilized. The streets—built for horses and wagons—were cluttered with unloading trucks and parked cars, left with absolutely no regard for posted signs. It was all familiar to the Cardinal—it reminded him of the Italian hill towns he'd seen.

They inched down a long, high-walled corridor that had almost become a pedestrian mall—there were so many tortilla stands and pastry carts and vendors' wagons. Then they drove out of the shadows of the corridor and into the plaza, and unlike the rest of the pueblo, the plaza was open and wide. Galvan parked before the small church and the three men got out. The Cardinal looked up at the church and said, "It's so small for such a bustling town."

"That's just the chapel, *padre*," Nuñez said. "It's been here since the twenties. The church is just behind it, and it's much larger, five times as big. And the building next door, we call it the Infirmary, but it's our school, and it's been enlarged, too."

Galvan frowned. "Did your Archdiocese approve these expenditures?"

Nuñez smiled proudly. "Oh, we did the work ourselves, Father. All the people in the parish. We're good Catholics in this town."

There was a burst of good-natured shouting from behind them and they turned to see, on the steps of an unremarkable dun-colored two-storied building across the *placita*, a short, gray-haired man in a tie, white shirt and creased slacks, with a black patch over his right eye. He was leaning on an ironwork railing, shouting down to the driver of a flatbed truck.

"*Pendejo!*" the man with the eye patch shouted with a smile. "Thief! You come in here and pay for that fucking license right now, or I'll confiscate your fucking truck!"

The man in the flatbed truck fired his noisy engine and yelled back, "Miguelito, *you're* the thief! You won't let an honest man earn a living." The trucker was laughing.

"Honest! Honest! What the fuck do you know about honest?! You don't pay your taxes! You refuse to renew your conveyor's license! You're a bum, Chato! A fucking bum!"

"Ah, hombre! I don't let people talk to me like that!" He grinned from behind the truck's steering wheel and shook his finger. "You better watch your mouth!"

The man with the eye patch lurched down from the steps in a rolling crook-legged lope—his right leg was bent—and raised his fist as the trucker rammed the truck into gear.

"Get out the truck! Get out the truck!" the man with the eye patch shouted. "I'll kick your ass all over this plaza!"

The trucker drove away laughing, and the man with the lame leg and the eye patch chuckled to himself, brandishing his fist high in the air.

"That," Nuñez said to the clerics by his side, "is our Mayor."

The man turned and his eyes fell on Nuñez.

"Claudio! You fucking drunk! I thought you were working on the sewage ditch?"

"*Sí*, Miguelito, but the foreman sent me home, and I'm not even drunk yet."

Miguelito looked askance at the man in the baseball cap, then he noticed the two strangers in black suits. He hurried across the plaza. "Father, Father. Welcome to Sagrado Corazón."

The Cardinal moved forward with his hand extended, but Galvan quickly moved in front of him.

"*Alcalde,*" he said to the mayor, "I'm Father Galvan, and this," he said importantly, "this is John Cardinal O'Rourke."

"Cardinal?" Nuñez was shocked. "Shit!" he said in English.

"I don't think we've ever had a Cardinal in our town before," Miguelito said. "No, I *know* we haven't." They shook hands.

"And you're Mayor Milagro," the Cardinal said. "How did you come by such a saintly name?"

Miguelito chuckled. "And me such a vulgar man? Well, it's an adopted name, and *that* is a very long story, which I don't think—" The mayor stopped in midsentence and stared at the Cardinal. When the moment became uncomfortably long, Nuñez haltingly asked, "*Qué te pasa,* Miguel?"

Miguelito didn't take his eyes off the old man. Finally he said, "Did you say O'Rourke?" *Oruque.*

"O'Rourke. Yes, why?"

"John O'Rourke?"

"Yes . . ." The Cardinal was feeling the beginnings of that displacement again, that sense of complete disconnection.

Miguelito smiled, as if he knew some secret. "Were you once a priest in New York City?"

The Cardinal slowly nodded.

"You had a parish in *la Cocina del Diablo?* In Hell's Kitchen?"

The Cardinal blanched. "How did—how'd you know that?"

Miguelito cocked his head. "Tell me, Cardinal O'Rourke, how did you come to visit our pueblo?"

"If it's any of your business—" Father Galvan moved to exercise the authority vested in him. "My Archbishop charted a complete tour—"

"I saw a strange boy under a eucalyptus tree," the Cardinal interrupted. "An albino boy— He told me to come here."

"O'Rourke?" Nuñez had been thinking. "Isn't that the same name as—"

"Come with me, John O'Rourke." Miguelito moved to take the Cardinal's arm. "I want to show you something."

◄〇►

INSIDE THE CHURCH WAS WARM AND WELL-LIGHTED. TOMMY TURNED to the congregation and offered everyone who wished to partake of Communion to approach the communion rail. There was a general rustling and the unmistakable sound of leather shoes dully striking wooden kneelers as almost the entire congregation began to file from the pews and approach the altar. Tommy gave young Father Aguallo, who was assisting him in the Mass, a look that said there they were going to be here for a while. The people of Sagrado Corazón were always devotional, but in the months leading up to Christmas they bordered on zealotry.

The two priests were almost finished dispensing the shards of wafer when the church door opened and four men entered from the blue-gray overcast of outside. Tommy recognized two of the men at a glance—Miguelito and Claudio Nuñez. Tommy gently laid a piece of communion wafer into the mouth of a dark-haired little girl he had confirmed only last June, then he looked up and squinted—he'd left his glasses in the rectory—to get a clear view of the other two. They were priests, he saw that immediately. A young Latin and an old Anglo. Tommy stepped to the next celebrant kneeling at the communion rail. It was the little girl's mother—a woman who confessed to Tommy each week that she had lain yet again with her husband's brother. As Tommy placed the shred of wafer on her outstretched tongue he offered a quick, silent prayer, imploring that this poor, good-hearted woman be delivered from the bondage of her flesh. He looked up again and the four men were still standing at the stone holy-water font, but the old man had taken a few steps forward. He was peering intently at Tommy. Tommy paused, his hand over the chalice, and stared back. There was something vaguely familiar about the old man. As

356

if Tommy had met him once, or a younger relative. He slipped the Host into the mouth of the next man at the communion rail and then there was a commotion at the rear of the church and when he looked up Miguelito and the young priest were holding up the old man.

—◄○►—

WHEN THE CARDINAL FOLLOWED THE MAYOR INTO THE CHURCH HE was struck instantly by the honest simplicity of the "chapel." The paintings were crude, the statuary hand-carved, the pews roughly finished, then polished smooth by decades of devout Catholic rumps. The Cardinal instantly and unconsciously compared it to the Vatican Palace, with its myriad chambers and churches, and found the Vatican wanting. This humble church was only three-quarters full, but it seemed almost everyone had taken Communion. The whole place was kneeling.

"Cardinal O'Rourke?" Miguelito had turned to him. "Do you know the priest who's giving Communion?"

The Cardinal was mystified by the devilish fire in the Mayor's one uncovered eye. He looked then at the priest at the communion rail. He was in his mid-sixties, his thick silver hair combed straight back from his forehead. He was on the thin side—he looked to be one of those men whose weight never fluctuates throughout their life. Then O'Rourke's eyes settled on the priest's face. He looked vaguely different from the other people in the church—though many of them were of European stock. The priest looked some-how—American.

And then the Cardinal began to experience that eerie dislocation again, that same separation from time and reality, only now it manifested itself physically. He felt it start at his calves and slip up his legs, like a chill or an electric shock. The silky white hairs on the old man's back tingled, and a wave of something akin to fear crept across his balding skull. Almost of their own volition, his legs moved his feet forward and he stared at the priest's face. His knees began to tremble. It was as if his flesh had acknowledged some truth that his mind hadn't yet accepted. Then the priest at the communion rail looked straight at him and the old man understood, and then he collapsed.

—◀○▶—

TOMMY LED THEM INTO THE RECTORY AND THEY LAID THE OLD PRIEST on a couch and Tommy looked at Miguelito and said, "What happened?"

Miguelito was concerned for the old man. "He got a shock."

"What do you mean?"

Before the Mayor could answer Father Galvan, who was opening the cardinal's collar, looked back at them in alarm. "This is a sick old man! Do you have a doctor in this town?"

Tommy moved to a sideboard and poured a glass of brandy. "Our doctor's recently passed away. The new doctor won't arrive until next week." He carried the brandy back to the couch. Galvan held out his hand to take it, but Tommy pulled up a chair and sat beside the couch. He gently lifted the old man's head and put the pony glass to his lips.

"Who is he?"

"He's a Cardinal!" Galvan sputtered, as if the man were only a title.

Tommy inspected his face. "I think I know him from somewhere."

"You do," Miguelito said.

Tommy poured a few drops of spirits into the old man's slack lips. "I do?" The old man coughed and Tommy turned to put the glass on the table.

"His name's O'Rourke."

Tommy's eyes flew up to Miguelito.

"John O'Rourke," Miguelito softly said.

Tommy stared at him a moment, then he whirled back and the old man was looking at him.

—◀○▶—

TOMMY CAME OUT OF THE ADJOINING BATHROOM CARRYING A WARM, damp facecloth. O'Rourke was sitting upright on the couch. They were in the room alone. Tommy held out the cloth and O'Rourke took it. He held up the empty pony glass. "I think I need another."

Tommy brought over the bottle and poured. "Are you all right?"

O'Rourke smiled and shook his head. "You have to admit, it's a surprising sight. Tommy Gun Coyne, dispensing Communion."

Tommy sat down and poured himself a drink. "No one's called me that in over forty years." He looked at O'Rourke. "We got old, Father—Your Eminence."

"I got older—seventy-six."

"I'll be sixty-seven in a few weeks, God willing."

A shadow flicked under O'Rourke's face. "God willing."

The two old priests held up their drinks in a silent toast.

"How the hell did you become a Cardinal?"

"How the hell did you become a priest?"

◄○►

THEY TALKED ALL THROUGH THAT GRAY AFTERNOON. TWO AGING MEN drinking brandy and smoking cigarettes. Father Galvan knocked once and stuck his head into the room, saying he'd found a small clean hotel only a few blocks away. Tommy informed him that His Eminence would be staying here at the rectory. Galvan stared suspiciously at Tommy and reluctantly went away. Around four o'clock Father Aguallo brought in sandwiches and bottles of beer. Tommy thanked him and the young priest quickly exited. They picked at the sandwiches and drank the beer and continued to talk.

Tommy told his story first. He touched on everything, but edited liberally. He didn't mention the shoot-out in the snow-covered Calgary Cemetery, although he knew O'Rourke had to be fully aware of it. He told of the train ride across America, the border crossing with the Indian woman who told him to take off his collar. He spoke of being captured in a little town whose name he didn't remember, and being brought to Guadalajara, and when he told O'Rourke of his hanging, of the weakened scaffolding collapsing under his weight, the old cardinal's eyes widened and he sat back and studied Tommy carefully. Tommy recounted coming to in this pueblo, his brother Frank being here, and a nun nursing him back to health. He told of the attack on the train, described the leaves of grass wet with water and children's blood and the sadness he felt, but he didn't mention Frank's cruelty, his dissipation, his murderous rampage. Tommy paused, and then spoke quietly of a boy injured in the attack on the train, who died three days later here in the pueblo and then came back to life as he was being buried. At that Cardinal O'Rourke raised his fingertips to his lips. Tommy told him of the great battle that raged on this mountaintop, a battle that

359

the government never acknowledged, a battle that historically never happened. He told of hand-to-hand fighting between the *cristeros* and the *agraristas,* of women in the street attacking the *federales* with butcher knives and hammers, of a lame boy with one clouded eye who jumped from rooftop to rooftop, firing a pair of nickel-plated automatics down at the enemy. Half the town's population was killed in the battle, including my brother Frank, Tommy said, and then the *federal* general fell and the tide of the struggle turned and finally the enemy broke and fled down the mountain and the people of the pueblo pursued them and hacked at them and clubbed them with rocks and rifle stocks until they were all dead. Tommy told him that it was on that day that he realized he could never kill again.

He described to O'Rourke the years after the amnesty, when there were still occasional raids on Catholic villages, and then the thirties, when Mexico was riddled with fascist nationalists. They came to Sagrado Corazón, hearing of a foreign priest in the pueblo, but after Miguelito and a man named Quintana went to talk to them they left and never returned. It was then that Tommy applied for Mexican citizenship. He claimed his church and identity papers had been burned in the *cristiada,* and he changed the spelling of his name to "Juan Oruque," and he became a Mexican.

"You could've picked any name. Why keep mine?"

Tommy shrugged. "Respect." He gave the Cardinal a small smile. "And anyway, everyone just calls me *Padre* Tomás."

"You could've used 'Thomas Coyne.' "

Tommy shook his head. "No. That man died."

Then he related to O'Rourke the quiet years of the forties and fifties, when he settled into the comfortable routine of baptizing babies, schooling children, marrying and burying.

"Weren't you ever challenged by the Archdiocese? By the Vatican?"

Tommy shrugged again. "Not really. From time to time Guadalajara would send a priest out to ask me questions, but you see, there was such chaos during the insurrection, so many priests were killed, they didn't have enough to minister to the people. I just kind of fell through the bureaucratic cracks. Finally, they just accepted me."

"That's incredible."

"That's Mexico."

They sat in silence for a while, then Tommy said, "The seminaries keep sending me their young priests to train."

"Unbelievable."

Tommy smiled. "I guess they think I'm a good priest."

"And you've never left Mexico?"

"I've never left this mountain. Oh, I travel to outlying areas of the parish, to little villages that don't have their own pastor. But why would I leave Sagrado Corazón? Everything I love is here."

O'Rourke didn't speak for a long moment, then, "And the gold from the train?"

Tommy smiled a larcenous smile and said, "Johnny lad, ye *still* don't trust me?" And O'Rourke thought he looked again like the Hell's Kitchen gangster who had held a .45 to his head so many decades before. Then the smile softened. "We kept it for the pueblo. At first it was for the *cristero* widows. And orphans. Then we dug into it to send promising kids away to the university." Tommy opened his hands and closed them, in a gesture of explanation. "And sometimes a local man working in the States gets into some kind of trouble, and we have to wire money for a lawyer or a doctor. Things like that." He smiled a very different kind of smile. "We make loans to people who couldn't otherwise get needed funds."

"And do they ever repay you?"

"Sometimes. . . . Sometimes. . . ." He raised his eyes to the ceiling. "A lot of it went to build this church. And the school. And the hospital. And—"

"I understand," O'Rourke said. "It's God's gold."

Then Tommy leaned forward on his knees and asked, "But tell me, how'd you become a Cardinal?" He grinned and shook his head. "A *Cardinal!*"

O'Rourke said that after the Police Commissioner realized that the priest had lied to give Tommy time to escape—the Cardinal paused, and they each knew the other was thinking of the killings in the cemetery—the Chief wanted to charge O'Rourke with being an accessory to murder, but the Archbishop called in a favor, explaining to the Mayor that it wouldn't be politically prudent to charge an Irish priest with murder in New York City, and O'Rourke was rushed off to a tiny parish in Indiana, where he promptly got into a feud with the mayor, who the priest had learned was the Grand Dragon of the local Ku Klux Klan klavern. O'Rourke was transferred to a number of places after that—Florida, Alberta, Louisiana—but there always seemed to be altercations or differences of opinion, and after what had happened in New York, O'Rourke was quickly stamped as a problem priest—rebellious, contentious, and disrespectful of tradition. He was finally posted to the Belgian

Congo and stayed there for almost twenty years, trying to bring
the message of Christ to people who filed their teeth and worshiped
crocodiles. In the mid fifties, when the fiery spirit of independence
swept across Africa and Roman Catholic missionaries became very
visible symbols of European colonization, O'Rourke's health began
to fail and he was sent to a clerical hospital just outside Venice for
recuperation. There he met Angelo Cardinal Roncalli, the patriarch
of Venice. The rotund, gregarious Italian took an immediate liking
to the American priest, who had been born on the same day, eleven
years later. He managed to get O'Rourke assigned to his staff, and
then, when Roncalli was elected by his fellow Cardinals to the papacy, he bestowed on him a monsignorial position, and finally
named him Cardinal of a small region in Sicily.

"Sicily?" Tommy was surprised. "What's it like?"

O'Rourke held up his hands and laughed. "I don't know. I've
never been there. It's just a title."

"But what a title!" Tommy grinned, then tilted the brandy bottle
on the table between them. It was empty. "Another dead soldier."
He rose and walked toward the liquor cabinet, saying, "Repeat of
the same, Your Eminence?" As he walked past the window he
peered out at the fallen night.

"My God, what time is it?" He looked at his cheap Japanese
watch and softly said, "Fuck me, Molly."

O'Rourke chuckled at hearing the old Hell's Kitchen profanity.

"I have to attend a birthday party," Tommy said, then looked at
the Cardinal. "Will you go with me?"

—◇—

IT WAS CHILL AND DAMP OUTSIDE. EVERY ONCE IN A WHILE THERE'D BE
a gust of wind accompanied by a smattering of fat raindrops. The
pueblo streets were alive with women hurrying to buy foodstuffs—
pork, milk, peppers, cornmeal—before the storm broke. Still, they
were not too harried to stop what they were doing and warmly
greet Father Tomás. They crossed the street when they saw him, as
if irresistibly drawn by some field of force that radiated out from
him. *"Buenas noches, Padre Tomás,"* they said, and then, O'Rourke
noted, they all *touched* him. They gently clasped his forearm, or
kissed his hand, or they might simply caress the cloth of his suit
coat between their fingers or brush their palms against his shoulder

as if dusting off a piece of lint. But they all felt some need—some physical, emotional necessity—to come in contact with his flesh, his person. As if he were a totem, a talisman, to be touched for luck, for security, for reassurance. As if he were a living shrine, and after they were granted his grace they walked away taller, more serene, wearing a smile. The men on the streets felt the same compulsion to press his flesh, only they expressed it in the manly Mexican embrace called an *abrazo,* or they draped an arm around his shoulders and patted his back affectionately, wearing that same reinvigorated grin. The two priests passed a workingmen's bar, with a large, square window bar that opened onto the street under a drooping awning where men on the sidewalk were passed down bottles of Corona and shots of tequila. These men were all dusty laborers, with muscled arms, beer guts, and reddened faces, but when they saw Father Tomás approaching they gave out loud welcomes and slapped him heartily on his back. The bartender reached down through the open window and shook his hand warmly, then several men came out the bar door to touch their priest. They tried to get him to come inside to drink with them but Tommy said he couldn't stay and the men moaned like children. O'Rourke hadn't seen a man so beloved since—well, since Angelo had died. John XXIII.

"*Cardenal!*" Nuñez pushed through the others to extend his hand to O'Rourke. "You've recovered!"

"Yes. I—"

"These are my amigos!" Nuñez was stumbling drunk. "And this." He put his arm around Tommy's waist. "This is my grandfather."

"Take it easy, Claudio." Tommy smiled. *"Calma, calma."*

"My special grandfather!" Nuñez's eyes were red and swimming. He pointed to Tommy and addressed O'Rourke. "My real grandfather, the great Victoriano Rojas, died in his arms. My uncles all saw it."

"My mother saw it, too," another man declared.

"My grandfather, too!"

Nuñez began to blubber. "Padre Tomás is a great man, like my grandfather was a great man." He laid his head on Tommy's shoulder. "And I am nothing."

"That's not true, Claudio." Tommy lifted the man's head and looked into his eyes. "You are my best Sunday morning usher. My very best. I depend on you."

Claudio fought back his tears. He smiled gratefully.

"Now go home, Claudio. I'll need you tomorrow morning."

"Yes, *padre* . . ." Then he said, "But just one more *cerveza*," and all the men broke into laughter.

◄○►

IT WAS A TALL, NARROW HOUSE ON A WINDING, UNDERLIGHTED STREET abutting the rear wall of the pueblo. The sporadic raindrops had become a steady drizzle. The door opened and the hallway light spilled out onto Tommy and O'Rourke, standing on the low step. A large, gray-haired woman in a black dress stepped into the doorway, backlit by the hall sconce.

"Father Tomás," she said. "You're late. I thought you'd forgotten."

"You think I'd forget your great-grandson's birthday?" He put his hand on O'Rourke's back and ushered him into the house. "John O'Rourke, I would like you to meet *Señora* Quintana."

"Ah, the Cardinal." She bent her head and kissed his ring in a perfunctory ritual. "The whole town is talking about you. We've never had—"

"—a Cardinal in your town before, yes I know." O'Rourke chuckled and then wouldn't let go of her hand. She was a beautiful woman, tall and imposing and attractive, even at sixty, and on impulse O'Rourke bent and gave a quick kiss to the back of *her* hand. When he raised his head he could see she was not pleased. He could also see, at that angle, in that light, that there was something wrong with the left side of her face. There was a blemish, a slurring of flesh. O'Rourke surmised that it had softened with years, with the aging of her skin, but that in her youth it had probably been much more pronounced.

"How European of you," *Señora* Quintana said, and her tone revealed her disapproval. "You've lived in Italy too long."

A door at the rear of the hall flew open and five children, all preschool age, rushed through and shouted, "Father Tomás! Father Tomás!" Tommy knelt on the polished floor and the children surrounded him like a litter of puppies. He rose with two in his arms, while the others clutched his legs, and managed to reach into his pocket for little foil-wrapped sweets. The children squealed.

"Where's your grandfather?"

"Watching *fútbol!* Watching *fútbol!*" they shouted, almost in unison.

"Television is the devil's worst creation," Lourdes said with a frown, and stepped solidly down the hall. "I'll get him."

"Where is everybody?" Tommy asked the children as he reached for a doorknob. "Are they in . . . *here!*" The children danced with excitement.

He opened the door and entered, nodding at O'Rourke to follow him.

The adjoining room was a dining room, and it stretched from the front of the house to the back wall. Around a long row of cloth-covered tables fifty well-dressed people were having predinner drinks. They were of all ages, all generations, and O'Rourke suddenly realized they were a family. Seeing Tommy, they all stopped their conversations and turned, smiling, to greet him.

During the next few minutes O'Rourke was stupefied by an endless round of introductions: sons, daughters-in-law, sons-in-law, daughters, grandsons and -daughters of ages from five to twenty. Tommy gave a running commentary as each was introduced.

"This is Héctor López. He's the second son of my friend Quintana's only daughter. Did I tell you Quintana is my best friend?"

"Yes, you did. Pleased to meet you, Héctor."

"It's an honor, Your Eminence. We've never had a Cardinal in Sagrado Corazón before."

"Really?" O'Rourke said with a smile to Tommy.

"And this, this is Paulino, Lourdes and Quintana's third son. Paulino, meet my friend Cardinal O'Rourke."

It went on like this for what seemed like an eternity, and after a while O'Rourke was even able to make a little sense of the endless round of dark-haired, dark-eyed, brown-skinned faces. The person named Quintana had married the woman who had greeted them at the door and they'd had five sons and a daughter—Enrique, Alberto, Paulino, Marcelino and Alicia, and a son who was not presently in the room. And these six offspring had together given their parents two-dozen grandchildren, and they were all gathered for the second birthday of one of the granddaughters' son—a chuckling little toddler in shorts and a tiny Nehru jacket. O'Rourke was wondering if he should even attempt to memorize the names of the grandchildren when *Señora* Quintana's authoritative voice rang out, "*Familia,* let Papa come through." The crowd quieted immediately, and then a tall, light-complexioned man in his early forties pushed a high-backed wooden-armed wheelchair into the center of the room. In the wheelchair, covered by a quilt comforter, sat a tiny, frail, skeleton of a man, with hair short-cropped but still ebony black, and skin the color of sweat-stained leather. With one look the Cardinal understood why the man's progeny were so dark, he was an Indian, and with that same quick look O'Rourke realized he had suffered a crippling stroke some time in the past. The man in the wheelchair wasn't able to move a single limb. In fact, he seemed incapable of any motion whatsoever. And then the Cardinal saw his eyes.

"John, I want you to meet my great friend, Aureliano Quintana."

The Indian's eyes were startlingly alive. Black and bright, they radiated humor, intelligence and soul.

Tommy stooped by the wheelchair and said to the Indian, "Amigo, this is the priest I told you about, the one who gave me sanctuary in the church in New York."

Quintana's eyes looked into O'Rourke's own, and the Cardinal felt that the Indian somehow knew him better than he knew himself. That he had looked into his very being. It was disconcerting.

"He just happened to come to Sagrado Corazón," Tommy said. "Isn't that a miracle?"

The Indian's eyes said he understood that it was.

"Hello, Your Eminence. I'm Francisco Quintana." The man behind the wheelchair held out his hand. "I'm Aureliano's eldest."

O'Rourke's eyes went up to the tall man's face, and his mouth dropped open.

"It's a great honor for you to dine with our family," Francisco said. "A great honor."

Tommy was adjusting the Indian's quilt. "He said an albino boy told him to come here. An *albino*. Isn't that right, John?"

O'Rourke finally was able to pull his eyes from Francisco's face, and when he looked down Quintana's eyes were laughing at him.

—◦—

LOURDES QUINTANA COMMANDED DINNER LIKE A MILITARY OPERATION. Each of her son's wives jumped to whatever task she snapped out, and if a drop of wine stained the tablecloth or if a pair of teenage granddaughters giggled too loudly, a withering glare from Lourdes's disapproving eyes brought immediate silence or more conscientious attendance to duty. The smaller children were relegated to an enormous round table in the corner of the room, doted over by the two maids. When all were seated at the long banquet table Lourdes rose and carefully prepared a plate from the numerous platters. At first O'Rourke began to feel embarrassed, because he thought she was preparing the plate for him, as the guest of honor, but when the plate was full she went to her husband in his wheelchair at the head of the table and showed him the food.

"How is this, Aureliano?"

The Yaqui's eyes said yes. O'Rourke could *see* them speak. Lourdes took the plate into the kitchen where there were several brief whirs of a blender, then she returned with the plate laden with what looked like several separate scoops of baby food. The pork in one, the beef, the vegetables, even the bread carefully blended into a soft custard.

During the meal Lourdes and Tommy, seated on either side of the Indian, took turns spooning food into his slack mouth between bites from their own plates. From time to time Tommy, never breaking his dinner conversation with the rest of the table, would softly pat Quintana's lips with his napkin, or Lourdes would gently massage his neck, easing the food down his throat.

As hard as he tried, O'Rourke couldn't keep his attention from straying back to Francisco Quintana, seated down the table and across from him. The tall man was thick-shouldered and blunt-fingered, as befitted his profession as a construction contractor, and as the eldest son of the paterfamilias he was accorded a trusting respect by his siblings, and the entire family. But that wasn't what keep drawing back O'Rourke's attention. It was his face that riveted the Cardinal—it was Tommy's face. One shade darker, of course, and with Lourdes's shape—but it could not be denied that Francisco was Tommy's son. It was like looking at a smudged pencil drawing of the man. O'Rourke glanced down the length of the table, absurdly astonished that no one else seemed to notice. They were aware of it, of course; there could be no other way. They must have known their whole lives. It was just a part of their reality, like the blue of the sky or the redness of the dirt.

Then O'Rourke felt someone watching him. He turned and the paralyzed Indian's eyes were sparkling with mirth. He was laughing at him again.

—◄○►—

THERE WERE A NUMBER OF TOASTS—TO THE BIRTHDAY BOY, TO THE Cardinal, to the several pregnant women at the table—then the cake was brought out and the children shrilled and got icing on their fingers and then one of the teenagers—Marcelino's classical pianist son Antonio—said, "The Olympics are on. I think it's basketball!"

One of Francisco's daughters—the one entering law school next year—pushed away her cake plate so violently that the clatter earned Lourdes's dark glare. "Cleotilde! You're at the dinner table!"

"I'm sorry, Grandmother," the brown-haired girl said, "but thinking about the Olympics going on, after what they did to those innocent kids at Tlatelolco, it just makes my blood boil."

O'Rourke was staring at the girl. He'd just realized that she reminded him of Peggy Coyne, her great-grandmother.

Lourdes noticed the Cardinal's stare, and said, "You'll have to excuse my granddaughter, Your Eminence. Our young people today seemed to have been bitten by the revolution bug."

"Well, didn't you and Grandpa fight for what you believed in? Didn't you have your rebellion?"

"That was for God!" Lourdes snapped. "They had outlawed Christ!"

O'Rourke cleared his throat. "I was at Tlatelolco."

Everyone stared at him as if he had said he'd walked on the moon.

"You were there, John?" Tommy finally said.

"Yes . . ." O'Rourke shook his head. "It was a massacre."

Then everyone asked questions at once. Lourdes slapped the table and called for silence, and O'Rourke told the story of what he had experienced that night in the Plaza of the Tres Culturas. When he was finished some of the women were crying.

THE PARTY WAS OVER. THE MAIDS WERE CLEANING UP. THE FAMILY WAS putting on their coats and leaving. O'Rourke sipped a final cup of coffee and admired the collection of crucifixes and Madonnas affixed to the wall. Tommy had told him earlier that they had hung in the home of *Señora* Quintana's father, in the city of León. When O'Rourke turned from the paintings all but Tommy and Lourdes had left, and they were huddled around *Señor* Quintana's wheelchair, whispering. The way they talked, always including the Indian in their gestures, their facial expressions, it was as if he were conversing, too. *Maybe he is*, O'Rourke thought. Then Lourdes looked up at the Cardinal, and he knew they were talking about him.

◄○►

THEY EXITED A SIDE DOOR AND CROSSED A SMALL FLAGSTONE COURT-yard and then Lourdes said, "My hands are full, Tomás." And Tommy handed the flashlight to O'Rourke and pressed on a panel of wood half-hidden behind a rain-dripping stone statue of the Virgin. The panel popped open and Tommy took back the flashlight and pointed it down a narrow winding staircase.

"We have a secret house guest," Lourdes said to O'Rourke, and then they started down. They had only taken a few steps when the Cardinal softly said, "A priest hole . . ."

"It was built in the thirties, when things looked like they were getting bad again."

"But we've never had to use it until now," Tommy said, and then they stepped down into a damp, dark room. Sleeping on a cot was a young man with a brutal cut down the right side of his face. It was sutured, swollen and inflamed. Lourdes set down on the floor a covered plate of food and an ancient, creased physician's valise. She sat on the bed beside the young man and started to inspect his face. He flinched and jerked up in fear.

"It's all right, Father. It's *Señora* Quintana."

O'Rourke looked at Tommy and Tommy nodded, *Yes, he's a priest.*

"Jesus the Savior," the young priest breathed, "I dreamt they were beating me again."

"The dreams will go away." Lourdes opened the doctor's bag and took out cotton and alcohol. "Eventually."

"Where's Dr. Muñoz?"

Lourdes shot a quick look at Tommy and then said to the young priest, "Dr. Muñoz died two weeks ago."

"Prostate cancer." There was a bench against the wall and Tommy dragged it across the concrete floor and he and the Cardinal sat down. "Remember, we said Requiem Mass together?"

The priest lowered his head and rubbed his skull. "I guess . . . I guess their clubs did some permanent damage."

"You'll be all right." Lourdes was washing the sutured slash with the alcohol. The young priest tried to jerk back from the sting, but her strong hands held his head in place. "You won't be so hand-

369

some anymore . . . but it's not good for a priest to be too handsome, anyway."

"*Señora* Quintana is as good as any doctor I've ever seen," Tommy said. "Better." Then, "The new doctor will arrive from Monterrey on Thursday. We have to see where his loyalties lie."

"They should lie with God!" Lourdes snapped. "We don't need another *comunista* doctor in this town."

"Lourdes." Tommy sighed as if they'd had this argument many times before. "Roberto became a very devout Catholic. Two of his daughters chose the veil."

Lourdes frowned. "Once a *comunista,* always a *comunista,* no matter how many nuns he whelps." Then she said to her patient, "A priest shouldn't be demonstrating with those hippies." She threw a quick glance at O'Rourke, then said to the young priest, "All you're doing is trying to look up those miniskirts! I know!"

"*Señora,*" the young priest said, "I was demonstrating for the freedom of the people."

She clipped the ragged end from a loosened suture. "You should be demonstrating for the glory of God. That's the only thing that endures."

The young man stared at her hands as she prepared a replacement suture and a needle for stitching, then he slowly said, "When they started shooting us . . . beating on us . . . it seemed . . . it seemed there was no God. And when that *granadero* put his bayonet to my face and slashed me, all I could think of was if there was a God, all I could think of was getting back at Him . . ."

Lourdes pierced his flesh with the suture needle and the young priest grimaced. "Don't fight with God, little Father," Lourdes said dryly. "He always wins."

"I was at Tlatelolco that night, too."

Without moving his head, the young priest looked at O'Rourke. "You were there?"

"I was there."

The priest grimaced again with the sting of the stitch. "Was God there that night?"

"No . . . The devil was there." O'Rourke looked at Tommy. "But God is on this mountaintop. Of that I'm sure."

Tommy leaned forward toward the injured priest and said, "The Federal police came to City Hall yesterday."

"Looking for me?"

"Mayor Milagro told them you were visiting relatives in Los

Angeles. When they came to the church and asked me, I told them the same."

"Do you think—do you think I'll have to leave the country?"

"We've been through times like this before," Tommy said. "The pueblo will protect you, and eventually they'll stop looking."

Lourdes tied off the suture and put away the medical implements in the antique physician's case. "They'll stop looking if you stop this foolishness and just serve your Savior."

"*Señora* Quintana," the young priest said, "to fight for the rights of the poor *is* serving my Christ. Wasn't His message to help the downtrodden? To relieve their suffering? To challenge the status quo? Or is my place only at the altar? Am I just to be a ritualist? A shaman?"

There was a moment of silence. Three priests and an ex-nun sitting in a cold, dank cellar built to hide just their kind. And then O'Rourke said, "No, you're not."

—◁○▷—

NOW THE STEADY DRIZZLE HAD DISSIPATED INTO A COLD GRAY MIST AND as they walked through the deserted streets the moisture collected on the shoulders of their black overcoats in a silvery glaze.

"So, not only are you a priest—" O'Rourke lightly chuckled. "You're a political priest."

Tommy smiled and gave his head a slow shake. "Please don't saddle me with that label. Radical priests don't last long in Latin America."

"Well, you're hiding one."

"I'm hiding a hotheaded young man who wouldn't listen to my advice and got himself into a lot of trouble. As I recall, John, you gave sanctuary to a much more dangerous criminal, once upon a time."

They walked in silence for a moment, then O'Rourke said, "Yes. Once upon a time."

Tommy had been thinking, too. "There will always be pain in this world. Grief, hunger, hatred . . . I take my job as trying to give people relief, and hope, and some measure of peace. . . . But when I see the fire in that young man's eyes, I wish I were young again. In these times." He chuckled. "Tommy Gun Coyne could have given those *granaderos* in Tlatelolco an interesting time."

Tommy had led them out of the pueblo walls and along a bumpy road lined with small simple structures on the left, and on the right a drop-off to the next level of houses.

O'Rourke cleared his throat and started to say, "The Quintanas' first son, Francisco—"

"It was a tumultuous time, John. Passions ran high. People made mistakes."

"Yes, I understand."

The road climbed a slight rise, and when they came down the other side there was a well-lighted cemetery encircled by waist-high walls. They walked through the jammed rows of tombstones and monuments glistening with rain. Then Tommy stopped before a marker that read *"Francis Aloysius Coyne S.J.—Beloved Brother, Patriot and Soldier of Christ."* They stared at the gravestone a long time, then O'Rourke said, "He was a good priest. A devoted priest."

Tommy waited a long time before he said, "Yes, he was."

"And he died much too young."

"Yes . . . Yes, he did."

O'Rourke noticed a big bouquet of flowers a few rows down. He stepped carefully over the well-kept but uneven burial ground and there was an open grave, outlined by thick and carefully tended grass, surrounded by flowers and wreaths. As O'Rourke looked down at the hole Tommy came up beside him.

"An open grave? You're expecting someone?"

Tommy smiled and shook his head, but he didn't speak. Then O'Rourke was struck by the realization and his eyes widened. "The boy . . . The miracle."

Tommy nodded. "Some call it that."

O'Rourke slowly crossed himself. Then he said, "What's 'Father Tomás's Vigil'?"

A shadow crossed Tommy's face and he said, "It's just a jumble of rocks on the other side of—"

"Take me there. I want to see it."

⊰⟨◇⟩⊱

THERE WERE NO LIGHTS ON THE BACK SIDE OF THE MOUNTAIN, AND with the moon lost behind the heavy skies Tommy had to hold the Cardinal's arm as they stepped through the rocky blackness. There was a warm yellow glow up ahead, half-hidden by the mountain slope, and as they came closer it revealed itself more and more. Then they were there and O'Rourke softly said, "My God."

The Devil's Throne had been turned into an open-air temple. There were hundreds of shrines—some large enough to stand in, others as small as a Christmas tree crèche—and they crowded the mountain behind and above the rock outcropping. They had been built to withstand the weather, with roofs and ingenious wind-breaks, and in at least half of them votive candles flickered. O'Rourke realized they were probably lit every few days and that each family in the pueblo, even the poorest, maintained their own individual shrine. All the candles burning together gave the mountainside a golden luminescence. And then O'Rourke saw that this whole part of the mountain was covered with the litter of generations of devotional offerings: icons faded by the seasons; fragile gold chains trod upon and broken; ancient rosaries; photographs of treasured ancestors, of the *Virgen,* of the mountain itself, like the ones sold down in the flatland market; generations of family heirlooms—offerings left for the gods to do with as they wished. O'Rourke looked around the glinting mountainside and asked, "What—what happened here?"

Tommy was looking out, at the unseen plain below, as he had all those years before.

"A man found himself here," Tommy said.

THEY WERE WALKING BACK PAST THE GRAVEYARD WHEN O'ROURKE stopped and stared at an oversized tomb. It was crowned by a stone cross and a rough rendering of an unsaddled, arched-neck horse. "Did the soul buried here love horses?"

Tommy chuckled. "No, the soul buried here *is* a horse."

O'Rourke's face knitted with confusion, then he thought he understood. "Ah, the red animal *Señor* Quintana rode. The one you told me about."

Tommy shook his head. "No, that's not the one."

O'Rourke waited for an explanation and was about to believe that one wasn't forthcoming when Tommy said, "The general of the *federal* forces rode this animal into the church. There was a man there with a weapon. The general intended to kill that man, and the man decided he would rather give up his own life than take yet another."

O'Rourke gave a slight nod, signifying that he knew who that was, then said, "But the horse—?"

"Just as that general was about to cut the man in two, the animal went down to its knees. Some people think he slipped on the clay floor. Others believe the mare was genuflecting, bowing before God and the altar. Saving the man's life."

"They believe it to be yet another miracle. And the general?"

"The general was thrown over the animal's head and broke his neck in the fall. After his death the *federales* broke and ran. The *pueblerinos* hung his body in the plaza and used him for target practice. . . . I couldn't stop them. . . . Afterwards, I managed to have his body taken to Guadalajara to be buried next to the remains of his two sons."

"Do you believe the horse was praying."

Tommy smiled. "No . . . she slipped."

—◁○▷—

THE CARDINAL SLEPT THAT NIGHT IN THE RECTORY, IN THE HIDDEN priest's room, and the next morning he woke up choking and managed to get to the bathroom in the hall before he retched and coughed up blood. He was hanging over the toilet bowl, watching the blood clots drift thickly in the water, when Tommy said, "Your liver?"

O'Rourke looked up at him and Tommy handed him a towel. The Cardinal wiped the blood from his lips and started to get up. Tommy helped him.

"No, I'm not one of those whiskey priests." He sat on the edge of the tub. "It's tuberculosis. I got it in Africa, twenty years ago."

Tommy flushed the toilet and watched the illness swirl down and disappear. "How long?"

"They don't know. Six months. Six weeks. They don't know."

"Isn't there any thing they can do?"

"They've been doing everything they can for years." He looked at Tommy. "My physician was Pope John's. And John died. . . . We all leave this world sometime. It's just my time."

"Are you comfortable with that?

"I wasn't, but I am now . . . I am now. . . ."

—◄◯►—

TOMMY ASKED O'ROURKE TO SAY MASS FOR HIS PARISH, AND THE Cardinal accepted. The new church—large, airy, and simple—was packed. The people of Sagrado Corazón stood along the side aisles and the rear wall. The news that an American Cardinal, an old friend of Padre Tomás, was going to celebrate morning Mass had swept the streets and *placitas* of the pueblo, within and without the town walls. Claudio Nuñez—seemingly not at all hungover, in an ill-fitting, shiny-elbowed blue suit—kept rearranging the crowd to make room for the newly arrived. The Quintana clan took up five pews in the front, with the patriarch himself seated crookedly in his wheelchair, in the center aisle beside his wife.

After the Mass there was a banquet in a *borrachería* and food was served, and *cerveza*, and then in the central plaza half the town had their pictures taken with the Cardinal. Afterward Miguelito and Tommy walked O'Rourke across the plaza to where Father Galvan waited by the car.

"Your Eminence," Miguelito said. "It was a great honor to meet you, and not because you're a Cardinal, but what you once did for my friend." Miguelito nodded at Tommy. "Good-bye, Your Eminence."

Miguelito limped smoothly back toward the crowd in the plaza. O'Rourke glanced over at Galvan and asked Tommy, "How many people know?"

"Just Miguelito and Quintana, and as far as I'm aware they've never told anyone else."

"Not even his wife—"

"She's the *last* one he'd tell. Quintana said she'd kill me." Tommy laughed and the Cardinal chuckled along, but he didn't know what he was laughing at, and knew better than to ask.

"And John, now you know."

O'Rourke raised his arms and embraced him as if he were saying a final good-bye. He whispered in Tommy's ear, "I had lost my faith. And after Tlatelolco I hated my religion. . . . You're given them back to me. Father O'Rourke, you're the best priest I've ever met."

As O'Rourke was slipping into the passenger seat, a score of little boys thundered out of a side street, kicking about a scuffed soccer ball. A small, dark-haired ragamuffin gave the ball a spirited kick and it sailed across the *placita*, and Tommy headed it back toward them. The children squealed, *"Padre Tomás! Padre Tomás!"* Tommy looked back once at the sedan, and then he was surrounded and someone kicked the ball back at him and Tommy shouted, "Oscar, are you challenging me?!" And the children laughed again, and the last thing O'Rourke saw as Galvan gunned the car out of the plaza was Tommy in his priestly black, tall in the midst of the Mexican children, kicking at the ball.

—◄○►—

GALVAN STEERED THE FORD THROUGH THE PUEBLO WALLS AND JUST outside the gate, where the mountain started to dip, the two women from the icon stand were inching up the mountain. They had tied the first set of cushions—now worn and bursting at the seams—to their knees with cords and were using a fresh set to inch forward on. They were wet from last night's rain and looked weary beyond human endurance. People came out on their porches and respectfully watched them pass.

"My God." Galvan shook his head in disapproval. "These people are in another century. I can't wait to get back to Mexico City."

O'Rourke watched the women over his shoulder until he couldn't see them anymore, then turned back. There was a rain-washed blue sky above, and before them the flatlands below, and it was breathtakingly beautiful.

"You don't like this pueblo, Father?"

Galvan snickered. "There's nothing to like. Just a bunch of pig farmers and *campesinos*. . . . Thank God I work for the Monsignor. I wouldn't want to be buried in a place like this."

They rode in silence for a long time, and then O'Rourke said, "I would."